I0586724

Other books by Keith Hoar

<u>NOVELS:</u>

Edge of Madness

<u>NONFICTION:</u>

DECEIVED: The Assault of Revisionist History

RAGE

Second Edition

Copyright © 2019
Zhetosoft Publications

Published by: Zhetosoft Publications

RAGE is a work of fiction. Names, characters, institutions, places, and events are either the product of the author's imagination, or, if real, are used fictitiously without any intent to describe their actual condition or conduct. Any resemblance whatsoever to names, characters, actual events, locales, businesses, organizations, or persons, living or dead, is entirely coincidental and beyond the intent of the author.

Copyright © 2019 by Keith Hoar

All rights reserved, including the right to reproduce this book or portions thereof in any form whatsoever. This book, or any parts thereof, may not be reproduced in any form without the express written permission of the author except for brief quotations in critical articles or reviews.

Interior format and cover design by Keith Hoar

1. Political Thrillers--Fiction 2. Conspiracy Thrillers--Fiction
3. Terrorism Thrillers--Fiction 4. Nuclear Terrorism--Fiction
5. Suspense Thrillers--Fiction

ISBN(13): 978-0-9994590-6-5 (paperback)
ISBN(10): 0-9994590-6-6 (paperback)
ISBN(13): 978-0-9994590-5-8 (eBook)
ISBN(10): 0-9994590-5-8 (eBook)

To

Kathie, my incredibly patient and loving wife

To

My sons: Derek, Darrin, and Daman

Without your support and encouragement,
this book would not exist.

Then more fierce the conflict grew;
the din of arms, the yell
Of savage rage, the shriek of agony,
The groan of death, commingled in one sound
Of undistinguish'd horrors.

Robert Southey,
Madoc In Atzlan, Vol. II, pg. 104

"…*and men loved darkness rather than light,*
because their deeds were evil."

John 3:19, KJV

RAGE

Cast of Characters

UNITED STATES ADMINISTRATION
Paul Cantwell, President of the United States
Donald M. Walsh, White House Chief of Staff
Edger D. Cordell, White House Communications Director
Jeffery T. Williams, Executive Assistant to the President
Arthur J. Mead, Vice-President of the United States
Matthew Tyler, National Security Advisor
John J. Elmore, Asst. to President for Counterterrorism
Fleet Admiral Douglas Bennington, Chairman Joint Chiefs
Andrew J. Holt, Director US Secret Service
Delbert R. McClain, Senior Secret Service Agent
James Sandberg, Director CIA
Thomas F. Calhoun, Director CIA Special Activities Div.
Margot Wilcox, US Representative, New Jersey District 7
TSgt. Emily Perkins, USNR, WHCA Operator
Kip Johnson, Gulfstream G550 Pilot

NATIONAL MILITARY COMMAND
Colonel Stephen S. Haywood, Pilot Air Force One
Lt. Colonel Alan R. Ross, First Officer Air Force One
Rear Admiral Charles Hadley, Director of Naval Intelligence
Captain Aaron Carpenter, Staff Aide
Captain Ronald Whitfield, Staff Duty Officer for CNO
Col. Jeffery Whalen, Commander, 90th Regional Support Group
Brig. Gen. Robert A. Gordon, Deputy Dir. for Operations NMCC
Col. Timothy V. Morris, Asst. Deputy Dir. for Operations NMCC
Lt. Colonel Donald Bell, Senior Controller, USSTRATCOM

SIXTY-NINTH BOMB SQUADRON, SCORPION FLIGHT
Major Chris Jones, Aircraft Commander, Striker One
Major Neil Dunlap, Co-pilot, Striker One
Captain Robert Perkins, Electronics Warfare Officer, Striker One
Captain Carl Boone, Radar Navigator, Striker One
Major Roger Freeman, Aircraft Commander, Striker Two

Major William Hutton, Co-pilot, Striker Two
Clifford Grubbs, Electronics Warfare Officer, Striker Two

NATIONAL RESPONSE CENTER
Commander Anthony J. Bradford USCG, Officer In Charge (OIC)
Lt. Jonathan C. Haydon USCG, Duty Watch Officer (DWO)
Edward D. Willis, USCG Senior Chief Intelligence Specialist
James L. Kean, USCG Intelligence Specialist First Class (IS1)
Andrew C. Reed, USCG Intelligence Specialist Second Class (IS2)
James E. Fischer, USCG Electronics Technician Second Class

USS WYOMING - SSBN 742
Commander Joseph Anderson, Commanding Officer
Lieutenant Commander James Barton, Executive Officer
Lieutenant Commander Paul Turner, Engineering Officer
Lieutenant Michael Gertz, Navigation Officer
Lieutenant David Murphy, Weapons Officer
Lieutenant Jg. Bill Chambers, Assistant Weapons Officer
Lieutenant Jg. Ted Mitchell, Electrical Division Officer
Mstr. Chief Damage Control Edward Benson, Chief of the Boat
Chief Machinist Mate Michael Warren, Machinery Division Chief
Chief Radioman, Thomas Dawson, Radio Division Chief
Reactor Operator First Class. Alan Turner
Radioman First Class Aaron Jiles, MAINCOMM Radio Supervisor
Radioman Second Class Gary Roosa
Machinist Mate Third Class Donald A. Lee
Engineman Third Class Mike Hall, Duty Helmsman
Missile Technician Third Class Peter Lefler

NUCLEAR EMERGENCY SUPPORT TEAM
Tony Larson, Senior Team Leader
Curtis Owens Team Logistics Coordinator
George Lee, Team Member
Samuel Gomez, Team Member
Drew Palmer, Equipment Support
Jeffery Mahone, Team Helicopter Pilot

CIVILIAN CHARACTERS

Zachariah James Templeton, Communications Consultant
Angie Templeton, Zach Templeton's Wife
Norman Glover (aka James Templeton), Undercover CIA
Susan Glover (aka Margaret Templeton)
Bill Morrison (aka Sotero Rojas), CIA Operative
Anthony Sterling (aka Frank Porter), former FBI Deputy Director
Dr. Marshall K. Woods, Emergency Department Physician
Dr. Ramona Berger, Emergency Department Physician
Carol Morgan, Emergency Department Nurse
Virginia Doyle, ICU Charge Nurse
Leonid Borodin, International Financier
Henry Tang, Shipping Magnet

FOREIGN CHARACTERS

Sharan Husam Ahadi, Radical Extremist
Mahmud Hakeem Antar, Radical Extremist Leader
Muti Nabih Daher, Radical Extremist
Abdul Suhaib Hadad, Extremist Proselyte
Simone Roux, Assassin for hire

Author's Note

Thank you for reading **_RAGE_**, Book 2 in the Zach Templeton thriller series. Book 2 is set in various locales in the United States, Quito, Ecuador, and Mexico. Seemingly incorrect grammar that is contained within quotes may reflect broken English this is used by some foreign characters. For example: "I not see you in long time." Would be typical speech for someone who has a poor command of the English language.

The events that occur in **_RAGE_** follow after those that take place in the novel **_Edge of Madness_**. To fully enjoy the Zach Templeton thriller series as intended, I recommend reading **_Edge of Madness_** first, the first book in the series, which introduces the key characters, their backgrounds, and their motivations. The challenges and dangers they face in the first book of the series lead directly into events that will take place in this book.

Thank you for taking the time to read this book and, hopefully, the next book in the Zach Templeton series. The author is very grateful for fans of his books, and would love to correspond with readers like you. Sample prologues and/or the first chapter of current and upcoming books can be viewed on his website at www.Zhetosoft.com. You are welcome to reach out to the author through his email address at author@zhetosoft.com.

Prologue

Terrace Room
The Plaza New York Hotel
Fifth Avenue at Central Park South
New York, New York

A steady, wind-driven rain fell from a dark overcast sky, drenching the concrete towers of New York City. Rain-soaked pedestrians dashed across busy streets, jumping over puddles, hurrying to work, meetings, or lunch dates. On the other side of the country in sunny California, beach-goers enjoyed the bright sun, families strolled through parks, while others, stalled in endless traffic jams, swore at their fellow commuters. All totally unaware of the horror that lay ahead. An atrocity so terrifying it would literally send them running for their lives.

Located a half-mile from Rockefeller Plaza, the century-old Plaza New York Hotel, frequent host to world leaders, public figures, leaders of industry, and the ultra-privileged of Broadway and Hollywood, was synonymous with luxury. Located in the heart of Manhattan and accessible to multiple subway lines within a four-block radius of the hotel, made it an ideal location for business meetings of all kinds.

A meeting of the Socialists of America filled the Plaza Hotel's Terrace Room to capacity. Not openly publicized like most organizational meetings, the Socialists of America meeting was attended by invitation only and, to a limited extent, approved guests of noteworthy attendees. A small nondescript, black and white placard sitting on a wooden easel at the entrance of the meeting room served as the only evidence the meeting was taking place.

Stanley Mercer, a hawkish man with a thin nose, black hair, and close-set, dark eyes, stood behind a wooden lectern on a small raised platform. He skillfully presented the assumed dangers of climate change. Mr. Mercer, dressed in a dark, custom-tailored suit, expertly held the crowd's attention. A label from one of New York's top fashion designers sewn inside his jacket bespoke his wealth and position. The meeting room, packed to capacity, became stuffy. Some attendees resorted to fanning themselves with their paper programs, attempting to lessen their discomfort.

Most of the attendees, dressed in expensive business attire, paid close attention to the information being presented. Mr. Mercer, a well-trained and gifted speaker, captivated his audience with his expansive knowledge of climate change and its purported dangers. At exactly the right places in his presentation, Mr. Mercer banged on the lectern with his fist for added impact. Knowing exactly when to change the inflection of his voice or when to increase the volume of his voice, he deftly manipulated the audience, keeping them on the edge of their seats.

Building to the conclusion of his presentation, he stepped down off the small platform and stood directly in front of the crowd. Becoming very animated, he extolled the virtues of Socialism, his voice raising to a fevered pitch. Nearly screaming, he drove home the point of his presentation by berating Capitalism and calling *anyone* who believed in Capitalism simpleminded, dim-witted, and a plague upon the Earth. Finishing with a resounding flourish, he wiped his forehead with his handkerchief.

He bowed slightly as thunderous applause filled the room. Attendees all over the room rose to their feet, expressing their concurrence with his ideology. The attendees not already standing also rose to their feet, until everyone in the room was standing. He bowed deeply as the applause continued. Straightening up, he waved to the crowd. The raucous applause continued for at least three full minutes. As the applause died down, attendees made their way to the exits at the front of the room.

Standing just inside the room's entrance, a rotund, balding man with a blotchy complexion closely watched the attendees as they exited the meeting room. He had slipped inside just as the applause ended. Obvious to anyone who might have looked his way, he was scanning the crowd for someone in particular. Upon locating the individual he sought, he waited and stepped in front of a well-dressed woman as she was about to exit the room.

"Excuse me ma'am," he said, slipping a business card into her hand. "I believe you will want to talk further."

"Why would I want to do that?" she sneered as she stepped sideways, attempting to avoid the man.

Again, the man stepped sideways in front of her. "I assure you we have mutual interests. I believe you have a plan to bring down our enemy. I believe you said it requires what you call a reset, yes?"

"Where did you learn of this?"

"Not here. We need somewhere private. Will you accompany me to the bar?"

"I don't know," the woman hesitated.

"I promise you it will be well worth your time. We will be in plain sight. You will have nothing to worry about, but much to lose if you refuse."

Somewhat intrigued by the man's knowledge of her position, she agreed, "Okay, Mister Black, is it," she said, glancing down at the business card in her hand. "I will give you fifteen minutes. No more."

The woman followed the man as he led the way toward the hotel's bar area. Despite knowing the name printed on the card was likely false, she needed to learn what he knew about her position and how he had learned of it.

Being early in the day, the bar's crowd was sparse, giving Mr. Black the opportunity to select a table well away from any other patrons. He pulled out one of the elegant, over-stuffed chairs and waited for the woman to sit down.

As she sat, he pushed the chair in for her. Taking a seat on the adjacent side of the table, he waved to a server circulating the area.

"What can I get you folks?" the server asked.

Mr. Black pointed toward the woman, "Whatever you would like. I'm buying."

"Chardonnay."

"I'll have a light beer. In a glass, please."

"I'll be right back with your drinks," the server said.

Mr. Black and the woman engaged in meaningless chatter, waiting for the server to return with their drinks. Several minutes later, the server returned and placed their drinks on the table. As she turned to resume her duties, Mr. Black spoke up. "Miss, we wish that no one disturbs us."

"Absolutely. Understood, sir," she replied as she turned and left.

Mr. Black waited until the server reached the other side of the bar. Glancing around the bar, satisfied everyone was well out of earshot, Mr. Black opened his mouth, about to continue.

Before Mr. Black could speak, the woman asked. "How did you learn of me and my position?"

"For now that is not important," Mr. Black answered. "If what I am about to tell you, does not convince you to join me, what I know and how I know it will be irrelevant. May I continue?"

"Go ahead. You now have ten minutes, Mister Black," the woman said, glancing at her watch.

"I'll get right to the point. I have recently learned you detest Capitalism and believe this country should work to abolish it. Is that correct?"

"Yes. I can agree with that as do many other people," she answered, taking a small sip of her wine.

Mr. Black slipped a sheaf of papers out of his jacket pocket and pushed them in front of the woman. "Have you seen this?"

"Yes. Not only have I seen it, I have read it."

"What is your take on the author's position?"

"The author develops an interesting premise, but he offers no method to accomplish it. There are far too many unanswered questions. It would require a major disruption to even get it started."

"Do you know any of the people from the meeting?"

"Yes, a few."

"Do they feel the same way as you?"

"Yes, I believe many do. They also have read this and believe it is mostly wild speculation, and that it is not possible to accomplish its conclusion."

To avoid saying anything out loud, Mr. Black slipped another piece of paper from his other jacket pocket, unfolded it, smoothed out the creases, and slid it in front of the woman. "What if I told you I could create the required fear to trigger a reset?"

The woman's eyes widened as she quickly scanned the piece of paper. She turned the paper over, shoved it under the other papers, glancing worriedly around the room. "You can't be serious! You can't really do that."

Mr. Black reached into his jacket pocket and retrieved yet another piece of paper. Putting his finger to his lips, he pointed to the top of the paper as he slid it in front of her. He watched the woman's eyes track back and forth as she took in the information in the document.

"That is where it will begin," Mr. Black said, pointing to a red-circled area on the paper. "I assure you everything you see here is ready, except for this last item. All I need is your help obtaining the items listed at the bottom of the paper."

"I don't know. I don't think I can…."

Mr. Black interrupted the woman, "I know of your recent good fortune. You will now be able to help us with this last obstacle."

The woman just sat there staring at Mr. Black, an incredulous look on her face. Mr. Black took a sip of his beer, waiting for the woman to respond.

"You said you wanted to destroy Capitalism. Is that not true?"

"Yes, but this…. I don't…. I can't…."

"Come on. This is your chance to realize your goal. How successful have you been so far?"

The woman did not answer. Mr. Black leaned closer to the woman, "Answer me. What success have you and the others really had?"

"Too little," she answered.

"Will you help us then?"

"Yes, I will consider it. When…."

"Be at this address. 7:00 p.m. sharp," Mr. Black said, pushing a different business card over in front of the woman. He retrieved the papers, stuffed them back in his pocket, tossed a twenty dollar bill on the table, stood up, and walked away without another word. Even after the man left, the strong scent of his cologne, heavy with citrus and spice, lingered. She slowly drew in a breath and wrinkled her nose, trying to identify the mixture of underlying scents. She knew she had smelled the fragrance before, but she could not remember where.

The woman sat there for a few minutes wondering if she had made a huge mistake. Remembering her lifelong passion to see Capitalism eradicated, she persuaded herself that if there was even the most remote prospect she could help bring down Capitalism, her participation in what Mr. Black suggested would be worth the risk. She convinced herself the size of the risk simply would not matter. "*Yes, I will meet with Mister Black again and I will help him anyway I can,*" she thought as she rose from the chair and hurried off for an important meeting.

Chapter One

Anthony Sterling strolled along Quayaquil Street on his way to the Plaza de la Independencia for his morning coffee. The sun was shining brightly. The weather was beautiful and Anthony was not in a hurry. Enjoying a leisurely walk, from his luxury apartment eight blocks away on Vicente Leon Street, he had stopped several times to look in the windows of various shops. Continuing his leisurely stroll, Anthony turned right onto Chile Street and walked past the Municipio de Quito, the city's center of government and administration. He approached the busy plaza from the southeast.

Plaza de la Independencia, called Plaza Grande by most locals, served as the central public square of Quito, Ecuador. The plaza, flanked on all four sides by impressive buildings, most of which dated to the colonial period, was located in the heart of the Old City. Anthony had chosen Quito as the location to establish a new life because of Ecuador's restrictive, and secretive, banking laws. The warm climate and the low cost of living also ranked high on Anthony's list of deciding factors.

Grand and majestic colonial mansions lined many of the streets surrounding the plaza. Anthony had selected a very sumptuous apartment in one of those mansions to serve as his residence. Life in Quito was slow and enjoyable. A sizable bank account guaranteed he could live in luxury for a long time. Despite his comfortable life, an overwhelming anger bordering on rage, boiled in Anthony's heart. A failed scheme to start a war, discovered by a simple communications technician, had forced him to abandon his beautiful house and successful FBI career and flee the United States.

Anthony had escaped from the United States with only minutes to spare using a forged passport in the name, Anthony Sterling. In actuality, he was Frank Porter, former Deputy Director of the FBI's National Clandestine Service. After fleeing to Quito, he dreamed of revenge against the country he held responsible for his failed plan, his anger focused on the one individual that had discovered his plan. He vowed he would get revenge and soon.

Anthony walked along the east side of the plaza. Spotting a break in the traffic, he crossed to the east side of the street. His destination, the outdoor café at the Hotel Plaza Grande, lay just ahead. He selected a table away from the street in a courtyard lined with metal barriers. A skinny young man wearing an apron, covered in stains, approached the table. Following the same routine he repeated every day, Anthony ordered a large coffee and an empanada. Anthony grabbed the copy of El Migrante Ecuatoriano, a local newspaper he had purchased from the newsstand at the corner of the plaza; and laid it on the table. Following another ritual he repeated every day, he scrutinized the other patrons of the coffee shop, looking for anyone he might recognize or anyone that might be paying him undue attention. He felt safe in his newly adopted city and he intended to keep it that way.

Satisfied no one was watching him, he reached in his left, inside jacket pocket, about to retrieve his cell phone when the server returned with his order. The server set Anthony's order on the table and rushed off to another table. Anthony picked up the cup and took a careful sip of the dark, steaming liquid. Delicious as always. The coffee was rich and dark, just the way he liked it. Deciding to let the call wait, he took another sip of the coffee, picked up the paper, and unfolded it to the front page. Twenty minutes and another cup of coffee later, he laid the paper on the table. He removed his wide-brimmed Panama hat, laid it on the table, and leaned back in the chair, feeling the warm sunshine on his face. The vibrating cell phone in his pocket interrupted his thoughts.

"Yes," Anthony answered quizzically, not expecting a call from anyone.

"The last item is on its way," a muffled, female voice on the other end answered.

"Understood. When?"

"Four days ago. It was carried personally. Should have arrived yesterday. Maybe today."

"When does the…."

Before Anthony could finish his question, the caller ended the call. He looked at the phone, swore under his breath, and dropped the phone back into his jacket pocket. Anger, relentlessly smoldering just below the surface, flashed into Anthony's consciousness. White-hot anger surged and boiled in his mind. Visibly shaking, Anthony retrieved a bottle from his pocket and shook out two antacid tablets into his hand. He threw the tablets into his mouth and chewed on them, hoping to relieve the acid churning in his stomach. Anthony's doctor had warned him he was developing an ulcer.

Months of suppressing the white-hot anger Anthony lived with every waking hour of the day had nearly driven him mad. It infected his thoughts, invaded the quiet night, and prevented sleep. It had reached the point where Anthony was becoming detached from reality. His initial scheme to punish the country he believed had murdered his real parents had failed. His mind drifted to the time when he was six years old. A commando team that swept through the small village in Iraq where he lived had killed his parents. He had been at school when the sweep took place. Overhearing several of the teachers talking about a military raid, he raced home as fast as he could. He found his mother lying dead in the street and his father lying dead in the doorway of their home. He loved his mother, but he adored his father. Often he would sit at his father's feet for hours, listening to his every word. His father had been his entire world.

After the death of his parents, Anthony, then known as Hajazi, lived in an orphanage in Jurf Al-Sakhar, Iraq. For two long years he endured the deplorable living conditions in the orphanage. Often he went days with nothing to eat. His mother was European and light-skinned. In appearance, Hajazi favored his mother, also being more light-skinned and more European in appearance than most Iraqi boys. His non-Iraqi appearance resulted in him being bullied and ignored by the other children. Being shunned and excluded, left little for young Hajazi to do, except to sit alone for hours and nurture his growing hatred for those who had murdered his father.

On one bright and sunny Friday, an American couple named Porter visited the orphanage and to his great surprise said they wanted to adopt him. At first, the thought of being transported to a country he hated did not sit well with Hajazi. However, the man and his wife appeared to be wealthy which would allow him to escape the deplorable conditions of the orphanage. To survive, Hajazi had become adept at lying and scheming. Believing he could use the Porter's wealth to his advantage, Hajazi hugged the woman and pretended to be excited. Inwardly, he laughed at how easy people could be manipulated. Hajazi and his new parents departed the next day for a city called Dallas in the United States.

Hajazi's new parents, Benjamin and Ruth Porter, were nice and bought him new clothes. The weather was warm. The food was good and plentiful. His bed was soft and clean. Hajazi had everything he needed to be happy, but still his hatred of America burned deep within his heart. Hajazi did not understand. Why would a people with such plenty need to bomb and murder his parents?

Several months after arriving in Dallas, Hajazi's new parents asked him if he would change his name. Hajazi agreed, not because he wanted to become an American, but because he had already decided he would use his good fortune to get revenge. Three weeks later he became Frank Porter. Several months after that, his adoptive father, a successful corporate lawyer, accepted a promotion to be chief counsel for the oil firm where he worked. The promotion required a move to the firm's headquarters in Houston, Texas. Using an influential, high-ranking contact, made through his membership in Dallas's most exclusive private club, his father called in a favor and had Frank's adoption records erased completely. Even the most meticulous background check would not reveal his true identity.

His family's move landed them in the stylish Cinco Ranch subdivision of Katy, Texas, a suburb thirty miles west of Houston. Enrolling in one of the best school districts in all of Texas, Frank Porter loved school and worked hard, excelling academically, and graduating at the top of his high school class.

Many scholarships presented from top schools allowed him to pick from the best colleges. He accepted a full-ride scholarship to Yale, believing that would offer him the best likelihood of accomplishing his desired goal.

While in college, his mother died and shortly after he graduated from college with a law degree his father died. As an only child and according to his father's will, Frank Porter was the sole beneficiary of his adoptive parent's wealth. Neither he nor his parents had ever spoken of his life before adoption. Now that his parents were dead, the last knowledge of his true identity vanished. He sold the big house in Houston and moved to Washington, D.C. After a short but highly successful career as an attorney, he joined the FBI and quickly rose to the level of Director. After all the years of hard work, long hours, glad-handing the rich and powerful, and making secret deals in posh clubs, his goal was finally within his reach. Then, to his utter disbelief, his elaborately crafted scheme to exact revenge on a country he hated had failed. Forced to flee with only minutes to spare, he used a pre-arranged escape plan which landed him in Quito, Ecuador with a new name and identity: Anthony Sterling, a retired businessman.

Anthony's chair slipped and nearly tipped over, interrupting his depressing reflection and bringing his mind back
to the present. Anyone and everyone had become the *enemy*.
He no longer cared who suffered from the retaliation he
longed for. Blinded by rage, he vowed this time he would
not fail. With the required final components delivered, the
nuclear weapons he would use to threaten the United States
were being constructed at that very moment.

Smiling, he savored the thought that his new and meticulously crafted plan was about to begin, but there was another piece of unfinished business still remaining. There was
one individual he wanted to see suffer more than anyone
else. The one person he blamed for his earlier failure.

Unwilling to wait until he was home in the safety of his
apartment, he scanned the café to see if anyone was close
enough to overhear. Satisfied no one could overhear, he retrieved the cell phone from his jacket pocket and dialed a
number from memory. There was one last detail necessary to
make his long-awaited revenge complete.

After five rings, a sleepy female voice with a slight
French accent answered, "Yes."

"It's time for that job I mentioned."

"When?"

"As soon as you can make it happen."

"Consider it done."

Anthony scanned the café again and lowered his voice.
"As a bonus, I will double the fee if you make it very slow
and very painful. I want him to suffer. I want his family to
suffer. I want everyone he knows to suffer. The more they
suffer the better," Anthony snarled, his face red and his
voice full of rage.

"Agreed."

He ended the call, his hands trembling as he dropped
the cell phone back in his jacket pocket.

Seated at a different street café thirty yards away, Sotero
Rojas had observed Anthony's every move. From the time
Anthony left his apartment, Sotero had shadowed him as he

strolled along Quayaquil Street, being careful to avoid detection. Sotero and his partners, Nestor Guzman and Omer Herrera, took turns surveilling Mr. Sterling to minimize any possibility of him noticing their presence.

Also in Quito using a false name, Sotero Rojas a deep-cover CIA operative, had a special interest in Anthony Sterling, aka Frank Porter. Sotero Rojas, aka Bill Morrison, had been part of the team that uncovered Frank Porter's evil scheme. If Bill's team members had arrived in Porter's office just minutes sooner, his escape would have failed. When they arrived in his office, Porter was already gone, leaving behind a successful career, a big house, and two luxury cars. The only things not left behind were whatever had been in a now open lockbox and a large sum of money. All attempts to trace Porter and the money failed. Both Porter and the money had simply vanished. After months of searching, the FBI and CIA gave up and labeled the case unsolved.

Mr. Frank Porter became a ghost. That all ended when Sotero Rojas spotted a man he believed to be Porter at an outdoor cafe while in Quito on another assignment. Rojas, a gifted linguist, spoke five languages fluently. Being fluent in Spanish, landed him in Quito to observe and infiltrate a terrorist cell that had fled the Czech Republic and set up operations in Quito, Ecuador. Rojas, using a camera with a telephoto lens, snapped a spread of ten photos. He hurried back to his apartment and uploaded the photos to his superiors to run through facial recognition software for corroboration it was in fact Frank Porter. The answer came in less than fifteen minutes. Yes, Rojas had accidently discovered the traitor he hated. With his identity confirmed, Rojas assembled a three-man team and began daily surveillance.

After weeks of watching, Rojas took notice when he saw Porter either receive or make two phone calls. Only once before had he made even a single phone call and now, there had been two short phone calls within seconds of each other. More conspicuous was that he seemed angry and agitated. Rojas had an earwig in his left ear connected to a highly directional listening device. However, there was so much activity and traffic on the streets around the plaza, he had only understood a few of Anthony's words. Rojas watched as his query got up, dropped several bills on the table, and hurried down Chile Street toward his apartment.

Anything this out of the ordinary definitely required a call to his superior. He lifted an encrypted SAT phone out of its leather case, punched a speed dial number, and waited.

In an office in the George Bush Center for Intelligence in Fairfax, Virginia, eighteen miles west of Washington, D.C., a phone rang. Thomas F. Calhoun, Director CIA Special Activities Division, glanced at the secure phone sitting on the corner of his desk. Instantly recognizing the incoming number, he grabbed the receiver and answered, "Good morning my friend, do you have something?"

"Yes sir, I do. Just now there were two short phone calls within seconds of each other. He looked as if he was furious and agitated. He left the café in a hurry. Looks like he's heading back to his apartment."

"Anything else?"

"Too much background noise to hear his entire conversations. I could only understand a few words. On the first call, all I could understand was *'arrived yesterday'*. On the second call, all I got was two words, *'soon'* and then *'suffer'*."

"Any idea what they might mean?" Director Calhoun asked, scribbling the words on a notepad.

"Sorry, no. I have no idea, sir."

"Okay. Keep eyes on him and report anything else that might give us a clue to what he's up to."

"Will do." Rojas answered. He ended the call, dropped the SAT phone back in its case, and hurried off to catch up with his query.

In his office, Director Calhoun stared at the words he had scribbled on the notepad, wondering what they might mean.

He knew Frank Porter had been involved in a scheme to start a war and had fled the Unite States just minutes before the Capitol Police had arrived in his office to arrest him. He also knew Porter was smart and cunning and would do nothing to jeopardize his cover. Unless something extraordinary was happening. Deciding he should check to see if his boss had any additional intel, he picked up the phone and dialed the number for the Director of the CIA.

"James Sandberg, can I help you?" The Director of the CIA mumbled, the stump of his ever-present cigar stuffed in the side of his mouth. Sandberg never lit the cigar, but the cigar grew shorter and shorter until he would discard a tiny stub and stuff a fresh one in his mouth. Everyone wondered what happened to the part of the cigar that disappeared, but no one ever asked.

"Hey, Jim. Thomas Calhoun here. I need to know if there's any recent intel on a man named Frank Porter."

"That stinking slime ball!" Director Sandberg snarled, jerking the cigar stub from his mouth and dropping it into an ashtray. "Not directly, but there has been increased chatter coming from the Middle East, Libya specifically. One of our assets thought they heard his name mentioned a few weeks ago in relation to something being smuggled. We tried to run it down, but it went nowhere."

"Anything more specific on Porter than that?"

"No. Why do you ask?" Director Sandberg queried.

"Just a few minutes ago, one of my assets observed Porter receive or make two quick phone calls. He also said Porter appeared to be furious and agitated. He could only catch a few words. One phrase *'arrived yesterday'* might seem worrisome. What do you think?"

"Are you on a secure phone?"

"Yes, I am. I'll activate encryption."

Director Sandberg did the same on his end of the phone call. A telltale echo signaled multi-layer encryption had been activated. Sandberg continued, "Several weeks ago hyperspectral satellite imaging detected a hot spot off the coast of Libya. Once the NIAG (Nuclear Interdiction Action Group) team arrived on scene, they got a hit on a freighter approximately fifty miles south of Malta. They stopped the freighter in international waters and boarded it. According to the captain, the vessel was bound for the Strait of Gibraltar and then on to Caracas, Venezuela. The interdiction team measured fairly high levels of background radiation in one compartment but that was all. A thorough search of the ship turned up no nuclear devices or weapons components. The ship's captain claimed they had transported medical imaging equipment a month earlier and that one container was severely damaged, causing it to break open and spill out some components. He claimed that had to be the source of the radiation. The team…."

"It's obvious he was lying, Jim. That event makes what I told you even more suspicious," Director Calhoun interrupted.

"Of course he was lying," Director Sandberg agreed. "But, with no evidence, the NIAG team had no choice but to let them go. If they had a nuclear device or any weapon components on board, they had been offloaded before they arrived on scene."

"I hope you put in a request to have the freighter tracked."

"I certainly did. Won't do any good though. Now that they know they have our attention, they won't go anywhere near their original destination. There have been five other detections, but each time the NIAG team arrived, it was the same as with the freighter. They measured some background radiation but could find nothing else. They had to know when we were coming."

"That's very alarming," Director Calhoun replied. "In view of these events, I think we need to proceed with extreme caution and assign some additional resources to see if we have a leak somewhere. What do you think Jim?"

"I concur, but we must do it outside normal channels. If there is a leak, and it's high enough to know what NIAG is doing, I can't use any of my normal resources. Let me know if you receive any further intel regarding Porter."

"Absolutely. I agree," Director Calhoun answered.

Both men switched off their end of the encryption system and hung up their phones. Director Sandberg knew he would have to be cautious and use only resources outside the usual chain of command. Director Sandberg returned to the stack of work on his desk with the question of what resource or resources he could use swirling in his mind.

An hour and two cups of coffee later, the answer popped into Director Sandberg's consciousness. He knew exactly the resource that would be perfect for what he needed. He got up from his desk and stuck his head into the outer office. "Jane, I need to make a private phone call. See I am not disturbed by *anyone* and hold all phone calls." He pushed the office door shut and locked it. Returning to his desk, he punched a number into the phone and waited.

"Admiral Charles Hadley, Naval Intelligence, may I help you?"

"Chuck, James Sandberg here."

"Hey, Jim. What can I do for you?"

"Can you talk privately?"

"Hang on a minute, Jim," Admiral Hadley said as he put Director Sandberg on hold. He called his assistant in the outer office and instructed her to close his office door and see that absolutely no one entered his office. He punched the blinking line on his phone. "Go ahead, Jim."

"I've got a problem, Admiral," Director Sandberg continued, becoming more formal. "What I am about to share with you is sensitive compartmented information. Your office establishes the access control systems for that type information. So, you know the risk I am taking."

"Yes, Jim, I do," Admiral Hadley replied. "What is so important to make you willing to take such a risk?"

"Just a few minutes ago, I received a call from the Director of the Special Activities Division. An asset that is shadowing a fugitive overheard fragments of two phone calls that are quite troubling when combined with other intel we are receiving. The bigger concern, however, is that it appears there is a high-level source that is leaking operational information. I need someone with resources outside my normal chain of command. Your name came to mind. If you will assist, I will give you the details. Otherwise, it was nice talking to you."

"I don't know, Jim," Admiral Hadley hesitated. "Sounds rather far outside the boundaries of what is legal."

"Let me give you a little incentive then," Director Sandberg urged. "The fugitive we have under surveillance is your old friend Frank Porter."

"That vile, traitorous rat?" Admiral Hadley snapped, the volume of his voice rising considerably.

"Yes sir, that Frank Porter. I thought his name might put a burr under your saddle."

"You bet. I nearly had my hands on that stinking traitor once. If I had been just ten minutes earlier, he would have been mine. I thought he was in the wind. Where is he?"

"Not now. If this plays out as I hope it will, you may have the opportunity again."

"The FBI and CIA gave up trying to find him. How did you locate him?"

"One of our under-cover assets, a Bill Morrison, stumbled across him by accident. Morrison is on loan to a deep-cover mission that is watching a growing terrorist cell. He was in an outdoor café and saw a man he believed to be Porter. He snapped a quick photo spread and sent it in for facial recognition. Facial recognition reported a ninety-nine percent match to Porter's employee file photo. I can't say anymore at this point. Are you in?"

"You bet I'm in," Admiral Hadley snarled. "I would throw away my entire career to put my hands around the neck of that scumbag."

"Okay then, Admiral. I am convinced someone is moving weapons grade nuclear material into the country. In my mind, it wouldn't be worth the effort unless they, whoever they are, have the means to use the material. Every time we identify a target and we get close to them, nothing! We measure some background radiation but, never any actual material or components. Someone has to be feeding them our operational plans. How else could they know exactly when to transfer the material? The interdiction team has come up empty six times. That's just not possible unless they are being tipped off."

"I agree. Sounds highly likely they're being warned," Admiral Hadley added. "What can I do to help?"

"I need you to assign a resource to investigate a lead we have. Maybe your resource can turn up something if we start from this end."

"I assume you want this *off-the-books*?" Admiral Hadley asked.

"Yes sir, very *off-the-books*," Director Sandberg answered, lowering his voice so the Admiral could barely hear. "I have an asset that has uncovered a lead pointing to the southern border as the entry point. I have specific details I will send you via hand-delivery. There will be no record of this."

"Jim, this is beginning to sound a mite dicey. Is my career at risk?"

"Yes, Admiral. Very likely. If anything leaks out, we never had this conversation. Admiral, this is as hot as it gets. I wouldn't ask otherwise. With that in mind, I suggest you chose your resource *very, very* carefully."

"Agreed. When will the details arrive?"

"Within the hour."

"How do I contact you if we learn anything?"

"That will be in the packet. I've got to go Admiral."

"Okay, Jim. I'll do what I can."

Admiral Hadley dropped the receiver back in its cradle, wondering if he had just flushed his career down the toilet. He sat there for a long time replaying the vision of his shoulder boards being ripped off, chains placed around his ankles, and then being led off to prison for a very long time. If it meant seeing Porter behind bars, it would be worth it. As Director Sandberg suggested, he would need a special individual for this assignment. Someone not officially connected to him or his department. His mind was blank. "*If I make a mistake….*," he thought. He decided it would be better if he did not think about that.

Admiral Hadley swiveled around and grabbed the carafe sitting on the credenza behind him. He filled his coffee mug, swiveled back around toward his desk, and took a sip of the coffee, his mind racing trying to decide what to do next. He needed to assign someone to track down the lead Director Sandberg would deliver to him and also any known associates that former Director Frank Porter had used in the past.

"Who should I call?" Admiral Hadley muttered out loud.

60 Riverside Boulevard
The Aldyn Apartments
Apartment 3203
New York, New York

"Pathetic, stupid idiot," the impeccably dressed woman laughed as she dropped a cheap, burner phone on the floor and stomped on it with the spiked heel of her expensive designer shoe. A tiny wisp of smoke curled up from the crushed phone. Touching the destroyed phone and finding it only mildly warm, she picked up the phone and dropped it in a sealable plastic bag she would discard later.

Holding a small, black notebook open with one hand, she pulled another cheap, burner phone out of her handbag. She punched in an underlined number and waited.

"Who is calling?" a heavily accented, male voice asked.

"Jane," the woman answered. "Is it done as I requested?"

"Exactly as instructed. He was only one on duty. Pretended he not see anything."

"Are you certain?"

"Yes. I watch closely. No one else see anything."

"What about the one who brought it north?"

"I pay him well. He gone. Back to home in Guatemala."

"When does he go off duty?"

"In two hours."

"You have the untraceable weapon I provided you?"

"Yes, I have."

"When he leaves, follow him. Make sure he stays silent permanently and make sure he is never found."

"Yes, I can do. Is much lonely desert here."

"Good. I have paid you half. When you have finished the job, someone will tell you how to collect the other half. Disappear and never mention this."

"Yes, it will be done."

The woman ended the call and destroyed the second burner phone just as she did the other one. Into the bag, the second burner phone went with the other destroyed phone.

"*It's amazing what people will do if you offer them enough money,*" she thought to herself. What was even more remarkable was that they would trust someone who would offer money to have someone killed.

"Poor, stupid man," she giggled as she dropped the bag of destroyed phones in her handbag. Little did the man know, he would never receive the last half of the money nor would he live to spend a single penny of the first half. He would join his victim in that lonely desert.

On her way out of the lavish apartment, she stopped in front of the hallway mirror to check her appearance. Pulling a tortoiseshell comb out of her handbag, she swirled several wayward strands of hair back into place in her elaborately coiffed blond hair. "*Perfect. Absolutely perfect,*" she thought, gazing at her reflection in the oversize mirror.

It had been a long, demanding, and sometimes demeaning, journey from the time she graduated law school, passing the bar exam on the first try. Expecting to jump right into an impressive office at a prestigious law firm turned out to be only a dream, or, more accurately, a nightmare. In Washington, D.C., lawyers were a dime a dozen or as thick as fleas on a dog's back as she was often and powerfully reminded. Left with little choice, she accepted a position as a lowly political aide. She absolutely hated it, but she bit her tongue and did anything and everything requested of her. Some things she did were legal, and some things were not.

Working alongside the most powerful lawyers and politicians in all of Washington, she learned quickly how to use people and, better yet, how to manipulate the system. What was good and right meant absolutely nothing in the nation's capital. Power. It was always about power. Being adept at reading people, allowed her to move up quickly, landing the desired lavish, corner office in less than eight years. Offered a full partnership in a very prestigious law firm just two years later, she quickly accepted. Finally, the prestige and power she craved were hers. Without a husband, and no desire for one, she moved effortlessly among the rich and powerful of Washington. Brandishing the power she possessed like a club, she used it to destroy anyone foolish enough to oppose her or get in the way.

"Now, look at me," she thought. *"A member of the United States House of Representatives and a member of a very important and powerful intelligence committee."* Despite an astonishing career and all the money she could ever need, an insatiable desire, bordering on insanity, fueled her desire for ever-increasing power and prestige. She refused to accept anything less than the total eradication of Capitalism, Like most single-minded ideologues, she yearned to destroy the monetary mechanism that had provided her the position, money, and power she craved. From birth, raised by parents that came out of the rebellious, free love and drugs hippy era, she had been saturated with the propaganda and philosophy of wild-eyed radicals. From early adulthood, she had secretly read and listened to all the fanatical socialist and communist philosophers until her inner soul became hopelessly blinded by their militant rhetoric.

The first step of her diabolical plan already underway, she beamed as she picked up her expensive, designer handbag and left the apartment. The knowledge, connections, and power required to execute such a plan were hers and she knew it. And she intended to use them.

"Consequences?" she laughed, heading for the elevator. "Who cares about consequences?"

Chapter Two

Arco Truck Stop
Three Miles north of Lodi, California

Sharan Husam Ahadi had driven the thirty-nine miles from Sacramento, obeying all traffic laws to avoid arousing even the slightest suspicion. After exiting State Route 99, Sharan pulled into an Arco truck stop and drove his 2003 Renault Espace around toward the rear of the restaurant on the south side of the truck stop, selecting a spot in the parking area away from prying eyes.

After arriving in the United States a year earlier, Sharan had assumed a Westernized appearance so he would not stand out. With great reluctance, he had shaved off his beard and had purchased a wardrobe of ordinary American clothes. Sharan loathed the Western clothes he was wearing. Every fiber of his being wanted to rip them off and burn them. In his mind, the clothing represented everything he hated about America, the Great Satan. Every day he had to force himself to dress in attire that represented the immoral lifestyle of the Western world because it was essential he blend in with the Americans.

Late getting started that morning, he had not taken the time to shave. He pulled off his sunglasses and stared into the rear-view mirror. The face staring back at him revealed a full day's growth of dark stubble and heavy dark circles under his eyes, the result of being up for twenty-four hours. He needed a shower, a meal, and then some sleep, but that would all have to wait. The last piece of his mission would soon be complete. Personal comforts would come later. He hoped he would look like any other midnight shift worker on his way home.

He sat in his car, impatient that his friend Muti had not yet arrived with the package. Every few minutes Sharan glanced at his watch, growing angrier each time. The longer he sat there in the parking lot, the more likely it was that someone would notice him and become suspicious. An hour had passed and still no Muti. About to start the car and leave the truck stop, Sharan sighed with relief when he saw Muti pull into an empty space in the opposite row.

Muti Nabih Daher got out of his car, hurried over to where Sharan was parked, and slipped into the passenger seat.

"Muti, I have been waiting for an hour. What kept you?" Sharan asked, anger clearly evident in his voice.

"I had to wait for the delivery. The man was late. There was nothing I could do. As soon as we transferred the container, I drove straight through without stopping," Muti offered in defense.

"Well, you are here now. Did you have any difficulty?"

"No. I was very careful to stay under the speed limit. I only stopped once for fuel."

"What about the delivery man? Did he have any trouble crossing the border? Did he raise any suspicion?"

"No, no trouble. He said he drove right across. He said the border guard looked at him and then turned away. Didn't even look in the car."

"Allah be praised," Sharan proclaimed. "It is as Mahmud said."

"I do not understand," Muti said, a puzzled look on his face.

"Muti, do you not remember," Sharan chided. "I told you about Mahmud Hakeem Antar. He confided in me that he has someone high in the government helping him. He paid people lots of money to look the other way and not see things."

"That is good, but he ah…., he ah…."

"Yes Muti, out with it. Did something happen?"

"Not with me, Sharan. The man that carried the container across the border said he opened it and looked inside."

"What?" Sharan gasped. "Why? Muti, you know they not allow this!"

"Sharan, there was nothing I could do. It had already happened."

"Did you question him?"

"Yes, I did. He is stupid and did not understand the danger. He knows nothing. He said he only opened it for a few seconds and glanced inside."

"Let us hope so, Muti. Let us hope so," Sharan moaned, shaking his head. "No one must know of this. Did you warn him to say nothing?"

"Yes. I told him someone would slit his throat if he said anything and then I showed him this," Muti answered, his eyes gleaming with hatred.

"Muti, put that away!" Sharan shouted, grabbing Muti's hand and shoving it down out of sight. "Do you want to get us caught?"

Muti quickly slid the gleaming dagger back into the scabbard behind his back.

"Let's get this done quickly," Sharan said as he backed out of the parking space. He drove his Renault around the row of cars and over to where Muti had parked his car. Muti watched for activity while Sharan struggled to get the heavy container up out of Muti's trunk and into the trunk of his Renault.

Sharan retrieved a large wad of bills from his pocket. He split the wad in half and handed half to Muti. "A little reward for your efforts, Muti. Spend it carefully. Do not attract attention to yourself."

Muti eagerly grabbed the wad of bills and stuffed them in his pocket. "May Allah grant us safety and great success," Muti said as he hugged his old friend.

"Yes. May it be always true," Sharan answered. "Hurry. We must go now. Quickly, before someone notices. Muti, go find our stupid friend and make sure he stays silent. Oh, Muti, before you do that, find that weak-minded Abdul Hadad. He likes America too much. He cannot be trusted. He is no longer needed. Make certain he also stays silent."

Both men climbed into their cars and headed for the highway frontage road. Upon reaching the highway frontage road, Muti, with a menacing grin on his face, turned south eager to silence Abdul and the stupid man that delivered the container. He despised both men and would enjoy very much making sure both stayed silent permanently. Sharan turned north and headed toward Sacramento. He also was smiling, knowing he was about to accomplish the great feat for which he had been born.

Suitland Federal Center
Office of Director of Naval Intelligence
Suitland, Maryland

Admiral Hadley sat at his desk staring off into space. He was having difficulty concentrating. The imminent threat of a nuclear weapon or at least the components necessary to build one slipping into the United States had him rattled. He needed to identify and quickly contact a trusted resource he could assign to track down leads. His mind had drifted off to the catastrophic consequences that would result if the extremists possessing nuclear materials could not be located in time. The horrible images of destruction flashing through his mind sent chills down his spine.

A knock at the door and the sudden entrance of his administrative assistant interrupted his sudden daydream, wrenching him back from the vision of cataclysm swirling before his eyes. Turning toward the door and seeing Jenny, his assistant, he remembered he had a meeting scheduled. A quick glance at his watch. "Good Lord," he exclaimed. "The meeting started ten minutes ago." Looking up at Jenny, he said, "Call the conference room and tell them to continue the meeting without me. I have an absolutely critical task I must attend to."

Jenny nodded her head, backed out of Admiral Hadley's office, and quietly pulled the door closed.

"Well, who can I call?" he asked himself for the second time as he picked up his coffee cup. About to take a swallow, he realized the coffee had gone cold. He pushed back from the desk, walked over to the small sink in the corner of his office, and dumped the cold coffee down the drain. As his hand touched the handle of the coffee pot, he stopped and stared at the photo hanging on the wall in front of him. A familiar face stared back at him.

"I know exactly who I need," he thought to himself as he rushed back to his desk. He tapped the space bar on the keyboard and waited for the computer to wake up. Opening his electronic contact list, he searched for the name that had just flashed into his mind. Reading from the screen, he quickly punched the number into his phone and waited. It would be a monumental and dangerous mission to dump on his new friend, but he did not know of anyone else better suited for the task.

"What if he refuses?" Admiral Hadley asked as he listened to ringing on the other end of the call. "But he can't. He must help," he begged out loud.

West Elgin Street
Tulsa, Oklahoma

Zachariah James Templeton gritted his teeth and pulled on the pipe wrench as hard as he dared, his face turning red. A heavy leak had developed at the water heater's cold water input fitting. "Why do these things always happen at the worst possible time?" he sputtered through clenched teeth, giving the wrench one last tug. He stopped and loosened the jaws of the pipe wrench, afraid to pull any harder for fear of breaking the fitting and creating a real disaster. He wiped the fitting dry with an old rag and waited. So far so good. The fitting appeared to have stopped leaking. He stood there watching the fitting for several minutes. Satisfied the fitting had stopped leaking, at least for the present, he dropped the pipe wrench in the bucket of tools sitting beside the water heater. He grabbed the bucket of tools and slammed the mechanical room door shut much harder than necessary.

After a quick stop in the garage to put the tools away, he headed for the bedroom to pack for a short three-day business trip. If no more interruptions arose and if traffic cooperated, he just might make his flight. Busy stuffing clothes into his suitcase, he did not notice Angie, his wife, enter the bedroom.

"Zach, you have a phone call," she announced.

"Huh, what?" he said, turning toward Angie.

"Phone call," she repeated, holding out his cell phone.

"Don't have time. Tell whoever it is to call back next week."

"Zach, it's Admiral Hadley. He says it's urgent, and he sounds frantic."

"Okay, okay," Zach answered, taking the cell phone and putting it to his ear. "Sorry to cut you off Admiral, but I don't have….."

Admiral Hadley interrupted Zach, explaining the bare basics for the unexpected phone call. As Zach listened, his eyes grew wider and wider.

"When did you learn of this?" Zach asked.

"Less than thirty minutes ago, Zach."

"Did you call anybody else, Admiral, or was I your first call?"

"There's nobody better for this and you know it."

"I'm not so sure, Admiral. I can think…."

"Zach, we don't have time to argue about this," Admiral Hadley interrupted again. "This is time critical. We absolutely have to get more intel on this threat, and quickly. What we currently know is several days old."

Zach just stood there staring at Angie, not saying anything. Angie walked over and poked Zach on the arm.

"Zach, what's the matter?" she asked, concern growing in her mind. She remembered vividly what had happened the last time Admiral Hadley had persuaded Zach to get involved in tracking down a depraved psychopath and stopping his plot to start a war. It cost Zach's friend his life and it nearly cost Zach his life.

"Admiral, hang on a minute. Angie is here with me," Zach said as he put the phone on mute and turned toward Angie. "Angie, this is beyond serious. I don't know what I am allowed to tell you. Can you give me a few minutes alone so I can get the rest of the details?"

"Zach, you can't do this again. You promised," Angie protested.

"Let me finish with the Admiral. Then we'll talk. Okay?"

"Okay, Zach. I'll be in the living room waiting," Angie grumbled as she walked out of the bedroom and pulled the door shut.

"Okay, Admiral, continue," Zach said.

"I probably shouldn't say this on an unsecure line but I don't have time to get you to a secure phone. A quick response team from the Nuclear Interdiction Action Group intercepted a freighter near Malta because satellite imaging detected a hot target near Libya. The NIAG team found evidence of radiation but nothing else. If there were nuclear weapons or components on the ship, they were long gone. However, what is more worrisome is two communications fragments picked up during surveillance of our old friend Frank Porter. It seems your old friend, Bill Morrison, stumbled across him while on another mission. You do remember Mister Porter don't you, Zach?"

"Oh yes, I remember him well," Zach replied, anger instantly flaring inside him. "I would very much like to get my hands on him, Admiral."

"I thought that would be the case," Admiral Hadley answered. He continued with the details of what he knew, "The message fragments your friend Bill intercepted are:

'arrived yesterday', 'soon', and 'suffer'. CIA Director Jim Sandberg believes those message fragments along with the hot freighter combined with some additional intel he did not share indicate a nuclear weapon or its components may already be in the country. What worries Director Sandberg more is that there is a high-level leak that is revealing operational plans. Every time the NIAG team got close to a suspected hot target, any material or components were long gone. Director Sandberg was concerned enough he called me and asked me for an *off-the-books* resource to track down a lead. Zach we desperately need your help on this."

"Admiral, if I were to agree, what exactly would be my objective?" Zach asked, uncertain he wanted to hear the Admiral's answer.

"We need you to interface with the Border Patrol and determine if there is any evidence of nuclear materials coming across the border, particularly in Arizona. I cannot tell you why Arizona specifically. Not yet, anyway." Admiral Hadley paused, uncertain he should say what he wanted to.

Zach waited. When Admiral Hadley did not continue, he asked, "Admiral, is there something else I should know?"

"Yes there is, but you must absolutely promise this goes no further. Even worse than the leak, he believes someone high up is helping terrorists get nuclear material maybe even weapons across the border."

"What?" Zach exclaimed.

"Zach, I only told you that so you will understand the need for absolute secrecy. You will need to be extremely careful when you question anyone. You will report anything you learn to me and to me only."

"Sounds like you believe I have already accepted your request, Admiral."

"I certainly hope so, Zach. In view of what I just told you, there is no one else I can trust. Will you agree to help us?"

"Okay, Admiral. If it means Porter will finally get what's coming to him, I will help you."

"That's great Zach. There's one more thing. You will need backup and protection. I can think of only one person who both you and I trust implicitly. Do you think Mister Glover would agree to join you?"

Zach wanted to disagree with Admiral Hadley, but he knew the Admiral was right. There simply was no one else. "I want to say no, but I know you're right, Admiral."

"Hang on, Zach," the Admiral said, searching through his contact list again. "Here's his phone number. I think it would be best if you talked to him."

Zach scribbled the phone number on a notepad sitting on the dresser. "There's one additional thing, Admiral. I need your permission to tell Angie something. We got back together and are doing great. If I run off after talking to you with no explanation, this time our marriage will be over for sure. If I can't tell her something that will convince her this is necessary, I won't help you. Non-negotiable Admiral."

"You have my permission, but only if she agrees to tell no one. It might surprise you to know I agree it is necessary for Angie to know. She will probably be in as much danger as you are if any of this leaks out. You have my direct number. Once you get Mister Glover to agree, let me know what you need and where you need it. I mean absolutely anything Zach. Just name it."

"Well, for starters, I will need total access to the Gulf-stream for the duration. Get it started toward McChord Air Force Base immediately. Call me and let me know when its wheels up."

"Done," Admiral Hadley agreed. "What else?"

"I will need high-level authority and immunity. This could get messy, Admiral, very messy."

"I will see to it that you have Special Agent authority by the end of the day tomorrow at the latest. As far as immunity, do what you need to do, Zach. I will clean up any mess later. Continue."

"I'll get you a list of everything else we will need as soon as I can."

"Fair weather and good hunting, Zach," Admiral Hadley offered.

"Thanks Admiral. Call you soon," Zach replied as he ended the call.

About to go face Angie, Zach stopped and stared at his reflection in the mirror sitting atop the dresser. He did not like the image that stared back at him. His thinning hair had grayed a lot during the past eighteen months and deep lines creased his face. The terrible events of those months flashed through his mind: his best friend murdered, forced to rely upon his SEAL training to stop a madman, a near divorce, seeing a despicable traitor escape, and perhaps worst of all, seeing his business, his lifelong dream, fail. The reflection staring back at him looked old and tired beyond Zach's forty-five years.

The call from Admiral Hadley revived all those haunting memories. When he returned from the last crisis he found himself embroiled in, all but a few small clients had cancelled their contracts with his communications support company. With debt mounting and the company beyond salvaging, he closed down the company and sold off its few remaining assets. He accepted a mid-level position with a local consulting firm and without the demands of the business, he and Angie were happy again. He had promised Angie there would not be any more sudden disappearances.

"*Now this*," Zach thought as he took a deep breath and headed for the living room to discuss the details of the current emergency with Angie.

Once Zach had Angie's assurance she would just sit and listen until he finished explaining the reason for Admiral Hadley's call, he spent the next fifteen minutes telling her what he had just learned from Admiral Hadley. The expression on Angie's face changed from shock to anger to horror and back to anger and finally to acceptance.

Angie could tell by the expression on Zach's face he had already accepted the mission. Even if she wanted to, how could she refuse if Zach had even the remotest prospect of helping stop the horror of nuclear weapons.

Knowing that Zach would be in great danger, Angie hugged Zach and begged him to be careful.

"You know I will Angie," Zach answered. "There's one other thing."

"What?" Angie blurted out, fearing something even worse.

"The Admiral asked me to call Norman Glover and ask him to help me," Zach answered.

"If it weren't so dangerous, I would say great. Do you think he will agree?"

"I certainly hope so. A plane is already on the way to pick him up. I need to go call him and convince him," Zach called out over his shoulder as he walked into the bedroom and pushed the door shut. He looked down at the number he had scribbled on the notepad, punched the number into the phone, and waited.

After eight rings, Zach was about to hang up.

"Hello," a winded voice answered.

Zach crossed his fingers and said, "Mister Glover, this is Zach Templeton. How are you?"

"Uh, I'm fine. Can't say I expected to hear from you," Mr. Glover answered.

"Are you alone?" Zach asked.

"Yes. Misses Glover is out in the garden."

"You know I wouldn't have called unless it was important. Well, this is beyond important. It is critical. I think maybe you should sit down."

Mr. Glover pulled a chair over by the desk and sat down, "Okay, shoot."

"I just got a call from Admiral Hadley. Seems there is a serious and imminent threat related to nuclear materials being smuggled across our southern border. Are you familiar with NIAG?"

"Yes, I know who they are and what they do."

"Several days ago satellite imaging detected a hot target coming out of Libya. The NIAG quick response team boarded a freighter, but found only residual radiation. Any nuclear weapons or components that might have been there were already long gone. It's also a concern that this was number six of six. After the initial detection, there was never a trace again. The Admiral didn't say so, but I think the satellite detections were just a ruse. The false positives kept the NIAG team chasing its tail. You know, keep them looking at the right hand while the left hand does something different. My feeling is that the material was shielded then moved by air to Mexico and then across the border. I think somebody wanted NIAG looking for another ship."

"Where do they think the material was headed?" Norman asked.

"Admiral Hadley and others think they were bound for the States."

"Is he certain? Exactly how long ago was this? What do you mean were?" Norman asked, emphasizing the word 'were'.

"One of the message fragments the surveillance team overheard was 'already arrived'. That means the material is likely already here in the States. At least the first five, anyway." Zach replied.

"That certainly is serious, but how do you figure into that or better yet how do I figure into all this?"

"Admiral Hadley asked me to run down some leads and see if I could find out where it might be. He said there is no one else he could trust because he and the CIA Director suspect a high-level official of helping terrorists get nuclear weapons into the country. He also suggested I convince you to help me."

"You can't be serious," Norman stammered.

"You bet I'm serious. The Admiral said this is to be an *off-the-books* op. If we can't locate the actors involved and where the materials' destination may be, the consequences will be catastrophic."

"Do I have any choice?" Norman quipped.

"Sorry, no. I requested total access to the Gulfstream for as long as we need it. It is already on its way to McChord Air Force Base to pick you up."

"Well then, I guess I better pack and head your way."

"Work up a list of anything you might need and pass it along to the pilot. I'll do the same on my end. We will combine the lists when I join you. The Gulfstream will stop here in Tulsa and pick me up."

"What is our final destination?"

"Not on the phone. I'll let you know when you get here. Sorry, but I can't talk any longer. I have a lot to do to get ready."

"Understood. It will be great to see you again," Norman said as he ended the call, shoving the phone back into its charger.

Norman headed for the garden to tell his wife he was taking a little trip. He dreaded the conversation to come, knowing his wife would be furious. After the last assignment, he had given his word there would be no more sudden disappearances. "I shouldn't make promises I can't keep," he muttered to himself as he pushed the door open.

Chapter Three

Copper Queen Community Hospital
100 East 5th Street
Douglas, Arizona

Dr. Marshall K. Woods sat alone in the Emergency Department break room at a small table in the corner. Exhausted and bleary-eyed, he caught himself nodding off, nearly slipping out of his chair. Easing out of the chair, he stood and stretched his tired aching muscles. Having nearly completed his third full day on duty, it was impossible to sit still without falling asleep.

Like most small town hospitals, Copper Queen Community Hospital was severely understaffed. Dr. Woods was one of only two emergency department physicians and the other physician, Dr. Ramona Berger, had called out sick with a severe case of the flu. It had been a busy night and Dr. Woods had gotten no sleep and little rest. If Dr. Berger didn't show up for her shift change, he would request the hospital assign one of its other physicians to the ER Department.

Under normal conditions, a hospital in a town with a population just shy of seventeen thousand, would not be swamped with cases on the 12:00 a.m. to 8:00 a.m. shift. However, Douglas, Arizona, being on the United States border across from Agua Prieta, Mexico, created a nearly constant flow of individuals, legal and illegal, suffering from exposure, sick from some disease, or injured during a scuffle with Border Patrol agents.

Dr. Woods was tall, standing six feet, three inches, and slim, partly due to the effect of two years internship and nearly two years at his current position. Upon graduation from the University of Houston Medical School he had accepted an internship in internal medicine at Texas Health Presbyterian Hospital in Dallas, Texas. To help finance his education, he had joined the U.S. Army Reserves. Under different circumstances, he would not have considered a position in such an out of the way place. To satisfy his U.S. Army Reserve requirements he had accepted the position at Copper Queen Community Hospital. He was also required to assist the United States Border Patrol in Douglas as necessary and as he had time.

Dr. Woods yawned as he ambled over to the counter where the coffeepot sat. He picked up the coffeepot and sniffed it. As usual, the coffee was old and burnt, but it was hot and he definitely needed the jolt of caffeine. He poured the cup two-thirds full, topped it off with artificial creamer, and slid the pot back on the burner. Dr. Woods grabbed a wooden swizzle stick, stirred the coffee until the creamer dissolved, and tossed the swizzle stick into the trash bin. He walked back over to the table and sat down. After blowing across the hot liquid several times, he took a small sip. If he had been near a sink, he would have spit out the bitter swill.

"Doctor Woods, I take it you don't like our wonderful coffee," Dr. Ramona Berger said, observing the sour look on his face, as she pulled out a chair and sat down opposite Dr. Woods.

"Oh, is that what you call this slop?" Dr. Woods shot back. "I think motor oil or, perhaps, road tar would be a much better description."

"Marshall, I'm sorry I couldn't make my shift yesterday. I don't think I spent over ten minutes out of bed all day. I stayed wrapped up in my blankets like a cocoon."

"I'm sorry you were sick," Dr. Woods offered. "However, I sure am glad you made it to work today though. I don't think I could…."

The sudden vibration and chirping from the pager clipped on the waistband of Dr. Woods' scrubs interrupted his reply to Dr. Berger mid-sentence.

"Sorry, looks like I have to go. EMTs are bringing in a patient with severe vomiting and disorientation. See you after turnover," Dr. Woods yelled over his shoulder as he ran down the hallway toward the emergency room entrance.

Arriving at the emergency room entrance at the same time as the EMTs, Dr. Woods grabbed one side of the gurney and helped guide the gurney into bay number two. The patient was trying to speak, but his words were slurred and unintelligible.

"Carol, O-Two, two liters, insert a Foley catheter. Get a sample for a full drug screen, CBC, arterial blood gas, chem screen, and a full tox panel."

Carol Morgan, one of three on-duty ER nurses, busied herself slicing the patient's trousers from ankle to waist and then his shirt from waist to neck. She gathered the shredded clothes and stuffed them into a white patient belongings bag.

As soon as Carol finished with the clothes, Dr. Woods jammed the stethoscope into his ears and listened to the patient's chest. With Carol's help, they rolled the patient on his side and Dr. Woods listened to the patient's breath sounds. After checking for any visible signs of trauma, they rolled the patient onto his back and Dr. Woods checked the patient's pupils' reaction to light.

"Any details we should know?" Dr. Woods asked the EMTs, pulling the stethoscope from his ears and draping it around his neck.

The EMT standing closest to the gurney answered, "We don't know much. The Border Patrol agents said they found him wandering in the desert three miles east of town. They said he was babbling nonsense. All they could get is that his name is Paulo Cordova Palomo and that he's from Juarez, Mexico."

"That's all?" Dr. Woods asked.

"Sorry, Doc. That's it."

The EMTs gathered up their equipment and exited the room as Dr. Woods continued his physical examination of the patient. While waiting for the labs to come back, he grabbed the chart and entered the available physical information: name, city, age - early forties, height - five feet, seven inches, weight - approximately two hundred twenty pounds. He drew a thermometer across Paulo's forehead and noted in the chart that his temperature was 100.9 degrees. Mr. Polomo's skin showed considerable reddening but there were no visible signs of rash or injury.

So far, all the physical symptoms suggested this might be a simple case of exposure. However, the temperature yesterday and overnight had been reasonably mild. Perhaps the lab results would point to something more definitive. Dr. Woods continued his physical exam of the patient while waiting for the results of the blood tests to come back. The patient's symptoms did not appear drug related, but the tox screen results would take two hours to complete. He added the physical exam observations into the chart.

Looking up from the patient's chart, he saw Carol rushing into the room holding up a yellow sheet of paper. The blood test results were back. He grabbed the sheet of paper and quickly reviewed the results. It did not take long for him to realize Mr. Palomo was even sicker than he looked. The preliminary blood test results indicated Mr. Polomo might have aplastic anemia. His hematocrit percentage, red blood cell count, and hemoglobin level were all significantly below normal levels. Shaking his head and still holding the blood test results, Dr. Woods returned to the patient and lifted the gown that was covering him.

"Something's not right. Carol, come over here and look at Mister Polomo's skin. What does that look like to you?"

Carol leaned over the bed and looked where Dr. Woods was pointing. "He is quite red. Looks more like a burn than a rash in my opinion."

"Exactly my thought," Dr. Woods answered.

Since entering the emergency department, Mr. Polomo had become progressively more unresponsive. His breathing had become shallow, his temperature had increased a half degree, and he was going into shock. Dr. Woods was about to order additional tests, when Mr. Polomo began seizing which lasted for less than a minute. When the seizing stopped, the alarm on the heart monitor began screeching.

Dr. Woods stomped the release pedal on the bed allowing the bed to go completely flat. "Carol, ET tube now," he shouted as he grabbed a laryngoscope. He tilted the patient's head back and quickly inserted the tube and affixed the Ambu bag to the tube. "Carol, take over while I start CPR."

Carol and Dr. Woods worked frantically for several minutes in their attempt to revive Mr. Polomo. The heart monitor stopped its screeching. Dr. Woods glanced up at the monitor, grabbed his stethoscope, and listened for heart sounds. It appeared the crisis was over, at least for the moment.

"Normal rhythm. Carol, get Mister Polomo hooked up to a ventilator," Dr. Woods said, backing away from the gurney, panting from the sudden and intense exertion. "Carol where's the chart?"

Carol pointed down at the floor where the chart had fallen during the commotion. Dr. Woods leaned over, picked up the chart, grabbed the lab results from the bed tray, and slumped into the chair that had been pushed up against the wall. Something was not right. Aplastic anemia was a serious condition but it would not account for Mr. Polomo's sudden deterioration and cardiac arrest.

Dr. Woods inserted the lab results into the chart and reviewed all the details of Mr. Polomo's case. There were precious few clues to review regarding an outward physical explanation of the patient's condition and there was absolutely no medical history. Turning to the only other source of information available, Dr. Woods studied the lab results carefully. He rechecked each of the abnormal values he had already observed that pointed toward a diagnosis of aplastic anemia. There was one value that was inconsistent with the other abnormal values. Mr. Polomo's MCV value was eighty-two right in the middle of the normal range. MCV, or mean corpuscular volume, is a measure of the average size of the sample's red blood cells. In cases of aplastic anemia, a patient's red blood cells would be smaller and would yield a low MCV value.

"Something just doesn't add up," Dr. Woods muttered to himself. "If Mister Polomo doesn't have aplastic anemia, what does he have?"

He got up, went over to the bed, and looked down at Mr. Polomo. "What are you not telling us?" he said, as he pulled back Mr. Polomo's gown and examined the reddened skin more closely. It looked like a sunburn but it had been cloudy for several days. A memory from long ago, during the first year of his residency, flashed into his mind. He remembered he had seen something similar. He lifted the receiver from the wall phone and dialed the hematology lab.

"Hematology lab," the on-duty technician answered.

"This is Doctor Woods. Do you still have Mister Polomo's blood sample in the lab?"

"It's ready to go to the freezer for storage. I was just walking out the door when you called."

"Great. I want you to run one more test. An 'E-Tr' assay. Do you have enough sample left?"

"Sure do. That test only takes a drop or two of blood, but the analysis will take two hours."

"That's fine. As soon as the results are back, call Carol Morgan in the emergency department or page Doctor Ramona Berger and give her the results."

"Yes, sir. Will do."

"Thanks," Dr. Woods said. He hung up the phone and headed for the emergency department admin desk.

Once Mr. Polomo was finally stable and had been turned over to Dr. Berger, a profound fatigue set in. Dr. Woods was mentally and physically exhausted. He felt as if he had barely enough energy left to walk to his car.

Heading for the locker room, he stopped at the ER doorway, "Hey, Carol, when the lab calls with the results of the test I ordered, call me. I hope I'm wrong, but I have an uneasy feeling about Mister Polomo's case."

Dr. Woods turned, shuffled off toward the locker room to change out of his scrubs, and head home to get some much-needed sleep. In the locker room, he slumped down on the bench and rubbed his tired eyes. He kicked off his shoes and threw them into the bottom of his locker. He sat there for some time going over everything that had transpired regarding Mr. Polomo. A nagging feeling that something was seriously wrong would not go away. Deciding there was nothing further he could do until the results of the last blood test came back, he finished changing into street clothes and headed for the exit.

Dr. Woods rushed out of the locker room and walked directly to the exit before anything else could happen. He pushed the exit door open and hurried to the last row in the parking lot where he had parked his faded, blue 1999 Chevrolet Tracker. Quickly unlocking the door, he tossed his backpack into the back seat, and slumped down into the front seat. He started the engine and waited a few minutes for it to warm up.

He could afford a better car, but the old car had been highly reliable all the way through medical school and his internship. Old Blue as he called it had become like an old friend. It ran well; it burned no oil, and it got reasonably good gas mileage. But most important of all; it was paid for and he hated spending money unnecessarily. He was not the least concerned about flaunting a successful doctor image. In his mind, spending tens of thousands of dollars on an expensive luxury car was foolish.

He backed out of the parking space and headed west toward Highway 80. Turning right onto Highway 80; he drove north for nine blocks then turned left onto Highway 191. He turned on the radio and tuned in the local country western station. He did not particularly care for country western music, but it was the only station he could pick up on Old Blue's radio. Knowing he would have difficulty staying awake, he rolled down the driver's side window and settled in for the thirty-minute drive to his rental house just east of Elfrida.

Even if he had been looking in the rear-view mirror, he likely would not have noticed the dark green Jeep Wrangler that followed him out of the hospital parking lot because Jeep Wranglers were an extremely popular vehicle in the desert southwest. The Jeep settled in behind him, following at a safe distance.

Dr. Woods' thoughts drifted back to his patient, Mr. Polomo. In his mind, he went over all the physical observations, the blood test results, and Mr. Polomo's sudden turn for the worse. The sunburn-like redness of Mr. Polomo's skin stood out like a beacon. It was the one item that just did not fit.

Upon volunteering for his current assignment in Douglas, Arizona, Dr. Woods had been temporarily assigned to the 90th Regional Support Group, headquartered at Fort Sam Houston, in San Antonio, Texas.

Several weeks earlier, Colonel Jeffery Whalen, Dr. Woods' unit commander, had instructed him to report even the slightest incident that seemed unusual. Mr. Polomo's case certainly stood out as unusual. Rather than wait for the results of the last blood test he had ordered, he lifted his cell phone out of its holster and punched the speed-dial key for Colonel Whalen. Dr. Woods reported the puzzling symptoms he had observed.

Sharan Ahadi's Residence
900 Block E Street
Sacramento, California

Sharan Ahadi slowed down and slipped into an opening in the center lane of Highway 99 as he approached the US Highway 50 interchange. Once through the heavy traffic of the interchange, he switched on his right-turn signal and merged into the far right-hand lane. One hundred yards further, he angled off onto exit 7B and stopped at the traffic light at Thirtieth Street.

The traffic signal turned green and Sharan followed Thirtieth Street for one block then turned left onto G Street and headed toward his rental house on E Street. He continued on G Street until it intersected with Twelfth Street. He turned right, drove into Neely Johnson Park, and pulled into a parking area. For twenty minutes, Sharan sat there watching traffic. Satisfied no one had followed him, he exited the park and drove the remaining four blocks to his rental house. He pulled into the alley, backed into his driveway, and parked beside the rear porch of the old, run-down house he had rented some months earlier. Standing at the back door, he checked for the slip of paper he had wedged under the screen door. Seeing it was still in place, he slipped a key into the deadbolt and unlocked the door. Sharan was fanatical about being careful. His final task, now his sole purpose in life, would soon take place. For Sharan, failure was unacceptable.

Sharan grabbed a two-wheeler sitting just inside the door, returned to his car, and opened the trunk of his 2003 Renault Espace. He struggled to lift the heavy metal container his friend Muti had delivered to him and set it on the ground beside the car. He closed the trunk, positioned the container on the two-wheeler, and headed toward the porch. He hauled the heavy load up the three steps to the porch landing.

Once inside the house with all the doors locked and double bolted, he wrestled the heavy container up three flights of stairs and into the bedroom on the south side of the house. He sat on an old wooden chair for some time staring at the shiny metal container, waiting for his breathing to return to normal. The time was drawing near. No longer fearing the material inside, he released the safety latches holding the lid closed and opened the container. He almost laughed. He found it hard to believe such a small amount of material would create such terrible destruction.

He closed and latched the container and carried it over and set it down next to the device sitting in the middle of the room. He turned and walked over to the south window and pulled back the heavy curtain. In the distance, he could see the dome of the state capitol building, a gleaming symbol of everything he hated. In Sharan's mind, California was the center of the evil he hated. Because of that, he had selected the state's capitol as his target. Soon, he would strike directly at the heart of the Great Satan his father had taught him to hate. As Sharan grew to adulthood, hatred for every American grew until it saturated every fiber of his being.

The name his father had given him on the day of his birth spoke of the mission of vengeance he was about to accomplish. As a small child, Suhaib, Sharan's father, had explained to him that his name meant on high or exalted. His father's teachings and the ranting of the wild-eyed mullahs had thoroughly convinced him greatness in the eyes of Allah lay just ahead. By the time he reached his teen-age years, Sharan boiled with hatred for the infidels that polluted the world with their immorality.

Sharan's hatred of the West grew exponentially more rabid on his sixteenth birthday. While preparing for the birthday celebration, he learned his beloved father was dead, killed in a bombing raid. Witnesses quickly spread word that United States aircraft had carried out the bombing raid. For days, Sharan wept bitterly. Each day the hatred that already filled his heart grew even deeper, finally evolving into a blind, seething rage.

From that day forward, everything he did, everything he learned prepared him for the great act for which he had been born. Finally, that great day of retribution was at hand. Sharan's focus was razor sharp. Nothing or no one could stop him now. He smiled with great satisfaction as he returned to his task.

Wells Cemetery Road
North of Douglas, Arizona

The previous day, Muti Daher had driven only as fast as he dared after delivering the container to Sharan Ahadi. Had the police pulled him over for speeding or for some other traffic offense, his superiors would have been furious. If he failed to follow his evil and short-tempered superiors' orders, they would have exacted a great price. The drive was long and exhausting. He did not feel well, and he was in a foul mood which was not all that unusual.

As he returned to his dingy rental house, Muti had attempted to call Abdul, his accomplice, who had been ordered to watch the man paid to move the container across the border. Muti needed to know where the man was so he could silence him. Three times Muti had dialed Abdul's number with no answer. Muti was livid, vowing Abdul would pay for his failure to follow orders. Knowing he could never find Abdul's house in the dark, he had climbed into bed, hoping he would feel better in the morning.

When Muti awakened the next morning, he felt far worse, a splitting headache and upset stomach amplified his foul mood. Despite a strong desire to crawl back into bed, Muti got dressed and left the shabby house, slamming the door so hard one of the window panes shattered. He turned and glared at the broken window, fuming with anger. "This is all Abdul's fault," Muti snarled. "That stupid moron will pay with his life for his stupidity!"

Reaching behind his back, Muti felt the gun underneath his jacket. He got into his car, started the engine, and squealed out of the driveway. Twenty minutes later he turned left off Highway 80 and drove west on Wells Cemetery Road, looking for the house Abdul had described.

Several miles after leaving the paved highway, he spotted a weathered house on the north side of the road. Abdul had told him the house was light green, but the house was so weather-beaten and faded it had no color left except a bleached out gray. The only identifying feature Abdul had described that was identifiable was the broken wagon wheel that had once been part of the mailbox.

Muti pulled in the driveway and drove up to the house. He stopped, turned off the ignition, and waited. Instructed to wait until Abdul recognized him and turned the porch light on and then off, he sat staring at the house. Muti saw the porch light blink on and then off. He climbed out of the car and headed for the house. Before Muti could grab the doorknob, Abdul opened the door and ushered him inside.

"Greeting my friend," Abdul offered.

"Yeah, sure," Muti responded, ignoring Abdul's greeting. "Abdul, what do you know of the man that delivered the container?"

"I know he was foolish to look inside," Abdul answered. "He said he only looked for a second and then closed it back up."

"Where is he now?"

"He is now sick. He is in the hospital in Douglas."

"What?" Muti shouted.

"I saw the Border Patrol pick him up," Abdul offered, sheepishly. "Then the ambulance came and took him to the hospital."

"Did he tell them anything?" Muti shouted again.

"I do not know, Muti. I was too far away. I could not hear," Abdul choked, backing away from Muti.

"Then what?"

"I entered the hospital and walked by the emergency room. I saw a doctor and a nurse working on him. I was afraid to stay in the hospital so I left and waited for the doctor to come out."

"And?"

"The doctor came out and drove away. I saw him make a phone call as he was driving."

"Where did he go?"

"Home, I think. A gray house. East of Elfrida. West Jefferson Road, south side of the road, third house."

"If that stupid idiot talked, it is your fault, Abdul," Muti sneered, jabbing his finger in Abdul's face. "It was your responsibility to watch him. Why did you not watch him?"

"He slipped away. I…. I…."

Muti pulled a black 9mm semiautomatic from behind his back and shot Abdul right in the middle of his forehead. Abdul fell in a heap in the middle of the floor.

Muti stuck his head out the back door, looking for a place to hide Abdul's body. He smiled when he noticed an old grain bin sitting along the back edge of the house. He dragged Abdul's limp body out the back door of the house and dumped it next to the old grain bin. After propping the lid open with an old shovel, he stuffed the body inside, dropped the shovel in the bin, and slammed the lid shut. Muti pulled a handkerchief from his pocket and wiped the sweat from his face.

Back inside the house, he stared at the blood stain on the floor. He would need to do something to disguise the stain. Standing in the middle of the room, he surveyed the contents of the house. An unopened bottle of ketchup sat on a dusty shelf over the cookstove. Muti grabbed the bottle of ketchup and squirted it over the pool of blood then dropped it on the floor beside the blood stain and stomped on it. If anyone were to enter the old dilapidated house, which was doubtful out in the sparsely populated desert, it would look like someone had dropped the ketchup bottle by accident.

Muti twisted the door lock and slammed the door shut. He climbed into his car and headed for the doctor's house to find out what he might know.

Chapter Four

Norman Glover sat in the hotel's breakfast area, nursing a lukewarm cup of coffee. Well streaked with gray, Norman's hair revealed his age. Despite Norman's age of sixty-four, he was lean and in great physical shape, the result of his two-mile run every morning and thirty minute sessions on the weight bench three times a week. Norman awoke early, unable to get back to sleep. An early riser for his entire career, it became a habit that extended into retirement.

Arriving in the hotel's breakfast area much too early, he had grabbed a copy of the local newspaper to kill time. As he read the newspaper, he kept an eye on the entrance door. When he saw Zach Templeton push the door open, he raised his arm and waved. Norman stood as Zach reached the table. He grabbed Zach and gave him a bear hug.

"Zach, it's great to see you again," Norman said as he released Zach, pointing toward an empty chair. "It would be more pleasant if it was under different circumstances though."

"I second that," Zach answered. "I need to….."

Norman interrupted Zach before he could finish. "Before we discuss anything, let's grab a donut, and I need to warm this up."

Zach and Norman walked over to the breakfast bar and grabbed donuts and coffee. As they returned to the seating area, Norman nudged Zach's elbow, directing him to a different table, one by the wall and away from the small crowd of people seated near the front of the room.

"I don't think we need to worry about anyone here. I've been here for almost thirty minutes and I have seen nothing I would consider suspicious. However, I don't think we can be too careful."

"Do we need to keep up the secrecy, Mister *Glover*?" Zach asked, emphasizing Norman's last name.

"Zach, you may call me James, but I really would prefer Dad," Norman answered with a wink. It would have been unnecessary to tell anyone that James and Zach were father and son. The likeness between them was striking, except for James' graying hair and Zach's slightly larger waistline, due mainly to his wife, Angie's fantastic cooking.

Norman reached across the table and laid his hand on Zach's arm. "I know the *agency* will be furious but your mother and I have decided the time for secrecy has ended. When we agreed I would get involved in this operation, we also decided the hiding and the constant fear of saying or doing something that would break our cover was over"

"Do you think that's wise?" Zach asked.

"We've been hiding long enough," Norman answered. "We hate the secrecy, the lying, the hiding, everything. Most of all, we hate not being able to spend time with you and Angie. As of today, Mister Norman Glover is dead! Zach, meet Mister James Fredrick Templeton, resurrected from the dead."

Zach stuck out his hand. "Glad to meet you Mister James Fredrick Templeton. I'm Zachariah James Templeton," Zach said with a laugh.

"I called the landlord and gave notice we are going to terminate our lease. When this mess is over, we will load up what is ours and find a place in Tulsa. Provided that is okay with you."

"You bet it is," Zach exclaimed.

James glanced at his watch. "It might surprise you to know your mother boarded an airplane for Tulsa before I headed for the Gulfstream. She should already be there."

"That's great, Dad. Angie will be thrilled."

The look on James' face became serious. "Now, we need to discuss our plan for the day. The pilot did not tell me much. He said you would have all the details."

"The Admiral didn't tell me much either. All he could tell me was that several weeks ago satellite imaging detected a hot spot off the coast of Libya. A quick response team from NIAG located the vessel, a freighter somewhere south of Malta. They boarded the freighter in international waters. Unfortunately, whatever had been on the freighter was long gone," Zach took a swallow of coffee and continued. "One of the CIA's under-cover operatives overheard three phrases from two separate phone calls made by our old friend Frank Porter."

"He's the one in the park in Washington, D.C., the one that got away, right?" James asked.

"Yes, he's the one," Zach answered. "Porter had already disappeared by the time the authorities reached his office. Everyone assumed he had disappeared for good. However, the under-cover operatives in Quito, Ecuador, recognized him in an outdoor cafe. As soon as the CIA Director was notified, he assigned three operatives to watch him. There was nothing unusual. No meetings. No phone calls. Then suddenly a week ago two phone calls back to back and in a public place. On the first call, all the operative could pick up was *'arrived yesterday'* and on the second call *'soon'* and then *'suffer'*."

"Does the CIA or the Admiral have any idea what they might mean?"

"Absolutely no idea from the second call. However, the Admiral said the phrase from the first call is worrisome when combined with some additional chatter. The chatter indicates something has been smuggled across our southern border."

"That's rather general. Could the Admiral be more specific?"

"The Admiral's gut feeling was somewhere in Arizona because of the wide open country and the easy access to the Interstate 10 corridor."

"That's still a lot of ground to cover. Where do we start?"

"I don't ….."

Zach's answer was interrupted by ringing from his cell phone. "Zach Templeton, can I help you?"

"Mister Templeton, this is Captain Aaron Carpenter. I'm the staff aide to Admiral Hadley. The Admiral is tied up in a critical meeting. He wanted me to get some new information to you as soon as possible."

"Go ahead, Captain," Zach said, pulling a small notebook out of his pocket.

"Sorry, this information is at least twenty-four hours old. It took time to percolate up through the chain of command. The Admiral just got this a few minutes ago. It seems a Doctor Marshall Woods in Douglas, Arizona, treated a patient with very odd symptoms. The doctor is an Army Reservist which required him to report his suspicions to his commanding officer. The doctor said the patient's symptoms could indicate radiation poisoning. He ordered a specific test to confirm. However, the results had not returned when he made his report."

"I need all the contact details you have for Doctor Woods, Captain."

Zach jotted down the details in his notebook as Captain Carpenter repeated them. "Thanks, Captain. Tell Admiral Hadley I will get back to him as soon as I have talked with Doctor Woods."

Zach quickly shared what he had just learned with his dad. Zach picked up his cell phone and punched in the number Captain Carpenter had given him. After fifteen rings, Zach gave up and ended the call. Thinking Dr. Woods might be at work, he punched in the number for the Copper

Queen Community Hospital. A short conversation with the Emergency Department revealed Dr. Woods had not shown up for his morning shift, he had not called in, and the hospital could not reach him.

"Doctor Woods did not show up for his shift this morning and they cannot reach him," Zach informed his dad.

James Templeton nodded and asked. "Do you have his address? I think we should go check on Doctor Woods."

Zach and his dad dumped their half full coffee cups in the trash bin on their way out the door. They hurried to their rental car, jumped in, and sped out of the hotel's parking lot, fearing the worst.

Sharan Ahadi's Residence
900 Block of E Street
Sacramento, California

Sharan looked around the cluttered bedroom on the third floor and smiled with satisfaction. He had spent months bringing in individual components for the device sitting in the middle of the room. Under the cover of darkness, he had carried in small pieces of the device. Often the components were small enough to fit under his coat or in a small grocery bag. He disguised the bigger pieces or hid them inside an even larger object.

Once Sharan had moved everything from his former residence on the other side of town, he had spent several days meticulously cleaning the old house to be certain no one would become suspicious. On the final day, Sharan spent two full hours opening every closet, every cabinet, and every drawer. Pens, pencils, rubber bands, a clothespin, even the smallest scrap of paper went into a plastic trash bag. He would discard everything he found in a dumpster ten blocks away. He left absolutely nothing to chance.

Sharan had spent days looking at various houses listed for rent. He excluded most of the houses after nothing more than a quick drive by. Others he excluded after a walk around the block because of too much traffic or nosy neighbors. None of the houses he looked at had come close to satisfying him. Discouragement set in until he walked into the south-facing, third-floor bedroom of a house on "E" Street. Looking out the south-facing window, there stood the state capitol building just twelve blocks away. The house was perfect. He immediately signed the lease and paid the landlord the required first month's rent and deposit in cash.

During the day, Sharan assumed his false identity as an electronics technician at a local assembly plant. He hated the job because it was far below his engineering skill level. The paychecks he received paid for all his food and gave him ample pocket money. He enjoyed having the extra money, so he worked hard and followed all the instructions his supervisor gave him.

One week earlier, Sharan walked into his supervisor's office and gave one week's notice. He lied and said he needed to return home to care for a sick family member. His supervisor made a half-hearted attempt to change Sharan's mind, but realized Sharan's mind was made up. He made Sharan promise to contact him after his family member had recovered. Sharan lied again and promised he would. He hurried to his locker and dumped the few things he kept stored there into his lunch pail and left the building, knowing he would never return.

In actuality, Sharan was a highly skilled electrical engineer. During the previous week, he had assembled the numerous stacks of components into the sophisticated device that now sat in the middle of the room.

Sharan once again released the latches on the metal container and lifted out the material stored inside. He carried the material over to the device and carefully inserted it into its designated spot, leaving the shield in place.

From a jumble of boxes and containers sitting against the wall, Sharan selected a stainless steel pressure vessel and carried it over to the device in the center of the room. Positioning the extraction port of the thermally insulated vessel toward the device, he picked up an object that remotely resembled a large hypodermic syringe. He pushed the object onto the port, rotated it until it clicked, and opened the valve. Pulling back on the plunger, he watched until the mark on the plunger aligned with the full mark. He closed the valve and released the object.

After removing the shield, he connected the object to a matching port on the device and injected the gas into the device. He dropped the object on the floor and pushed the pressure vessel aside.

Needing to connect the control mechanism next, he walked over to a pile of cartons stacked along the north wall. Kicking the empty cartons out of the way, he verified the label of the carton he needed that had been at the bottom of the stack. After slicing through the tape that sealed the carton, he pulled back the flaps, revealing an electronic control box and a control harness. The harness's wires were grouped into several bundles of a dozen wires each.

With the control box and cables in hand, he returned to the device. He laid the cables on the floor and secured the control box to a bracket on the left side of the device. Referring to a diagram that had also been in the carton, he positioned the cable harness on the rear of the device and began to connect the individual wires.

Working group by group, he inserted each wire into its numbered position and soldered it in place. He connected all the wire groups except for the wire bundle with the red tape around it. A note on the diagram instructed him to connect the wire bundle wrapped with bright red tape last. The final connections would require great care because they would connect directly to the ignition controller circuits.

Sharan straightened up, rubbing his back. He had been bent over working on the wiring for nearly two hours. His back was killing him. Connecting the last wire group would require great care because the internal shield would no longer be in place. One wrong move could be disastrous. Rather than risk making a stupid mistake, he took a break to steady his nerves.

He did not know when the *others* would complete their devices and be ready. The identity, locations, and even the number of *others* was never mentioned. Sharan only knew *they* existed. His superiors had instructed him to complete the device and wait to be notified of the exact date and time.

There was no reason to hurry so Sharan went downstairs and brewed himself a cup of tea and returned to the third-floor bedroom. He pulled an old wooden, straight-back chair over to the middle of the room and sat down. Great pride and anticipation washed over him as he gazed at his accomplishment, carefully sipping his tea.

Soon, very soon the glorious purpose for which he had been born would be complete.

I-10 Southern Arizona / Dr. Marshall Woods' Residence West Jefferson Road Elfrida, Arizona

Driving east on Interstate 10, James Templeton glanced to his right at his son Zachariah. The unspoken tension inside the car was palpable. Zach had not spoken a word since they left the hotel in Benson and had joined the eastbound traffic on the interstate highway. Unable to bear the tension any longer, James said, "Okay, out with it. If you have something to say, say it."

Zach opened his mouth to speak then stopped, turning his head and staring out the window at the passing scenery.

"Come on, Zach," James urged. "This will be a long assignment if you don't tell me what's eating at you."

Zach started to answer, stopping twice. On the third attempt he blurted out, "How could you just walk away in D.C.? You gave me the pocket knife I gave you when I was eight years old and then you turned and just walked away. You never looked back. Not once. You just walked out the door of the airport, climbed in the limo, and disappeared."

"I'm sorry, Zach," James answered. "You do not understand how hard that was. If I had looked back or if you had said anything, I wouldn't have been able to leave. I had no choice. I had to. I still can't tell you why your mother and I had to go into hiding. Just know this: if I hadn't walked away that day, it would have put not just me and your mother in danger, it would have put you and Angie in grave danger. More danger than you can imagine."

"Come on, Dad. It can't have been that bad."

James sat there not speaking for a long time, debating within himself how much he should, or could, say.

"Now who's not talking?" Zach chided.

"I know," James answered. "I'm trying to decide how much I am willing or able to tell you. I…."

"Good grief, Dad," Zach interrupted. "We're investigating the possibility of nukes coming across our border. How much worse can it get?"

"Well, I suppose you're right. Your mother and I went into hiding after I discovered a substantial threat to our country. What would you say if I told you I discovered a plot to destroy this country?"

Zach started to say something, but James held up his hand and continued, "That plot reached high into the government and I mean the highest level. Admiral Hadley and I didn't know who all the players were, and we didn't have enough evidence to go public. Somehow *they* found out I was digging and they attempted to silence me. So, the Admiral and I decided your mother and I should go into hiding until we could expose their entire group. I have worked with Admiral Hadley off and on, but the people behind the plot are smart and have become more careful about covering their tracks. We believe we were getting close. The Admiral believes and I concur that our digging may have pushed them to try something significant."

"Like smuggling nukes into the country," Zach suggested.

"Exactly my thinking," James remarked. "Several names come to mind, but I'm not willing to reveal them just yet. I'm certain this new plot involves them, but I don't have enough hard evidence."

"Fair enough," Zach responded. "Now back to the airport in D.C."

"Like I said before. If I had looked back even once, I wouldn't have been able to leave. I desperately wanted to turn around and join you and fly back to Tulsa and hug Angie and be a family again. These people are dangerous and powerful. Please believe me, Zach, I had no choice. Back then I had to leave, but no more. Your mother and I have talked and decided we're done hiding. Like I said at the hotel, as soon as this mess is over, we will move to Tulsa and be a family again. I can't tell you how proud I am of you, Zach." James reached out and put his hand on Zach's shoulder. An unspoken communication passed between father and son through a simple touch, melting the tension that had existed earlier. Zach wanted to know more, but they had a vital mission to complete. There would be time later to talk.

Zach looked up just in time to see the upcoming exit sign. He punched his dad's shoulder, "Hey, Dad, Exit 331 is coming up. That's the one we want."

James stepped on the brake and pulled off Interstate 10 and onto the exit ramp for Highway 191 South. He stopped at the stop sign at the end of the exit ramp and turned right onto Highway 191. Neither one said anything as they drove south along the west side of Wilcox Dry Lake, passing through the communities of Cochise, the east side of Sun Sites, and Pearce, Arizona. Finally arriving in Elfrida, James saw the road sign for West Jefferson Road. He turned left and continued driving for another mile and a half.

"Not bad," James said as he pulled into the gravel driveway of a light gray ranch-style house. "Seventy miles in one hour and twenty minutes."

"Yeah," Zach answered. "Let's hope Doctor Woods is home."

James and Zach climbed out of the rental car. As they walked toward the house, they saw an old, faded blue Chevrolet parked in a detached garage at the end of the driveway.

Inside the house, Muti Daher heard the crunch of tires on the gravel as the car pulled into the driveway. He peered around the corner of the kitchen wall and ducked back when he saw two men walking toward the house. His superior would be furious if anyone spotted him or worse yet, captured him. Muti's superior had told him in no uncertain terms he must avoid capture, even if it cost him his life.

He would have already been long gone, but when he had been about one quarter mile from the doctor's house, the doctor pulled out of the driveway, drove into town, and stopped at the local grocery store. Muti waited while the doctor spent nearly an hour in the grocery store before returning home.

After Dr. Woods returned home, Muti had parked in the doctor's driveway and knocked on the door, pretending to be a salesman for a filtered water delivery service. The doctor told him he was not interested and tried to shut the door. Muti pulled his gun and forced his way inside. The stupid fool tried to grab the gun so Muti had had no choice but to kill him. He did not get to ask him a single question. To make everything appear normal, he had moved his car around behind the detached garage and out of sight.

Muti was frantically searching through the house's contents to see if there was any evidence of what the doctor might have learned about that stupid idiot, Polomo, when he heard the crunch of tires on gravel. Muti hoped that when no one answered the door, they would just leave.

James stepped up onto the concrete slab and banged on the front door. No answer. He banged on the door again but with more force. Zach walked over and peered in the front window and saw a body lying on the floor.

"There's a body on the floor. Kick it in," Zach yelled.

James pulled the screen door open and kicked hard right next to the doorknob. The door jamb splintered as the door slammed open. James pulled a gun out of his rear waistband and rushed into the house with Zach right behind him. James stood guard while Zach knelt down and checked for a pulse.

"He's dead," Zach said. "Looks like a single gunshot to the chest." Zach grabbed one of Dr. Woods' arms and rolled him over. "No rigor. Still warm. He's not been dead more than a few hours." Zach straightened up and pulled a gun from behind his back.

"Do you see anything suspicious?" James asked.

Zach looked over at the bookcase sitting against the wall. All the books lay in a pile on the floor. The end table drawers lay upside down, their contents scattered on the floor. "Someone ransacked this place," Zach answered.

James heard something, held up his finger to his lips and then pointed toward the kitchen. Zach acknowledged and moved up closer to the kitchen wall. As James and Zach were about to rush into the kitchen, Muti bolted and ran out the back door.

James and Zach rushed through the kitchen and out the back door, trying to catch the fleeing man. As they exited the back door, they saw a man's form disappear into the garage.

Muti ran into the garage, grabbed the backpack he had laid on the hood of the Chevrolet, and ran to the back of the garage. He reached in the backpack and clutched the trigger in his right hand. The men he feared far more than the police had been clear about what would happen if he got caught. Left with no other option, he triggered the device, threw it in front of the Chevrolet, and dived through the back door of the garage.

With Zach about two steps behind him, James rushed toward the garage. James was only ten feet from the garage when the backpack Muti had thrown exploded.

The garage erupted into a wall of flames. The walls exploded outward from the force of the blast. Large pieces of the roof flew into the air. The blast knocked James over backward. Instinctively, Zach hit the ground, but the concussion knocked him unconscious. Dirt, wood splinters, and debris from the garage rained down upon James and Zach.

As the dust and debris settled, Muti jumped into his car and sped off. His tires screeched as he hit the paved road and roared off toward the East. Several minutes passed. Zach stirred and struggled to his knees. Wild thoughts and distorted images danced before Zach's eyes. As his vision cleared, he saw his dad laying a few feet away. He crawled on his hands and knees over to his dad and listened to his chest. For some time, Zach could find no signs of life.

"Oh, God no!" Zach wailed. "No, not now!"

James groaned and moved several fingers of his right hand. Zach noticed and put his hand to the side of his dad's face. "Don't move. I'll call for help."

Zach frantically pulled out his cell phone and dialed 911. Nothing. He pulled the phone away from his ear and looked at the screen. A message displayed on the screen said 'No Service'. "What do I do now?" Zach screamed. "The house," he thought. "*A doctor has to have a phone.*" Zach forced himself up, limped into the house, and tore through its contents like a wild man. "Where could it be?" he bellowed. In the living room, he spotted a phone line plugged into a wall plate. He jerked the line, seeing it led underneath a pile of books. Frantically, he tore through the pile of books and located the phone. He lifted the receiver, dialed 911, and waited.

"Cochise County dispatch what is your emergency," a male voice asked.

"Explosion. West Jefferson Road. East of Elfrida. One patient seriously injured." Zach shouted into the phone.

"Stay on the line while I get fire and ambulance started your way," the dispatcher advised, putting the line on hold. The dispatcher accessed another line and alerted the fire department and also requested an ambulance.

The dispatcher took the initial line off hold, "Fire department and ambulance are on the way. What kind of explosion?"

"Someone triggered a bomb. This is Zach Templeton, special investigator for the Director of Naval Intelligence. I also need the Sheriff's department ASAP. I'll be outside waiting." Zach answered.

"I will send the Sheriff as well," the dispatcher said.

Zach dropped the phone and ran out the back door of the house to comfort his dad until the ambulance arrived.

Sharan Ahadi's Residence
900 Block of E Street
Sacramento, California

Sharan Ahadi hurriedly gulped the last swallow of his luke-warm tea, eager to get back to completing the wiring of the device's final control assembly. He set the empty teacup on a small table, got up off the chair, and dragged an old stool over next to the device.

He sat on the stool and looked over at his soldering iron. While he had finished his tea, the iron had switched off and become cold. Annoyed, he angrily punched the switch to turn the iron back on. Waiting for the iron to become hot, he spent some time looking over the wiring instructions. The indicator light on the soldering iron flashed green. The soldering iron had come up to temperature. Sharan lifted the soldering iron out of its holder and wiped the tip on the wet sponge. Steam curled up from the sponge, the tip gleaming a bright silver color. He bent over the device, ready to begin.

According to the assembly diagram, the last cable bundle of the wiring harness required direct connection to the initiator which would propel the fissile sparkplug into the tamper. Because the initiator was deep inside the device, the final connection required removal of the interior shield. Sharan reached inside the device, pressed the release tabs, and slid the shield up and out of the way. He tossed the shield on the floor beside the stool, then positioned the final cable bundle in proximity to the initiator. He took a deep breath to steady himself and began carefully inserting each of the remaining eight control wires into their numbered positions.

With all the wires in place, he reached over and grabbed the soldering iron. Acrid smoke curled up from the tip of the soldering iron as he soldered each of the first four wires in place. Physical access to the initiator was very limited, making it difficult to get the soldering iron in place and still be able to see. The difficult task required all of Sharan's concentration. A small bead of sweat rolled down Sharan's forehead and into the corner of his eye. He leaned back and blinked several times, attempting to clear his vision.

He leaned back over the device and began again. Unfortunately, Sharan, in his rush to complete the device, had completely overlooked the warning on the assembly instructions that explained how sensitive the initiator was. The assembly diagram listed step-by-step instructions on how to remove the backup battery *before* connecting the control cable to the initiator assembly. Another bead of sweat rolled into Sharan's eye. He leaned his head toward his shoulder to wipe the sweat from his forehead, causing the tip of the soldering iron to short out two connections. Sharan's retina registered the spark but before the nerve impulse could reach his brain, the room erupted in a blinding blue-white flash.

Chapter Five

Lloyd Wilson and his wife Cheryl, visiting from Eagle Lake, Texas, stood on the east side of Ninth Street near the traffic circle of Capitol Mall Boulevard discussing where to grab lunch. Lloyd and Cheryl, in their seventies and retired, were in Sacramento visiting family. Having just completed a stroll through Capital Park, they were catching their breath before heading for a restaurant to meet their son and his wife for a late breakfast.

Lloyd was remarking to his wife how beautiful the park looked when he noticed a blinding blue-white flash from the North.

Four blocks away, Judith Brendell and her husband, Edgar, had just finished breakfast and had stepped out of a restaurant onto Sixth Street. Judith was the first out of the restaurant and also noticed a blinding blue-white flash from the North.

Riding his bicycle east on Q Street past Fremont Park, Jerry Clayton, startled by the blinding flash from the North, ran up over the curb and crashed into a trash receptacle.

The blinding, blue-white flash also startled dozens of people in Southside Park. Some playing softball. Others fishing in the park's pond. Some sitting on benches in conversation. Others sprawled on blankets enjoying a picnic.

Grace Harris, pushing a double stroller holding her twins Alicia and Abigail, had stopped to pet a rambunctious golden retriever dragging its owner down the sidewalk. The happy dog stuck its nose into the stroller, sniffing and licking each twin's face.

Not ten feet away, Nora and Harold Wilcox, in their eighties, exhausted from a walk around the park had stopped to sit on a wooden bench to rest. They laughed as the owner of the dog attempted to corral the excited dog.

Less than one and one-half seconds later the blast wave thundered by, traveling several times faster than the speed of sound, creating wind speeds over five hundred miles per hour.

The nuclear device triggered by Sharan Ahadi's carelessness would have been in the twenty kiloton range had it been a normal gun-type device. However, Sharan's skill and training as an electrical engineer had allowed him to assemble a boosted, implosion type device. After being supplied with deuterium and tritium gas by someone he did not know, he had injected the gases into the hollow space in the center of the fissile pit. Boosting increased the quantity of high-energy neutrons released, speeding up the fission chain reaction. Boosting could lead to as high as a hundred-fold increase in the yield of a fission weapon, depending on the quality of the fission materials.

The high explosives in the initiator detonated and slammed the uranium tamper into the primary target mass of uranium 235, creating a nuclear fission chain reaction. The pulse of tremendous over pressure, generated by the staggering amount of energy released, produced the deadly blast wave. Because of the massive amount of energy released by the growing chain reaction, a temperature of tens of millions of degrees Centigrade developed in microseconds in the immediate area of the detonation; mind-boggling temperatures, comparable to those inside the core of the Sun.

Fortunately Lloyd Wilson, his wife Cheryl, Judith Brendell and her husband Edgar never felt a thing. Jerry Clayton never had time to cry out in pain over his skinned knee. Neither Grace Harris and her twins nor Nora and Harold Wilcox nor any of the other people in the park had time to comprehend the flash. The extreme temperatures instantly incinerated them and thousands of others. Death came so swiftly it produced no awareness in their brains. No pain. No terror. No sensation. One instant they were alive, then in less than a thousandth of a second they were not, consumed by a temperature in the tens of thousands of degrees. The raging nuclear fire reduced their bodies to dust and the violent inrush of wind sucked the dust up into the debris cloud.

In zones one and two of a nuclear blast, called the "*killing field*", fatalities are instantaneous and complete. It did not matter if people were out in the open or if they were inside buildings. The devastation inside the "*killing field*" was absolute. The blast wave destroyed every single building, turning them to dust and rubble from the incredible heat and high winds. As the super-heated gases began to swell, an expanding fireball developed and began to rise like a monstrous balloon. Because it was a surface blast, enormous amounts of soil, water, and debris became vaporized and contaminated by radioactivity, rapidly sucked up by the winds feeding the expanding fireball, giving it the appearance of the familiar mushroom cloud.

For those not killed by the high temperatures and the destructive effects of the blast wave, lethal doses of electromagnetic, flash radiation killed them where they stood. Everyone out to a distance of nearly three miles would succumb to the blast's effects.

Beyond the "*killing field*", the wind speed gradually decreased, but at a distance of three miles the wind speed still exceeded one hundred fifty miles per hour, as strong as the winds in a severe F3 tornado. Even at a distance up to four miles from ground zero there were countless deaths and large-scale injuries. Beyond four miles, the over pressure dropped, but it was still high enough to blow out windows and cause serious injuries. Human beings that were unfortunate to find themselves outside might have been able to withstand the over pressure, but they could not withstand being thrown against hard objects nor could they withstand buildings falling upon them.

Those within fifteen miles of the blast who died instantly were the lucky ones. Many thousands more would eventually die from severe, traumatic injuries or fatal infections because of being blasted by wind-blown debris. Days and weeks later, many thousands more would die from severe radiation poisoning. A large, unknown number would suffer the radioactive fallout's cancer producing effects for a lifetime. A high radiation exposure over the whole body brings with it an eighty percent chance of contracting cancer of some form. The cancer risk would hit first responders and emergency personnel especially hard as they cared for those irradiated by the initial blast; themselves then becoming radioactive.

As the blast wave expanded, it also decimated areas beyond downtown Sacramento. The blast wave obliterated Sacramento Executive Airport, just south of downtown. It shattered every window of the terminal and many of the structures collapsed as the high winds roared past the airport. The fierce winds reduced small planes tied down along the airport perimeter to twisted lumps of metal no longer recognizable as airplanes. Five lone survivors crawled out of the destroyed terminal.

At Sacramento International Airport, northwest of the nuclear detonation, United flight 4160 bound for Chicago had communicated with Airport Tower Control and had received clearance to take off on runway Sixteen-Right.

Seated in seats 23 E and 23 F, Bernard Devoe and wife Estelle from Saulx-les-Chartreux, France, twenty kilometers south of Paris, spoke in hushed tones. Bernard had his hand on top of Estelle's, doing his best to comfort her. Estelle's knuckles were white from gripping the seat arm so tightly. She hated flying and was especially nervous during takeoffs and landings.

Arthur B. Townsend, from Bartlesville, Oklahoma, sat in seat 11A, on his way home from a business conference.

Arthur, a frequent flyer, was studying some materials he had picked up while attending the conference, oblivious to the takeoff roll.

United flight 4160 was halfway down runway Sixteen-Right and increasing speed. Both the pilot and copilot were preparing for liftoff when they observed a blue-white flash ahead and slightly to their left. Less than two seconds later the blast wave slammed into the Boeing 737-700. The blast wave ripped through the fuselage like it was butter, splitting the aircraft into three pieces. The nose of the aircraft, including the flight deck and rows one through five, tumbled end over end down the centerline of the runway. The tail section, including rows nineteen through twenty-four, slammed down onto the runway and slid off the left side of the runway toward the terminal. The remaining and largest center section, including the wings and rows six through eighteen, flipped over and landed upside down, half on the runway. Jagged metal fragments, luggage, seats, some with bodies and some without, clothing, and various objects from broken luggage littered the airport.

Many of the objects had not even stopped rolling before the heat from the flash radiation ignited the spilled jet fuel into a massive wall of flames. There was not one survivor of the one hundred eighty-five passengers that had been on board United Flight 4160.

The blast ripped apart other aircraft parked at gates or taxiing around the airport, reducing them to smoking, twisted piles of metal. The blast ripped jetways from their attachments and hurled them many feet away. Not one soul survived of all those that had been in one of those jetways or onboard one of those aircraft.

Nearly all the people in the airport terminal also died in the initial blast wave and ensuing fires caused by the intense heat from the flash radiation. Those few people working in deep underground areas of the terminal survived the initial blast wave and resultant fires but would later die, suffering the horrible effects from the radioactive fallout that fell on them as they crawled out of the rubble.

The speed and direction of the winds aloft over the city of Sacramento over the coming twenty-four hours would determine the total number of people sickened by the radio-active fallout spread by the mushroom cloud. Even with nominal winds, the fallout plume would expand to three miles wide and reach as far as twenty-five miles away.

In mere seconds, the blast decimated most of the city of over one-half million people. Buildings not destroyed and reduced to rubble were burning or severely damaged and beyond repair. Structures not directly damaged by the blast had become radioactive and would be uninhabitable for many years to come.

Beyond the far edge of the blast zone, in less than an hour every highway leading out of or into Sacramento be-came hopelessly clogged with miles-long lines of stopped and abandoned cars. Many drivers who first saw the fireball rising above the city stomped on their brakes, stopping dead in their lane. Others mesmerized by the rising fireball slammed into the back of cars stopped on the roadway. Ear-ly in the melee, panic-stricken drivers attempted to turn around and flee by speeding across the median and into the outbound lane. The result was hundreds or, perhaps, thou-sands of additional collisions, choking off all roads leading into or out of the city. Any hope of escape became impossi-ble. The terror that ensued in the dying city was chaotic and growing.

For those outside the area of immediate destruction and out in the open, an unspeakable horror flooded their minds. Frozen in place by the horrific scene, onlookers were unable or unwilling to grasp what they were seeing. Some ran screaming, looking for a place to hide. Others fell on their knees and prayed, while many others stood silently weeping.

For every living soul that witnessed the terrifying event, there was but one question - *what had just happened to their be-loved country* and there was but one emotion - *absolute horror*!

Dr. Marshall Woods Residence
West Jefferson Road
Elfrida, Arizona

Zach flew out of the back door of Dr. Woods' house and ran over to where his dad was lying. He dropped to his knees and checked his dad's pulse. At first he could not feel a pulse. He pushed a little harder. He took a deep breath and concentrated. There was a pulse, but it was faint and uneven.

"Dad, Dad," Zach screamed.

No response. Zach pinched his dad's arm and shouted at him again. Still nothing. He pushed his knuckle into his dad's chest. Still nothing. He pushed harder. James moaned softly, one eyelid fluttered open.

"Dad, stay with me," Zach shouted. "The ambulance is on its way. Dad, stay with me." Zach was unaware of the blood running down his arm until it dripped on his dad's shirt. He glanced at his arm and wiped it across his pants. Ignoring his injury, he returned his attention to his dad. Zach was becoming even more frantic as the minutes passed. He held his breath and listened for the sound of a siren.

Nothing. Just the crackling created by the small fires burning in the rubble that had been a garage. Zach felt for his dad's pulse again. It felt as if it was getting weaker.

"Come on. Come on!" Zach begged. He glanced at his watch and saw it had been over fifteen minutes since he called 9-1-1. "Why is it taking so long?" he choked, tears forming in his eyes. "You can't die. Not now," he wailed.

He straightened up and listened again. In the distance, Zach heard the faint but unmistakable wail of a siren. Over the next several minutes, the wail grew louder until the ambulance turned into the driveway and slid to a stop on the gravel. The two EMT's of Medic 2 piled out of the ambulance. The lead EMT, Paul Sparks, grabbed a drug box and rushed toward Zach and his dad while the other EMT, John Sutton, ran around to the back of the ambulance and slid the gurney out and loaded several pieces of gear onto it.

"His pulse is thready and his breathing is shallow," Zach shouted out as the EMT Sparks arrived and dropped to his knees beside James.

"Sorry it took so long," EMT Sparks offered. "We're out of Copper Queen Hospital in Douglas. We're the only ambulance service for the entire county. How long ago did this happen?"

"Maybe twenty minutes," Zach answered.

EMT Sparks busied himself assessing James' condition. With a stethoscope stuffed in his ears, he had listened to James' breathing, determining there were no breath sounds on the right side. He felt James' extremities, checking for broken bones. After slicing James' shirt open, he noticed a large bruise on his side. Pressing on the center of the bruise revealed at least two broken ribs.

EMT Sutton arrived with the gurney. "The first thing we need is a C-Collar," EMT Sparks shouted. "I'll hold his head still while you slip the collar under his neck."

EMT Sutton grabbed a C-Collar from an equipment bag sitting on the gurney, kneeled down beside James, and slid the collar under James' neck while EMT Sparks held James' head still. With the initial assessment complete and the C-Collar in place, EMT Sparks pushed the transmit button of the microphone clipped to the epaulette of his right shoulder. "County EMS, Medic 2."

"County EMS," the duty dispatcher answered.

"County EMS, we have one patient severely injured by an explosion. Right pneumothorax, internal bleeding, multiple contusions and lacerations, labored breathing. C-Collar is in place. Stand by for vitals."

"Medic 2, understood. Go ahead with vitals," the duty dispatcher answered, lifting his hand to signal the supervisor he needed help.

EMT Sparks jotted the vitals down on a notepad as EMT Sutton gave them to him. With all the vitals recorded, EMT Sparks called County Dispatch. "County Dispatch, vitals are: blood pressure ninety over fifty-seven, pulse ninety-two, respirations 11 and labored. Request permission for two IVs, one with normal saline, one with Ringers."

During the time it took for the exchange of information, the hospital dispatcher located a staff resident who was now listening to the communications from Medic 2. The resident bent over and spoke softly to the duty dispatcher. The duty dispatcher nodded in agreement and pushed the transmit button on the console, "Medic 2, I authorize the use of IVs. Transport immediately. Code Red. Repeat, Code Red."

"Transport immediately. Code Red acknowledged," EMT Sparks barked into his microphone. "Let's go Sutton. Get the saline IV started on the left. I'll get the Ringers started on the right. We've got to get this guy bundled and loaded."

The EMTs got the IVs started quickly. They laid the IV bags on the gurney next to James and tightened up the straps to hold James and the bags in place.

Zach had listened to the conversation and had watched the EMTs perform their tasks. "How is he?" Zach asked, worry clouding his face.

"I won't lie to you. He's in serious condition. We will transport Code Red. That means we can exceed our normal speed limit. Law enforcement will watch traffic ahead of us to make sure we have clear roads," EMT Sparks replied. "Don't worry. Copper Queen Hospital has one of the best trauma teams in the State."

Zach had other questions, but the EMTs were already pushing the gurney down the gravel driveway as quickly as they could. EMT Sutton recognized Carl Brooks, the responder that had arrived five minutes after the EMTs.

"Hey Carl, we've got a Code Red," EMT Sutton announced. "Can you give us some traffic control?"

EMTs Sparks and Sutton pushed the gurney into the ambulance and latched it down so it wouldn't roll around. EMT Sutton hopped in the back to monitor the patient while EMT Sparks ran around to the front and jumped into the driver's seat. He put the ambulance in reverse and backed out onto West Jefferson Road while Firefighter Brooks stood in the middle of the road to stop any oncoming traffic. EMT Sparks switched on the siren as he sped off down West Jefferson Road, headed for Copper Queen Community Hospital.

Zach was heading for his car when an arm reached out and stopped him. Zach turn and stared in the face of a man dressed in a crisp, starched uniform. Light brown trousers with a dark green stripe down each leg. Medium brown, highly shined boots. Dark green uniform shirt with a bright gold badge above the left pocket. On top of his head sat a dark brown "Smokey the Bear" hat.

Zach leaned a little closer and looked at the silver nameplate above the officer's right shirt pocket and read the name Lopez.

"Sheriff Francisco Lopez," the man said, holding his hand out.

"Sheriff." Zach answered. "That's my father in the ambulance. I really need to go."

"Not yet," the Sheriff said. "I need to get some information before I can let you go. Just exactly what happened here?"

"My name is Zachariah Templeton." Zach answered as he took out his wallet and displayed his identification to the sheriff. "My father's name is James. We are in Arizona investigating at the request of the Director of Naval Intelligence. We were following a lead that brought us to the house of Doctor Marshall Woods. We knocked on the door. When there was no answer, I looked in the front window. I saw a body lying on the floor so my father kicked in the door. While we were investigating, a man ran out the back door. We followed. Halfway to the garage over there it blew up."

"What are you investigating?"

"Sorry, Sheriff I can't tell you that without clearance from my superiors."

"I've got to have more than that Mister Templeton."

"Sorry, I can't. What I can do is give you a phone number you can call."

Zach took a business card out of his wallet and scribbled a phone number on the back. "Here Sheriff. This is the direct line for Rear Admiral Charles Hadley, the Director of Naval Intelligence. You can call him. He will verify my identity. Whether he will tell you what we are investigating will be his call. That's the best I can do."

The sheriff took the business card and stuffed it in his pocket. "Okay, Mister Templeton. I will call him as soon as I get back to the office. Can you give me a description on the man that ran out of the house?"

"Six foot tall. One hundred ninety to two hundred pounds. Full beard. Dark olive skin. Small scar under his left eye. Faded jeans and a light brown shirt, long sleeves."

"That's quite a description, Mister Templeton," the Sheriff remarked, while writing the description Zach gave him in a small notebook.

"That's my business, Sheriff. I'm trained to see things," Zach answered. "Sheriff, I need you to lock down this crime scene. Absolutely no one in or out without clearance from me or someone I designate. We need to get a federal forensics investigation team out here. There is a grave threat to national security. I believe Doctor Woods' death is related. When you call Admiral Hadley, he will confirm."

"Okay, Mister Templeton. I believe you, for now. We found some tire tracks out behind the garage. Somebody left in a real big hurry. We'll take molds of the tire treads but it probably won't help much."

"I've got to get out of here and to the hospital," Zach pleaded.

The Sheriff motioned to the driver of one of two additional patrol cars that had arrived at the scene. "Hey Ben, come over here."

"Mister Templeton this is Deputy Ben Jenkins. He will escort you to the hospital. Get going! Oh, I assume one of these is yours and one belongs to your dad. You might need them," the Sheriff added, handing Zach the 9mm Glock he had dropped during the explosion and his dad's Walther PPK .40 caliber.

Zach grabbed the guns and stuffed his Glock behind his belt. He ran over to his rental car, jumped in, shoved his dad's Walther PPK under the seat, and backed out on West Jefferson Road, backing up far enough to allow the deputy to get in front of him. The deputy made a wide u-turn and positioned his patrol car in front of Zach's car.

The Sheriff stepped over to the deputy's patrol car and waited for him to roll the window down. "Ben, the ambulance left here Code Red. So, step on it!"

Andrew Laughlin Residence
Big Cut Road
Two miles south of Placerville, California

Andrew Laughlin was bent over scribbling in his logbook, adding the latest contact he had made on his Amateur Radio system. Andrew was part of the ARRL (American Radio Relay League) and was fastidious about keeping his contact logbook up to date. He finished the entry and slipped the logbook back on the shelf.

Andrew's ham shack was a windowless addition he had built at the back of his house much to the protestations of Julie, his wife. The sparsely furnished addition contained only a tattered, thrift-shop love seat in the corner and a wobbly, hardback chair that sat beside it. Andrew spent the bulk of his radio budget on the radio equipment that sat on the shelves built along the north wall of the addition. Even more than the large amount of money spent on radio equipment, Julie complained about the time Andrew spent with his radios, to the neglect of their two-year-old son Taylor. Just fifteen minutes earlier, Julie had left in a huff when Andrew refused to join her and Taylor in the living room for some family time.

Andrew turned his attention to the six meter band radio that sat in the center position on the lower shelf. He turned the knob of the frequency indicator of the 50-54 MHz radio, to the frequency of his next contact in the Falkland Islands. "Whiskey-Echo-6-Xray-Sierra,   calling   Victor-Papa-8-Foxtrot, Whiskey-Echo-6-Xray-Sierra. Calling…"

Andrew heard a loud pop and then everything went dark except for the battery-powered lantern sitting on the top shelf. Five seconds later the entire house shook. Loose material on the shelves fell off onto the floor. Andrew assumed it was another one of California's frequent earthquakes. He stuck his head through the door into the main house and called out to his wife, "You guys all right in there?"

"We're okay, Andrew," Julie answered. "Did you see the bright flash?"

"Flash. What flash?" Andrew replied, stepping completely into the living room.

"It was in all the windows, Andrew. It was so bright. I'm scared." Julie cried, picking up their son Taylor who wailed at the top of his lungs."

"Maybe the earthquake caused some power lines to short out. Stay here. I'm going outside to have a look around." Andrew walked over to the front door, pulled it open, stepped halfway through, and froze as if he had become stone.

Andrew couldn't speak as he looked toward the west. Forty-two miles away directly over Sacramento, a giant fireball was rising into the sky. The clouds roiling at the top of the fireball flashed with lightning. Andrew had watched a documentary about the old Cold War and the disaster drills school children performed where they had scrambled under their desks. The documentary had also shown the frightening fireballs produced by the nuclear tests conducted in the desert.

Seeing Andrew frozen and not saying a sword, Julie ran over and grabbed Andrew's arm. "Andrew, what is it?"

Andrew turned, stunned, unable to speak. Julie pushed Andrew aside and looked outside. She saw what had Andrew so rattled. "Andrew, Andrew, they have attacked!" she screamed. "What are we going to do?"

Andrew did not move. He just stood there. "Andrew, Andrew, do something!" she screamed again, punching him in the arm.

Andrew realized he had to do something. He needed to call someone on the alert system. "Power, power! We need power!" Andrew bellowed as he ran toward the back door. Slamming the back door open, he ran over to the generator, ripped off the canvas cover, and yanked on the starter handle. Nothing. He yanked again. Still nothing. "Stupid moron," he yelled as he leaned over and turned the fuel supply valve to the 'on' position. Another mighty yank on the starter handle. The generator sputtered for a few seconds and stopped. Andrew yanked frantically on the starter handle. Again and again he yanked. "Come on, you stupid piece of junk," he sputtered. He yanked again as hard as he could. The generator sputtered, blue smoke belching from the exhaust pipe. "Come on. Come on," Andrew begged.

The generator sputtered again, backfired with a loud crack, blew a large cloud of blue smoke, and finally ran up to speed. A quick glance at the voltage meter to be certain it was functioning correctly and Andrew was off. He raced back through the house and ran into the ham shack, finding all the lights on and the equipment dials glowing brightly.

Andrew sat down and attempted to tune in his designated ARRL contact. Frantically, Andrew tuned through all the frequencies. Nothing; not even static. He tried all his other radios on all bands. Nothing but silence. The high energy, electromagnetic pulse, traveling along with the blast wave, caused high voltage surges in every radio in the ham shack. The circuit boards in every single radio smoked, fried to a crisp by the electromagnetic pulse.

Andrew was helpless. All he and his wife could do was sit and wait for what was to come.

Chapter Six

National Response Center
Coast Guard Station
McGuire Ave. SE
Washington, D.C.

Commander Anthony J. Bradford, the current Officer In Charge of the National Response Center, sat in his swivel chair gazing through the large viewing window at the manned communications stations in the National Response Center (NRC). Responsibility for oversight of all inbound communication related to potential emergencies or disasters was enormous, something Commander Bradford did not take lightly.

Despite his diminutive size, Commander Bradford, standing five feet five inches tall, presented a commanding image. His hair, meticulously trimmed in the high-and-tight style, acknowledged his military heritage. His gig-line, the line formed by shirt, trousers, and belt buckle, perfectly aligned. Shoes shined to a mirror-like finish. Insignias, buttons, and service ribbons perfectly positioned. All facets of Commander Bradford's appearance exemplified career military, three generations before him having served with distinction in the United States Navy. His eyes, dark and intimidating, confirmed his no-nonsense character. As expected, Commander Bradford's office also mirrored his personality; no pictures of family or friends, no knickknacks, and no memorabilia of any kind. The few photos on the wall were of officers in the chain of command. Everything about Commander Bradford conformed to his by-the-book, no excuses style of leadership.

Within the National Response Center, situations considered urgent, were forwarded up the chain of command for consensus and further action. Commander Bradford's stern mannerisms and vivid red hair gave rise to his nickname '*Fireball*', a nickname that fit him perfectly. Expecting top-notch performance from everyone, he tolerated no nonsense in the day-to-day operation of the response center. Despite his strict manner, everyone under his command liked Commander Bradford because he was as fair as he was demanding.

Operating according to its mission statement, the NRC Coast Guard Station, part of Joint Base Anacostia-Bolling, located directly across the Potomac River from Reagan National Airport, dealt with any emergencies related to the environmental security and safety of the country. Highly trained communications specialists, under the direct supervision of the NRC Duty Watch Officer, guided callers to the NRC through a series of detailed questions.

Before being assigned to the NRC, all potential staff submitted to a thorough screening process. After several rounds of grueling interviews, a selection committee meticulously examined a potential assignee's service record. Enlisted members ultimately selected as NRC staff were the best of the best in their various specialties. Successful candidates considered an assignment to the NRC a huge honor and a virtual guarantee of a promotion during the next annual review cycle.

Glancing down at the communications center below, Commander Bradford spotted a pair of legs blocking the walkway between two rows of communications consoles. He swiveled around to his desk, picked up the phone, and dialed the duty watch officer's phone number.

"Lieutenant Haydon, Duty Watch Officer."

"Lieutenant, Commander Bradford. There's a pair of legs blocking the walkway between console rows two and three. I thought you completed repair of console Two-Charley yesterday."

"Yes, Sir, it was. It seems the repair completed yesterday didn't fix the problem. Someone reported the issue again this morning at 0915. I will go check on it immediately, Sir."

"Notify me of the status when you know something further, Lieutenant."

"Will do, Sir," Lieutenant Haydon answered. He dropped the receiver in its cradle and headed for the communication center. Arriving in the communications center, he walked between the two rows of consoles and kicked Electronics Technician Second-Class (ET2) James E. Fisher's foot.

"Ow," ET2 Fisher wailed, slicing his finger on a support brace. "What's the matter with you? What do you think you're....?" the rest of the sentence dying in his throat as he slid out of the console and noticed Lieutenant Haydon standing over him. Lieutenant Haydon picked up a rag draped across the lid of ET2 Fisher's toolbox and handed it to him.

"Sorry, Sir," ET2 Fisher stammered, grabbing the rag and wrapping it around his bleeding finger. "You startled me. I didn't know it was you, Sir."

"Commander Bradford called me. He's not happy the problem with this console has not been corrected."

"We thought we had it fixed yesterday, Sir," ET2 Fisher answered. "It was operational throughout the night watch then reported out of service with the same problem this morning."

"Any idea what's wrong and how long it will take you to get it back online?"

"I've traced the problem to the first stage of the inbound amplifier. I think a short fried the whole module. I sent someone down to the basement to look for a replacement."

"So, how long?"

"Ten minutes if the replacement module fixes the problem. Another thirty minutes to test and verify. Say an hour tops."

"Okay, Petty Office Fisher. Call me as soon as it has been tested and deemed operational."

"Yes, Sir," ET2 Fisher replied, slipping the rag off his finger to see if it was still bleeding. The slice in the tip of his finger still oozed slightly, a trail of blood running down his finger. Electronics Technician Third-Class (ET3) Randy Anderson, the newbie assigned to assist ET2 Fisher, came running into the room, holding up the replacement module ET2 Fisher sent him to locate.

"Anderson, my finger's still bleeding," ET2 Fisher said, re-wrapping the rag around his finger. "Do you think you could crawl in the console and replace the module?"

"Absolutely," ET3 Anderson beamed, dropping to his knees and wriggling the upper half of his body into the console.

Intelligence Specialist First Class (IS1) James L. Kean, seated at Console One-Baker, of the primary row of the communications center, sat answering calls and logging the times and locations of reported events. Immediately to his right, at Console One-Charley, his roommate in the enlisted housing complex, Intelligence Specialist Second Class (IS2) Andrew C. Reed, sat waiting for the next call to arrive at his console.

During a lull in inbound calls, IS1 Kean leaned over and tapped IS2 Reed's left arm. "Hey, any plans for the weekend?"

"No, I have not made any plans as yet," IS2 Reed answered.

"I thought maybe we could drive over to DC and go to the Smithsonian."

"I don't know. I'm a little short on cash," IS2 Reed complained.

"No problem," IS1 Kean shot back. "I'll drive and I'll even pay the admission."

"That would be......"

A sudden surge of inbound calls cut off IS2 Reed's answer. The communications center lit up like a Christmas tree.

Call indicators began flashing on every console. The senior operator alerted on-break operators sitting in the break room. The on-break operators rushed back to the communications center to fill positions at vacant consoles.

IS1 Kean punched one of the three flashing call indicators on his console. "Operator Kean, please state your emergency."

"Angela Franklin, Fresno County California emergency operating center. We have multiple reports of a large mushroom cloud over Sacramento."

"What?" IS1 Kean stammered. "Are you certain?"

"We have multiple reports. Five Sheriff's department deputies report confirmed sightings."

"Understood," IS1 Kean answered, scribbling frantically in his logbook as he punched the next flashing call indicator.

"Operator Kean, please state your emergency."

"Dispatcher Ramon Alvarez, Santa Clara County California emergency center. We're receiving numerous reports saying there is a large mushroom cloud rising over Sacramento. Sheriff Maxwell said it looks like a nuclear explosion."

"You can't be serious," IS1 Kean exclaimed, momentarily losing his composure.

"You bet I'm serious, Operator Kean," Dispatcher Alvarez shouted. "The Sheriff said he stood and watched it grow himself. He heard the roar clear down here in San Jose."

"Okay, understood," IS1 Kean acknowledged, about to punch the next flashing indicator.

IS2 Reed leaned over and shook his friend's arm. "Jimmy, what is going...."

IS1 Kean shook his head, turned back toward his console, and went back to answering calls. Panic grew quickly as every operator in the communications center received identical frantic calls.

Lieutenant Jonathan C. Haydon, the Duty Watch Officer, alerted by the senior operator, rushed into the communications center from his office. The vision of every line on every console flashing, sent a chill up his spine. The last time he had seen anything remotely similar, two airplanes had crashed into the twin towers of the World Trade Center. Checking the logbooks of several operators, quickly revealed a full scale catastrophe had occurred. He grabbed a free telephone and called Commander Bradford, the OIC.

"Commander Bradford."

"Sir, this is Lieutenant Haydon the DWO. We have a level one alert. Multiple stations; multiple lines reporting a mushroom cloud over Sacramento. Multiple law enforcement eyewitness confirmations."

"On my way," Commander Bradford answered, dropping the receiver on the desk as he ran for the door. Rather than wait for the elevator, he slammed the door to the stairwell open and leaped down the stairs three at a time.

Panting and out of breath he ran into the communications center. He slid up next to Lieutenant Haydon, nearly knocking him over. "When did this start?"

"About twelve minutes ago."

"Do we have sufficient justification to skip the normal chain and alert the White House?"

"More than enough, sir. Way more!" Lieutenant Haydon answered, horror growing in the pit of his stomach.

Commander Bradford reversed the direction of his earlier sprint, arriving back in his office in less time than his dash down to the communications center. He picked up the receiver still lying on the desk and mashed the button on the phone to release the old connection. Holding the receiver while flipping madly through the Command and Control Manual, he located the page he was searching for. With his finger under the number for the White House Communications Agency (WHCA) switchboard, he hurriedly punched in the number and waited.

The White House
1600 Pennsylvania Avenue
Washington, D.C.

In a windowless basement room, a team composed of members of all branches of the military busied themselves supporting the White House Communications Agency (WHCA). According to its mission statement, the WHCA provided secure normal, secret, and emergency communications requirements to support the President. On her third duty day in a row, Air Force Technical Sergeant Emily Perkins punched a flashing button on her switchboard and became the unfortunate one to receive Commander Bradford's frantic phone call.

"Tech. Sergeant Perkins, White House Switchboard. How may I direct your call?"

"Commander Anthony J. Bradford, Officer In Charge, National Response Center. I need to speak to the president's executive assistant," Commander Bradford panted, still out of breath from his dash to his office.

"Commander, not just anybody gets to...."

Overwhelmed by the gravity of the situation, Commander Bradford's voice increased in volume as he interrupted Tech. Sergeant Perkins and roared into the phone, "I don't have time to argue Sergeant Perkins. I'm reporting an exceptional catastrophic incident. There's been a nuclear detonation in or near Sacramento. It's imperative I speak to the President's executive assistant, NOW!"

"Right away Commander," TSgt. Perkins conceded as she put Commander Bradford on hold. Had it not been for the staggering nature of the commander's call, she would have protested. She pressed another button on the switchboard and punched in the number for the White House Communications Director.

Edger D. Cordell, the White House Communications Director, also serving as Assistant to the President for

Communications, answered on the second ring, "Edger Cordell."

"Sir, I have Commander Bradford, Officer In Charge, National Response Center on another line. He's reporting an exceptional catastrophic incident. He claims there's been a nuclear detonation in Sacramento," TSgt. Perkins explained.

"Hang on," Communications Director Cordell said as he put his hand over the receiver's mouthpiece. He turned and waved at Donald M. Walsh the White House Chief of Staff who was in his office for their weekly staff meeting. "Hey Don, the White House Communications Switchboard is on the line. The operator says a Commander Bradford from the National Response Center is calling demanding to speak to the President's executive assistant. Claims there's been a nuclear detonation in Sacramento."

"Huh, that's crazy," Chief of Staff Walsh countered. "Is he…." Walsh stopped mid-sentence and dug the ringing cell phone from his pocket. "Walsh," he answered. He ended the call without saying a word. He looked at Director Cordell with a stunned look on his face. "People all over the building are getting reports of a nuclear blast. Have the switchboard put the Commander through."

Director Cordell took his hand off the receiver and put it up to his ear. "TSgt. Perkins, we're getting additional unconfirmed reports. Put the Commander through to the President's assistant *immediately*."

"Yes, Sir,"

TSgt. Perkins took Commander Bradford's call off hold. "Commander, I'll transfer you to the President's executive assistant."

"President's office," Jeffery Williams answered.

"Sir, TSgt. Perkins, White House operator, I have Commander Bradford on the line reporting a catastrophic incident."

"Understood. I've got it," Williams said. "Commander Bradford, explain please."

"Mister Williams, this is not, I repeat not, a drill. Every console in the NRC is lit up. We're getting calls from all over the West. We have multiple *confirmed* eyewitness reports from law enforcement agencies of a nuclear detonation in or near Sacramento."

"Commander, incident verification code please," Williams requested, confident a true catastrophe was unfolding. He wrote the code as the Commander read the six character code. "Repeat please." He compared the repeated code to the one he had written. "Verified, Commander Bradford. Report directly to me if you have reports of any additional detonations." Williams gave the Commander the number to his personal cell phone and ended the phone call.

Mr. Williams picked up the phone again, punched in the number for Andrews Air Force Base, and waited, tapping his foot on the floor nervously.

"Joint Base Andrews, 89th Airlift Wing, Master Sergeant Pollard."

"Master Sergeant this is Jeffery Williams, Executive Assistant to the President, we have an alert level one incident. I need the CDO (Command Duty Officer) now!"

"Right away, sir," MSgt. Pollard acknowledged.

Less than thirty seconds later, a deep voice tinged with a Texas drawl came on the line, "Captain Phil Whitman, may I help you?"

"Captain, this is Jeffery Williams, Executive Assistant to the President, we have an alert level one incident," Williams repeated. "Get Air Force One prepped and ready for immediate departure. The FAA will get a call within the next five minutes to issue a ground stop for all traffic inbound and outbound to Dulles and Reagan until Air Force One is airborne and out of the area. You will receive clearance for a straight-out, hurry-up departure as soon as the team arrives. Depart Marine One for the White House immediately."

"Yes, sir," Captain Whitman responded. He dropped the phone receiver back in its cradle and raced off to alert the crew.

Mr. Williams yanked open the bottom drawer of his desk and grabbed his copy of the National Security Presidential Directive 51 and also his copy of the National Continuity Plan. Without bothering to push the drawer closed, he turned and ran out the door.

He stopped beside the desk of his executive assistant. "Betty, there is an alert level one incident. Notify the team to drop whatever they are doing and head for Marine One. It's departing Andrews now. I will notify the President and get him started toward Marine One. Anyone not onboard when the President and I arrive will be left behind. As soon as someone makes the notification, head for your designated emergency relocation facility."

"Mister Williams, what do…."

"Sorry, Betty, no time," Williams shouted, already racing out the door. "God help us!" He exclaimed as he ran down the hallway toward the Oval Office.

Jeffery Williams ran at full speed into the President's Secretary's office and directly to the door leading into the Oval Office. Without waiting for approval, he pushed the door open and barged into the Oval Office. President Paul Cantwell looked up from the budget documents he was studying and turned his head to see who was disrupting his meeting unannounced. Likewise, the heads of the other meeting attendees turned toward the source of the commotion.

Williams rushed over to the President's side, leaned toward him, and whispered into his ear.

"What?" President Cantwell bellowed, bewilderment showing on his face. "Where, when?"

"Sacramento, probably fifteen to twenty minutes ago," Williams answered. "Where's John Elmore?"

"Left here thirty minutes ago. He should be back in his office by now," President Cantwell answered.

President Cantwell stood up, looked at the men seated around his desk and shrugged. President Cantwell stood a head taller than anyone else in the room at six foot five inches. He walked with a slight limp, the consequence of a high ankle sprain that occurred during the third year of his college basketball career. The injury had refused to heal completely, ending his basketball career and hopes of joining the NBA. After graduation, the injury had improved considerably leaving him with a hardly noticeable limp. Able to hide the ankle weakness, he joined the United States Navy and began a career as a line officer.

"We'll have your secretary notify Elmore. Once we're airborne, I will activate Presidential Directive Fifty-One. Elmore has to depart with us. He's the designated National Continuity Coordinator. He will be critical to assure the continuity of government. Marine One is on the way. We've got to go! Now!" Williams barked as he grabbed the President's arm and ushered him toward the door.

As they rushed into the outer office, Williams shouted at the President's secretary. "Notify John Elmore to drop whatever he's doing and proceed to Marine One without delay."

"Marjorie, call FEMA and notify them to be ready to activate the Emergency Response System," President Cantwell added. "We must put out a national warning soon. Jeffery, we need to implement Directive Fifty-One now." President Cantwell stopped and reached for the phone.

"No time," Williams protested, grabbing the President's arm. "We've got to get you on Marine One and headed toward Andrews. Then, we worry about implementing emergency plans."

"How many casualties?" President Cantwell asked as they ran down the hallway.

"If it detonated inside the city, my guess would be at least seventy-five to one-hundred thousand dead, injured probably double or triple that," Williams answered. "Long-term death toll estimate will depend on wind speed and direction."

"Any claim of responsibility? Are there more nukes out there?"

"Way too early to know that," Williams answered as he continued pushing President Cantwell down the hallway. "The Crisis Response Team will work on that as soon as they mobilize and arrive on scene. The first step will be to identify the type of nuclear material used. Then maybe we'll have some idea of where it came from."

"I never dreamed I'd see this day," President Cantwell choked, his voice wavering as a deep fear and sadness settled over him.

Jeffery Williams and President Cantwell exited the White House. A squad of marines armed with semiautomatic weapons surrounded the two men as they headed for the South Lawn to meet Marine One, circling for its final approach.

Marine One approached from the south and hovered over the South Lawn as two F-16s from the 113th Combat Support Wing flew close cover air support around the White House. The large Sikorsky VH-3D Sea King helicopter, operated by Marine Helicopter Squadron One, settled smoothly onto the beautifully manicured grass. The pilot reduced power and the huge rotors began to slow, but to ensure a quick departure the engine remained running.

Encircled by the Marine squad, Jeffery Williams and President Cantwell ran toward Marine One, ducking as they ran under the spinning rotors. The two men hurried up the five steps and scrambled into the interior, the Marine squad already retreating toward the White House exit to wait for additional National Essential Functions (NEFs) team members.

Dropping into his seat, President Cantwell asked, "How long do we wait for the rest of the team?"

Jeffery Williams held up his hand and answered his cell phone. "Understood," he said. "Mister President, five of six are on their way. We wait five minutes. Not one second more."

Intending to ignore an incoming call, President Cantwell lifted the vibrating cell phone out of his jacket pocket.

About to dump the call, he noticed the calling number. Had it been anyone other than his lifelong friend Admiral Charles Hadley, he would have ignored it and sent it to voice mail. Cantwell and Hadley had attended the US Naval Academy together. An unfortunate accident aboard the Navy frigate where Cantwell served as executive officer provoked his old ankle injury. Despite several months of intense physical therapy, his ankle continued to deteriorate, leading to reconstructive surgery. After the surgery, a Navy medical board declared him unfit for command. Faced with the prospect of an unsatisfying career commanding a desk, he accepted a RIF (reduction-in-force) discharge and went into politics. His old friend Hadley had made the Navy a career. Cantwell felt his friend deserved a warning.

"I don't really have time to talk. There's…"

"Sorry to interrupt, Paul, I'm hearing horrible reports of a nuke going off," Admiral Hadley interrupted. "At this moment, I have a team tracking down leads on nuclear material coming across the southern border. I think it's related."

"You're correct, Chuck. There's been a catastrophic incident. I'm sitting on Marine One ready to depart for Air Force One. I've only got a minute or two. What do you need?"

"I need high-level authority and clearance for my team. They might be able to find the source of the nuke."

"Call Andrew Holt, Director US Secret Service. I will instruct him to give your team whatever it needs. Chuck, there's probably seventy-five to one hundred thousand dead from the initial blast alone. Most of Sacramento is gone. I want the perpetrators of this unspeakable and cowardly event found. Your guys have full authority to do anything they need to and I mean *anything*. Understood?"

"Yes sir, Mister President."

The President ended the call as the first of the remaining team members, Lieutenant Colonel Thomas Martin, the President's military aide and carrier of *The Football*, arrived. Two minutes later John J. Elmore, Assistant to the President for Homeland Security and Counterterrorism, and also National Continuity Coordinator, exited the White House and was escorted to Marine One by the Marine squad. Over the next three minutes three additional members of the NEFs team arrived: Delbert R. McClain, Senior Secret Service Agent, Donald M. Walsh, White House Chief of Staff, and Matthew Tyler, National Security Advisor.

Seeing the President had ended his phone conversation, Jeffery Williams asked, "Mister President, should we activate the Emergency Response System?"

"Is there any reason to believe there are other devices?" President Cantwell questioned in return.

"We don't know that. There has been no communications from terrorist organizations. Nobody's taking responsibility yet. No threats or warnings."

"Jeffery, if we were to send out a warning, what exactly do we tell them? If there are more devices out there, where do we tell them to go? We will only create a larger panic."

"I don't know, Mister President," Jeffery Williams replied shrugging his shoulders.

"Exactly. I don't know either with the information I have at this time. I will wait until we get to Air Force One and I meet with the NEFs team. After evaluating all information at hand, and *if* the NEF team concurs, I will instruct FEMA to send out the warning."

"Understood, Mister President," Jeffery Williams answered, settling into his seat and cinching up his seat belt.

At the five-minute mark, Andrew J. Holt, the Director of the US Secret Service had not arrived. "Can't wait any longer Mister President. According to SOP, Mister Holt must go to a designated alternate location," Jeffery Williams shouted over the noise of the still running engines. He signaled the pilot with a "thumbs up" signal. The Marine contingent withdrew as the doorway pulled up and locked into place. The pilot opened the throttle to increase the rotor speed, while scanning the instrument panel. With his right hand, he pulled up on the collective, causing the big helicopter to rise. As the big helicopter went "light on the skids", he pushed on the right anti-torque pedal to compensate for the torque created by the spinning rotor. As the helicopter lost contact with the Earth, he applied force with his left hand to the cyclic to balance all the forces and keep the helicopter fixed relative to the ground. Deftly hovering a meter above the ground, the pilot made one last check of the instrument panel. The rotor and engine RPMs were normal, pressures and temperature all in the green. Satisfied all systems were operating normally, he applied force to both collective and cyclic and quickly rose above the surrounding trees and buildings. Clear of all obstructions, Marine One banked toward the East and headed off toward Andrews at top speed.

227 West 77th Street
New York, New York

In a posh, luxury apartment in the Upper West Side of New York City, a portly, balding man pushed the shower door open and leaned out, listening for what he thought was the telephone. He listened for a few seconds but heard nothing. About to pull the shower door shut, the phone rang again. He turned the water off, stepped out of the shower, wrapped a towel around himself, and ran toward the foyer.

As the man rounded the corner of the hallway, his foot, still wet from the shower, slipped on the polished marble floor. His foot flew out from underneath him and he went down in a heap, sliding across the foyer and up against the wall. The phone stopped ringing before the man could get his feet under him and stand up. He stood up, wrapped the towel back around his waist, and glared at the phone, waiting for it to ring again. He gave up and limped down the hallway toward the bathroom rubbing his knee and muttering under his breath.

Halfway down the hallway the phone rang again. He turned and hobbled down the hallway as fast as he could. He stepped around the corner into the foyer and snatched the receiver off the phone. "Hello, who is it?" he growled into the phone, still annoyed about his tumble.

"It's me," a female voice screeched in his ear so loudly he had to hold the receiver away from his ear. Without stopping for an acknowledgment, the woman continued, "What on Earth is going on? Are you completely insane? The device was not to be detonated. You said you were just going to take photographs of it and warn them. It was just supposed to be for leverage."

"I have no idea what happened," the man offered in defense. "It must have been some kind of accident. The idiot was not supposed to connect the controller. Neither I nor my colleague gave an order to even arm the device let alone detonate it."

"I don't want to hear any excuses," the woman screamed. "What are we going to do now?"

"It is unfortunate, but we can use it to our advantage," the man replied. "Now, we will have their attention. When we show the government officials photos of the other devices, they will gladly accept our demands. They will not have any choice."

"Others? What others? You said nothing about any other devices. Where are they?"

"It is better that you do not know where they are. I assure you they are well hidden. We need them to convince the officials we are serious."

"No. I never agreed to that. I will no longer be part of this insanity."

"You have no choice, madam. Remember our meeting after the climate change meeting? Do you think I was stupid enough to not have a record of that meeting?"

"What do you mean you have a record?" the woman gasped.

"I had a recording device in my jacket pocket and a colleague was up in the mezzanine with a video camera. If you go to the authorities, you will lose your prestigious position and you will go to prison for a very long time or worse."

"Listen here, you sniveling weasel. You can't threaten me. I have a powerful position. I'm a…"

"Shut up," the man snarled, cutting the woman off. "If you do not believe me, I can email you a copy of the video. Perhaps I should send a copy to the local news media. I can tell them you threatened me and coerced me into helping you. I have friends in very high places. I guarantee you will take all the blame and I will disappear without a trace. Is that what you want?"

"No. I ahh….," the woman stammered, trying to decide what she should say.

"Well, I'm waiting. Should I send the video or not?"

"No, that will not be necessary. I believe you."

"Good. One final warning. You are to remain silent. My organization has people who love to inflict pain. If you tell anyone, you will regret it. Prison will be the least of your worries. Do you understand me, madam?"

"Yes, I understand," the woman snapped. She was about to say more but the line went dead. After hanging up, the man picked up the receiver and laid it on the table beside the phone.

Intense anger boiled up within the woman as she dialed the man's number again, receiving only a busy signal. She tried three more times, receiving a busy signal each time. After the forth unsuccessful attempt to reach the man, overcome by anger, she slammed the receiver down so hard, an expensive antique vase sitting on the table began to wobble. She attempted to grab it, but her hand hit the side of the vase. The vase flew off the table and crashed onto the floor, exploding into hundreds of tiny pieces. She balled up her fists and screamed, fearing her life was about to explode like the vase.

The man snickered as he limped back to the bathroom, knowing the dreadful woman's usefulness had ended. He would very much enjoy watching her demise. Soon he would leave the apartment for the last time. When that time came, he would call Nikola and have him put an end to the horrible woman's screeching.

He grabbed another towel and returned to the foyer to mop up the puddle he had dripped while talking on the phone. He stood there admiring the palatial, penthouse apartment, sad that the original artwork, priceless oriental rugs, custom-built mahogany furniture, and other expensive trappings would soon be abandoned. He could accept the loss, knowing he had a luxurious apartment in Brussels, a beach house in Saint Tropez, France, and a villa in Milan.

The early detonation in Sacramento would hinder getting more materials and it would force them to move earlier than they had planned. However; the fear, chaos, and rioting the blast created could be used to their advantage. He smiled as he returned to the bathroom to finish his shower. The intricate scheme, working out exactly as planned, would culminate soon. Humming his favorite tune, he stepped back into the shower.

Chapter Seven

Copper Queen Community Hospital
100 East 5th Street
Douglas, Arizona

Zach Templeton roared into the parking lot of Copper Queen Community Hospital, tires screeching. He pulled into the first empty parking space he saw and stomped on the brake. Misjudging his speed, the car slid up against the curb and bounced up over it and onto the grass. He switched the engine off, bailed out of the car, and rushed toward the emergency entrance.

Arriving only moments before Zach, the EMTs had just unloaded Zach's father and were pushing the gurney toward the double doors. Running up behind the EMTs, Zach followed them into the emergency department entrance.

The ambulance having radioed ahead, Carol Morgan, one of the emergency department nurses, and Dr. Ramona Berger, ER Physician, stood in the hallway waiting. As they rolled the gurney down the hallway, Dr. Berger already barking orders, directed the EMTs into one of the trauma bays. Zach attempted to follow the medical personnel into the trauma bay. Halfway into the trauma bay, Nurse Morgan grabbed Zach's arm and spun him around, pushing him out. "You can't be in here," Nurse Morgan ordered.

"He's my father. I have to be in there," Zach begged.

"Doesn't matter. You'll only get in the way."

Zach twisted out of Nurse Morgan's grasp and started into the trauma bay. Seeing Zach entering the trauma bay, Dr. Berger stepped over in front of him. "No sir. You can't come in here."

"But he's my dad. I...."

"I know you're concerned, but your presence will only hinder our efforts if we have to work around you. You don't want that do you?"

"I ahh, I ahh…"

"Come on, sir. Let the doctor do her work. I'll keep you informed. I promise," Nurse Morgan said, pushing Zach out of the trauma bay and pointing him toward the admin desk. "Go give the admin nurse all the pertinent details."

"Okay," Zach answered, realizing the trauma nurse was not going to allow him in the trauma bay. He turned, walked over to the admin desk, and smiled weakly at the admin nurse.

"Sorry, I know it's difficult," the admin nurse offered. "While you wait to hear something, can you give me some personal information for your *loved one* is it?"

"Yes, he's my father," Zach answered. "His name is Norman Glover." Zach stopped, uncertain how much he should say. Their identifications would not match, so knowing he had little choice, he continued, "No. Actually, his name is James Templeton."

"What?" The admin nurse asked, looking up at Zach, a puzzled look on her face. "I don't understand."

Zach took a deep breath and began, "This *must* remain confidential. My father is in the witness protection program. We are here investigating a top secret matter at the request of the Director of Naval Intelligence. We were at Doctor Woods' residence. Someone set off a bomb. The…"

"Huh, Doctor Woods? Our Doctor Woods?" the admin nurse interrupted. "Is he all right?"

"Lower your voice please," Zach insisted. "The fewer people that know about this the better. I'm sorry to tell you, Doctor Woods is dead. The Sheriff will confirm later."

The admin nurse looked devastated. Doubting if she could continue, Zach asked if there was someone else that could assist. After some weeping and several tissues, she gave Zach a name and number for someone in the business office. Zach called the business office and asked that person to come to the ER admin desk.

The new person arrived and after several minutes of explanation, Zach got the new person to agree to record minimal information until a later time. Pacing back and forth in the emergency department, Zach tried to peek into the trauma bay through the small window in the double doors separating the admin area from the trauma bays.

The scene inside the trauma bay could be described as organized chaos. Once James's breathing had been stabilized, Dr. Berger had requested several blood tests. She palpated James' chest and found three broken ribs. Stuffing the stethoscope in her ears, she listened to his breath sounds, finding diminished sounds in his right chest. She grabbed the ultrasound probe, squirted some gel on it, and positioned the probe against James' chest. Watching the ultrasound screen, she pushed the probe around to different areas of the chest. Reaching the area just below the broken ribs, she stopped and leaned closer to the screen.

"Carol, he's bleeding into his chest," Dr. Berger shouted. "Grab a chest tube now."

While Nurse Morgan rushed to grab a chest tube, Dr. Morgan, swabbed an area of James' chest with betadine, grabbed a syringe filled with lidocaine from the drug cart, and injected the skin around the location where she intended to insert the chest tube. She picked up a scalpel and made a one and one-half inch long incision. She dropped the scalpel on the bedside tray, inserted her gloved finger into the incision to widen the opening, and then gently pushed the end of the chest tube into the chest cavity, stopping when blood began to flow into the tube. Nurse Morgan attached the other end of the tube to the drainage system while Dr. Berger placed a stitch into the skin to hold the tube in place. Satisfied with the chest tube placement, Dr. Morgan placed a sterile dressing over the site and moved on to the next issue, a large scalp laceration.

"Doctor Berger, Can I go update the patient's family?" Nurse Morgan asked.

"Yes, go ahead," Dr. Berger answered. "This head lac will take me a few minutes to suture."

Zach had been pacing for fifteen minutes when Nurse Morgan pushed the door open and walked over to where he was standing.

"So far, it doesn't look as serious as it could be," Nurse Morgan explained. "A large head laceration, three broken ribs, and bleeding in his chest. May be a lacerated lung, liver, or a ruptured spleen. We don't know yet. He will need surgery as soon as he is stable enough. Right now I would say his condition is guarded. That's all I can tell you at this time. I've got to get back."

"Thank you, Carol," Zach said, leaning forward slightly to read her name tag. "I really appreciate your letting me know."

Zach exhaled, thankful his dad was still alive. Somewhat relieved by the news the nurse had delivered, he suddenly felt very shaky. Hoping a cup of coffee would settle his nerves, he headed for the break room. Once in the break room, Zach weaved his way through the tables and walked up to the coffee station sitting on the far side of the room. He lifted a styrofoam cup off a stack of cups sitting beside the coffee machine and set it on the counter. Shaking badly, he slopped coffee all over the counter. He slipped the coffeepot back on the burner and just stood there staring at the mess he had made.

The admin nurse who had taken his father's information earlier, glanced through the doorway and noticed Zach standing there. She pushed back from her desk, got up from her chair, and walked into the break room. Stopping beside Zach, she tapped him on the arm. "Sorry, I don't mean to intrude, but I couldn't help but notice," the nurse said. "Please, let me help."

Grabbing a rag from the cabinet underneath the counter, the nurse picked up the half-full cup and threw it in the trash bin. She wiped up the spilled coffee, set a new cup on the counter, and filled it.

"Anything in your coffee?" Mr. Templeton.

"No, just black thank you," Zach responded.

The nurse pointed at a chair at an empty table. She carried the cup over, set it on the table in front of Zach, and slipped into the chair across from him.

"I'm so sorry Mister Templeton," the nurse offered. "I know it's difficult to sit and wait for news when a family member is in the emergency room. Even though this is a small hospital, Doctor Berger is one of the best trauma physicians in the state. She is also a certified trauma surgeon. Your father is in good hands."

"Thank you for your help," Zach said. "I'm a mess. My dad and I just got back together. If I lose him now, I….." Zach stopped as his voice choked up and his eyes began to tear up.

The nurse reached out and patted the back of Zach's hand. "I know it's difficult; but like I said. Dr. Berger is one of the best. You just have to trust her."

"Thank you Gwen," Zach said, glancing at her name tag. "You've really helped."

"I'm glad," Gwen answered, rising from her chair. "I have to get back to my desk. I hope your dad gets better quickly." Nurse Gwen turned and disappeared through the doorway.

Zach picked up the coffee cup and took a careful sip. Thankful it was freshly brewed, he took another sip. Not the best coffee he had ever drank, but it was better than most waiting room coffee.

Left alone to his thoughts, Zach's emotions swirled from fear about his father's condition to anger over the way the cowardly thug at the house in Elfrida had tossed the bomb at them. Twenty minutes passed as Zach fidgeted, drank some coffee, then fidgeted some more, waiting for news from the emergency room.

About to throw the empty cup in the trash bin after draining the last swallow of coffee, Zach turned and watched as the emergency room doors swung open. Pushing a hospital bed containing Zach's father, two nurses used a free hand to steady IV bags and the many tubes hanging from support rods on both sides of the bed. Following behind the nurses, Dr. Berger stopped beside Zach.

"Your father's condition is still guarded," Dr. Berger said. "But he is stable enough to go to surgery."

"What is the prognosis?" Zach asked, fearing what Dr. Berger might say.

"Other than three broken ribs and some internal bleeding, things don't look too bad," Dr. Berger replied. "In surgery, I'll locate and stop the source of the bleeding. There could be serious internal damage. I won't know until I get him open. However, at this point I don't think the damage is too extensive. He will go straight to ICU after surgery. You can wait in the ICU waiting room. If the surgery turns out to be extensive and looks like it will take over an hour, the circulating nurse will find you and give you an update. I have to go." Dr. Berger rushed off down the hallway to prep for surgery before Zach could say anything further.

Following the signs pointing to various departments in the hospital, Zach located the ICU waiting room. Hesitating as he stood in front of the coffee station, he decided he wanted no more coffee. He located an empty chair and flopped down into it, rubbing his tired eyes. He was exhausted and his emotions were frazzled, but he still needed to call Angie and update her on his father's condition.

Zach retrieved his cell phone and tapped the icon for Angie's number.

"Zach, I've been sitting here waiting for your call," Angie bleated the apprehension obvious in her voice. "How is your dad? Is he going to be okay?"

"I just talked to Doctor Berger, the ER doc, a few minutes ago," Zach answered. "She is also a trauma surgeon. They worked on Dad for thirty minutes in the ER to get him stable enough for surgery. Doctor Berger said Dad has three broken ribs and internal bleeding. She said they won't be certain how extensive the injuries are until they get inside. The good news is that she said his condition is guarded, and she thinks the injuries are not too serious."

"Well, I guess that last part is encouraging. What happened, Zach? When you called earlier, you were frantic, and you didn't make any sense. Something about a bomb."

"Dad and I were checking out a lead Admiral Hadley gave us; a Doctor Marshall Woods who works at the hospital here in Douglas, Arizona. He didn't answer his phone, and the hospital said he didn't show up for work. So, Dad and I drove to his house. Dad knocked on the door and I looked in the front window and saw a body lying on the floor. Dad kicked the front door in and we went inside to investigate. We had just started to examine the scene when someone ran out the back door. We chased the person out the back door of the house. Dad was several steps in front of me, headed toward a garage when it exploded. It had to be a bomb."

"Zach, that is exactly why I didn't want you and your dad to get involved in this," Angie protested. "Why does Admiral Hadley need you to do this? He could get trained agents for something this dangerous."

"Angie, we can handle this," Zach asserted. "There wasn't time to explain after Admiral Hadley called. Dad is capable of things you cannot imagine. I have seen him in action. The simple truth is we were not as careful as we should have been. That will *not* happen again."

"Zach, I still don't think you….."

"Hang on, Angie. Someone's calling," Zach interrupted as he pulled the phone away from his ear to see who was calling. "Angie, its Admiral Hadley. It is likely important. I'll call you right back. Okay?"

"Okay, Zach. I will be waiting."

Zach dumped Angie's call and swiped across the screen of his phone to answer the Admiral's call. "Admiral, I'm on the…"

"Hang on, Zach," Admiral Hadley interrupted. "I have some startling news. You might want to sit down."

Zach stopped his pacing, found an empty chair in the waiting area, and sat down. "Go ahead, Admiral."

"Zach there has been a nuclear detonation in Sacramento."

"What? You can't be serious," Zach shouted, causing several other people in the waiting area to stop what they were doing and look at Zach. Covering the phone with his hand, Zach turned toward the people and offered an apology, "Sorry, I didn't mean to be so loud." Placing the phone back against his ear, he continued, "Admiral, what are you talking about?"

"I can't be any more plain, Zach. Someone detonated a nuclear device in or near downtown Sacramento. Early reports say the blast decimated the city. Early estimate says at least one hundred fifty thousand dead just from the initial blast. How many more that will die from injuries or radiation is unknown."

Zack stood there frozen, his mind reeling, overwhelmed and unable to cope with the magnitude of events happening around him.

"Zach, are you still there?" Admiral Hadley questioned. "Zach, can you hear me?" Admiral Hadley waited, but still no answer. "Zach, I will hang up and call back."

"No, wait, Admiral," Zach blurted. "I'm at the hospital. Dad's in surgery. A bomb." Again, Zach just stood there wide-eyed.

"Zach, what are you talking about," Admiral Hadley demanded.

Snapping out of his trance-like state, Zach answered, "We were trying to contact Doctor Woods. You know. The person you said called his superiors about a man with a suspicious medical condition. He didn't answer his phone and didn't show up at work. Dad and I drove to his house and found him lying on the floor. We were investigating when a man ran out the back door and into a garage. We chased him. Just short of the garage with Dad in front, the garage exploded. The ambulance took him to Copper Queen Community Hospital in Douglas. He's in surgery now."

"Zach, I'm so sorry. What does the doctor say?"

"She said he is in guarded condition. I guess you could say she's cautiously optimistic. She thinks he will be okay."

"We will hope and pray for the best, Zach. Now, back to our current disaster. I must assume you agree with me that your situation has to be related to the incident in Sacramento, yes?"

"Yes, Admiral, I agree. It is obvious someone wanted to make sure Doctor Woods didn't talk to anyone. What's next?"

"I talked directly to the President. I informed him I had a team running down a lead, and that I was convinced it was related to the Sacramento incident. I asked for and received full authority for you and your dad. The President, himself, authorized you to do anything you needed to do and I mean *anything*. Absolutely anything you need. Just ask and it's yours."

"Okay, Admiral. I need some hardware and credentials. I will still need full access to the Gulfstream for the duration."

"The *hardware* and credentials are on their way via my personal courier. The Gulfstream is yours for as long as you need it, and if you need any FAA clearances, ask and it's done." Admiral Hadley replied. I will contact the courier and direct him to the hospital. He's close and should be there in an hour or two."

"What about the ability to travel, Admiral? Have they activated the Emergency Response System?"

"Not that I know of, but travel will probably be difficult. There is no doubt people will panic. So far, the only air traffic ground stop issued is for the Washington, D.C., area, but I suspect there will be a full ground stop issued for the Southwest Sector as a minimum. That is the President's call. When I spoke to him he was on his way to Air Force One.

Once he arrives, he will activate Presidential Directive Fifty-One. As I said earlier, if you need an FAA clearance *anywhere*, call me. Keep me informed, Zach. Finding the source of that weapon is crucial."

"Okay, Admiral. I will have Angie fly down here before there is any disruption in air travel. Once she arrives and can be here for my dad, I will break away and talk to the Sheriff and see if I can learn something from him or the crime scene."

"Agreed. Call me the instant you learn anything."

"Will do, Admiral," Zach agreed as he ended the call and was about to call Angie back.

A tall, well-dressed woman walked into the waiting area. As she crossed thru the room, headed for the coffee station, she bumped into Zach, causing him to drop his cell phone.

"Sorry, sir," the woman apologized, bending down to pick up the wayward cell phone.

"You should be more….," Zach interrupted his complaint as he turned to see who had bumped into him. He stopped when he saw the woman standing there holding his cell phone.

"Sorry again, sir," she said as she held out Zach's cell phone. "I am so clumsy sometimes. My mother is sick and I am so worried about her I can't seem to concentrate."

"My condolences," Zach said, taking the phone from her outstretched hand. "My dad is in surgery. I know how you feel."

"Well then, it seems we are in the same boat," the woman answered as she straightened her knee-length black dress.

"Yes, I guess we are. Do you live here?"

"No. My dad and I are here on business."

"It is sad that you must be alone at a time like this."

"My wife and mother are on their way. Should be here soon."

"That is good. I must go," the woman said. "I need to grab a cup of coffee and get back to my mother's room."

"I hope your mother gets well soon," Zach said to the woman's back as she walked over to the coffee station.

"I hope your dad recovers soon as well," she answered over her shoulder. She busied herself pouring a cup of coffee, adding a spoonful of sugar. Dropping a stir stick in the cup, she turned and walked out of the waiting area. Returning his attention to his phone, Zach did not notice the woman stop just outside the doorway to the ICU Waiting Room and drop the untouched cup of coffee into a trash receptacle.

As quickly as she could, she slipped a cell phone out of her purse and snapped several photos of Zach as he dialed his cell phone. She dropped the cell phone back in her purse, turned, and walked hurriedly down the hall toward the elevators.

Waiting for someone to answer, Zach sat in one of the waiting room chairs. After five rings, the call to Angie went to voice mail. As Zach was ending the call, he noticed a voice mail icon at the top of his phone's display. He dialed his voice mail and listened to the short message from Angie. The message informed him that Angie and his mother were already on the way to Arizona.

Air Force One
Andrews Air Force Base
SE of Suitland, Maryland

A gleaming blue and white 747-200B, standing six stories tall and almost as long as a football field, accelerated down runway Zero-One Left. The instant the President had stepped foot on board the aircraft, it assumed the air traffic control call sign Air Force One. The Boeing VC-25, highly customized and electronically hardened, operated under authority of the 89th Airlift Wing stationed at Andrews Air Force Base.

Colonel Stephen S. Haywood, hands steady on the aircraft's yoke, glanced across the cockpit assessing the many flight instruments, satisfied all aircraft systems were operating normally. As the airspeed indicator reached one hundred sixty knots (one hundred eighty-four MPH), Colonel Haywood pulled back on the aircraft's yoke. The massive aircraft lifted free of the runway. Seven seconds later, at thirty-five feet, he retracted the landing gear and increased the climb angle to fifteen degrees. Maintaining a steady pressure on the yoke, he kept the aircraft at a rotation angle of fifteen degrees. A normal rotation angle was ten degrees, but given the gravity of the situation, Departure Control authorized a hurry-up departure which would allow Air Force One to proceed to a safe altitude and depart the D.C. area quickly. Once at altitude, two F-16s, already circling the Washington area, would rendezvous with Air Force One to provide close air support.

"Air Force One, Departure Control, fly runway heading. Climb and maintain ten thousand. Contact Washington Center en route on one-two-one point zero-two-zero."

"Air Force One out of two for ten. Contact Washington Center en route roger."

Colonel Haywood maintained the fifteen degree climb angle, climbing at fifteen hundred feet per minute. Six and one-half minutes later, Air Force One leveled off at ten thousand feet. Flying level at the assigned altitude, he dialed in the Washington Air Traffic Control Center frequency, and thumbed the transmit button, "Washington Center, Air Force One, heading zero-one-zero level at ten thousand."

"Air Force One, Washington Center, proceed direct to your final altitude. Hurry up climb and maintain four-one-thousand, turn right heading zero-seven-six, increase speed to five-two-zero knots."

"Washington Center, hurry-up climb and maintain four one thousand, turn right heading zero-seven-six, increase speed to five-two-zero knots, roger." Colonel Haywood pushed the throttles forward and pulled back on the yoke, increasing the climb angle to twenty degrees and increasing the climb rate to eighteen hundred feet per minute. As the four powerful General Electric CF6-80C2B1 engines responded producing a combined thrust of almost two hundred thirty thousand pounds, Colonel Haywood eased the yoke to the right, turning the aircraft toward the assigned heading of zero-seven-six. He pushed the inter-aircraft comm button to advise the passengers of the unusual maneuver. "This is the Captain. Washington Center has cleared us for a hurry-up climb to our assigned cruising altitude. It will likely get a little bumpy. Stay seated and keep your seat-belts fastened."

Six minutes later flying on a heading of zero-seven-six and passing through twenty-one thousand feet, Air Traffic Control called Air Force One with an ominous warning. "Air Force One, Washington Center, traffic above and behind you and descending toward you. We are not in contact with them. I repeat, we are not in contact with them. They display no 'ident' and are not responding. We must classify the contact as hostile. Turn right heading one-three-eight, maintain two-three thousand."

"Washington Center, Air Force One, turn right heading one-three-eight, maintain two-three thousand roger." Colonel Haywood released the comm button and glanced over at Lieutenant Colonel Alan R. Ross, Air Force One's first officer. Lieutenant Colonel Ross leaned forward and looked out the cockpit window on the starboard side of the aircraft and watched as one of the F-16s shadowing Air Force One banked hard right and disappeared behind them. Washington Air Traffic Control Center had ordered one of the F-16s to investigate the unresponsive aircraft encroaching on Air Force One's airspace and shoot it down if it did not respond.

Colonel Haywood banked Air Force One hard right, turning toward the ordered heading. "Alan, arm the countermeasures."

Colonel Haywood pushed the inter-aircraft comm button, "This is the Captain. Air Traffic Control has advised there is an unresponsive aircraft closing on our position. We may need to take evasive action. Stay in your seats and make certain your seat belts are securely fastened."

Air Force One crossed over the coast of Maryland and flew out over the Atlantic Ocean. With his eyes glued to the incoming threat radar screen, fed from four conformal antennas mounted mid-fuselage on the port side of the aircraft, the flight engineer scanned for any sign of inbound threats. The President and his fellow passengers could do nothing but wait as the minutes dragged on.

The F-16 instructed to intercept the aircraft encroaching on Air Force One's airspace located a passenger airliner whose transponder had failed. To compound the transponder failure, the pilot had failed to switch to an alternate frequency as directed by FAA regulations. The airliner's pilot was more than a little shocked and embarrassed when the F-16 flew within one hundred feet and waggled his wings to get his attention. A short but quite terse conversation ensued between the two pilots, ending with the airliner's pilot being instructed to land at the closest available airport and wait until contacted by FAA officials.

Flying three hundred feet off the airliner's port wingtip, the F-16's pilot followed until the airliner approached the downwind leg of the airport's landing pattern. The F-16 pilot called airport arrival control and secured clearance for the airliner and informed them of the pilot's error, also instructing them to notify the appropriate FAA officials to meet and hold the pilot. The F-16 orbited just to the west of the airport, waiting until the airliner's wheels touched down on the runway. After calling for and receiving a direct vector to rendezvous with Air Force One, the F-16 pilot pushed the throttles forward beyond the detent, engaging the afterburner. The F-16 streaked off toward the Northeast to rendezvous with Air Force One.

Lieutenant Colonel Ross tapped Colonel Haywood on the shoulder and gave him the thumbs up signal when he saw the F-16 pull up and assume its escort position on the starboard side of the aircraft.

"Washington Center, Air Force One, level at two-three thousand, heading one-three-eight, escort aircraft has returned. Request return to base course."

"Air Force One, Washington Center, climb and maintain four-one thousand at your discretion, turn left heading zero-one-six."

"Washington Center, Air Force One, climb and maintain four-one thousand, turn left heading zero-one-six roger"

Colonel Haywood pulled back on the yoke and pushed the throttles forward, resuming the hurry-up climb rate of just over eighteen hundred feet per minute. "This is the Captain. Washington Center has verified the threat as being false. We are returning to original heading and should be at cruising altitude in approximately ten minutes."

Just over eleven minutes later, Colonel Haywood leveled Air Force One off at forty-one thousand feet, cruising at five hundred sixty-five knots. He engaged the auto-pilot, turned off the seat-belt sign, and announced, "This is the Captain. We are level at our assigned altitude of forty-one thousand feet. You may unfasten your seatbelts and move about the aircraft. I will assess additional threats as they arise. Be ready to return to your seats if requested to do so."

With an armed guard standing in front of the door to Air Force One's soundproof conference room, the President convened a meeting of his essential staff to discuss the catastrophic emergency taking place.

"Gentlemen, our first order of business is to assure continuity of government," President Cantwell began, looking directly at John J. Elmore, Assistant to the President for Homeland Security and Counterterrorism. "Where are we headed?"

"We will fly a prescribed, albeit secret, flight plan until any identified threats have been eliminated," John Elmore answered. "At that time, we are en route to one of the Presidential Relocation Facilities. By direction of Presidential Directive Fifty-One, the Vice President and other designated, key officials are moving to their alternate safe facilities as we speak. As you know, Mister President, geographic dispersal of key government leaders and their functions is essential for continuity of government."

Following directives outlined in Presidential Directive Fifty-One, an unnamed number of PRFs (Presidential Relocation Facilities), hardened underground bunkers, were constructed to serve as critical command centers in catastrophic emergencies. The relocation facility selected as the President's destination, known only to a few key individuals, would already be in its "warm up" mode. Assigned personnel, already on site, would be bringing key systems on line. The presidential directive required all systems to be fully operational upon the President's arrival.

"What is our designated PRF, Mister Elmore?" President Cantwell asked.

John Elmore lifted a plastic card from his shirt pocket, held his finger above the code 'Majestic One' on the card, and pushed it in front of the President. Despite being in a soundproof conference room, no one was to speak out loud the President's and his team's destination.

President Cantwell looked at the card, nodded, and continued, "While we were waiting on Marine One, Jeffery Williams asked whether I should activate the EAS. I was then, and still am, hesitant to do so. At the current time, we do not know the delivery system of the detonated device. We also do not know if more devices exist. Bottom line, gentlemen, we know very little."

Matthew Tyler, the National Security Advisor, spoke up. "Mister President, prior to departing the Whitehouse, NORAD advised they had no indication of inbound threats and the early warning system showed no inbound targets."

"I believe we can then assume there are currently no airborne threats. Considering we do not know if there are any additional devices or where they might be, I do not believe activating the EAS is wise. That would only create more confusion, but I will order all financial markets closed until further notice. Gentlemen, do you concur?"

President Cantwell looked at each person seated at the conference table. No one spoke or showed any disagreement with the President's decision.

"Okay, moving on," President Cantwell said. "What about communications?"

"Most landline and cell phone systems are hopelessly jammed," Donald M. Walsh, White House Chief of Staff, answered. "In proximity to the blast, the EMP generated by the blast overwhelmed all electronic systems. Communications circuits in that area will likely be out for months or even years. We will have to rely on hardened communications systems."

"Exactly as expected," President Cantwell added. "Given NORAD says the weapon was not air-delivered, someone smuggled it into the country. If someone could smuggle in one weapon, we have no choice but to believe there are more weapons somewhere in the country. Does anybody disagree?"

Everyone seated at the conference table nodded their heads, agreeing with the President's assessment.

"Everyone is in agreement there are likely more weapons. The next step is to determine the source of the weapon and who is responsible *before* they can detonate another one."

Matthew Tyler looked at the President and responded, "Mister President, the Army has a nuclear incident response team gearing up to proceed to the blast zone. They will collect samples to determine the signature of the fissionable material used. That should give us a likely source of the nuclear material but it may not identify the individuals responsible for planting and detonating the device."

"I understand that, Mister Tyler," President Cantwell exclaimed, looking directly at Matthew Tyler. "When the meeting concludes, I want you personally to contact incident command and inform them there is nothing more important than identifying the source of the nuclear material. I will order our forces to be ready when that information becomes available. Am I clear?"

"Yes, Sir," Matthew Tyler replied, scribbling on the pad lying in front of him."

The momentous decision to launch nuclear weapons weighed heavily on President Cantwell. His skin was pale, his face was drawn, and small beads of perspiration glistened on his forehead. He picked up a bottle of water and sipped slowly, trying to wash down the acid rising in his throat. The men seated around the conference table murmured in low voices as they waited for the President's decision.

Matthew Tyler looked up from his notepad and addressed the President. "Mister President, I have conferred with the Joint Chiefs and they assure me we have more than ample capability to obliterate the enemy."

"I have no doubt about that, Matthew," President Cantwell snapped. President Cantwell pulled a handkerchief from his pocket, wiped his forehead, and regained his composure. "Sorry, Matthew, I know you're just passing along information. I'm not worried in the least regarding our forces' ability to deliver their payloads on target. What worries me is what it will leave after that. What will we leave our children?"

President Cantwell hung his head and closed his eyes. The other men around the table sat in silence not knowing whether he was thinking or whether he was praying. A long thirty seconds passed with no movement from the President. The men began to exchange worried glances. Mathew Tyler was about to speak when the President looked up. His expression had a different appearance. The hesitant look gone, replaced by a look of determination and resolve.

"Gentleman, I have made my decision. We cannot, we will not allow such an atrocious act to go unpunished. I will order our Armed Forces to DEFCON 3. No, ignore that. I will order our Armed Forces to DEFCON 2 This incident may be a prelude to war. Our forces must be ready to strike. We must implement Operation Vigilant Strike. Our bombers will be scrambled with pre-designated target packages. Our submarine strike forces will be ordered to their pre-designated launch coordinates to await launch orders."

Even though the President's decision was exactly what they expected, everyone seated around the conference table looked visibly shaken. They had all taken part in numerous drills and planning sessions for this eventuality, but no amount of drills or preparation could truly prepare anyone for what they now faced. This was not a drill. This was real. Nuclear war had just become a very real possibility.

Chapter Eight

National Military Command Center
Emergency Conference Room
Alternate Safe Facility - Defender One
Location - Classified

The National Military Command Center (NMCC), housed in the Pentagon under normal conditions, had moved to a hardened, alternate location because of the declaration of a catastrophic emergency. Activity in the ECR (Emergency Conference Room) operated with a heightened sense of urgency.

Maintained by the Department of the Air Force, the NMCC operates as a command and communications center for the National Command Authority under direction of the President of the United States and the United States Secretary of Defense. Divisions of the NMCC answer to the Chairman of Joint Chiefs of Staff in his role as the principal military advisor to both the President and the Secretary of Defense.

NMCC has three main missions: monitoring worldwide events which may be of defense significance, operating a crisis response unit, and operating a strategic watch unit. The NMCC generates Emergency Action Messages (EAMs) to launch control centers, nuclear submarines, recon aircraft, and battlefield commanders worldwide and also maintains the infamous "*Red Phone*".

Under normal conditions, the NMCC would receive commands from the White House Situation Room. Because of the current extreme conditions, the White House Situation Room sat in total darkness, its functionality having already moved to an alternate safe location. Commands now came directly from the President or the Chairman of the Joint Chiefs.

Brigadier General Robert A. Gordon viewed the frenzied activity in the CAC (Current Actions Center) of NMCC. Large volumes of inbound communications, resulting from the nuclear incident, threatened to overwhelm the personnel on duty. From the outset of the incident, General Gordon alerted all on-call personnel to return to the NMCC immediately. A few communications specialists had arrived, but many still displayed on the duty board as "en route". General Gordon paced back and forth nervously, fearing an operational collapse of the CAC. The more he paced, the more nervous he became. With his stress exploding dramatically, he had perspired through his uniform, large wet circles under his arms stained his uniform jacket.

He began to relax somewhat when he saw four additional communications specialists run into the CAC and plug their headsets into unmanned consoles. Mopping his face with a handkerchief, he pulled a rolling chair over in front of the viewing window. About to sit down on the chair, an earsplitting alarm sounded as the "*Red Phone*" lit up. Startled, his hand slipped off the chair's arm and he fell to his knees. He stood up quickly and glanced around the room to see if anyone had seen him fall.

"Are you kidding me?" he squawked as he scrambled to answer the phone.

"NMCC, General Gordon."

"General Gordon, this is Fleet Admiral Bennington."

General Gordon's heart sank the instant he realized he was speaking to the Chairman of the Joint Chiefs. Considering the frantic activity already underway, he feared the situation was about to get much worse. "Go ahead, Admiral," General Gordon advised, expecting the worst.

"General, I have been in secure communication with Air Force One. The President has ordered the Armed Forces alert level raised to DEFCON 2. The order is to go out immediately."

"Yes, Sir, Admiral."

"General Gordon, in conjunction with raising the military alert level, the President has ordered Operation Vigilant Strike implemented immediately. Nuclear Strike Forces are to use pre-assigned targeting packages. All ballistic missile submarine units are to cease current operations immediately and proceed directly to designated launch stations and await orders. B-52 squadrons are to scramble and proceed to their assigned failsafe coordinates. Did you get all that, General?"

"Yes, Sir, Admiral. The orders will go out immediately."

"Very well, General. Wish our troops Godspeed."

"Will do, Sir."

Shaking slightly, General Gordon dropped the *"Red Phone"* receiver back in its place and took a deep breath. Not willing to rely on anyone else to give such a weighty order, he took off at a run, heading for the CAC. All eyes in the action center followed the General when they saw him run into the room at full speed. Once he located an unmanned console, he leaned over and punched a large red button labeled USSTRATCOM (United States Strategic Command).

Several states away, deep inside the United States Strategic Command Center housed on Offutt Air Force Base near Omaha, Nebraska, another *"Red Phone"* rang. That phone was the Primary Alerting System, a direct line to the National Military Command Center. Lieutenant Colonel Donald Bell, the Senior Controller on duty, grabbed the receiver and listened intently.

"My God," Lieutenant Col. Bell gasped when the voice on the other end of the alert system advised him the scramble order was not a drill.

Before he could cradle the primary alert phone, Lieutenant Colonel Bell grabbed for the microphone that would scramble the B-52 squadrons stationed on Air Force bases at Minot, North Dakota, and Barksdale, Louisiana. The scramble order was transmitted via a secure, single-sideband radio transmitter on the High Frequency Global Communications System. Once the B-52 aircraft were scrambled and airborne,

NMCC would send the targeting EAM directives in secure digital format via AUTODIN (the military's secure Automatic Digital Network).

Back in NMCC, General Gordon transmitted additional orders, alerting both COMSUBPAC and COMSUBLANT, the Navy's Pacific and Atlantic fleet commanders, advising them to order their ballistic missile submarines to proceed to their designated launch stations.

Once all the Nuclear Strike Forces had confirmed receipt of the scramble order, General Gordon leaned back in his chair, sweat drenching his face.

"World War Three, here we come," he stammered as he got up and rushed back to his office.

Copper Queen Community Hospital
100 East 5th Street
Douglas, Arizona

Zach Templeton paced back and forth across the hospital's ICU waiting area, awaiting an update on his dad's condition. He could not remember how many trips he had made back and forth across the waiting area or how many cups of lukewarm coffee he had drunk. About to start another trip across the waiting area, he looked up when Virginia Doyle, ICU Charge Nurse, pushed open the sliding door to his dad's room.

"Mister Templeton?" she asked.

"Yes," Zach answered, fearing the worst because of the look on Nurse Doyle's face.

"The good news is that your father came through the surgery okay," Nurse Doyle advised. "The bad news is that he is in a medically induced coma to allow his body to heal. Doctor Berger has your father listed in guarded condition."

"How serious are his injuries?"

"He has a collapsed right lung, multiple broken ribs, and internal bleeding. The bleeding is under control for now. The doctor is cautiously optimistic."

"How long will he be in a coma?"

"That depends on how he responds. The doctor said the next two to three days will be critical. I have to get back to ICU. If you have questions, contact the ICU admin desk."

"Thank you, Nurse Doyle." Zach stood there numb, watching Nurse Doyle as she returned to his dad's room and slid the door shut. The anguish of not knowing whether his dad would survive his injuries reignited the memory of the horrifying day many years earlier when the Coast Guard notified him that his parents and their beloved sailboat, *Tipsy*, had disappeared somewhere off the coast of San Francisco. After three weeks of searching without a trace, the Coast Guard ended the search, and they declared his parents lost at sea.

Unanswered questions had flooded Zach's mind: Did they run into a sudden squall? Did they have mechanical problems? Was there an explosion? Why did the sailboat sink? Why was there no trace? After months of sleepless nights wondering what could have happened to his parents, he was forced to accept the agonizing truth. He realized he would never see his parents again. A profound emptiness had settled over him, knowing the affirmation from his father he longed for would never come. Unconsciously, he transferred that unfulfilled longing into a craving to succeed and gain respect. He left the Navy and opened a fledgling, communications installation and support company. Zach's craving to succeed drove him to spend more and more time on company matters. Serious problems with a DOD contract consumed even more of his time, worsening the neglect Angie, his wife, felt. Unhappy and frustrated, Angie moved out and asked for a divorce.

Just when Zach believed his life could not get any worse, a sinister plot plunged him into a chilling struggle that would pit him against a depraved military officer and a rogue FBI agent. Two men driven to madness by hatred. Their depraved scheme threatened to destroy Zach's shaky marriage, everything Zach had worked for, and, even worse, it would instigate a global war.

With his best friend murdered and his company in ruins, Zach stood face to face with his enemy. Failure was imminent and then suddenly, like a ghost, his father appeared. Together Zach and his dad thwarted the scheme. While the FBI captured one man, the other man escaped without a trace. For a few short minutes, Zach had felt the love of a father for his son. Then, his father disappeared as quickly as he had appeared.

Then, only days ago the worried call came from Admiral Hadley. During that call, the Admiral gave Zach a contact number for his father. Once again, a madman's evil plot reunited them, but this time his father promised he would not disappear. Just one day later, his father lay in a hospital bed a few feet away with death a very real possibility. *"When will this nightmare merry-go-round ever end?"* Zach asked himself.

Zach did not know how long he had been standing there with the nightmare of past events swirling in his mind. A hand touched his shoulder, startling him out of his daydream. Turning to see who had touched him, he saw Angie, his wife, standing there in front of him. Just behind Angie stood his mother, Margaret.

"Oh, Zach. I'm so sorry about your dad," Angie choked. "How is he? Have the doctors said anything?"

Zach reached out, drew Angie toward himself, and held her tightly, resting his head on her shoulder. He drank in the warmth and softness of her neck and the soft fragrance of her perfume. The tender embrace reminded him of another embrace at the Miami International Airport after he had learned his comrade and best friend was dead, supposedly the result of an automobile accident. As hard as he had tried not to, tears had rolled down his cheeks, soaking into Angie's blouse. This time there was no sobbing or crying. Just the tears of pain, driven by the worry he might lose his father again.

"Zach, I....,"

"Just give me a minute, Angie," Zach sniffed.

As Zach stood there composing himself, another hand touched his shoulder. He did not need to look to see who touched him. A son always knows his mother's touch. He released his embrace of Angie and turned to face his mother. It seemed like a dream, but he was awake. Right there in front of him, in the flesh, stood his mother.

"Zachie," his mother called out softly.

Zach stepped into his mother's open arms and instantly felt the warmth and protection only a mother's arms can provide. No longer did a grown man stand there. Zach was the little boy in a mother's arms being comforted for whatever bump or bruise or nightmare had befallen him. The subtle scent of honeysuckle transported Zach backward in time. Zach had not seen nor spoken to his mother in over five years. Despite the long time span, Zach instantly felt safe and protected in his mother's arms. He did not want that feeling to end.

"Zach," his mother urged, shaking him slightly. "Zach, how is your father?"

"Oh, okay. I'm sorry, Misses Susan Glover," Zach quipped, a smile spreading across his face. "Or is it Misses Margaret Templeton? I forget."

"It's Margaret Templeton, Zach. I believe your father told you that," his mother stated as she grabbed Zach's ear and tweaked it.

"Hey, that hurts," Zach squealed. The strained smile on Zach's face faded as he began to fill them in on his dad's condition, "Dad has a collapsed right lung, multiple broken ribs, and internal bleeding. The nurse said the bleeding is under control for now. She also said the doctor is cautiously optimistic."

"Well, Son, are you going to leave an old woman standing in the middle of the room with no coffee?"

"Oh, sorry. Sure," Zach answered, pointing to a table in the corner of the ICU waiting area. With his mother and wife seated, Zach walked over to the coffee station and poured two cups of coffee. He set the steaming cups in front of them and sat down beside his wife, Angie. He looked at his mother and said, "You don't seem very bothered by this. I don't understand."

"You may not see it, but I am extremely worried," his mother replied. "When you have been through this as many times as I have, you get somewhat numb. I can't count the number of hushed phone conversations, the middle of the night disappearances, the cryptic phone calls from God knows who, the secret stash of weapons, the…." His mother's voice grew silent. "I have said way too much. You must promise to forget what I just said."

"I think it might surprise you to learn how much I know," Zach replied. "I have been…."

The sudden entrance of a slender, young man in a dark suit, white shirt, and dark tie interrupted Zach's attention. Everything about the man's appearance implied government agent. With a laser focus on Zach, the man walked directly over to Zach, pulled a leather wallet from inside his jacket, and flopped it open for Zach to inspect.

Zach looked at the credential, comparing the photo on the left side of the wallet to the man's face, a full day's growth of beard, the only variance between the photo and the man's face. "Agent Martinson," Zach said, offering his hand. "I assume Admiral Hadley sent you."

"Yes, sir. Mister Templeton," Agent Martinson replied. "Admiral Hadley said it was vital I reach you as soon as possible. We will need somewhere private to talk. Come with me."

Agent Martinson, with Zach following close behind, walked over to the ICU Admin desk. He flopped his credentials open for the on-duty nurse to see and asked if there was somewhere private he and Mr. Templeton could talk. The on-duty nurse directed them to a patient conference room off the hallway just outside the ICU waiting area.

As Zach entered the conference room, Agent Martinson pulled the door shut and stood in front of it to prevent anyone else from entering.

"Mister Templeton, Admiral Hadley instructed me to deliver this to you personally."

"Thank you, Agent Martinson. I was expecting….", Zach hesitated as he flipped the leather wallet open and examined the credential. "Wow! I was not expecting that!" Zach read the credential again, out loud to be certain he was not mistaken. "Secret Service - Special Agent, Presidential Detail."

"Pretty impressive, Mister Templeton," Agent Martinson affirmed as he reached in his pocket and retrieved a plastic card that had a single six character code embossed on it. He handed the plastic card to Zach. "That's as high as it gets. I assure you your credentials and that access code will get you absolutely anything you request and I mean *ANYTHING!*"

"Yes, I suspect it will," Zach agreed, stuffing the credentials and plastic card in his jacket pocket. "What about *special* hardware?"

"First, we need to make your appointment official. Raise your right hand, Mister Templeton."

Agent Martinson stated the oath while Zach repeated the oath in his own words. With Zach's appointment official, Agent Martinson stuck out his hand, "Welcome to the service, Special Agent Templeton. It's a pleasure to have you join us."

"Thank you. It's an honor," Zach answered. "Now, what about that hardware?"

"I almost forget. Here is the SAT phone the Admiral wanted you to have. Cell phone coverage is spotty and undependable and where it is working, it is hopelessly overwhelmed. Admiral Hadley may need to contact you on short notice. As far as the *hardware* goes, I have a pretty extensive array of items in the trunk of my car. You can view them later and select whatever you need."

"Agreed. I'll go make a quick check on my dad's condition and then we can go have a look."

As Zach pushed the conference room door open, he noticed the woman he had bumped into earlier in the ICU waiting area. Zach saw the woman crouching against the hallway wall pointing a long menacing handgun toward the ICU waiting area. A nurse entered the hallway and screamed when she saw the woman pointing the gun. Startled, the woman with the gun lost her concentration. She fired anyway, her hand jerking upward twice, clouds of smoke rising from the end of a heavy cylinder attached to the end of the barrel.

"Gun!" Zach screamed, reaching behind his back to grab his weapon only to find nothing there, having locked his weapon in the trunk of his rental car before entering the hospital.

Agent Martinson turned his head and looked at the woman. An old memory flashed in his mind as their eyes made contact. He had seen that face before. Agent Martinson reached behind his back and pulled out his weapon. Zach saw the woman turn and point the gun in their direction.

Adrenalin pumping, Agent Martinson hurriedly pointed his weapon at the woman and fired, but the round bored harmlessly into the wall just above the woman, creating a cloud of splintered tile and plaster. The woman smiled as she fired two rounds into Agent Martinson. Agent Martinson gasped, falling against Zach causing him to lose his footing. They both fell to the floor. Agent Martinson's weapon clattered to the floor beside them. The sudden mêlée awakened Zach's Navy SEAL instincts. With as little movement as possible, he felt around and located the loose weapon. His hand tightened around the weapon. Zach rolled sideways, quickly firing four rounds as the woman fired again. Zach felt a searing pain as the weapon fell from his hand and clattered on the floor.

USS Wyoming (SSBN 742)
Southeast of Bermuda

Chief of the Boat, Master Chief Damage Controlman Edward Benson, reached up and twisted the yellow, general alarm handle, giving it one full revolution, setting off a series of fourteen gongs.

"Bong, Bong, Bong, Bong….," the flooding alarm, the most feared alarm for all submariners, rang throughout every compartment of the USS Wyoming.

Several seconds after the blaring alarm, Master Chief Benson's excited voice blared over the 4-MC, "All hands, flooding in the engine room, starboard side!"

Wyoming's commanding officer, Commander Joseph Anderson, responded without thinking, the result of many hours of practice drills. "Conn, Dive, blow all variable ballast tanks. Ten degree up bubble. Helm, ahead full, make turns for fifteen knots," Commander Anderson shouted into the 1-MC. His first, and most critical, priority was to point the boat upward and increase speed to counteract the extra weight of the water streaming into the engine room.

Submarines were designed to carry a considerable amount of extra weight; but only if the boat was moving at an upward angle with adequate speed. If the amount of water pouring into the boat became excessive, the speed and angle of the boat would not matter. Uncontrolled flooding would add extra weight and would soon exceed what the boat could compensate for. If the damage control party could not bring the flooding under control in a few minutes, the extra weight of the sea water would drag the Wyoming to the bottom.

Lieutenant Commander Paul Turner, Wyoming's Diving Officer with an urgency in his voice, called out the boat's depth as it began to slide backward into the dark water, "Seven hundred feet and sinking!"

Standing right beside the diving officer, Chief of the Watch, Chief Machinist Mate Michael Warren, shouted, "Blowing all variable ballast tanks. Connecting trim pumps to the drain system. Trim and drain pumps at maximum RPM."

Trim pumps, pumped ballast water forward and aft to balance the boat, but during flooding emergencies, the Chief of the Watch would connect them to the drain system. Being centrifugal pumps, the trim and drain pumps added only minimal pumping capacity. The amount of water they could pump decreased in direct proportion to the external pressure of the seawater outside the boat.

"Nine hundred feet and sinking!" Lieutenant Commander Turner shouted.

As *Wyoming's* depth increased, the output from the trim pumps decreased rapidly. The inflow rate of the water pouring in from the leak increased because of the increasing pressure of the surrounding seawater, magnifying the pumps' decreased output.

"Eleven hundred feet. Rate of depth change is increasing!" yelled Lieutenant Commander Turner.

As *Wyoming* sank deeper into the frigid water, the pressures increased rapidly, increasing the rate at which she was sinking. Soon there would be nothing anyone could do.

Damage control teams, equipped with multiple sizes of banding clamps, used to seal leaking or split water lines, ran frantically toward the engine room. The damage control teams would have to seal the leak quickly before the extra weight exceeded the critical point. The water streaming into the boat made all the surfaces wet, impacting the damage control teams' ability to control the flooding. Water streaming through a high pressure leak could literally cut off limbs. Working in close proximity to the leak required extreme care. The great danger and understandable panic created a scene of sheer terror.

"Passing test depth! Two hundred feet to crush depth!" screamed Lieutenant Commander Turner

"Conn, Quartermaster, Give me a sounding," Commander Anderson called out.

The Quartermaster glanced quickly at the fathometer and replied, "Seven hundred fifty fathoms Captain."

The possibility that *Wyoming* could settle out on the sea bottom before her hull collapsed did not exist. The current ocean depth of forty-five hundred feet under *Wyoming's* keel was more than triple the boat's crush depth. *Wyoming's* situation deteriorated from grim to desperate. Their only hope hinged on the damage control teams' ability to stop the flooding within the next twenty seconds.

"Conn, Damage Control, band clamp has slipped. Flooding is not under control, I repeat, flooding is *not* under control," a desperate voice screamed over the 4-MC.

"Approaching crush depth!" shrieked Lieutenant Commander Turner.

With large beads of sweat running down his face, Commander Anderson glanced around the control center. Terrified faces stared back at him, begging him to call out some procedure to try next, but there was nothing left to do. *Wyoming* had just run out of options. She was dying and heading for the bottom.

Chapter Nine

Copper Queen Community Hospital
100 East 5th Street
Douglas, Arizona

Haze from the gun battle swirled in wispy clouds near the ceiling. The heavy, acrid smell of cordite filled the air. Hospital security, weapons drawn, converged on the hallway and the ICU waiting area. Medical personnel gathered at the far end of the hallway waiting for security personnel to advise them they could proceed.

The first hospital security guard to arrive seized the weapons lying on the floor. Assessing no further threat existed, one of the security guards signaled the medical personnel to advance.

Zach looked up at the security guard standing over him. "The woman., the woman! I need to see her weapon, now!" Zach demanded, as he held out his new credentials.

The security guard pulled the weapon out from behind his back and looked the weapon over. "Don't see many of these around here," he said as he leaned over and handed the weapon to Zach.

"A Heckler and Koch, Mark 23, with sound suppressor," Zach remarked. "I'll take custody of that. This weapon is US Army Special Operations issue. How on earth did that woman over there get one of these?"

Ignoring the blood running down his left arm, Zach pushed himself up and walked over to where the woman was lying. He stepped around the nurse who was attempting to administer aid to the woman. "She needs medical attention," the nurse countered. "You can't talk to her."

"This is a national emergency," Zach barked. "I have to talk to her now." Holding the gun in front of the woman's face, he poked her in the arm and asked, "Who are you? Where did you get this?"

Receiving no answer, he poked her harder, "I said where did you get this?"

The woman's eyes fluttered open and then closed. Zach jabbed her even harder. The woman winced and her eyes fluttered open again. With great effort she sputtered, "*Voutré vieil ami* Frank Porter *dit qu'il va vous voir dans l'enfer.*"

"What did you say? What does Frank Porter have to do with this? Answer me!" Zach screamed at the woman.

"Beware *mon ami*, he has many friends," the woman gasped. One long breath escaped from her lips as her eyes opened wide and became fixed. The blank stare of death was obvious. The woman would answer no more questions.

"Does anybody here speak French?" Zach asked. "I have to know what this woman said."

"But you're bleeding," the nurse said, looking up at Zach, pointing at his left arm.

"That will wait," Zach snapped. "I have to know what that woman said!"

"There's a woman from the islands that works in the laundry. I think she speaks French," the nurse answered.

"Get her here. Now!" Zach bellowed.

"Okay, I'll go get her."

Zach pulled a handkerchief from his pocket, placed it over the wound in his left arm, and walked back over to where Agent Martinson laid. He looked down at the nurse that had been working on him. She looked up and shook her head.

"Great. Just great," Zach exclaimed. "Sorry, but I need the keys to his car." Zach patted the right side of his jacket then the left side. Feeling a large lump in the left pocket, Zach reached his hand into Agent Martinson's left jacket pocket and drew out a set of keys with a rental car company's information tag attached. He turned, starting toward the exit as the nurse from earlier came running down the hallway with a tall black woman in tow.

"Sir, this is Clarice Lachapelle," the nurse announced. "You know, the woman from the laundry. She's from Martinique. She speaks French".

"Thanks. I appreciate you finding her," Zach said, turning to address the black woman. "I understand you speak French."

"*Oui monsieur*, I do."

"The woman lying over there said something before she died and I need to know what it means. Can you translate it?"

"*Oui*, I will try, sir."

"The woman said *Voutré vieil ami* Frank Porter *dit qu'il va vous voir dans l'enfer.* What does that mean?"

"She used the name - Frank Porter. She said this 'Frank Porter' will see you in Hell."

Zach balled his fists and clenched his jaw as anger rose within him. Twice, in a few short days, someone had mentioned the name of that vile, traitorous rat. If that weasel were standing there right that instant, Zach would have choked the life out of him with his bare hands. Mr. Frank Porter was the contemptible traitor that had escaped his and Admiral Hadley's grasp. Still raw and painful in Zach's mind, he would never forget the unbearable sting of that failure.

"Sir, are you okay?" Ms. Lachapelle asked.

"Huh, oh, yes ma'am, I'm okay. I appreciate your help in translating. I don't want to keep you from your job."

"*Oui*, glad I could help," Ms. Lachapelle said as she turned and started down the hallway.

"Mister Templeton, Mister Templeton," the ICU charge nurse hollered, running out of the ICU waiting area. "Your mother has been injured. Come quick."

Zach remembered seeing the woman with her gun pointed toward the ICU waiting area when he had opened the conference room door. "Oh my God," he shouted as he ran toward the ICU waiting area, fearing the worst.

The ICU waiting area was in shambles. Chairs over-turned and tables shoved haphazardly in all directions. At the front of the waiting area, several nurses on their knees attended to Mrs. Templeton. Zach ran over and dropped to the floor beside his mother.

"She'll be fine. It looks like the wound is a through-and-through. The bullet didn't hit the bone," one nurse said as she wrapped a bandage around his mother's leg.

"Angie. Where's Angie," Zach cried out.

"Right here behind you, Zach," Angie answered as she laid her hand on Zach's shoulder. As Zach turned slightly and looked up at her, she noticed the blood on Zach's arm. "Nurse," she said, pointing at Zach's arm. "I guess we'll have a family affair in the emergency room."

Two nurses loaded Zach's mother on a gurney and wheeled her toward the emergency department with Zach and Angie following close behind. As the nurses pushed the gurney through the double swinging doors of the emergency department, a chaotic scene presented itself. Even though Douglas, Arizona, was a small town, the waiting room more resembled a large city hospital's emergency room. People filled nearly every chair as they waited for treatment. Several babies wailed at the top of their lungs, a construction worker with his hand wrapped in a towel, a young boy with his foot on a pillow, people coughing into their hands, and others with various maladies. Zach and his mother received more than a few dirty looks when the nurses directed them straight through the waiting room and into the emergency department.

Twenty minutes later, Zach's mother's leg had been cleaned and bandaged and Zach's arm had also been dressed and bandaged. Both Zach and his mother were given tetanus boosters and injections of antibiotics just to be safe. The doctor had advised Zach to take it easy for several days. Considering the gravity of current events, the doctor was not at all surprised when Zach told him that would be not possible. The doctor shrugged, grabbed several charts, and headed for the admin area to finish the patient records.

Angie walked over and stood beside the gurney on which Zach sat. "I don't suppose I could talk you into taking it easy either," she said.

"I which I could, Angie. I really do," Zach answered. "Did you hear about Sacramento?"

"Yes. Your mother and I saw it on the television while we were waiting for our flight. It's just awful, Zach. So many people dead."

"This mess is related. That's why I can't sit around."

"What are you talking about, Zach?"

"The dead woman in the hall was carrying this," Zach said, holding up the H&K Mark 23.

"Zach, that is awful. What is that thing?"

"It's a US Army Special Operations weapon. Nothing that woman should have had. She's a professional assassin."

"What are you talking about? How do you know that?"

"Right before she died, she gave me a message. She said my old friend Frank Porter would see me in Hell."

"Frank Porter?" Angie questioned. "That Frank Porter? The one that got away in Washington D.C.?"

"Yes, that one."

"How is he involved in this?"

"I'm not exactly sure, but that is why Dad and I were sent here by Admiral Hadley. Porter's name came up in surveillance operations. The Director of the CIA believes he is involved in smuggling nuclear material across the border. We were here to talk to a Doctor Woods, but we found him dead at his residence. Dad and I chased someone out the back door and into a garage and then the bomb went off."

Dr. Ramona Berger had been standing close by and perked up when she heard Dr. Woods' name mentioned. She walked over and stood in front of Zach and Angie.

"Sorry, I didn't mean to eavesdrop, but did I hear you mention Doctor Woods' name?"

"Yes, my Dad and I were sent here to talk to him. We are the ones who found him dead."

"Did I also hear you mention nuclear materials?" Dr. Berger asked.

"Yes. Doctor Woods reported to his superior in the US Army Reserve he had a case that showed signs of radiation poisoning. It took several days for the information to filter down to us."

"Doctor Woods treated a Mister Polomo in the emergency room several days ago. The last blood test he ordered confirmed that Mister Polomo had radiation poisoning."

"You said *had*?" Zach questioned.

"Yes. He died that same day."

Zach pulled out his new credentials and flipped them open for Dr. Berger to see. "Did Mister Polomo have any personal effects with him?"

"Nothing except for the clothes he was wearing. There was absolutely nothing in his pockets. The Border Patrol picked him up in the desert three miles east of town. All they could get from him was his name and that he was from Juarez, Mexico."

"Thank you, Doctor Berger."

As Dr. Berger left to attend to other patients, Angie tapped Zach on the arm. "Can I see that?" She said, pointing toward the leather wallet. "Wow, impressive. Mister Zachariah Templeton, secret agent man." she said with a frown on her face, handing the wallet back to him. "I guess I can't say I am surprised."

"These credentials are necessary to get me clearance and access to whatever I need. Angie, the people responsible for Sacramento must pay for what they have done. Admiral Hadley and others are concerned there may be more devices hidden in other cities."

"This time I am in total agreement, Zach."

"You are?" Zach answered, a look of amazement spreading across his face.

"Yes, absolutely. This is bigger than you and me. Way bigger. Whatever you need to do, Zach, I am behind you. Just please be careful."

"Thank you, Angie. You don't know how much your support means. I promise I will be as careful as I can be. The first thing I need to do is call Admiral Hadley."

Zach kissed Angie gently and gave her a hug. He held on to Angie for a long time savoring the warmth of her neck against his face and the soft fragrance of her perfume. It had taken months to rebuild their relationship after the last crisis. He wanted to just stand there and hold the woman he loved, but once again evil threatened his country causing him to accept his old friend's plea for help.

Zach gently kissed her neck, stepped back, and looked directly at her. "Angie, I wish I could stay. I promise I will do everything in my power to get back as soon as possible," Zach said as he turned and disappeared in search of a quiet place to confer with Admiral Hadley.

Zach located a patient conference room on the opposite side of the hallway from where the earlier melee had occurred. He punched in Admiral Hadley's number and waited.

"Zach, I've been hoping you would call. Did you get the credentials?"

"Yes, Admiral. A secret service agent delivered them just today. I'm afraid I have some bad news, Admiral. Agent Martinson is dead."

"What?" Admiral Hadley blurted. "He was a close friend. What on Earth happened?"

Zach described the details of the gun battle with the female assassin. Admiral Hadley became furious when he heard Frank Porter's name mentioned as being the perpetrator behind the assassination attempt. Zach explained that the woman had no ID of any kind. Upon learning she had a Heckler and Koch, Mark 23, including sound suppressor, Admiral Hadley became even more concerned.

"That's US Army Special Ops. How did she get a weapon like that?"

"I wondered that myself, Admiral," Zach added. "My speculation is that Porter is still calling in favors."

"Be that as it may, we have much bigger problems, Zach."

"How so, Admiral?"

"Reports from the Western US show civil order is breaking down. Law enforcement is overwhelmed. The President has issued a Southwest Sector ground stop for all airlines, but it hasn't helped. The news media is ranting about more bombs being hidden somewhere in the country. People are headed for a full-out panic and the panic is spreading east. Soon, there will be no controlling it."

"What can I do, Admiral."

"You can track down any leads related to the man reported to have radiation poisoning. Somehow his radiation poisoning relates to the smuggled nuclear materials."

"The doctor here said the Border Patrol found him. I'll start there."

"Oh, Zach, another thing. The President has ordered the alert level raised to DEFCON 2 for all Armed Forces and he has initiated Operation Vigilant Strike."

"I don't like the sound of that, Admiral," Zach said, apprehension suddenly clouding his face. "Exactly what is Operation Vigilant Strike?"

"Our worst nightmare, Zach," Admiral Hadley answered. "The President is livid such a reprehensible act could happen in this country. Operation Vigilant Strike activates our nuclear strike forces. As we speak, orders are going out to COMSUBPAC and to COMSUBLANT to direct our ballistic missile submarines to their launch points and to the Air Force Global Strike Command to scramble all B-52 squadrons. I'm not sure how long I can get the President to hold before releasing them to their targets. Whatever you can discover, you must do it quickly! Am I clear, Zach?"

"You bet, Admiral. I understand. I've got to go, now! I'll call you the instant I learn anything," Zach said as he ended the call without waiting for the Admiral to respond.

"Holy Crow!" Zach choked as he headed off to find Angie. He slammed the conference room door open and ran as fast as he could toward the emergency room waiting area. Nearly knocking two people over, he ran into the waiting area looking for Angie. Helping Zach's mother into a wheelchair, Angie looked up to see Zach slide to a stop in front of her.

"Angie, worse than I thought," Zach panted. "The President — activating nuclear forces — more bombs — panic — crazy…"

"Zach, slow down," Angie urged, grabbing Zach's arm. "I don't understand what you're saying."

Zach took a deep breath and continued. "Admiral Hadley said civil order is breaking down. Panic is spreading. The President has activated our nuclear strike forces. Angie, time's running out. I've got to go. Can you take care of my mom?"

"Zach. Go do what you need to."

Zach bent over and kissed his mother's cheek. "Sorry, Mom. I have to go."

Zach hugged Angie, turned, and ran for the exit door. Once in the hospital's parking lot, he ran up and down the rows of cars pressing the remote he had taken from Agent Martinson's pocket. Halfway down the third row, the lights of a black SUV with dark-tinted windows flashed. Noting the location of the SUV, Zach ran back to his rental car and drove it down the third row to where the SUV was parked.

Stopping in the middle of the drive between the rows, Zach got out and opened the rear hatch of the SUV. He looked over the impressive array of weapons: assorted handguns, long guns, sound suppressors, bang sticks, ammunition, and other lethal looking items. Unable to decide what would be most useful, he piled everything in the trunk of his rental car. He jumped into the car and sped off in search of the local Border Patrol office.

USSTRATCOM
United States Strategic Command
Offutt Air Force Base
Omaha, Nebraska

Deep inside USSTRATCOM, the United States Strategic Command, routine monitoring activities gave way to a panicked flood of activity as reports of a nuclear detonation in Sacramento besieged all inbound communication circuits.

USSTRATCOM is one of ten unified commands in the United States Department of Defense, housed at Offutt Air Force Base, Omaha Nebraska. The command center is responsible for the Nation's strategic deterrence and global strike capabilities. Providing a host of resources: including strategic warning; integrated missile defense; and global strike authority, the command center provides national leadership, aka the President, a unified resource to respond to specific threats around the globe, and to meet all threats rapidly.

GOC (the Global Operations Center), the nerve center of USSTRATCOM, is principally responsible for global situational awareness, exercising operational command and control over the Nation's global strategic forces.

Frayed nerves and emotions ran high as reports continued to pour in regarding the nuclear detonation in Sacramento. Only the professionalism of the highly trained and dedicated military personnel, kept the operations center from imploding into chaos. The noise level increased as reports continued to flow in. Despite the rising noise level, the instant the '*Red Phone*' blared its distinctive wail, all conversations ceased and every eye in the center turned toward Lieutenant Colonel Donald Bell, the Senior Controller on duty. On the very rare occasion when the "*Red Phone*" blared its warning, it typically turned out to be a drill, but considering the catastrophe in Sacramento, not one soul in the operations center thought it would be a drill this time.

Lieutenant Colonel Bell scrambled to the Primary Alerting System console to answer the blaring phone. For a brief few seconds he thought of the brand new house he and his family had moved into. Then came terrifying visions of his beautiful wife and six-month-old son being vaporized in a mushroom cloud. He took a deep breath and tried to steady his nerves as he grabbed the receiver and put it to his ear.

"USSTRATCOM, Lieutenant Colonel Donald Bell, Senior Controller," he announced, his voice shaking with anxiety.

"Lieutenant Colonel Bell this is General Gordon, NMCC, I have a verified scramble order for B-52 squadrons at Minot, North Dakota, and Barksdale, Louisiana. Operational order is Vigilant Strike, GO code is ECHO-ALPHA-WHISKEY-HOTEL-ROMEO. I repeat, Operational order is Vigilant Strike, GO code is ECHO-ALPHA-WHISKEY-HOTEL-ROMEO. NMCC will transmit final targeting packages via a secure link."

"Operational Order is Vigilant Strike," Lieutenant Colonel Bell repeated, his voice quavering as he madly flipped through the operational control and verification manual. Praying he would find a routine drill authorization code, his finger ran quickly down the list of verification codes, stopping on the code EAWHR General Gordon had just repeated. His voice froze in his throat.

"Lieutenant Colonel Bell, I need you to verify receipt and verification of the operational order. Now, Lieutenant Colonel Bell. This is not a drill. I need that verification now!"

"Operational order Vigilant Strike verified, ECHO-ALPHA-WHISKEY-HOTEL-ROMEO. Nuclear weapons are authorized. Confirmation Code is, PAPA-QUEBEC-ECHO-ECHO-BRAVO," Lieutenant Colonel Bell acknowledged, visibly shaking.

"Confirmation Code is, PAPA-QUEBEC-ECHO-ECHO-BRAVO," General Gordon repeated. "Scramble order confirmed. Get to it Mister Bell."

"Yes, Sir. Immediately, Sir," Lieutenant Colonel Bell replied. He dropped the receiver back in its cradle and hung his head. Like many others before him, he had trained time and time again for this eventuality. But all those times had been just routine drills. This time it was not a drill. It was real, and it had occurred on his watch. He lifted his head determined to do exactly what he had been trained to do.

Every pair of eyes in the Global Operations Center stared at Lieutenant Colonel Bell, fearing the confirmation they hoped would not come. As he lifted the microphone for the High Frequency Global Communications System, a deathly silence enveloped the operations center. Lieutenant Colonel Bell steadied himself and pressed the transmit button on the microphone.

Chapter Ten

Air Force Global Strike Command
Fifth Bomb Wing, 69th Bomb Squadron
Minot, North Dakota

Fifty miles south of the Canadian border on the alert ramp, also called the alert apron, Minot Air Force Base's twelve B-52H Stratofortress aircraft sat parked and waiting. The B-52 aircraft is the United States Air Force's principal strategic nuclear weapons platform. With a weapons payload of over seventy thousand pounds, a B-52 can carry the most diverse range of weapons of any combat aircraft, including advanced nuclear cruise missiles, air-launched nuclear cruise missiles, and conventional heavy bombs. The B-52 had been designed around a singular mission - to carry as large a weapons payload as possible.

Located close to the alert ramp, deep below ground, is the Fifth Bomb Wing command post, an element of the Air Force Global Strike Command (AFGSC). The AFGSC provides combat-ready forces to conduct strategic nuclear deterrence and global strike operations in support of national defense.

Ready to respond at a moment's notice, twelve five-man flight crews, one for each of the aircraft, spent their on-duty hours in the Readiness Crew Building (RCB), the on-alert crew quarters. The on-alert crew quarters, jokingly called the "Mole Hole", consisted of sloped entrance tunnels and underground, self-contained crew facilities. Half-way through a normal duty day, the twelve five-man flight crews and their associated maintenance and support personnel had finished lunch. The maintenance personnel had gathered in the maintenance shop conference room to plan for the upcoming quarterly inspections. On the other side of the crew complex, the aircraft flight crew members had completed the first hour of a routine training session. The doors to the training room flew open and the flight crews headed toward the break room for a short fifteen minute break.

Major Chris Jones, Aircraft Commander of Striker One, the lead aircraft of Scorpion One Flight Group, walked into the break room and headed straight for the soda machine. At forty-five Major Jones was trim and fit, owing to his three times a week sessions in the base's gym. Flying the mammoth B-52 did not take a lot of physical strength, but it required immense concentration and endurance for the missions that could exceed twenty-four hours.

"Hey, Rob, I hear you're taking some leave," Major Chris Jones, remarked to a fellow crew member. "Where are you headed?"

"Yeah, I haven't taken leave for a while," Captain Robert Perkins, Striker One's Warfare Officer answered. "My wife, kids and I are going to Barbados. Going to spend some time on the beach soaking up rays. The kids are so excited I think I will have to tie them up."

"Maybe you should spend some time in the gym while you're there," Major Jones teased. "You know the Air Force is getting rather hard-nosed about weight. If the flight surgeon puts you in the fat-boy program, it could cost you your flight status."

"I'm okay. There's nothing to worry about," Captain Perkins replied, taking a large bite of the candy bar in his right hand.

"I'm not so sure. I think you….," Major Jones was interrupted by a load, piercing wail.

With no forewarning, the "*War Horn*", the B-52 Alert Klaxon, blared throughout the on-alert crew quarters and the alert maintenance facility. Without hesitation, the twelve flight crews assigned to the B-52 aircraft parked out on the alert ramp immediately ceased whatever they were doing and sprinted toward the twelve support vehicles parked just outside the alert building. In the alert maintenance facility, startled maintenance personnel dropped tools, notebooks, repair parts, cables, or whatever was in their hands and sprinted toward the exit. Absolutely nothing was more important than getting their assigned aircraft off the ground.

Even though the mad scramble appeared to be chaos, it was a well-practiced chaos. In less than two minutes, all flight crews and maintenance personnel were in their assigned vehicles and already speeding toward the aircraft alert ramp.

Each one of the twelve support vehicles screeched to a stop in front of its respective aircraft, the crews piling out before the vehicles had come to a complete stop. As each flight crew approached their respective aircraft, the ground crew chief gave the pilot a 'thumbs-up' signal, indicating all the pre-flight, maintenance checks had been completed. Each flight crew climbed up a small ladder just aft of the nose wheel and entered the lower level of their assigned aircraft. The bombardier navigator slipped into his position. The rest of the crew climbed up another ladder to the main deck of the aircraft. The radar navigator and the defensive weapons coordinator clambered into their aft-facing positions. Then the aircraft commander and copilot struggled down an extremely narrow, six-foot crawl space and dropped into their positions in the cockpit.

Due to the B-52's mission design to maximize its weapons payload, the five members of the flight crew had to squeeze into a combined workspace the size of a small minivan. Despite the restricted space, less than one minute later, the flight crews were in their seats, buckled in, and beginning the engine startup process. Each B-52 aircraft was equipped with a quick start capability, allowing all eight Pratt and Whitney turbofan jet engines to be started simultaneously. Billowing clouds of blue smoke belched out behind the aircraft as the engines ignited and began to spool up to speed.

In another two minutes, all eight engines on each one of the twelve aircraft were running at MRT (Military Rated Thrust). The avionics suites began warming up as soon as the engines ignited and the generators came on line. From that point, the only thing holding the aircraft back would be traffic in front of it, post-startup checklists, and the final scramble order authentication from the command post.

"Minot Ground, Striker One cleared to taxi Runway Two-Niner via Alpha. Scramble order is confirmed. Repeat, scramble order is confirmed. Upon reaching Runway Two-Niner you are cleared for immediate takeoff. Be advised, this is a quick-away launch, and you are directed to use Minimum Interval Takeoff procedures."

As Aircraft Commander of Striker One, Major Chris Jones also assumed the role of Flight Leader of Scorpion Flight. Major Jones pushed himself up against the shoulder straps of his harness and pulled on the legs of his trousers to straighten out the wrinkles. It would likely be a long and grueling flight and he wanted to get as comfortable as possible.

Major Jones settled back down into his seat and keyed the microphone button, "Striker One, Scorpion Flight Leader, Minot Ground, cleared to taxi Runway Two-Niner via Alpha. Scramble order confirmed. Use Minimum Interval Takeoff procedures roger."

Major Jones looked out the cockpit window and signaled the ground crew to remove the chocks. When the ground crewman reappeared, Major Jones saluted him and looked over at the copilot and nodded his head.

Major Neil Dunlap, first officer and copilot of Striker One, pressed the transmit button for the inter-aircraft comm system. "Brakes off, ready, roll now." he spoke into his lip microphone.

Major Jones eased the throttles for the eight powerful Pratt and Whitney TF33s engines forward until the huge Boeing B-52 Stratofortress began to roll away from the parking ramp. Easing the throttles back slightly, he steered the huge aircraft onto the taxiway. One by one, just seconds apart, the remaining eleven B-52 aircraft rolled away from the parking ramp and lined up nose to tail along the taxiway.

At the same instant the "*War Horn*" had blared in the crew alert facility, an alarm had also sounded in the Fifth Bomb Wing control tower. All outbound traffic had been ordered to hold in place and all inbound traffic had been routed to holding patterns south of the airfield to clear the airspace for the departing B-52 aircraft. When Striker One reached Runway Two-Niner, Major Jones required no further clearance. He made a wide sweeping turn and steered the aircraft onto the runway threshold. Lined up on the centerline he released the brakes and pushed the throttles all the way forward. Huge clouds of black smoke swirled behind the aircraft as the powerful jet engines spooled up and the huge B-52 began its take-off roll down Runway Two-Niner.

Positioned at the end of the taxiway, Striker Two waited its turn. Major William Hutton, Co-pilot of Striker Two, took a time hack when he saw the clouds of black smoke billow out behind Striker One. The pilot of Striker Two rolled onto the runway, stopped on the threshold, and set the aircraft's brakes. Major Hutton stared at his watch intently. At exactly the fifteen second mark, he called out, "Brakes off, ready, roll now."

Major Roger Freeman, Aircraft Commander of Striker Two, pushed the eight throttle levers all the way forward. Once again, great clouds of black smoke billowed out behind the aircraft as Major Freeman released the brakes and Striker Two lumbered down the runway. When Striker One's wheels lifted off the runway, Striker Two was already one-third of the way down the runway. Mission parameters for a normal training scramble would call for each B-52 to be thirty seconds behind the aircraft in front. However, the current scramble was not a drill. This was the real thing, requiring a take-off interval of fifteen seconds. The critical, mission objective was to get all aircraft in the air, formed up, and heading toward their target as quickly as possible.

As each aircraft lifted off, the aircraft commander flew a slightly different heading in a fan pattern to avoid the worst of the turbulence caused by the heavy aircraft that had just lifted off. A short two minutes and five seconds after Striker One lifted off, all eleven remaining Scorpion Flight aircraft were airborne and forming up with Striker One. Only five of the aircraft had missed the targeted fifteen second takeoff interval. From the time the "*War Horn*" had sounded until all twelve aircraft were airborne, only nine minutes and twenty-five seconds had elapsed, less than the prescribed mission parameter of ten minutes.

"Minot tower, Striker One, Scorpion Flight, all aircraft airborne and in formation. Awaiting further instructions."

"Roger Striker One, confirm all aircraft outbound, and in formation. Climb and maintain flight level two-seven-zero. Proceed to Waypoint Three. NMCC will contact you with the final targeting package and final authentication."

Per MILCOM regulations, the aircraft were not allowed to broadcast any heading information over radio frequencies. All heading and coordinates were to be flown according to pre-assigned mission parameters. At Waypoint Three, Scorpion flight would rendezvous with Brickyard Zero-Eight, a KC-135 Refueling Tanker from the 161st Air Refueling Wing. Brickyard Zero-Eight would fly in a long racetrack pattern at flight level three-one-zero. Upon rendezvous with Brickyard Zero-Eight, each Scorpion Flight aircraft would ease up underneath the tanker and top off their fuel. With full fuel tanks, Scorpion Flight would then climb to flight level four-one-zero and proceed to Waypoint Four and await final confirmation and targeting packages.

Personnel in the tower at Minot Air Force Base relayed the scramble confirmation to NMCC (National Military Command Center), via secure communications link. As other bomber squadrons confirmed they were airborne, NMCC personnel transmitted the EAM messages and any changes to final targeting packages. Onboard the aircraft the crypto-graphic protocols would be decoded, confirming the final target coordinates and authorizing the release of nuclear weapons.

Major Jones keyed Striker One's internal communications system, "Rob, is there anything on the HF comm system yet?"

Striker One's Electronic Warfare Officer, Captain Robert Perkins, eyes glued to the AUTODIN decoder responded, "Nothing yet, sir."

Three minutes later, Captain Perkins' excited voice came over the aircraft's internal comm system, "Sir, incoming EAM message. Final SIOP targeting package is uploading now. Nuclear launch directive is confirmed. No terminate or stand-down codes. This is not a drill! Sir, this is the real thing!"

"Captain Perkins, focus. Read me the EAM Code," Major Jones ordered.

Captain Perkins ripped the paper tape off the authenticator and read the code. "Whiskey-Zulu-Hotel-eight-niner-seven-Foxtrot."

"EAM is authentic," affirmed Major Jones. "Authenticate and lock in targeting packages and switch weapons release to armed."

In the cockpit, Major Jones settled down in his seat and tightened his safety harness. "Striker One flight crew, stay sharp, focus on your duties," Major Jones announced over the inter-aircraft comm system. Hesitating only for a second, he keyed the air-to-air comm system, "Scorpion Flight, this is Scorpion Leader, This is not a drill! I repeat this is not a drill! We have received a valid and authenticated nuclear launch order! Be alert. We may encounter hostile aircraft en route. Scorpion Flight climb to flight level four-five-zero."

Onboard the twelve B-52 aircraft, nervous crews busied themselves checking and re-checking the final targeting packages and preparing the lethal nuclear weapons loaded in the belly of their aircraft. Once the weapons officers authenticated the targeting package and locked it into the guidance computers, they would set the nuclear weapons to the "*armed*" mode. At that point, the aircraft needed no further launch orders from the ground. All that remained was for the aircraft to reach the target launch point and activate the "release" command.

Ground Zero
Sacramento, California

Six hours after the detonation of the nuclear weapon in Sacramento, the Federal Radiological Monitoring and Assessment Center activated the closest NEST team (Nuclear Emergency Support Team). As members of the NEST team arrived at the operations center, they busied themselves assembling their response gear.

The team's logistics coordinator, Curtis Owens, inspected the radiological detection equipment arranged in the response bay, marking off each item as he made his way down the rows of equipment. All but one of the team members had arrived and were checking their personal equipment.

"Any word from Randy West?" Tony Larson, the senior team leader, asked, glancing at his watch.

"Not a word," Curtis Owens answered. "We have called both of his emergency contact numbers. Neither one is working. His cell phone doesn't answer either. We assume communication circuits in his area are down."

"Is everyone else here?"

"Yes. They're in the other bay making final checks of their personal gear. They said traffic is crazy. People are panic-stricken. Abandoned vehicles are jamming the roads already. By nightfall, there won't be anything moving."

"What about the alternates?"

"No answer there either."

Not thrilled by the prospect, Team Leader Larson did not want to go into a hot zone short-handed, but being the initial entry team, they had no other choice. How rapid their response time was would determine whether they could identify the detonation products. "Okay. We'll go with what we've got. Tell the rest of the team we go in ten minutes. Jeff, go warm up the bird."

"Yes, sir," Jeffrey Mahone the helicopter pilot answered as he turned and sprinted out the double doors.

The rest of the NEST team members came running out of the other bay dressed in their radiological protection suits and carrying their respirators.

"Let's get this equipment on the bird," Team Leader Larson shouted above the noise of the helicopter idling just outside the door. "We need to be off the ground in ten minutes. Sam, what about the repelling gear?"

"It's already on board," Samuel Gomez, the team's newest member shouted.

Team Leader Larson watched as team members loaded the last piece of equipment on the helicopter. "Okay, let's saddle up."

The team members scrambled onto the helicopter and buckled themselves in. Team Leader Larson shoved the side door shut and gave the thumbs-up signal to the pilot. The pilot operated the helicopter's flight controls, lifting the helicopter straight up to twelve hundred feet before pointing the nose down and heading toward the blast zone. There was no need for clearance as there would be no air traffic anywhere near the blast zone.

One hour and ten minutes later the NEST helicopter approached the edge of the blast zone from the upwind side, flying at twelve hundred feet. The pilot avoided any rising smoke to avoid sucking contaminated particulates into the helicopter's engine. The pilot slowed the helicopter and descended to five hundred feet as the team members observed the destruction, attempting to locate the epicenter of the blast zone.

"Good Lord," Team Member George Lee exclaimed. "There's nothing left."

"Move five hundred feet to the northwest," Team Leader Larson said over the intercom. "I see the edge of a crater."

The pilot flew the helicopter sideways five hundred feet as requested. "How's that?"

"Another one hundred feet."

Team Leader Larson looked at the other team members. "What do you think?"

"Looks like we're over the center of the crater to me," Curtis Owens advised.

"I agree," Team Leader Larson answered. "Hold your position here and mark the coordinates, Jeff. What would you estimate the diameter of the crater to be?"

"I'd estimate it to be four to five hundred feet, give or take," pilot, Jeffery Mahone answered.

"That's my estimate as well," Team Leader Larson replied. "Ease us back to fifty feet west of the crater's rim. After you drop us off, report the coordinates and estimated size of the crater to headquarters and confirm it was a surface blast. We'll confirm the crater's size when we're on the ground. Take us down to two hundred feet."

The pilot eased off on the collective and the helicopter descended to two hundred feet. Holding the helicopter in hover mode, the pilot called back to crew, "Okay, hovering at two hundred feet. Go now!"

The team members were already in their harnesses and waiting for the *go* signal. Tony Larson, the senior team leader, hooked the repelling line onto its attachment point and threw it out of the helicopter. He reached out and yanked on the repelling line several times to be certain he had attached it firmly. He hooked onto the repelling line, leaned out of the door, and disappeared from view. One by one, each of the team members hooked onto the repelling line and descended to the ground.

Drew Palmer, the team's equipment support technician, hooked on the first bundle of test equipment and lowered it to the team waiting on the ground. Seeing the *okay* signal from the team member on the ground, he hooked on the second equipment bundle and lowered it to the ground. Seeing the second *okay* signal, he pulled up the repelling line and stuffed it into a shielded, isolation bag. After he stowed the isolation bag, he tapped the pilot on the shoulder.

"Team leader, radio check," pilot Jeffery Mahone spoke into his lip microphone.

"Read you loud and clear," Tony Larson replied.

"Repeat. No Copy. Repeat. No Copy."

"I read you. Some static, but understandable."

"Team leader, your transmission is garbled," Jeffery Mahone spoke into his lip microphone. "I will transmit these coordinates to the collection vehicle. It has already started into the blast zone and should arrive at your location in approximately one hour. I repeat, one hour. Acknowledge, please."

Team leader Tony Larson clicked the transmit button twice. He looked up and watched the helicopter bank right and head East toward a safe landing area outside the contamination zone. He lowered his head, turned in a full three hundred sixty degree circle, and stood there stunned. Many times he had read about the effects of a nuclear explosion, but it had failed completely to prepare him for the scene before him. The ground, dead and barren, appeared not unlike the surface of the moon, except it was not gray. The ground was light brown, the color of dirty sand. Everywhere he looked there was nothing but level, barren ground, except for what appeared to be an occasional piece of twisted metal or broken chunk of concrete.

He kicked at the ground with the toe of his boot. Packed hard, and crusty by the blast, it looked like soft limestone with occasional shiny clumps scattered about. He kicked one of the shiny clumps loose, bent over, and picked it up.

"Hey, Curtis, look at this," Tony Larson exclaimed, his voice picked up by the microphone mounted inside the large hood of his protective suit.

Curtis Owens turned and looked at the three centimeter long greenish lump of glass-like material Tony Larson held in his hand. "What is it?"

"It used to be sand. The heat from the blast melted it and fused it into glass. They call it trinitite. That happens at ground zero at the instant of ignition. These lumps are important. If we're lucky, the lab can find traces of the bomb's tamper mechanism in the trinitite. The tamper is the spherical metal shell that keeps the weapon's core from flying apart too quickly which would allow the nuclear reaction to fizzle out. The ratio of isotopes in the tamper will vary depending on the origin of the material. If these lumps contain any traces of the tamper, the lab should be able to identify the origins of the weapon. That would be huge. So, be on the lookout close to the crater's rim. Bag and label any lumps you find."

With a startled look on his face, Curtis Owens looked around and said, "This is unbelievable! There's absolutely nothing left! The ground looks like a giant blowtorch blasted it clean."

"You're exactly correct. Inside zone one, the destruction is complete. The blast consumed everything. Plants, trees, building material, even most of the steel supports, and *humans*. Everything. There's nothing left."

"Shouldn't we get a sample at the bottom of the crater?" Curtis Owens asked, peering over the crater's rim.

"I don't think that would be advisable, Curtis," Tony Larson advised, putting out his arm to prevent him from falling into the deep crater. "Let me check the residual radiation before anyone even thinks about going into the crater." He took a portable radiation survey meter out of its protective case and placed the probe close to the rim of the crater. "Wow, that's hot," he announced. "The meter registers one hundred fifty rads. That's high, especially considering the fact that after seven hours the residual radiation should be only ten percent of the amount it was at one hour and after forty-eight hours the residual radiation will only be one percent. That means the yield of the device had to be between thirty and fifty kilotons. That's twice the size of Hiroshima. It's probably several magnitudes hotter at the bottom. Nobody's going down there. Our protective suits are not rated for that and I doubt we have ropes long enough to reach the bottom."

"So, what's next, boss."

"Spread out and take two samples each here, from the rim of the crater. Then we'll go one hundred feet in each direction and take two more samples. If we see anything unusual and it's small enough to fit in a sample bag, pick it up and dump it in a sample bag."

The team members fanned out several steps in different directions around the edge of the crater. Each team member then scooped up two samples and dumped them into individual sample bags, labeling each bag with location and direction from assumed ground zero. They regrouped and stacked all the sample bags next to the east rim of the crater. The team walked two hundred feet north of the crater, being careful to not overlook anything unusual or remarkable. With two samples each collected and labeled, the team returned to the crater. As soon as the team returned to their mobilization point, someone would fly the samples to the testing laboratory.

The initial estimate of the yield of the device, as determined from the size of the crater and the residual radiation, suggested it was an HEU (high-enriched uranium) nuclear weapon. The laboratory would analyze the samples and determine the ratios of the U-235, U-236, and U-238 fission products produced by the detonation. The ratios would identify the original attributes of the material used in the device. The original attributes of the weapon would significantly increase the probability of identifying the perpetrator of the attack. Identifying the perpetrator of the attack was critically important and needed as soon as was humanly possible.

"Hey, what's that?" Samuel Gomez hollered as the team walked toward the west. He stopped and pointed toward several round, black, marble-like objects a few yards south of their path.

Tony Larson walked over to where Gomez was point-ing and bent over to look at an object. Using his hand shov-el, he scooped up several of the round objects and dropped them into a sample bag. "It's called Black Rain, Sam," Lar-son answered. "Because of the intense heat created by a nu-clear explosion, airborne debris gets sucked up into the rising cloud. The debris particles act as condensation nuclei. More and more debris particles get combined with the oily, black soot particles from incomplete combustion in the firestorm until they form a black mass approximating the size of mar-bles. Once the updraft dissipates, they drop out and cover a wide area, extending outward from the hypocenter in the direction of the prevailing winds. Hence, the name Black Rain."

"Wow. That's incredible," was all Gomez could say, as he poked at one of the black masses with his hand shovel.

"Okay, let's go," Tony Larson said. "We need to get the rest of the samples collected before the helicopter returns."

The team walked two hundred feet from the crater's rim in each of the three remaining directions and collected two samples each. With all the samples collected and labeled, the team returned to the east rim of the crater and stacked the additional sample bags next to the collection box.

"Hey, Sam," Tony Larson called out. "Walk around to the west side of the crater and stand there so I can get an accurate measurement of its width."

Gomez turned and walked counterclockwise around the crater until he was standing directly across from Tony Lar-son. Larson grabbed a laser measuring device from a tool bag, pointed it at Gomez's chest, and looked at the readout. "Holy Crow! The crater measures eight hundred twenty-eight feet," he remarked. "I had hoped I was wrong, but that confirms my yield estimate based on residual radiation. A crater diameter of over eight hundred feet for a surface blast suggests a yield of thirty to forty kilotons."

Larson pointed the laser measuring device toward the bottom of the crater. Several times he moved farther around the crater and took additional measurements. "One hundred fifty-seven feet," he announced to no one in particular. "No way our ropes would reach the bottom of that."

He walked toward where the team had piled all the sample bags. The rest of the team stood waiting, having stopped several times along the way to take residual radiation measurements, noting any unusual observations using the microphones inside the hood of their protective suits. Upon reaching the rest of the team he said, "Okay everyone, let's get these sample bags stowed in the protective crate. I want to be ready the instant the collection vehicle gets here. The radiation is high here and I don't want to spend any more time here than necessary." Once all the sample bags had been stowed into the protective crate, Tony Larson closed the latches on the lead-lined box, slid an official seal through a latch, and crimped it closed.

Samuel Gomez released the latches on a second, smaller lead-lined crate. The team members placed all the hand scoops and any other tools they may have used into the second crate. Tony Larson also placed the laser measuring device and radiation survey meter into the case. Gomez circled the team members looking for anything that might have been overlooked. With all items stowed in the protective crate, he closed and latched the lid. Larson stepped over the case, pulled a second plastic seal from a pocket in his protective suit, slipped it through the latch, and pressed the locking clip until it clicked.

Larson looked at his watch. The collection vehicle was twelve minutes overdue. He went around to all the other team members and looked at their radiation measurement stickers. They were all approaching two hundred rads. He tapped Gomez on the shoulder, pointing to his own sticker.

Gomez bent forward and peered at Larson's radiation sticker. "Looks like it's getting close to three hundred rads.

We need to get out of here soon. What do we do if the collection vehicle doesn't come soon?"

"We still have some safety margin left, Gomez. Another thirty minutes, then we will worry."

The team members stood there staring at the unbelievable sight of destruction around them. Curtis Owens moved a few feet from the rest of the group and bent over to look at a lump of the greenish trinitite, kicking at it with the toe of his boot. Returning to the group, he noticed a cloud of dust in the distance. "Hey, I think the collection vehicle is coming. I see a cloud of dust," he said, pointing toward the east.

The rest of the team members turned to see what Owens was pointing at. At the base of the dust cloud, they could see the collection vehicle lumbering toward them. "Okay, men, let's be quick when the vehicle arrives. We need to get out of here and get these samples to ARG as quickly as possible," Tony Larson ordered.

The critical piece of the entire mission was to get the samples they had collected to ARG (Accident Response Group) for analysis. The Accident Response Group, a group of scientists, technical specialists, and sophisticated equipment, waited at the edge of the safe zone. They would analyze the samples as quickly as they could and report the results to the President.

Slightly over an hour later the collection vehicle arrived at the Response Management Center, just inside the hot zone. The team offloaded the protective sample case first and rushed it to the lab for analysis. Then the team members were transported to the edge of the hot zone. They entered the decontamination station and began the long process of washing off any contaminated particles that might remain on their protective suits. The decontamination team used radiation detectors to check the team for any residual radiation. Finding no residual radiation, the team crossed into the safe zone and climbed out of their protective suits.

As the initial entry team showered, the lab personnel had already unloaded the samples from the protective case and had begun analyzing the post-detonation material. The lab personnel's critical duty was to assess the sample material quickly and determine the device's type and verify how powerful the device was. The most important analysis would be where the nuclear material came from.

Using complex algorithms, the lab scientists determined the ratio of fission product residue in the samples. Once the scientists had measured the isotopic ratios in the fission product residue, they could calculate the original attributes of the fissionable material used in the device.

The last step, comparing the original material's attributes to a master database of stolen or missing nuclear material, would yield the country of origin. International researchers claimed the master database was the world's most complete database of lost, stolen, and misplaced nuclear material. The astonishing amount of stolen or missing nuclear material depicts a world awash in weapons-grade uranium and plutonium that nobody can account for.

The senior scientist reviewed the results and refused to accept the results. He stood beside the scientist that had completed the original computations and verified the measurements and calculations at every step as they repeated the analysis.

"Nobody will believe this," the senior scientist remarked. "Repeat all the calculations with the screen recorder on. I'm certain someone will challenge us on the results."

The senior scientist rushed over to the temporary command structure and handed the analysis results to the on-site, incident commander.

"This can't be correct," the on-site, incident commander gasped. "Are you certain?"

"We repeated the measurements and calculations twice," the senior scientist replied. "I stood there and verified every step myself. Those results are correct. I'd stake my career on it."

"You just might have to," the on-site, incident commander cautioned. "I've got to phone this in immediately."

The on-site, incident commander grabbed the SAT phone and retreated to a small enclosed area of the temporary command structure to get as much privacy as possible. Knowing the critical nature of the incident and the fact that the President had scrambled all strategic nuclear forces, he called the highest level contact available on the notification list. After multiple explanations and several transfers, he finally reached someone on the President's staff. He read off the results of the sample analysis. The staff member argued with him saying the results had to be wrong. The argument went back and forth several times. Knowing the information was vital and must be reported immediately, he demanded direct access to the President. After several reasonable and calm attempts to explain the urgent need, he lost his temper and threatened the staff member with being responsible for the start of World War Three.

As the conversation became more and more heated, the two men shouted at each other. The shouting interrupted the President's discussion with the other staff members. He walked over and stared at the staff member, a displeased look on his face. The staff member put his hand over the phone and explained to the President who was calling and why. Without speaking a word, the President held his hand out. Without hesitation, the staff member handed the receiver over to the President.

The President listened for a few minutes, a look of alarm spreading across his face. "You can't be serious!" he exclaimed. "Hang on a minute." He put his hand over the receiver and spoke to the staff members. "Gentlemen, I need the room, please." The staff members quickly grabbed their notebooks and left the room. When the last member exited the room, and the door closed, the President put the phone back to his ear. "Go ahead. Give me the exact details again." The President stood there stunned as the on-site commander repeated the results of the analysis a second time.

"Is there any possibility of error in running the analysis?" the President questioned.

"Absolutely not," the on-site commander replied. "The lab personnel performed the analysis twice, and I personally observed a third repeat of the analysis. All three runs of the analysis produced exactly the same result, Mister President. I would stake my career on the accuracy of the analysis."

"I just can't believe…."

"There's something else you should know, Mister President," the on-site commander interrupted. "We are certain boosting elements were used to increase the yield of the device."

"What do you mean boosting elements?"

"It's called fusion boosting. Fusion boosting is achieved by introducing deuterium gas into the fission reaction. Deuterium gas is injected into a hollow cavity at the center of the sphere of fissionable fuel called the pit. The deuterium speeds up the effectiveness of the late stages of the chain reaction, increasing the reaction's efficiency which increases the yield of the device."

"How much increase are we talking about?"

"At the Sacramento detonation site, we estimate two to three times. Whoever assembled the device must have crudely constructed it. Otherwise, the yield could have been tenfold. We'll never know exactly because, as you might imagine, the initial blast incinerated the device. Using the size of the crater as a rough indicator, we estimate the blast at thirty to forty kilotons."

"That's double the size of the bomb dropped on Hiroshima," the President gasped. "How big is the area of destruction?"

"The area of physical destruction is not as big as you might think because it was a surface blast. However, the deaths from fallout will be far worse because a surface blast draws much more debris up into the fireball."

"Where would the deuterium come from?"

The President listened to the on-site commander's answer, his face growing pale as he slumped down in his chair.

The President advised the on-site commander to immediately mark all copies of the report as "*eyes only*". He requested a hard copy to be delivered by military courier ASAP. He dropped the receiver into its cradle and placed his face in his hands.

"My God. What do I do now?" he choked.

Chapter Eleven

U.S. Customs and Border Protection
South Kings Highway
Douglas, Arizona

Zach roared into the parking lot of the Douglas, Arizona, Border Patrol Station and slammed on his brakes, sliding up against a concrete parking stop and nearly onto the sidewalk. He climbed out of the car and rushed toward the entrance to the patrol station. Not taking notice of the carefully maintained desert landscape surrounding the building, he flew right past the large sign announcing the border patrol station in Douglas. One of six such border crossing stations in Arizona, the Douglas station was operated by the Customs and Border Protection Division of the Department of Homeland Security.

Zach yanked the main entrance door open, located the information office, and stepped up to the information counter. Zach tapped the bell sitting on the counter. An agent of average height and average build with short sandy colored hair looked up from the paperwork that held his attention. He rose from his chair and walked over to the counter.

"May I help you, sir," the agent asked.

Zach read the name embroidered above the agent's right shirt pocket. "Agent Winfield, My name is Zachariah Templeton," Zach said, offering his hand.

Agent Richard Winfield reached out his hand and shook Zach's hand vigorously. "Glad to meet you, Mister Templeton. What brings you to the Douglas Border Patrol Station today?"

"It's urgent that I speak with the Sector Chief Patrol Agent," Zach answered as he reached into his jacket, pulled out the leather wallet containing his Secret Service ID, and held it open for Agent Winfield to see.

"Holy Moly," Agent Winfield exclaimed, revealing his southern upbringing. "We don't see creds like that around these parts. Agent Harold Lynch is the SCPA for this sector. He's in his office, but I think he's busy."

"Please interrupt him, Agent Winfield," Zach insisted. "This is a matter of national security. I assure you he will want to see me."

"Yes sir, Mister Templeton," Agent Winfield replied. He turned, walked to the rear of the building, stopped in front of a closed office door, and tapped on the door twice. A few seconds later he opened the door, entered the office, and pulled the door shut. Zach studied the station while he waited for Agent Winfield to return. The main station seemed somewhat small for the amount of activity that occurred at the Douglas border station. The furnishings, brightly colored, but tasteful, looked like what would be found at a high-end furniture store. Beautiful framed prints, depicting mountain streams, hung on three of the walls. A large framed print of the President of the United States hung on the other wall.

Zach saw Agent Winfield emerge from the rear office with a tall, muscular man with jet black hair following close behind him. As the men approached the front counter, Zach noticed the tall man's olive-green uniform, bearing a blue stripe down each leg and a gold badge affixed to the uniform shirt just above the left pocket. Zach assumed the tall man must be Agent Lynch as he carried himself with an air of authority. When the men reached the front counter, Agent Winfield returned to his desk and the other man reached under the counter and pressed a button, releasing a waist-high door at the far end of the counter.

The tall man stepped though the doorway and stuck out his hand. "I'm Chief Patrol Agent Harold Lynch. I understand you need to speak with me about a matter of national security."

"Yes, absolutely, Agent Lynch," Zach answered, shaking the man's hand and holding out his wallet for Agent Lynch to inspect.

"I agree with Agent Winfield. We don't often see IDs with this level of clearance here in Douglas. What exactly can I do for you, Mister Templeton?" Agent Lynch asked as he handed the wallet back to Zach.

"The matter is highly sensitive and classified. I can't talk out in the open."

"Very well, follow me to my office."

Agent Lynch stepped over in front of the doorway through the counter and snapped his fingers. Agent Winfield jumped out of his chair, rushed over to the counter, and pressed the release for the door.

Agent Lynch pushed the door open and held it open for Zach to pass through. "This way, Mister Templeton," he said, heading toward the rear of the building.

Zach followed Agent Lynch to the rear of the building and into his private office. "Have a seat, Mister Templeton," Agent Lynch said, pointing to a chair in front of this desk. "How about a coffee, Mister Templeton?"

"That would be great and call me Zach," Zach said, stopping to admire a large aquarium sitting against the wall.

"Very nice aquarium. Salt water, right?"

"Yes it is," Agent Lynch answered. "A hobby of mine. A rather expensive hobby I might add." Agent Lynch walked over and stood beside Zach.

Pointing at a brightly colored fish, Zach asked, "What is the bright purple and orange fish there in the corner?"

"That's a Royal Gramma Basslet. It comes from the Caribbean. It's a hardy fish, great for beginners, and it's fairly inexpensive. At only twenty dollars, it's the cheapest one in the tank."

"What about the orange one with the blue swirled stripes?" Zack asked, pointing at a fish at the other end of the tank.

"That's a Green Mandarin Dragonet. Dragonets are incredibly difficult to adapt to an aquarium because they're so finicky about what they will eat. That's my third one and at seventy dollars each, it will be my last one."

"They sure are beautiful," Zach said as he straightened up.

"Yes they are," Agent Lynch agreed. "It would be a great hobby if it weren't so expensive. Now, I'm certain you didn't come here to admire my fish." Agent Lynch returned to his desk and again pointed to the chair in front of his desk. Zach tore his gaze from the aquarium and sat in the chair Agent Lynch pointed toward.

"Zach, you take anything in your coffee?"

"No. Black and bitter is good for me."

Agent Lynch picked up the phone, pressed the intercom button, and waited. "Agent Winfield, bring two cups and a carafe of coffee to my office, please."

"So, Zach, where do you call home?" Agent Lynch asked.

"I live in Tulsa. I flew into Tucson on a Gulfstream 550. Perks of the job."

"Impressive," Agent Lynch said. "I hear that aircraft is very luxurious."

"Yes it is," Zach added. "I've only had use of it twice for special projects. It's assigned to my boss."

"And who might that be?"

"Rear Admiral Charles Hadley. He's the Director of Naval Intelligence. He recruited me and my dad, James Templeton, for a special assignment. My dad's in the hospital here. We intended to talk to a Doctor Marshall Woods, but when we stopped at his house in Elfrida, we found his body. While we were investigating, we surprised someone. The man ran out the back door and we gave chase. He ran into a garage and threw an explosive device out the door."

"I heard about that. Is your dad okay?"

"The doctor has said very little. My dad has broken ribs, a collapsed lung, and a couple of large lacerations. He hadn't regained consciousness before I had to leave."

"I hope he gets better soon. I'm guessing you were involved in the shootout at the hospital."

"Yes, that was me. A professional assassin tried to kill me and my family. She killed a Secret Service agent, but I grabbed the agent's weapon and I killed her before she could kill anyone else."

"Professional assassin? Naval Intelligence?" Agent Lynch questioned, a shocked look on his face. "What on earth are you involved in and what would Naval Intelligence be investigating at the border in Arizona?"

"I assume you heard about the nuclear detonation in Sacramento."

"Of course I heard. Everyone in the whole country heard about that."

"What I am about to tell you next is extremely sensitive. You aren't cleared for this, but time is critical and I need information. I must have your assurance that what I tell you will not leave this office."

"You have my word."

Zach was about to explain to Agent Lynch why he was in Arizona when two knocks on the office door interrupted him.

"Enter," Agent Lynch hollered.

Agent Winfield pushed the door open, carrying two coffee cups and a carafe. He walked over to where the two men were seated, handed a cup to Zach and one to Agent Lynch, and set the carafe on the edge of the desk.

"Thank you, Agent Winfield," Agent Lynch said as he got up from his chair and followed Agent Winfield to the door. When the door closed, Agent Lynch locked the door, returned to his desk, and picked up the phone. "Hold all my calls," he ordered. He dropped the phone back in its cradle and looked at Zach. "Okay, tell me why you're here."

Fifteen minutes later Zach concluded telling Agent Lynch the reason for his presence in Douglas. Zach tipped his cup and drained the last swallow of lukewarm coffee, waiting for Agent Lynch's reaction.

"I assume you believe the device or components to build it came across the Douglas sector of the border," Agent Lynch declared, a defensive tone in his voice obvious.

"There's no time to worry about blame," Zach countered. "My chief concern is that there may be more devices. My task is to identify and locate *anyone* who may have assisted or been involved in smuggling nuclear devices or materials across the border. I need your full cooperation. If another device is detonated, blame will be the least of your worries."

"Fair enough," Agent Lynch conceded. "We are a satellite office of the El Paso sector. The Douglas station has the third highest number of border crossings of the six stations along the Arizona border. Ever since implementation of 'Operation Hold the Line', our agents are stretched thin, heavily focusing on deterring crossing at more remote locations. The directive assumed it would be easier to capture illegal entrants in the wide open deserts than through the urban alleyways. In actuality, the operation merely shifted the illegal entries to other areas, resulting in our agents no longer reacting to illegal entries at designated border stations."

"If that is the case, do you believe the materials would likely have come across in a vehicle of some kind?"

"Yes, I think that is a likely possibility."

"Do you remember a Mister Polomo that was captured east of town? "

"Yes, I scanned the arrest report. There didn't seem to be anything out of the ordinary. A lot of the individuals we catch crossing the border illegally are sick. EMTs were called and he was transported to the hospital."

"Are you aware that Mister Polomo died of radiation poisoning?"

"No, I did not know that. Once detainees are transported to a medical facility, they become the responsibility of local law enforcement. We don't receive reports on their medical status once that occurs."

"Do you have a record of the time he was apprehended and the time EMTs were called? It should be within the past few days."

"We keep a detailed log of calls for medical services. Hang on a minute." Agent Lynch picked up the phone and requested Agent Winfield to bring in the medical services request logbook. Agent Lynch got up from his chair, walked over to the door, unlocked it, and waited for Agent Winfield who arrived with the logbook in less than a minute. With the medical services request logbook in hand, Agent Lynch returned to his desk. He laid the three-ring binder on the desk and began flipping through its pages. Locating the last page that contained entries, he backed up two pages and began running his finger down the column of names. Finding no one named Polomo, he flipped to the next page and continued. Halfway down the page, he stopped.

"Here he is," Agent Lynch announced. He picked up a yellow highlighter and drew a line across the page then handed the open binder to Zach.

"Good. Based on the assumed radiation exposure he had to have received, it couldn't have been more than twenty-four hours before he arrived at the emergency room. We're assuming he crossed the border somewhere around that time. Do you have video surveillance of the bridge for that time frame?"

"Yes, no problem. We can go back that far."

"Who was on duty during that period?"

Agent Lynch swiveled his chair around and grabbed his copy of the past week's duty roster from a table sitting behind his desk. He swiveled back around and searched through the roster until he located the day corresponding to Mr. Polomo's assumed crossing.

"Being short handed, we assign the agents here to twelve-hour shifts, so there are only two agents that could have been on duty during that time period. Agents Greg Mills and Richard Cummings."

"Can I speak to them?" Zach asked.

"Hmmm, there's something here that may be suspicious. Agent Greg Mills didn't show up for his shift this morning and we have been unable to reach him."

"Do you have an address for Mister Mills?"

"Sure, I know exactly where he lives. He just bought a house west of town, just north of Highway Eighty on Becki Lane. It's the only house on that road."

"Do you have a card with your phone number on it?"

Agent Lynch lifted one of his business cards from a brass holder sitting on his desk. He scribbled a number on the back and handed it to Zach. "That's my personal cell phone number on the back. Call me anytime if you learn something or if you need any additional information."

"I'll go talk with Mister Mills while you look over the video for anything suspicious."

Zach stood up and stuck out his hand. Agent Lynch grabbed Zach's hand and shook it. "It was a pleasure to meet you Zach. I wish it was under different circumstances."

"Thanks, Harold, I agree," Zach reciprocated. "I appreciate your help. I will be in touch after I talk to Agent Mills."

Zach turned and hurried out of Agent Lynch's office, stopping at the counter to wait for someone to release the door. In a hurry, Zach decided to not wait. He reached his hand under the counter and pressed the release button himself. Agent Winfield looked up from his work and noticed Zach passing though the door. "Hey, Mister Templeton, have a great day. I hope you got what you needed."

"Thank you. I did," Zach answered as he turned and exited the border patrol station, pressing the unlock button on the rental car's key fob as he stepped through the exit door. He jumped into the car and backed away from the parking stop. He dropped the car into drive and sped out of the parking area, spitting up rocks and dust and leaving ruts in the gravel.

He drove through town slightly over the speed limit and headed west on Highway Eighty. Nearly missing the small sign identifying Becki Lane, he stomped on the brakes, sliding partly onto the shoulder, two car lengths past the intersection. Glancing in the rear-view mirror, he saw no other traffic on the highway. He shoved the car into reverse and mashed down on the accelerator. Backing up into a cloud of dust, he stopped at the intersection. He dropped the car into drive and stomped down on the accelerator, fishtailing through the intersection. Black streaks trailed out behind the car as he sped off toward a house he could see in the distance.

Zach pulled into the driveway leading to the only house on Becki Lane. He pulled in behind a light green car parked in front of the house, blocking it in. Zach reached under the seat, retrieved his weapon, and climbed out of the car. He shoved the weapon behind his back as he headed for the front door of the house. Standing beside the door, he reached over with his left hand and rapped three times on the door. Receiving no response, he reached out and rapped on the door again. He could hear footsteps approaching the door.

The door opened a tiny crack and the man inside called out, "Who is it?"

"My name is Zach Templeton. It's important that I talk to you," Zach announced, holding his credentials out for the man to see them.

The man peered through the crack, trying to read the wallet, giving Zach the opportunity he needed. He stepped in front of the door and pushed it open. The man backed up and tripped over a pair of shoes sitting beside a small kitchen table.

"What do you think you're doing?" the man sputtered as he pushed himself up using a chair as leverage.

As the man stood, Zach made a mental note of the man's physical characteristics: five foot eight inches tall, probably one hundred eighty pounds, curly brown hair, green eyes, and heavy stubble on his face, indicating he had not shaved for several days.

"Agent Greg Mills I assume," Zach said.

"How do you know who I am?"

"I just came from the border patrol station in Douglas. Agent Lynch told me where you lived. Seems you didn't show up for your shift this morning. You aren't answering your phone and you don't look sick. All that is a bit suspicious, don't you think?"

"I think it's none of your business whoever you are. Now get out of my house!" the man yelled.

"It is my business, Agent Mills. I don't have time to argue. You *are* going to answer my questions."

"Like I said. It's none of your business and I am not going to answer any of your questions. Now, get out!"

"I suggest you might want to rethink that. We have reason to believe you looked the other way when a Mister Polomo sneaked nuclear materials across the border. How does twenty years in prison sound? Or maybe life. Or better yet, let's just make it a lethal injection seeing as how you are responsible for the deaths of several hundred thousand people. How does that sound, Agent Mills?"

Zach could see that Agent Mills was visibly shaking, his eyes darting back and forth, sweat glistening on his forehead.

"Come on, Agent Mills, we know you are guilty. Agent Lynch is reviewing the video surveillance tapes right now. If you confess and help us find the people behind this, we might be able to take the death penalty off the table or maybe you would rather die. Well, Agent Mills, what's your choice?"

Agent Mills was trapped, and he knew it. There was no way out. If only he had left the previous night like he had planned. He didn't believe he would be offered leniency considering the catastrophe in Sacramento, leaving him only one option. It was not a good option, but he really had no other choice.

"I swear I didn't know they were carrying anything. They just said they wanted to get someone across the border. I assumed it was somebody's relative," Agent Mills bawled, visibly trembling. "They offered me a lot of money. They said they would get me fired if I didn't help them. They threatened me and my family. They showed me a photograph of my mother in Orlando and said they would slit her throat in the middle of the night. What choice did I have?"

"Give me a name," Zach demanded.

"I don't have one. They never used names. They just showed up at my house one night."

"You've got to give me something."

"I was watched every day. One night I sneaked out the back of the station and I saw a license plate. I've got it written on a piece of paper in the bedroom. It's right in here," Agent Mills said as he turned and headed for the room on his right. Zach followed close behind.

In the bedroom, Zach noticed a partially packed suitcase lying on the bed. Agent Mills turned and pointed toward a dresser against the wall. "It's written on a piece of paper. It's lying on the dresser."

When Zach glanced toward the dresser, Agent Mills seized his last and only option. He dived for the bed, pulling out a 9mm pistol hidden under the suitcase. Unfortunately for Agent Mills, Zach had expected him to try something stupid. Zach already had his hand on the weapon behind his back making his reaction much quicker. Zach fired twice before Agent Mills had fully extended his arm. Agent Mills fell onto the bed and rolled off onto the floor. Zach walked over to where Agent Mills was lying and placed two fingers against Agent Mills' neck, finding no pulse.

"*Probably better for Agent Mills, considering either a lethal injection or life behind bars*," Zach thought as he walked over and examined the top of the dresser. "Well, what do you know," Zach exclaimed. "He wasn't lying." In plain sight on top of the dresser laid a small scrap of paper with a license plate number written on it. The paper said, "Ohio plate: JKD492."

Zach pulled out the business card Agent Lynch had given him and dialed the number written on the back. Waiting for the call to connect, he stuffed the business card and the small scrap of paper into his shirt pocket.

"Hey, Zach, calling already?"

"Yeah, got some bad news. I found Agent Mills at home. I suspected he would try something stupid. He tried to pull a gun and now he's dead. But I did get a license plate number for the men that paid him to look the other way."

"I'm sorry to hear that. Are you okay?"

"I'm fine. I will call the sheriff and get him to run the license plate number and I will notify him regarding Agent Mills."

Zach dialed the number for the Cochise County Sheriff's Office.

"Cochise County Sheriff's Office. May I help you?" a female voice answered.

"This is Zachariah Templeton. I need to speak to the sheriff. It's urgent. I have a dead body to report."

As he waited for the sheriff to answer, he laid one of his business cards on the top of the dresser and wrote his cell phone number on it.

"Sheriff Francisco Lopez. What's this about a dead body, Mister Templeton?"

"I'm at a house on Becki Lane west of Douglas. Three-quarters of a mile north of Highway Eighty. I came here to speak with a Border Agent Mills. He was stupid and tried to pull a gun. I had no choice. I came here from the border patrol station in Douglas. Agent Lynch and I determined he was the likely suspect in allowing a Mister Polomo to smuggle illegal materials across the border."

"Is that the man that died at Copper Queen Hospital?" Sheriff Lopez questioned.

"Yes, that's the one. What he smuggled may be dangerous," Zach lied. "I'm now on the Presidential Detail of the Secret Service and I am trying to find out who paid Agent Mills to look the other way. We need to locate those materials. Before he died, Agent Mills claimed he had written down the license plate number of one of the man that recruited him."

"Read it to me and I'll have someone run it while I get more details from you."

Zach pulled the slip of paper from his shirt pocket and read off the numbers to the sheriff. "Ohio plate: JKD492." Zach heard the sheriff call out the numbers to someone.

"What else can you tell me, Mister Templeton?"

"Not much I'm afraid," Zach offered. "All I got from Agent Mills was that license number. Right after that, he made his move, and I killed him. Unless the number I gave you leads me somewhere, it will likely be a dead end."

"That was quite a mess you got into at the hospital. And then the explosion up in Elfrida. It seems trouble follows you around."

"It certainly does," Zach remarked.

"How's your dad doing?"

"I don't know much. I had to leave before I could talk to the doctor."

The sheriff started to say something but stopped and told Zach to hang on. Thirty seconds later the sheriff returned to the line. "Mister Templeton, that plate is registered to a red Hyundai Sonata. It belongs to Easy-Rents, a small rental car company that operates at Tucson Airport. My deputy called the rental agency and put a little pressure on them and got the renter's name and a local address."

"That's great," Zach exclaimed. "Read me the name and address, please."

"The name on the rental contract is David L. Park. It's probably a phony. The local address he gave is the Welcome Inn Tucson. It's a small hotel on South Country Club Road near the airport. The deputy also called the hotel. The day manager said there is a Mister Park registered in room two twenty-eight. He said it's on the north side of the hotel."

"Thanks Sheriff," Zach said. "And thank your deputy for the extra effort. Can you call the sheriff for the Tucson area and let him know I will be in the area?"

"That would be Pima County. Sheriff Robert Potter. I will call him personally," Sheriff Lopez answered.

"Tell Sheriff Potter I would like them to be on the lookout for that car. Tell them to just observe and not make any contact or let the owner know they're watching. I need to take this one alive, but these types generally refuse to be taken alive. It's imperative I get to Tucson ASAP. I won't be here when the deputy gets here."

"Understood. Good luck, Mister Templeton."

Zach took the time to call Admiral Hadley and fill him in on the discovery of Agent Mills and his role in allowing Mr. Polomo to cross the border unchallenged. He also had to share the news of Mr. Mills' untimely demise. The additional time it would take to track down the new lead in Tucson caused Admiral Hadley deep concern considering the country's nuclear strike forces had been activated and assigned targeting data. A look of apprehension clouded Zach's face.

Zach ended the call on the SAT phone, ran out of the house, and leaped into his rental car. Rather than take the time to back up and turn around, Zach roared through the yard and onto Becki Lane. Barely slowing for the stop sign at Highway Eighty, he drifted into the opposite lane as he slid through the intersection. Once straightened out and in the proper lane, he called Sheriff Lopez again and asked him to call the state patrol and notify them he would be exceeding the speed limit as he drove toward Tucson. He pushed the big, black SUV to twenty miles per hour over the speed limit on the two-lane highway. Once he reached the interstate highway, he would push the SUV to its limit, praying he would not be too late. Time was running out, and he still had no answers, only questions.

Chapter Twelve

Welcome Inn Tucson
South Country Club Road
Tucson, Arizona

Halfway between Benson and Tucson, an Arizona State Patrol trooper pulled up beside Zach. The state trooper waved at Zach, motioning for him to look behind him. A second state trooper waved for Zach to move over into the fast lane in front of him. Zach moved over into the fast lane between the two state patrol cars, matching their speed. As Zach and the state troopers raced toward Tucson, he noticed additional state troopers clearing traffic ahead of them.

Zach glanced down at the instrument panel to verify the SUV was performing okay at such a sustained high speed. None of the gauges revealed any problems. He took a quick look at the speedometer and saw they were doing one hundred ten miles per hour. The state troopers were maintaining a four car-length distance in front of and behind Zach. If they were to encounter an obstacle in the road, the result would not be pretty.

As they approached the outskirts of Tucson, the traffic increased and the troopers slowed down to ninety miles per hour. Zach's cell phone rang. He tapped a button on his Bluetooth headset. "Zach Templeton," he answered.

"Mister Templeton, this is Trooper Richard Ruiz. I'm the patrol car in front of you. Where are you headed?"

"The Welcome Inn on South Country Club Road," Zach answered.

"Okay, we will take the East Irvington Road exit. It's coming up soon. Follow me onto the exit. We will turn left onto East Irvington Road and cross under the interstate.

South Country Club Road will be the second left. When we pass under the interstate, we will turn off our emergency lights and siren. You will turn left onto South Country Club Road. We will not follow you, but will remain in the area."

"Thank you, Trooper Ruiz. I appreciate the escort."

"Glad to be of assistance, considering the importance of your visit. Sheriff Potter passed along the details. We have all troopers on alert for the car you described. We have also advised the Tucson City Police."

"That's great, but do not attempt to stop him. It's imperative I get him cornered somewhere. He is the last lead I have. If anyone spots him, notify me. I will cruise the hotel's parking lot and if I don't see his car, I will park out of sight and wait for him."

"Understood. If you need additional assistance, do a call back to this number. I will be close by."

"Will do. Thanks again for the escort," Zach answered as he reached up and tapped the Bluetooth headset to disconnect the call.

Two miles later Trooper Ruiz signaled Zach to follow him over to the exit lane. Another half mile and Trooper Ruiz exited the interstate and turned left at the end of the exit lane. As they passed under the interstate, the two patrol cars switched off their emergency lights and sirens, to the surprise of several confused motorists who had pulled to the side of the road and stopped. At the intersection with South Country Club Road, Zach turned left while the patrol cars continued on East Irvington Road, turning left at the next intersection.

Zach continued driving south on South Country Club Road until he spotted the Welcome Inn in the next block. In the middle of the next block, he pulled into the nondescript hotel's entrance. Despite a recent paint job, the hotel still looked old and worn out. The flower beds were unkempt and full of weeds and trash littered the parking lot. For a hotel only ten blocks from the airport, a half full parking lot late in the afternoon suggested a less than four-star hotel.

Zach made a complete loop around the parking spaces in front of the hotel, looking at the license plates on the cars. Not seeing a single Ohio plate, he drove around the south side of the hotel and then around the north side. He did not see an Ohio license plate parked anywhere. Having noticed there were several open spaces on the north side of the hotel, he circled the hotel again. To be as inconspicuous as possible, he backed into an empty spot at the far west end of the north parking area. Switching off the SUV's engine, he settled in to wait for his quarry.

Exhausted after a long and trying day, Zach had trouble staying awake as he watched the parking lot for a car matching the description Sheriff Potter had given him. Darkness settled in, making it even more difficult for Zach to stay awake. Unable to stay awake, he nodded off, his head leaning against the doorpost. Several minutes later, he was startled awake by the Bluetooth headset buzzing in his ear. He tapped the answer button. "Zach Templeton."

"Mister Templeton, one of our units just spotted the car you described. The license plate matches. It's six blocks south on South Country Club Road, heading north toward your location. Remember, if you need assistance, call me."

"Thanks, I will," Zach answered. Zach slipped out of the car and closed the door as softly as he could. He hid behind a dumpster enclosure and watched the entrance to the parking lot. In the darkness, no one would notice him. Zach breathed deeply and slowly to control his heart rate. Five minutes passed. A flash of red passing through the light cast by the hotel's sign got Zach's attention. He watched as a red car continued past the hotel office, stopped partway down the row of parking spaces, and backed into a parking space, the car's license plate was clearly visible. Zach read off the plate's letters and numbers silently, "JKD492". "Here we go," Zach whispered to himself.

Earlier, Zach had changed into a pair of shoes with soft rubber soles to eliminate the sound of his footsteps. He watched a man climb out of the red car and slam the door.

Instinctively, Zach's right hand reached behind his back and touched his weapon to verify its presence. He eased out from behind the dumpster enclosure and followed the single occupant of the car toward the hotel. Zach watched as the man slid the key into the lock and unlocked the door. The instant he saw the door open, Zach rushed out of the darkness, pushed the man into the room, and slammed the door.

The man, much quicker than Zach had expected, turned and pointed a gun directly at Zach's chest. Attached to the barrel of the man's weapon was a sound suppressor. *"Only a professional assassin would need a sound suppressor on his weapon,"* Zach thought.

"Who are you and why did you push your way into my room?" the man demanded. "Maybe I should just shoot you and not worry about who you are."

"Easy. I'm reaching for my credentials," Zach announced.

"Very slowly and don't try anything."

Zach slowly reached into his jacket and pulled out the leather wallet containing his credentials. He flopped it open for the man to see. When the man leaned forward to reach for the wallet, Zach made his move. Zach's cat-like reflexes, developed during two tours assigned to the Navy's SEAL Team Four, were just slightly quicker than the man standing in front of him. Fortunately for Zach, the long sound suppressor attached to the end of the gun made it awkward in a close struggle. The man slipped out of Zach's grasp, spun around, and fired as he fell against the bed. The slug missed its mark, slamming into the wall beside the door.

The man straightened up, ready to fire again. Zach pushed the man's arm down and away and lunged toward him, grabbing him by the throat. The two men lost their balance, falling against the side of the bed and then toward the floor. The two men hit the floor as they struggled for control of the gun. The gun fired again. The struggle ceased and silence filled the room

A smoky haze from the gunfire filled the room. After some time, Zach took a deep breath and pushed himself up. He rolled the man over. "Great, just great!" Zach moaned when he saw a gaping hole where the man's left eye used to be. Zach reached out and pressed two fingers against' the man's throat. The man was dead and would not be answering any questions. A quick check of the man's pocket revealed absolutely nothing just as expected.

Zach pulled out his cell phone, located the most recent call from Trooper Ruiz, and pressed call back. Zach explained to Trooper Ruiz the struggle and unfortunate death of the man now lying on the floor. Trooper Ruiz advised Zach to stay put and wait for him to arrive.

"*Now what do I do?*" Zach asked himself as he waited for Trooper Ruiz to arrive. The man lying dead on the floor had been his last lead. With no more leads to follow, Zach was at a dead end. What would he tell Admiral Hadley? Zach mulled over the events of the last several days trying to come up with an explanation he could give Admiral Hadley that would explain the unfortunate turn of events. An idea flashed into his mind. Frantically, he dug his cell phone out of his pocket and made another phone call.

USS Wyoming (SSBN 742)
28° 0' 30" N, 60° 12' 45" W
Southeast of Bermuda

"Alert One! Alert One!" MAINCOMM Supervisor, Radioman First Class Aaron Jiles' excited voice echoed throughout the compartments of USS *Wyoming*.

Commander Anderson reached up and thumbed the 1-MC, "All stations, this is the captain. Secure from the flooding drill. I repeat, secure from the flooding drill."

The crewmen assigned to the damage control party that had been working furiously in the engine room immediately stopped their work and hurried back to the maintenance spaces to stow their tools and supplies, doing their best to avoid the officers running toward the control room. Receiving an EAM message during a patrol, always created a sense of urgency. The *Wyoming* would remain at a heightened alert status until the message had been properly decoded and authenticated.

All officers not on watch in their respective departments hurried into the control room. To minimize the potential for errors, a two-man team of officers would decode the incoming EAM. Lieutenant Bill Chambers, Assistant Weapons Officer, and Lieutenant Jg. Ted Mitchell, Electrical Division Officer, formed decryption team one. They stopped and waited outside the Op Center, a small room next to the radio room.

Radioman Chief Thomas Dawson, Radio Division Chief, recognized the two officers waiting outside and opened the hatch, allowing them into the cramped space. Lieutenant Chambers, the senior team member, entered the combination into the safe containing the EAM codebook, jerked the door open, and withdrew the codebook. He handed the codebook to Lieutenant Jg. Mitchell.

Chief Dawson stepped out of the Op Center into the radio room and tore the EAM message off the radio room printer. A few seconds later he returned with the EAM in his hand.

"Here is the EAM, sir," Chief Dawson announced, handing the sheet of paper to Lieutenant Chambers.

Lieutenant Chambers carefully read the letters, comparing them to a list of three-letter codes in the codebook. Lieutenant Jg. Mitchell, standing right beside him, confirmed the translation, a look of fear spreading across his face. Outwardly Lieutenant Chambers appeared calm, but on the inside he struggled desperately to stay calm. Maintaining control of the situation fell on him as the senior member of the encryption team. Together they had decoded many EAM messages, but they had always turned out to be training drills. This EAM was not a drill. This one was the real thing.

The message had decoded properly. Next, the message would need to be authenticated using the codes sealed in the double walled safe. Lieutenant Chambers stood in front of the safe to prevent anyone from seeing the combination as he spun the dial back and forth to the numbers he had memorized at the beginning of the patrol. He pulled the safe's outer door open and stepped aside. Lieutenant Jg. Mitchell moved over in front of the safe and spun the dial on the inner door. His hand shook so badly, he failed on his first attempt. He spun the dial several times in the opposite direction and repeated the combination. The combination correctly entered, he pulled the inner door open. He reached in and retrieved the appropriate plastic authenticator. Lieutenant Chambers and Lieutenant Jg. Mitchell, with authenticator in hand, exited the Op Center, leaving custody of the open safe to the secondary decryption team.

Together, the two officers made their way to the control center and stood facing the captain. A feeling of unease spread over everyone in the control center as the two officers were pale and visibly shaking.

Lieutenant Chambers spoke carefully, attempting to hide the fear and anxiety rising inside him, "Sir, we have received a valid Strike Message. The message is a properly formatted and valid EAM."

"I concur," Lieutenant Jg. Mitchell stammered. "The message is a properly formatted and valid EAM."

Commander Anderson took the message and codebook from Lieutenant Chambers and slid the authenticator down to the matching line in the codebook. Satisfied the two officers had correctly translated the EAM, he looked up at Lieutenant Commander Barton, *Wyoming's* Executive Officer. Lieutenant Commander Barton checked the codebook and after a long pause agreed, "I concur, Captain. The message is a properly formatted and valid EAM."

The last statement got everyone's attention. All eyes were riveted on the four officers. Even a valid EAM, meant nothing until it was authenticated. Only that final step remained.

"Request permission to authenticate," Lieutenant Chambers announced, holding the authenticator in his shaking hand.

"Authenticate," Commander Anderson directed.

Lieutenant Chambers snapped the authenticator in half and pulled out a red card with black, block letters. Slowly and deliberately he read off the letters, "Alpha-Tango-Tango-Foxtrot-Sierra-Whiskey-Bravo."

He handed the card to Lieutenant Jg. Mitchell, who swallowed hard and repeated the process, "Alpha-Tango-Tango-Foxtrot-Sierra-Whiskey-Bravo."

The codes that had been read off twice by different officers matched perfectly to the letter sequence printed at the bottom of the EAM message.

"The message is authentic," Lieutenant Chambers announced, visibly stunned by the words their operating procedures required him to say.

"I concur," Lieutenant Commander Barton confirmed. "The message is authentic."

Commander Anderson stared at the decoded EAM, studying the message's launch instructions.

Except for the soft whirring of the ventilation fans, a deathly quiet gripped the control room. The *Wyoming* had just received an authenticated order to launch its nuclear missiles. The crew of *Wyoming* had trained many times for such an eventuality. Before arriving on board, every crew member knew full well the boat's lethal mission, but no one on board ever expected such an order would come.

Commander Anderson knew the launching of nuclear weapons would inflict a heavy toll on the crew. They had trained long and hard for this possibility and they could perform their duties blindfolded, but actually launching nuclear weapons and unleashing such devastating destruction would prove to be an entirely different matter.

Commander Anderson reached up and thumbed the 1-MC, "All stations, this is the captain. We have received an Emergency Action Message directing us to launch our nuclear weapons. We will immediately proceed to our designated launch point and then fire our missiles. Details will be disseminated as soon as the targeting and launch packages have been loaded and confirmed. Crew of the *Wyoming*, you have trained long and hard for this eventuality and you will be expected to perform accordingly. Captain out."

"Mister Chambers, deliver the targeting and launch instruction to the Weapons Officer ASAP."

"Helm, Conn, right standard rudder, come to course zero-nine-zero. All ahead full, make turns for twenty-five knots."

"Conn, Helm, right standard rudder, come to course zero-nine-zero. All ahead full, make turns for twenty-five knots, aye."

Commander Anderson studied the crew as they went about their assigned duties, looking for any sign of fear or resistance. Any crew member not able to perform their duties, would be replaced instantly. "*Would they be able to launch Wyoming's deadly missiles?*" he asked himself. "*Would he be able to turn the launch key and issue the final command to launch such horrible destruction upon the world?*" Silently, in his mind he prayed their launch order would be countermanded before they reached their designated launch zone. If not, he would perform his duty, because that was what he was trained to do.

Copper Queen Community Hospital
100 East 5th Street
Douglas, Arizona

Angie, curled up in an uncomfortable recliner, dozed fitfully. The nurse who had come into James Templeton's room to check his vitals, knocked a book off the bedside tray, startling Angie awake. Angie struggled to a sitting position, rubbing her sore neck caused by the odd position she had fallen into.

"How's he doing?" she asked the nurse.

"He's still pretty heavily drugged to allow him to rest and his body to heal. He opened his eyes briefly when I checked his blood pressure. The doctor has been easing up on the drugs somewhat to see how he tolerates it."

"When is the doctor coming again?"

Looking up at the clock, the nurse said, "Anytime now, I believe. She got out of surgery thirty minutes ago. I would imagine as soon as she dictates her surgical notes she will stop in."

Angie got up from the chair, stretched her stiff muscles, and walked over to the side of the bed. She gently laid her hand on James's arm. His eyes fluttered open slightly, he grunted, and smiled ever so slightly, or, at least, Angie thought he smiled. Just that quick, his eyes closed and his breathing returned to a shallow rhythm. Angie squeezed his arm, waiting for a reaction. Once again, his eyes fluttered open, but quickly fell closed. Angie patted his arm and returned to the chair. She was thirsty and would like to go to the cafeteria but she did not want to leave Zach's dad alone.

Tired of sitting, she stood up and walked over to the window. The sky, colored a dreary, lifeless gray, made the desert landscape seem even more bleak than usual. A few rain drops spotted the glass. The weatherman Angie had watched earlier that morning had predicted on and off rain showers for the entire day. Angie did not believe in omens, but still, an odd feeling overpowered her and she shivered. Something felt very wrong. A nuclear bomb had decimated the city of Sacramento, a crazed assassin had shot Zach's mother in the leg, Zach's dad lay in a hospital bed a few feet away in critical condition, and Zach had left in a near panic at the behest of Admiral Hadley. Would Zach also end up in a hospital bed, or worse? A persistent sense of foreboding nagged at her consciousness. She shivered again as she stared out the window, trying to imagine what Zach might be doing. Buzzing from inside her purse interrupted her reverie. She reached inside her purse, intending to silence the vibrating cell phone. Recognizing Zach's number, she answered the call and slipped out into the hall.

"Zach, where are you?" Angie demanded. "I've been sitting here with your dad imagining all kinds of horrible things."

"Sorry, Angie," Zach apologized. "I don't think you would believe me if I told you."

"Try me," Angie protested.

"I promise I'll explain, but first, how is my dad?"

"He's still critical. The nurse was just in his room and told me the doctor is easing up on his drugs to see how he tolerates it. I squeezed his arm then he grunted and opened his eyes, but only for a second or two."

"That's a good sign, right?"

"I don't know, Zach. The doctor hasn't been in yet. She's supposed to be here anytime according to the nurse."

"Dad's tough," Zach offered. "He's been through a lot worse than this and pulled through. He'll be all right. I know he will."

"I hope you're right. Now, how about that explanation you promised me?"

"Time is short, so I will just explain the highlights." Zach described the recent events to Angie: the man with radiation poisoning brought to the hospital in Douglas; finding Dr. Woods dead; the bomb that injured his dad; the gun battle at the hospital in Douglas, which she already knew about; the conversation with the sector chief at the Douglas border patrol station; tracking down the corrupt border patrol agent; how he had to kill the border patrol agent when he pulled a gun; and, finally, the license plate number that led to the man in Tucson.

"Good grief, Zach," Angie commented.

"Oh, wait. I'm not finished," Zach interrupted. "I'm at the hotel room of the man that rented the car. I waited for him and followed him into his room. Before I could question him, he pulled a gun, we struggled, and now he's dead as well. Angie, he was the last lead I had."

"Everyone around you seems to either end up injured or dead," Angie interjected. "So, what are you going to do now?"

"I have one last idea," Zach answered. "That's the reason for my call. When Dad and I were driving from the hotel in Benson to Doctor Woods' house, Dad insisted on talking about the incident in Washington, D.C., and how he had just turned and walked out of my life. Well, one thing led to another, and he finally divulged the reason he and my mother disappeared all those years ago. He told me he had discovered a serious and credible threat to destroy our country. He worked with Admiral Hadley off and on trying to uncover the people involved. He and the Admiral believe their digging may have pushed the people behind the original plot to try something significant, like the nuke in Sacramento. He said he had two names, but he wouldn't tell me their names. Angie, I have to have those names."

"But, Zach, your dad is unconscious," Angie protested.

"I know that. If at all possible, the doctor has to reduce the medications and allow him to wake up."

"He's in critical condition. Waking him up might be too dangerous."

"Angie, there's no other choice. There might be more nukes. Admiral Hadley informed me the President scrambled our nuclear strike forces and they are on their way to their targets right now. There is not much time left. If I can find out the individuals behind this, we might avoid a nuclear war. Angie, I absolutely have to know those names."

"Hang on, Zach. Doctor Berger just walked into your dad's room. You should talk to her." Angie put her hand over the phone, hurried back into the room, and tapped the doctor on the shoulder. Angie quickly explained what Zach wanted and handed her the phone. Dr. Berger and Zach argued back and forth for several minutes regarding the danger of allowing his dad to wake up. Dr. Berger would not give in. She refused to reduce James' meds.

Zach got Dr. Berger to agree what he told her must be kept secret. Zach told her about the current threat, but still she resisted, saying it would cause his dad too much stress and she would not be responsible for the outcome. Left with no other choice, Zach demanded that Dr. Berger summon the hospital administrator to James' room immediately. Dr. Berger handed the phone back to Angie, pulled her own cell phone from her jacket pocket, and called the hospital administrator. After a brief conversation, she ended the call and dropped the cell phone back in her pocket.

"He said he would be right here," Dr. Berger announced.

In less than five minutes, a small thin man with a round, oval face and a thin strip of scruffy gray hair just above his ears hurried into the room. A narrow, outdated tie, loosened at the knot, hung askew below the collar of his ill-fitting white shirt that looked two sizes too big. Completing his unkempt appearance, the man wore shapeless gray slacks and black loafers with deep scuffs across the toes.

"What is the meaning of this?" the man demanded

"Missis Angie Templeton, this is Doctor Floyd Rotter, the hospital administrator," Dr. Berger announced.

"Pleased to meet you, Missis Templeton" Dr. Rotter said, sticking out his bony hand. After shaking Angie's hand, he repeated his initial question, "Why am I here?"

"Mister Zach Templeton, the patient's son, demanded to speak with you. He said it is a matter of national security," Dr. Berger replied, pointing at Angie. Angie handed the cell phone to Dr. Rotter.

"Mister Templeton, this is Doctor Rotter, the hospital administrator. What is so important?"

Dr. Rotter stood silent, listening to what Zach had to say. After hearing that there might be more nukes waiting to be detonated, and being asked if he wanted the FBI to descend on the hospital, he relented and agreed to Zach's demands. He handed the cell phone back to Angie and turned toward Dr. Berger.

"Reduce the patient's IV drip," Dr. Rotter ordered.

"But, Doctor Rotter, the stress will not be good for the patient," Dr. Berger protested.

"I understand your concerns Doctor Berger. Reduce the patient's IV drip. I will take full responsibility." Dr. Berger started to protest again, but Dr. Rotter held up his hand, signaling that the debate was over. He turned and walked out the door, the frayed cuffs of his baggy pants dragging the floor. Had Dr. Berger not introduced Dr. Rotter as the hospital administrator, Angie would not have believed it. The man looked more like he should be the manager of some flea-bag hotel. She hoped his administrative skills were better than his fashion sense.

Dr. Berger stepped over to James Templeton's bed and grabbed the IV tubing. Turning toward Angie, she said, "I want you to know I am against waking Mister Templeton up. I won't be responsible if his condition worsens. It will be Doctor Rotter's problem."

"We understand, Doctor Berger," Angie acknowledged.

Dr. Berger adjusted the IV drip to less than half what it had been.

"Zach, Doctor Berger just reduced the drip. I hope this goes well."

"Okay, let me know when he starts to wake up."

Dr. Berger had summoned the nurse assigned to James's room in case there were complications. Several minutes passed as everyone stood quietly, waiting for James Templeton to awaken.

"Nothing yet," Angie advised. Several more minutes passed. James's eyelids fluttered, the fingers of his left hand pulling at the blanket covering him. He moaned as his eyelids opened slightly. His left hand balled into a fist.

Dr. Berger instructed the nurse standing on the opposite side of the bed to increase the pain meds. The nurse located the control for the patient-controlled analgesia (PCA) pump and pressed the button, delivering an additional dose of the pain medication. Almost immediately, James's hand relaxed and his eyes opened a little wider.

"Zach, your dad's beginning to come around," Angie said as she stepped over beside the bed and laid her hand on James's arm.

"Is he lucid? Can he talk?" Zach asked.

Angie leaned over and squeezed James's arm several times. "How do you feel? Can you understand me?" Angie could see that James was trying to open his eyes wider with little success. His eyes fluttered a few times and went closed. "I don't know about this, Zach. His eyes are closed again."

"It's crucial, Angie. Try again," Zach urged.

"Okay," Angie said as she squeezed James's arm a little harder. His eyes opened a little wider and he blinked several times. "James, can you understand me?" When Angie realized he was trying to say something, she leaned closer and asked, "What are you trying to say?" She leaned her ear close to James' mouth. "Say that again."

"Dry," James croaked, the word barely distinguishable.

"Can he have some water, Doctor?"

"Only a sip," Dr. Berger replied.

Angie grabbed a cup of water from the bedside tray and held the straw to James's mouth. "Just a sip." James struggled to get his lips closed around the tip of the straw and then pulled a tiny bit of water into his mouth. Angie pulled the straw away as he swallowed the water. James opened his mouth, indicating he wanted another sip. Angie looked at Dr. Berger.

"One more and that is all," Dr. Berger advised.

Angie repeated the process with the straw. James swallowed the second sip of water and seemed satisfied. "Is that better?" she asked. James held up the thumb of his left hand, managed to half close his right eyelid, and tried to say something. Angie leaned her ear close to James's mouth again. She straightened up with a smile on her face.

"Zach, I don't believe it," Angie remarked. "He winked at me. His words were slurred, but he definitely said 'Hey gorgeous'."

"That's my dad. See, I told you he would be okay. Ask him if he can talk."

"Zach wants to know if you can talk to him."

"Yes," James whispered with great difficulty.

"Ask the nurse and Doctor Berger to leave the room for a minute or two. They can't be allowed to hear this."

"Zach asks that you both leave the room for a few minutes. Sorry, you can't hear this."

"No more than two minutes," Dr. Berger demanded, glaring at Angie. "We'll be right outside." She pointed toward the door. The nurse followed Dr. Berger out and pulled the door partially closed, leaving a small gap open.

"They're gone."

"Tell Dad all the leads are dead and I must have the names he told me about when we were on the way to Doctor Woods' house. Then ask him if he understands."

Angie did as Zach had instructed and asked James if he understood. James acknowledged by raising the thumb of his left hand. She told Zach his dad understood.

"Okay. Put the phone down next to his mouth and lean close so we both can hear and then tell him to speak the names of the people involved in the plot."

Angie complied and instructed James to speak the names. James's eyes opened wide, he took a deep breath, mumbled something, and his eyes closed. Angie leaned close to the phone and said she could not understand. Zach had not understood either.

"Listen here James Templeton," Zach shouted into the phone. "I need those names. I'm depending on you. You will tell me those names."

James's eyes open wide again and he spoke a name, but only one name. His eyes fell closed again.

Angie pulled the phone away from James's mouth, straightened up, and spoke into the phone, "Zach I understood the name. Did you hear it?"

"No, Angie, I didn't. Tell me what he said." Angie repeated the name his dad had spoken and asked Zach if it meant anything to him. Zach told her he had never heard the name before, and it meant nothing to him. They both agreed they had pushed Zach's dad as hard as they dared and Zach would have to be satisfied with just one name.

"What now?" Angie asked.

"I'll call Admiral Hadley and see if the name means anything to him. Thanks, Angie. I couldn't have gotten the name without you. I have to call Admiral Hadley immediately and determine what the next step is. I'll get you a message somehow when I know anything."

Angie responded, but Zach had already ended the call. Somewhat annoyed that Zach had ended the call so abruptly, she pulled the door open and told Dr. Berger and the nurse they could return to the room.

Welcome Inn Tucson
South Country Club Road
Tucson, Arizona

Before he could punch Admiral Hadley's phone number into the SAT phone, a knock on the hotel room's door interrupted Zach. He stood up, walked over to the door, and peered through the door's peephole. Recognizing Trooper Ruiz's nameplate, he opened the door and ushered the trooper into the room.

Trooper Ruiz glanced at the body lying on the floor and said, "I thought you wanted to take him into custody."

"Yes, I did, but I guess he had other ideas. I followed him into the room and he pulled a gun before I could say anything. We struggled and fell against the bed and then onto the floor. The gun fired and there is the result."

"Who is he?"

"I don't have a clue. He has no ID or identification of any kind on him, but I would guess he is a professional killer," Zach said, holding out the weapon with a sound suppressor attached to the barrel. "If he hadn't snagged the suppressor in his jacket, it would probably be me lying there on the floor."

"What about prints?" Trooper Ruiz asked.

"You can check, but I seriously doubt if you will find his prints on file."

Trooper Ruiz leaned over the body and pulled out his portable fingerprint scanner. He lifted the man's right arm, about to place his thumb on the scanner. "Hey, Mister Templeton, come have a look at this."

Zach walked over by the bed and leaned over. "Wow! Do all his fingers look like that?"

Trooper Ruiz looked at all the fingers on the man's right hand. He dropped the man's right arm, picked up the man's other arm, and examined the fingers on his left hand. "Every single one," Trooper remarked. "This man has no prints on his fingers. I'll try facial recognition." He lifted a cell phone from a holster on his belt and snapped a photo of the dead man's face. From a menu on the cell phone, he opened a new text message, attached the photo, and pressed send.

"There's so much damage to his face I doubt if the photo will match anyone. Wait a minute," Trooper Ruiz said, turning the man's head to the side and then the other. "Look at the fine lines here and here. He's had plastic surgery."

"Somebody went to a lot of trouble to conceal this man's identity," Zach remarked.

"The only thing left is a DNA analysis," Trooper Ruiz said. "When we're done, I'll call the crime scene unit and have them go over the room. I doubt we will find anything useful, though."

"I suspect you're right," Zach agreed. "I need to make an urgent phone call to my superior."

Zach grabbed the SAT phone, walked into the bathroom, pushed the door shut, and punched in Admiral Hadley's number. On the eighth ring, an out of breath Admiral Hadley answered. "Zach, sorry. I was in the other room. I'm in the middle of something rather pressing. Do you have something important?"

"Yes, I do Admiral. With the Douglas sector chief's help, we identified the border patrol agent that let Mister Polomo across the border without being checked. That led me to a man in Tucson. They both pulled a gun and they're both dead. The man in Tucson is, or was, a professional. He has no fingerprints and he has had plastic surgery and he carried a weapon with a sound suppressor. He was my last lead, Admiral. Until another idea popped into my mind."

"And what was that?" Admiral Hadley asked.

"My Dad and I had a discussion about the incident in Washington, D.C., with Frank Porter. He told me about the plot he uncovered and about going into hiding. He said he thought the plot was related to the detonation in Sacramento and he knew two names, but he wouldn't tell me who they were. With no leads left to follow, I called Angie at the hospital where Dad is and I convinced the doctor to allow Dad to wake up. With Angie's help, we got Dad to tell us one name." Zach told Admiral Hadley the name his dad had spoken. There was no response from the Admiral, only silence.

"Admiral, are you still there?" Zach asked. Still no response. "Admiral, can you hear me? Do you know that name?"

"Yes, Zach, I hear you," Admiral Hadley stammered. "This is.... This is.... Zach, this will have to go to the President. I will call him and have him call you on the SAT phone. Stay put."

"How long, Admiral," Zach asked, but the Admiral had already ended the call. Zach pulled the SAT phone away from his ear and stood there staring at it. The mention of the name elicited a response completely out of character for the normally stoic Admiral. The name had definitely rattled the Admiral. Zach had no idea why the mention of a name would have to go to the President. He did not know how long it would be before the President called. Rather than sit around waiting, he decided he would drive to the airport and have Kip Johnson get the Gulfstream pre-flighted and ready for departure.

He pushed the bathroom door open and walked over to where Trooper Ruiz was sitting. "I'm afraid something rather urgent has developed," Zach said. "I need to get to the airport. I have a private jet waiting. Is there anything else you need from me?"

"I don't think so Mister Templeton. Is there a way I can reach you if I find I need any additional information?"

Zach dug one of his business cards from his credentials wallet and wrote the SAT phone number on the back. "If the number on the front doesn't work, try the one on the back," Zach said as he handed the card to Trooper Ruiz.

Trooper Ruiz stuck his hand out and shook Zach's hand. "It was nice to meet you, Mister Templeton. I wish it could have been under better circumstances."

"I agree. Thanks again for the escort and for your quick response here," Zach said as he exited the hotel room and headed for his rental car. He climbed into the car and sped out of the hotel parking lot, hoping he would reach the Gulfstream before the President called.

Chapter Thirteen

Luxury Apartment
Vicente Leon Street
Quito, Ecuador

Anthony Sterling's (aka Frank Porter) anger grew intense after having failed four times to reach the assassin he had contracted to mete out revenge on Zach Templeton and his family. Determined to find out why his plan was unraveling, he tried to reach his other contact in the United States, also failing after four attempts.

Already outraged because the nuclear device had been detonated before the ransom demands could be delivered, Anthony was fuming. The early detonation had ruined his plan to use the devices for blackmail and leverage. Any hope of attaining his original goal lost forever and unable to reach any of his contacts, Anthony's blood pressure climbed higher and higher as he paced the floor of his apartment. Knowing he had to get his emotions under control, he decided to wait a few minutes and try his contacts later.

No matter how hard he tried to calm himself, faced with the intolerable thought of yet another defeat, the anger and frustration inside him grew uncontrollable. Overwhelmed by seething anger and frustration, Anthony did something desperate. He ran into the bedroom and yanked the top drawer from his dresser and dumped it upside down on the bed. He peeled off a small notebook taped to the underside of the drawer. After locating a number he had been instructed never to call, he punched the number into his cell phone and waited.

"Yes," a gruff, male voice answered on the fourth ring.

"This is Sterling. I need…."

"You idiot," the man bellowed. "I told you to never call this number."

"I don't care," Anthony snapped back. "I paid you a lot of money to follow my instructions. The device was to be detonated only if my demands were not met. Now, my entire plan is ruined."

"I was not there. I don't know what happened."

"You must find the individuals responsible," Anthony screamed. "I want to know what happened."

"There's no point," the man answered. "Travel into that area would be impossible. I can't do anything about it now."

"Yes, there is," Anthony snarled. "I want you to detonate the remaining two devices."

"Are you crazy!" the man exclaimed. "That's utterly insane. I'm not going to do that."

"You will do exactly what I tell you to do or I will expose the entire plot and you will get the death penalty."

"I couldn't detonate them if I wanted to. The elements to boost the devices have not been delivered."

"What? You promised me they would be there a week ago. Why don't you have them?"

"I don't know. Nobody contacted me."

"I don't care. Just detonate them as is."

"I can't. I don't have the triggers to activate the devices. I don't know where they are. I've lost contact with the man in Arizona."

"You imbecile! I paid you generously to follow my instructions. You will find those triggers and you will do what I paid you to do."

Anthony's face grew flushed as he waited for the man to answer. "Hello. Hello. Are you there?"

Nearly incoherent, Anthony screamed into the phone again but received no answer. The man had ended the call and Anthony heard a dial tone in his ear. Anthony cleared the call and dialed the number again but heard a busy signal. He tried two more times, each time hearing a busy signal.

Losing control and lapsing into a fit of rage, Anthony slammed the cell phone down so hard the glass screen shattered, scattering shards of broken glass across the top of the dresser. He grabbed the broken phone and threw it as hard as he could, embedding it halfway into the wall. He slammed his fists down on the dresser so hard the top split. Rubbing a growing lump on his left hand, he stormed out of the bedroom, vowing someone was going to pay dearly.

Back in the living room, Anthony, hands balled into fists, paced back and forth across the apartment, shaping a new plan in his mind. Rushing back in the bedroom, he rummaged through the spilled contents of the dresser drawer searching for the backup cell phone he kept hidden there. He rushed back into the living room and grabbed the local phone book from the bookcase. Flipping through its pages, he located the section he wanted, punched in a number, and waited.

"Quintero Aviation, this is Jacinto. May I help you?"

"May I speak to Adulfo Caldera?" Anthony asked.

"One moment, please."

Several minutes later a heavily accented voice answered the phone. "This is Adulfo. How I help you?"

"Adulfo, this is Sterling," Anthony answered. "I need an aircraft fueled and ready as soon as I can get there. Say, thirty to forty-five minutes."

"Sorry, Senor Sterling. I cannot do that."

"Yes you can and you will," Anthony demanded.

"No, Senor, all our planes are ready for other customers."

"Adulfo, I will not argue with you. You will do as I ask. You will get an aircraft fueled and ready."

"No, Senor. Is not possible."

"Listen carefully, Adulfo. You know I do not make idle threats, right?"

"Yes, Senor Sterling. I know this."

If an aircraft is not ready and waiting when I get there, I will find you and I will kill you and your entire family and it will not be pleasant. Do you doubt me, Adulfo?"

"No, Senor Sterling. I know you. I no doubt you. I will do my best to have a plane ready."

"That's good, Adulfo. Your life depends on it. Tell the pilot to file a flight plan for Panama City. I will be there as soon as I can. Adulfo, it had better be ready," Anthony warned as he ended the call. He consulted the hidden notebook again, punched in another number, and waited.

Anthony discussed his estimated time of arrival and need for transportation with the individual that answered the phone. He ended the call and called a taxi for an immediate pickup. Anthony looked around the apartment wondering if he would ever see it again. One thing of importance that he would need came to him. He retrieved the item from a hidden compartment in the bookcase and stuffed it behind his back. He exited the apartment without looking back and pulled the door shut. Only one thing now drove Anthony: a blinding rage that could only be satisfied by revenge.

Anthony exited the apartment building and leaned against the taxi stand waiting for the taxi he had requested. Across the street and a block away, Sotero Rojas perked up at the sudden appearance of his quarry. Just as suddenly, a white taxi pulled up to the taxi stand and stopped. His quarry jumped into the taxi and it sped off. Sotero dug out his cell phone and called his partner, Nestor Guzman.

Yes, Sotero. What is it?"

"Porter just exited the building and jumped into a taxi. Come and pick me up quick."

Nestor came roaring around the corner, having been parked less than a block away. Sotero leaped into the car and Nestor gunned the engine before Sotero had even closed the door. Sotero pointed out the white taxi two blocks ahead as Nestor raced down the street. Weaving in and out of traffic, they followed the white taxi at a safe distance. Twenty-five minutes later the white taxi pulled up and stopped in front of the general aviation terminal at Quito's Mariscal Sucre International Airport. They watched as Porter jumped out, threw some bills into the passenger window, and disappeared into the terminal.

"Where do you suppose he's going in such a rush?" Nestor asked.

"I have no idea," Sotero answered. "This I have to report in." Sotero retrieved a cell phone from his pocket, pressed a speed dial number, and waited.

"Director Sandberg."

"Director, this is Sotero. I just saw our friend Porter run out of his apartment building and jump into a taxi. We followed the taxi to the airport. Porter got out and entered the general aviation terminal."

"Any idea where he might be headed?" the director asked.

"Not a clue," Sotero answered.

"Find a location where you can observe the duty runway and watch the outbound traffic. Record the tail numbers of all outbound private aircraft. Then report back to me."

"Will do," Sotero replied. "Nestor, circle the airport and park in the waiting area. The boss instructed us to record the tail numbers of all outbound private aircraft and report back to him."

Nestor slipped the car into gear and drove around the access road that circled the airport. He pulled the car into the parking area designated for people waiting for inbound passengers. Sotero retrieved a pair of binoculars from the glove compartment and busied himself watching private aircraft departing the airport.

Scorpion Flight
Flight Level 450 (45,000 ft.)
Location - Classified

"Scorpion Flight Leader, Striker Eight, be advised we have an engine exhaust overtemp warning light on engine number two."

"Acknowledged, Striker Eight. Striker Ten, Scorpion Flight Leader, Striker Eight reports engine exhaust overtemp on engine number two. Do you have a visual?"

The copilot of Striker Ten, trailing one-half mile behind and slightly below Striker Eight, looked out his starboard window and reported, "Scorpion Flight Leader, Striker Ten, Striker Eight is trailing heavy black smoke from the inboard engine in the far starboard pylon."

"Striker Eight, did you copy Striker Ten?" Major Chris Jones, Aircraft Commander of Striker One queried.

"Scorpion Flight Leader, affirmative," Major Roy Mayhall, Aircraft Commander of Striker Eight, reported. "Scorpion Flight Leader, engine two's exhaust temp is continuing to climb. I am going to shut down engine number two. Per mission parameters, with seven engines we are still a go for the mission." Major Mayhall reached up to shut down engine two when a loud bang reverberated throughout the aircraft.

"Scorpion Flight Leader, Striker Ten, there was a bright flash from outboard tip of Striker Eight's starboard wing. The outboard pylon is now streaming flames."

Inside Striker Eight, Major Mayhall glanced at the instrument panel in front of him and discovered that the fuel flow rate for engine two was surging beyond redline. At that moment, a compressor blade failed in engine number two and broke loose from the shaft, shredding internal components as it travelled through the jet engine. By instinct, Major Mayhall reached up to activate the fire suppression switch for engine two, but he was a few seconds too late.

"Scorpion Flight, there was a large fireball from Striker Eight's starboard wing," came the excited voice of Striker Ten's aircraft commander. "Half of the starboard wing is missing, and the aircraft is pitching down and right."

"Attention all Scorpion Flight aircraft," announced Major Jones. "Watch for parachutes from Striker Eight. I want an exact count." Major Jones, ignoring proper radio protocol, pressed the inter-aircraft comm switch and shouted, "Boonie, get a fix of our current position so we can radio it in for the rescue team."

Captain Carl Boone, Striker One's Radar Navigator, consulted his navigation charts, calculated their current coordinates, and reported back to the aircraft commander. Major Jones reported the emergency and their coordinates to the command center via the encrypted, CONECT satellite datalink, a multi-function digital interphone system, which would allow the crew to survive and function during nuclear conflicts. Major Jones switched back to the flight control frequency and communicated to all flight crews, "Gentlemen, focus on your mission. It is critical that you maintain situational awareness."

Crewmen in all Striker aircraft, their faces plastered against windows, watched and waited, looking for the telltale puffs of smoke from Striker Eight's ejection systems and then parachutes opening. Striker Eight continued to plummet toward the ground swinging in large circles. Striker Three's demoralized crew reported to Flight Lead they only spotted two parachutes before losing sight of the crippled aircraft.

"Scorpion Flight Leader, All Striker Aircraft, Confirm two parachutes only. Repeat, confirm two parachutes only."

Over the next thirty seconds, three additional flight crews reported seeing only two parachutes emerge from Striker Eight.

"All Striker aircraft," Major Jones announced. "There's nothing we can do for Striker Eight. We *must* focus on the mission. We have been assigned a job to do and we will do it. That is all."

Many of the crew members closed their eyes for a few seconds and whispered silent prayers for their comrades, hoping that they had missed the other parachutes deploying. Being highly trained professionals, they returned to their duties and focused on delivering the lethal payload stored in the belly of each aircraft.

General Aviation Terminal
Mariscal Sucre International Airport
Quito Ecuador

After entering the general aviation terminal, Anthony had walked to the far end of the terminal and took a seat beside a small snack bar. Several minutes later, Adulfo stepped out from a door labeled 'Airport Personnel Only' and motioned at Anthony. Anthony got up and walked through the door as Adulfo quickly pulled it shut behind him. Adulfo hurried Anthony through the restricted area before anyone could see them.

Anthony Sterling exited the general aviation terminal's maintenance area and hurried past three private jet aircraft parked on the ramp. He spotted the aircraft Adulfo had arranged for him parked at the far end of the row of aircraft. He walked up to the Learjet 75, verified the tail number, and walked up the stairs, and stepped into the cabin.

Glancing toward the aft end of the passenger cabin, he confirmed he was the only passenger on board. He stowed his small bag, threw his jacket over a seatback, and dropped into the starboard side seat in the front row. As Anthony was buckling his seat belt, a short, excited man stepped out of the cockpit and glared at Anthony.

"I'm Selesio Espinosa, your pilot," the man said. "Elido Mena is in the cockpit. He will be the copilot."

"I'm Anthony Sterling. I'm in a hurry. Let's get started," Anthony replied, ignoring the man's offered hand.

Espinosa pulled his hand back and said, "Senor Sterling, the copilot and I were not pleased to be pulled from a flight already scheduled to depart. I had already filed a flight plan, I might add. We tried to refuse, but Adulfo was adamant. He said you were very important and we must accommodate you. We have agreed to fly you where you want to go. You should not be so rude."

"I'm sorry," Anthony lied. "My mother is quite sick. She is dying and may not survive another day. The doctors said I must hurry."

"Well then, we will depart immediately. Adulfo said you wish to fly to Panama City. Is that correct?"

"Yes, Panama City. That's correct."

"See that you are buckled in," Espinosa said as he turned and stepped back into the cockpit.

Espinosa settled down into the pilot's seat, slipped on his communications headset, and called the flight service center. Having already verified there would be clear weather all the way to their destination, he had filed a VFR flight plan for a direct flight from Quito, Ecuador, to Panama City, Panama. Ground control approved Espinosa's request for a first-in-line taxi because of a critical medical issue suffered by their passenger's close relative.

Espinosa steered the Learjet 75 onto the taxiway and proceeded to the south end of the airport and held short of Runway Three-Six. A large 767 jetliner flared over the end of the runway and touched down, large clouds of blue-white smoke billowing up from the wheels. Espinosa taxied the Learjet onto the runway, lined up on the centerline, and set the brake. Once the large jetliner had cleared the runway, the Learjet received clearance to take off. Espinosa released the brake and pushed the throttles forward. The Learjet rolled down the runway, gaining speed. Two-thirds of the way down the runway, the Learjet's nose wheel lifted into the air, the rear wheels lost contact with the runway, and it departed into the northern sky.

As the Learjet lifted off the runway, Anthony pushed the stopwatch button on his watch. Forty-five minutes later, while uninterestedly browsing through a travel magazine, the stopwatch alarm on the watch sounded. Anthony cleared the alarm, unbuckled his seatbelt, and stood up. He went to his small bag, retrieved a .22 caliber Beretta Model 70, and held it behind his back. Anthony loved his Beretta Model 70. Being lightweight, accurate, and easily concealable, made it the signature terminator weapon of the Mossad, the premiere intelligence agency of the State of Israel.

Anthony pushed the curtain aside and stepped part way into the cockpit. Before either man could react, he pressed the end of the sound suppressor against the base of the copilot's neck and pulled the trigger. The .22 caliber slug bounced around inside the copilot's torso destroying organs as it went. The angle of the muzzle at which he held the weapon assured the slug would penetrate the heart, killing the copilot instantly.

"What the....", the pilot started to object until he saw the bloody end of the muzzle pointing directly at his face.

"I suggest you do exactly as I tell you," Anthony commanded. "Put the aircraft on autopilot."

"You wouldn't dare fire that," the pilot exclaimed. "The bullet will damage the aircraft."

"No, sir, it won't. It's a twenty-two caliber. It will bounce around inside your head like a rubber ball. Turn on the autopilot and don't try anything stupid. I'm a pilot. I will know if you do something incorrectly," Anthony shouted.

Left with little choice, the pilot conceded and did as Anthony commanded. Anthony watched the pilot's motions carefully. He continued watching the flight controls for several seconds to be certain the autopilot was in control of the aircraft.

"Get out of your seat carefully," Anthony ordered. Anthony pushed the curtain out of the way and backed slightly out of the cockpit, watching as the pilot released his safety harness and slipped out of his seat.

"Now, drag the copilot out of his seat and dump him in one of the rear seats in the passenger cabin." Anthony watched as the pilot released the copilot's safety harness and struggled to get him up and out of the seat. Anthony backed down the aisle, keeping his Beretta trained on the pilot. Anthony stepped sideways behind the first seat to let the pilot by. The pilot dumped the copilot's body in the port side seat.

"Buckle him in and then cover him with a blanket," Anthony ordered. The pilot complied. As the pilot was about to straighten up, Anthony put the suppressor to his head and squeezed the trigger. The pilot fell in a heap in front of the copilot's body. Anthony grabbed another blanket and covered him up. He hurried back to his bag, pulled out an aeronautical chart, and made his way back to the cockpit.

He slipped down into the pilot's seat and buckled the safety harness. He unfolded the aeronautical chart and noted the coordinates for the mid-point of the flight track from Quito to Panama City. Comparing the coordinates indicated on the automatic flight guidance system to those written on the chart, told Anthony the aircraft was still ten minutes away from his target. He waited eight minutes, put his hand on the yoke, then released the autopilot.

Exactly two minutes later, Anthony reached up and switched off the transponder and the comm system. He put the aircraft into a left turn while descending from flight level three-two-zero to flight level one-eight-zero. Steadying the aircraft up on a heading of three-one-nine, he settled in for the rest of the flight to his true destination.

A little over an hour later, aircraft tail number Hotel-Charlie-Whiskey-Foxtrot-Golf would not check in for approach clearance to Panama City's Tocumen International Airport. A search would be initiated, but they would find nothing. After several days of searching, they would assume the aircraft had crashed and sank without a trace.

Alternate Safe Facility - Majestic One
Location - Classified

Exhausted from long hours, the stress of the emergency relocation to the alternate safe facility, and the mental trauma
from watching videos of the unimaginable destruction in
Sacramento, the President sat behind a battered desk with
his chin resting on his chest. Several other members of the
President's staff had also succumbed to the long hours and
mounting stress, their heads leaning against the back of the
leather couch on which they were seated. Those staff members not napping ignored the soft snoring and continued to
review intelligence reports.

The alternate safe facility was of moderate size. The dé-
cor in its smallish rooms had a rather beaten and worn look,
suggesting an age far beyond the ten years since the facility
had been built. In the windowless conference room, a
scratched lectern had been shoved into the front corner of
the room. The scarred, wooden conference table looked as if
it had been purchased at a flea market. Arranged around the
table, a few equally beat-up chairs also showed their age. At
the back of the room, a thirty-cup coffeepot sat on a worn
and water-spotted library table. Half-empty cups of bitter
coffee and plates with partially eaten stale pastries littered the
conference table.

A tomblike pall hung over the conference room.
Hushed voices drifted around the room as the President's
staff members discussed recent events. Tired and frazzled
from the sudden exodus from the nation's capital, tempers
threatened to explode. The President had been angry when
he entered the facility and observed its shabby and unkempt
condition. Had circumstances been different, he would have
had someone's head. Exhausted and disheartened he had
slumped down into a threadbare office chair sitting behind
the desk and almost immediately drifted off to sleep.

The phone on the corner of the President's desk rang.
One of the staff members rushed over and snatched the re-

ceiver before the phone could ring a second time. He spoke quietly into the receiver so as not to wake the President unnecessarily. He listened for a short time, laid the received on the desk, and shook the President's shoulder.

"Sorry, Mister President. It's General Gordon from NMCC. He needs to speak to you regarding Operation Vigilant Strike."

The President stood up, raised his arms over his head, and stretched to chase the cobwebs of sleep from his mind. Yawning as he sat down, he reached for the phone. "Yes, General, President Cantwell here," he said, trying to suppress another yawn.

"Mister President, this is Brigadier General Robert Gordon. I am calling to advise you that per your order to execute Operation Vigilant Strike, our airborne nuclear strategic forces have been scrambled, appropriate targeting packages have been transmitted, and the aircraft are now on their way to their targets. COMSUBPAC and COMSUBLANT have acknowledged that EAM's have been sent to all appropriate ballistic missile submarines instructing them to proceed immediately to their designated launch zones and launch their missiles."

"Understood General," President Cantwell acknowledged. "Is there anything else?"

"No, Sir. Without a countermanding order, the strategic forces will immediately execute their launch orders upon arriving at their respective launch coordinates," General Gordon answered.

"Thank you, General," President Cantwell said. He hung up the phone, leaned back in his chair, and spoke to no one in particular, "May God forgive us for what is about to happen."

The sleeping staff members, awakened by the phone ringing and the President's conversation, stared at President Cantwell, his usual upbeat and cheerful demeanor gone. His face looked drawn and haggard, dark shadows visible under his eyes. Salt and pepper stubble from not having shaved since arriving at the safe facility only added to his fatigued appearance. He rubbed his tired eyes and turned toward the center of the room. He was about to speak when the phone rang again.

"President Cantwell," he spoke into the phone.

"Mister President, this is Admiral Hadley. I have an update regarding Mister Templeton's investigation."

"I hope you have some good news, Admiral. I could sure use it."

"Sorry, Sir, I do not. With the help of the sector chief at the Douglas Border Station, they identified a border agent that looked the other way when the man we believe smuggled the nuclear material crossed the border. Mister Templeton questioned the agent and persuaded him to give up some information. The agent wrote down the license plate number of the vehicle the man who coerced him was driving. Mister Templeton tracked that man to a hotel in Tucson and confronted him."

"But, isn't that good news," President Cantwell protested.

"Unfortunately, both men pulled a gun and Mister Templeton had no choice but to defend himself. Both men are dead."

"So, we're at a dead end. Is that what you're telling me, Admiral?"

"Well, not exactly. Does the name Norman Glover ring any bells?"

"Um, I don't think so. Jog my memory, Admiral?"

"He was investigating a plot to destroy the United States. He got really close and had to go into hiding. We faked a boating accident, gave him and his wife new names, and put them in WITSEC."

"Still nothing. Can you provide anything else?"

"Do you remember the incident with Vice Admiral Harlan Beckwith and Frank Porter?"

"Oh, yes, I remember that very well. If memory serves me, Beckwith was arrested and Porter disappeared without a trace."

"You are correct. Well, a few days ago, a CIA operative observed someone he thought looked like Porter. He took a photo spread and sent it in for facial recognition. It proved to be a match. The CIA now has full-time surveillance on Porter. I called Mister Glover out of WITSEC to shadow Mister Templeton and protect him. He was instrumental in keeping Mister Templeton alive until Beckwith's plot was uncovered. Norman Glover's real name is James Templeton."

"I'm guessing there's a relationship of some kind between them."

"Right again. James Templeton is Zach Templeton's father."

"Okay, so what does that have to do with our current situation?"

"When all of Zach's leads ended up dead, he recalled a sensitive conversation he and his father had while heading to question someone. Zach called the hospital where his father was admitted after the bomb exploded and had the doctor reduce his meds and wake him up."

"Huh, hospital, bombs exploding?" President Cantwell questioned.

"Sorry, Mister President, I don't have time to explain that. Anyway, Zach remembered his father divulged that he had been investigating a plot and knew two names he believed were likely involved in the Sacramento detonation. At the time, his father refused to tell Zach their names. Once the doctor reduced the meds, his father became lucid enough to talk. Zach's wife held the phone to James Templeton's ear and Zach insisted he tell him the names. He only spoke one name before lapsing back into unconsciousness."

"Well, what was the name, Admiral," President Cantwell insisted.

"You will not believe it. I think it best if you hear it straight from him. I told him I would have you call him and to stay put. I'll give you the number for the SAT phone he's carrying."

President Cantwell wrote the SAT phone number down as the Admiral repeated it. He pressed and held his finger on the phone's hook-switch and looked up at the staff members. "Gentlemen, I need the room." He kept his finger on the hook-switch until the last staff member had exited the room and closed the door. Immediately, he released the hook-switch and punched in the number he had written on the desk pad.

Several thousand miles away the SAT phone lying on the passenger seat of Zach's rental car began to ring. Zach had just driven through the gate for Tucson International's General Aviation parking lot. Pulling into the first empty space he saw, he grabbed the SAT phone and answered, "Zach Templeton."

"Mister Templeton, this is President Cantwell."

"Yes, Sir, Mister President. Admiral Hadley told me to expect your call."

"Admiral Hadley told me you were at a dead end but then you got a name from your father."

"Yes, I was. The man I confronted here in Tucson was definitely a professional. I had hoped to question him and find out who hired him, but he gave me no choice. He had no ID and no fingerprints. His fingers had been polished smooth."

"I understand that," President Cantwell broke in. "Admiral Hadley said you got a name from your father. The Admiral wouldn't tell me. Zach, I need that name."

Responding to the President's request, Zach told the President the name his father had spoken. Silence, just like when he told Admiral Hadley the name. Zach waited, but the President did not respond. "Sir, did you hear me?"

Zach repeated the name and again asked, "Mister President, did you hear me? Do you know that name? Mister President are you still there?"

"Yes, yes, I'm still here Mister Templeton," President Cantwell answered, shaking his head, stunned by the name Zach had told him. "Absolutely, I know that name. I just can't believe it. Are you certain that was the name your father spoke?"

"Yes, Sir, I'm certain," Zach insisted. "My wife was leaning over the bed and she verified that was the name I heard."

"Now that I think about it, this new information might shed some light on the analysis results of the samples the NEST team collected from the blast zone. Mind you I said might, Mister Templeton."

"Understood, Sir. Are you able to share those results?"

"Normally, I would say absolutely not, but given the grave nature of what we are facing and how critical it is that you track down the perpetrators of this despicable act, I will tell you. But be aware, if any of this leaks out, you will likely spend a long, long time in prison."

"I understand, Sir." Zach sat in his rental car, silently listening and becoming more and more dumbfounded as the President shared the results of the NEST team's analysis of the nuclear blast debris.

"But how can that be?" Zach stammered.

"I thought the same thing, many times," President Cantwell added. "But, considering the name you just gave me, maybe it isn't so preposterous. Zach, if this all ties together as I think it might, we have a monumental problem! I believe Admiral Hadley informed you that our strategic nuclear forces have been scrambled and are on their way to their targets as we speak."

"Yes, Sir, he told me that."

"Unless some verifiable evidence presents itself, and soon, and NMCC issues a countermanding order, the strategic nuclear forces will deliver their payloads. Zach, there is not much time."

"Do you have an address for the name?" Zach asked.

"Not right at the moment, but I will get it. The instant I have it, I will send it to you. Good luck, Zach."

"Thank you sir, I will need it."

"Oh, by the way," President Cantwell added. "A word of warning, Zach. The World is watching what we do. You had better get it right, and soon!"

"I'll do my best, Sir," Zach answered as he ended the call. Rather than look for a parking space closer to the Gulfstream, He scrambled out of the rental car and started to sprint across the parking lot. Failing to notice an empty bottle lying on the ground as he dodged between cars in the next row, he tripped, tumbling to the ground. He lost his grip on the SAT phone and watched it bounce out into the middle of the lane between the rows of parked cars. Zach watched in shock as a white pickup truck's wheels ran directly over the SAT phone. The pickup screeched to a stop. The driver's side door flew open and a tall skinny man jumped out and ran to where Zach laid on the ground.

"Are you all right?" the man asked.

Zach looked up at the man dressed in dark blue work clothes. "I think so," Zach answered.

"Here, let me give you a hand," the man said, offering his hand to Zach.

Zach grabbed the man's hand and struggled to his feet. Zach read the man's name from the large white patch over his shirt pocket. "Thank you, Steve," Zach groaned, noticing the gaping hole in the right leg of his trousers. "I guess I should be more careful." While Zach rubbed his sore knee and brushed the dirt from his clothes, the man bent over and retrieved the crushed SAT phone.

"I don't know what this thing is, but it doesn't look too good," the man said, holding it out toward Zach. "I'm sorry. I didn't see it until it bounced right out in front of me."

Zach took the SAT phone from the man and examined it. "It's a SAT phone and you're right. It does look a little worse for wear. It's not your fault. Don't worry about it."

"You sure you're okay? I'm late for work. I really need to get going."

"Yes, I'm fine, except for my pride and ripped pants. I really appreciate your stopping to check on me."

"I'm glad you're okay. Hope your knee doesn't give you too much trouble," the man answered as he ran around the truck, jumped into the cab, and sped off toward the airport terminal.

Zach limped past the last three rows of parked cars as fast as his painful, bruised knee would allow, hurrying toward the gleaming private jet parked three hundred feet away. Zach looked up and saw Kip Johnson, the pilot, standing in the forward doorway waving at him.

"Great," Zach muttered. "He saw my graceful swan dive." Zach waved back, held up his right hand making a circular motion, and continued hobbling toward the aircraft.

Kip Johnson ducked back inside the aircraft and began preparing the aircraft for takeoff.

Chapter Fourteen

USS Wyoming (SSBN 742)
Southwest of Bermuda

The *USS Wyoming*, making turns for twenty-five knots on a heading of zero-nine-zero, had just undergone a watch change. Some crewmen immediately headed to the mess deck to grab some chow. Others that had not yet qualified for their dolphins had trudged off to attend yet another class on critical submarine systems. Those not in either of those two groups headed to their personal bunk spaces to write letters that might never get mailed, to change clothes, or, most important of all, to get some much-needed sleep.

Whenever a submarine was at sea operating at a heightened alert, the on-duty rotation schedule defaulted to port and report, which equated to six hours on, six hours off, six hours on, and six hours off. Many sailors complained that it felt like they were living two days every twenty-four hour period. Adding to the difficult and grueling on-duty schedule was the fact that without looking at a clock it was impossible to know if it was day or night. Sleep was difficult because crewmen were always coming and going, and noise was never-ending as machinery operated twenty-four hours a day. Adding to all that difficulty, was the mental strain of knowing they were about to launch the most destructive weapons ever devised by man.

Commander Anderson, captain of the *Wyoming*, had checked with the navigation officer and learned the boat was approaching the edge of their designated launch zone. He reached up and thumbed the lever for the 1-MC, "Crew of the *USS Wyoming*, this is the Captain. We are now one hundred nautical miles from the edge of our designated launch zone. I want everybody not on watch or assigned to special duty to stay in their personal spaces. I want the boat operating at peak efficiency. There is to be no unnecessary movement or noise. Captain out."

Commander Anderson leaned over, about to speak to Lieutenant Commander James Barton, *Wyoming's* executive officer. Suddenly the control center went dark. Two seconds later, the emergency battle lanterns switched on, casting eerie orange shadows in the control center.

"Conn, Reactor Room," boomed Reactor Operator Second-Class Michael Warren's voice over the 1-MC. "There was a significant short on the main electrical buss. The reactor SCRAMed. A repair party is being organized to locate and isolate the short."

"Reactor Room, Conn, make it quick. We are time critical on reaching our launch zone."

In the short time it took Master Chief Damage Controlman Edward Benson, also Chief of the Boat, to organize a damage control party, smoke had begun to fill the engine room spaces. The damage control party donned their emergency breathing apparatus, entered the engine room, and removed panels from equipment bays, looking for the source of the smoke.

"Conn, Radio, There is smoke coming from the Main Radio equipment rack," Radioman First Class Aaron Jiles' voice announced over the 1-MC.

"Radio, Conn, secure power and wait for the damage control party," Commander Anderson ordered.

Radioman Jiles moved over next to the main radio panel and reached for the main power breaker just as the equipment rack erupted, showering sparks on the floor. The equipment cover panel blew off and struck Radioman Jiles in the face, knocking him backward into Radioman Second Class Gary Roosa. Stunned by the sudden explosion, the two men fell against the partially open radio room hatch and out into the passageway. Radioman Roosa, only startled and knocked off his feet, struggled out from underneath Radioman Jiles and stood up. Radioman Jiles had not been so fortunate. He lay on the deck unconscious, blood streaming from a large laceration across his forehead. Radioman Roosa tore off his shirt and pressed it against the injured man's forehead and screamed for a corpsman.

Two additional small fires broke out in *Wyoming's* equipment spaces. The initial short had generated an enormous voltage spike which caused system failures all throughout the boat. Many of the newer systems had automatically switched offline, protected by overload protection circuits. However, circuit boards and components in older systems, overwhelmed by the surge, melted and arced, creating additional small fires.

The stench and smoke from burning electrical equipment spread rapidly throughout the boat. Crewmen on duty at critical stations, unable to reach emergency breathing apparatus, pulled their tee shirts up over their noses and strained to keep their eyes open in the stinging smoke.

Engineman Third Class Mike Hall, the duty helmsman, shouted, "Conn, Helm, we're losing steerage way."

"Helm, Conn, losing steerage way acknowledged," Commander Anderson replied. He thought for a moment then reached up and thumbed the lever for the 1-MC, "Attention damage control parties, this is the Captain, we are drifting off position. It is imperative you get those fires under control quickly."

Relying on often-practiced procedures, the damage control parties battled the fires using fire suppression, fogging systems. Over the next sixteen minutes, damage control parties reported all fires as under control. Once the fires were out, the damaged systems were switched off and isolated from the main power buss. Despite the quick action of the damage control parties, the smoke generated by the electrical fires had turned *Wyoming's* air toxic. Commander Anderson watched as crewmen in the control room coughed and retched from the acrid, stinging smoke.

"Reactor Room, Conn, All fires have been extinguished and faulty equipment has been isolated. How quickly can we do a reactor restart?"

"Conn, Reactor Room, the reactor did a hot shutdown and transitioned to mode three. The reactor core is still at normal operating pressure and temperature. With the lighting, air-conditioning, and ventilation systems shut down we can initiate a fast recovery startup. The reactor should be back online and able to answer maneuvering bells in five to six minutes."

"Reactor Room, Conn, we need maneuvering in less time than that," Commander Anderson urged. He tugged the top of his tee shirt up and covered his nose, tapping his foot involuntarily as he waited impatiently for the reactor to come back online. Crewmen in the control room continued to cough and sputter. Two of the crewman succumbed to the toxic air, collapsing onto the floor.

Four and one-half minutes later the reactor room reported the reactor had been restarted and was back online, ready to answer maneuvering bells. Only one action remained that could save *Wyoming's* crew from the polluted air.

Commander Anderson yelled, "All ahead flank. Chief of the Watch, EMERGENCY BLOW!"

Machinist Mate Third Class Donald Lee turned toward the one-foot high platform in the center of control, known as the Conn, when he heard the Captain yell. Being Machinist Mate Lee's first patrol, he had not yet learned all the submarine's critical systems. His current assigned duty was to shadow the maneuvering watch as part of his qualification requirements, still having much to learn before he would qualify to wear the silver dolphins. Despite his limited overall systems knowledge, he knew exactly what protocol required to execute an emergency blow. A serious emergency on board a submarine could sink the boat within minutes. Instant reactions to emergencies were essential. The emergency blow procedure was the first thing a newly reported crewman learned as part of his qualification. Machinist Mate Lee glanced over to the position where the on-duty diving officer should have been standing and saw Chief Machinist Mate Michael Warren lying on the floor. Machinist Mate Lee rushed over to the diving officer's position reached above his head, and grabbed the two "T" handles, one for the forward main ballast tanks, one for the aft main ballast tanks.

The control valves used to initiate an emergency blow were wired shut to prevent an accidental roller coaster ride to the surface. Machinist Mate Lee tripped the quick release mechanisms, twisted both "T" handles counter-clockwise ninety degrees, and pushed them upward as hard as he could, releasing the extremely high-pressure air stored in two separate clusters of tanks located forward and aft. The high-pressure air screamed through several one-way check valves causing a horrendous bang that made everyone in the control center jump. Machinist Mate Lee then reached up and mashed the diving alarm, setting off the familiar ahhh-OOOggg-aaahh, ahhh-OOOggg-aaahh.

The high-pressure air rushed into the main ballast tanks, forcing the seawater out of the tanks through vents in the bottom of the boat. As the seawater was displaced, the boat quickly achieved positive buoyancy. Machinist Mate Lee grabbed a stanchion to his right and screamed, "Grab on to something!" The boat pitched upward and shuddered violently as the fifteen thousand shaft horsepower applied to the screws propelled the boat toward the surface. In less than ten seconds, the emergency blow procedure had the boat pitched upward at a forty-degree angle. Those crewmen not belted in grabbed whatever they could, hanging on with both hands to prevent being thrown against bulkheads or equipment racks.

Forty-five seconds later, *Wyoming* broached the surface, the bow reaching thirty or more feet in the air before slamming back down to the surface of the ocean, creating an enormous cloud of saltwater spray. *Wyoming* rolled slightly several times on its longitudinal axis and then settled out on the surface. Commander Anderson ordered all ventilation systems to high to exchange the contaminated air inside the boat with fresh air from outside. Rescue parties were spreading out through the boat to tend to injured crewmen that had been unable to snag a handhold during the emergency blow maneuver.

The *Wyoming* spent slightly over an hour on the surface clearing smoke from the electrical fires and assessing damage to critical systems. All systems not having serious damage were brought back online one system at a time. Commander Anderson authorized necessary testing for critical systems only. While systems testing was underway, the navigation officer used the opportunity to obtain a satellite GPS location and reset *Wyoming's* inertial navigation system. As soon as all critical systems were deemed operational, he ordered *Wyoming* back to patrol depth and resumed course back toward their launch zone.

All uninjured maintenance personnel were ordered to work non-stop until all nonoperational systems had been repaired. The most important systems that remained nonoperational were the communications systems. Even though the communications system was considered a crucial system, it's unavailability would not prevent *Wyoming* from firing its missiles. Damage in the radio room had been extensive and would require a herculean effort to overcome. As senior electronics technicians identified and removed charred circuit boards and wiring, more junior personnel made frequent trips to the supply closet in search of replacements.

With the boat back on course toward the launch zone, Commander Anderson turned the Conn over to Lieutenant Commander James Barton, *Wyoming's* Executive Officer, and circulated throughout the boat to commend the crewman for a job well done and to combat the growing anxiety. Life onboard a U.S. Navy SSBN was generally rather boring, just the way its crew liked it. An SSBN's mission was to transit to the patrol area, stay extremely quiet for a few months, and then go home, safe and sound. This mission was different. A sudden equipment failure had nearly crippled the boat and they were about to launch weapons that could plunge the world into a global war. Many crew members feared there might be no home to return to.

As many of the members of *Wyoming's* crew that were not busy with repairs and that could fit into the control center had assembled at the Captain's request. Commander Anderson raised his hand and waited for the gathered crewmen to quiet down.

"Machinist Mate Third Class Donald Lee, front and center," Commander Anderson barked. Machinist Mate Lee pushed his way through the crowded control center and stood at attention before Commander Anderson. "Machinist Mate Lee, as commanding officer of the *USS Wyoming*, I hereby commend you for your quick thinking and swift action in stepping in for an incapacitated crewman. Your bravery and quick action likely saved the *Wyoming* and its crew from a watery grave. An official letter of commendation will be added to your personnel file."

As applause began, Commander Anderson held up his hand to silence the gathered crew. "Crew of the *Wyoming*, from this day forward, Petty Office Lee will no longer be called a NUB. He is now to be treated as a full member of the crew." On board a U.S. Navy submarine, the term NUB, an acronym for Non-Useful Body, described a submariner that had not yet passed his submarine warfare qualification, thereby earning his Dolphins.

Commander Anderson stepped down off the platform and held out his hand to Petty Office Lee, "Job well done Petty Officer Lee. It is a privilege to serve with you."

Thunderous applause broke out in the control center amid shouts of hooyah, hooyah, hooyah. Machinist Mate Lee received many slaps on the back and handshakes as he made his way through the control center. The brief revelry provided the crew with a much-needed release from the tension that had built up over the past several hours. Commander Anderson allowed the commotion to continue for several minutes. "Okay gentlemen, we have a job to do. Let's get to it."

Gulfstream G550
Tucson International Airport
Tucson, Arizona

The gleaming white and blue private, business jet sat parked on the general aviation ramp at the northwest end of the airport, next to the U.S. Customs Office. Located along the northern edge of the airport, Davis Monthan Air Force Base buzzed with activity. A steady stream of military jets departed, patrolling the southwestern corridor to identify and eliminate any further threats. Zach ducked instinctively as a low-flying F-15 screamed overhead.

Zach climbed the three stairs and stepped into the lavishly appointed passenger cabin of the Gulfstream G550. No matter how many times he flew on the Gulfstream, its elegance always stunned him. "*Someday I need to get Angie a ride on this aircraft. She'd love it,*" he thought to himself as he headed for the cockpit.

"Hey, Kip, are we ready to go?" Zach asked.

"Just about," Kip Johnson answered. "By the way, I saw your tumble in the parking lot. Are you okay?"

"Yeah, I'm okay. Tore the leg of my pants. My knee is a little sore, but nothing I can't handle. I can't say the SAT phone fared too well though," Zach said, holding out the smashed SAT phone.

"Wow. All that damage from a little fall?"

"No, the thing slipped out of my hand, bounced out into the road, and some guy in a pickup truck speeding between the rows of cars ran over it. You wouldn't happen to do phone repair, would you?"

"No, I don't," Kip laughed as he climbed out of the pilot seat. "The pre-flight is complete except for an exterior check of the aircraft." Kip exited the aircraft and ran his hand along the leading edge of both wings. Ducking under the aircraft, he shined a flashlight up into the wheel wells looking for any signs of hydraulic fluid leakage. He made one final walk around of the aircraft looking for visible signs of damage to any of the control surfaces. Kip gazed lovingly at the sleek aircraft, ready for flight in all respects. After climbing back into the aircraft, he stopped in front of Zach. "Where are we headed?"

"New York City," Zach replied. "I think Newark would be the best airport. The traffic out of LaGuardia is brutal and JFK is much further from downtown. What do you think?"

"I agree one hundred percent. Newark is the best choice."

"Well then, let's saddle up and hit the trail, mister," Zach joked.

"Yes, sir, pardner, I'll mosey up front and get them there engines started," Kip shot back with a huge grin on his face. "While I do that, can you go pull the chocks?"

Zach hurried off the aircraft, ducked under the aircraft and pulled the chocks away from the wheels. He grabbed the yellow rope tying the two chocks together, dragged them out of the way, and climbed back aboard the aircraft. Once inside, he pulled up the stairs and secured the front hatch. As he settled into his seat, his cell phone alert chirped. He lifted the cell phone out of its holster and tapped the icon to open the text app. As promised, President Cantwell had sent him the address of the individual Zach had mentioned to the President earlier.

"Are we ready to depart?" Kip hollered from the cockpit.

"Give me a minute. I need to send Angie a message," Zach answered as he opened a new text, selected Angie's number, and typed a quick message telling her where they were headed. "Okay, I'm ready. Let's go."

Kip pressed the transmit button on the yoke, "Tucson Ground, November-four-six-Mike-Lima, requesting clearance for taxi to active runway One-One Left."

"Negative, November-four-six-Mike-Lima, there is a full ground stop in effect for this sector. Only military aircraft are allowed clearance for departure."

"Tucson Ground, November-four-six-Mike-Lima, my passenger is on a special presidential detail for the President."

"November-four-six-Mike-Lima, no exceptions."

"Tucson Ground, November-four-six-Mike-Lima, acknowledged. Stand by."

"Hey, Zach, I'm having difficulty getting ground clearance release to taxi to the duty runway. There's a full ground stop for the southwest sector. I don't think we're going anywhere."

Zach unbuckled his seat belt, pulled a plastic card from his jacket pocket, and poked his head into the cockpit. "Here, give this a try."

"Tucson Ground, November-four-six-Mike-Lima, requesting clearance for taxi to active runway One-One Left. Presidential authorization code as follows: Baker-Romeo-Alpha-Alpha-Golf-Three-Seven-Three."

"Stand by November-four-six-Mike-Lima." Ten seconds later the radio crackled to life, "November-four-six-Mike-Lima, Tucson Ground, taxi to runway One-One-Left via Delta, hold short runway One-One-Left."

"Tucson Ground, November-four-six-Mike-Lima, taxi to runway One-One-Left via Delta, hold short runway One-One-Left roger."

Kip Johnson pushed the throttles forward, twisted the steering yoke to the right, and slowly eased the Gulfstream toward the taxiway Delta. He straightened out the steering yoke and increased the throttles slightly. The Gulfstream bounced slightly as it rolled down the taxiway. Kip taxied the plane to the taxiway's intersection with the runway and stopped short of the active runway.

"November-four-six-Mike-Lima, Tucson Ground, hold short for military traffic inbound on final two and one-half miles."

"Tucson Ground, November-four-six-Mike-Lima, hold short for military traffic inbound on final two and one-half miles roger."

Kip keyed the cabin intercom, "Zach, military traffic inbound on final and then we're next. Make sure you're buckled in."

Zach leaned forward in his seat to watch the military traffic as it landed. Two F-15s flared over the threshold of the runway and flashed by the Gulfstream. Tires screeched and puffs of smoke rose into the air as the two F-15s settled onto the runway.

"Tucson   Ground,   November-four-six-Mike-Lima, cleared for takeoff runway One-One-Left. Fly heading one-two-three, climb to three thousand two hundred, then direct to radar vector SID VEYLE."

"November-four-six-Mike-Lima,   Tucson   Ground, cleared for takeoff runway One-One-Left. Fly heading one-two-three, climb to three thousand two hundred, direct to radar vector SID VEYLE, roger," Kip repeated.

Kip eased the throttles forward, steering the Gulfstream onto runway One-One-Left. Lined up on the centerline, he set the brake, and pushed the throttles all the way forward. He waited for the twin Rolls-Royce BR710 engines to spool up. Upon reaching seventy percent thrust, he released the brake and the sleek Gulfstream began its take-off roll. Kip scanned the gauges and indicators as the Gulfstream accelerated toward V1, the decision speed where he could still abort the takeoff. With everything normal and no warning indicators, he pulled back on the control yoke and the nose wheel lifted off the ground. A few seconds later, the Gulfstream's rear wheels lifted from the runway and the jet began its climb out to the southeast. At two hundred feet, Kip retracted the landing gear.

At precisely three thousand two hundred feet, Kip thumbed the transmit button and called departure control, "Tucson Departure, Gulfstream November-four-six-Mike-Lima, three thousand two hundred, at SID transition."

"Tucson Departure, November-four-six-Mike-Lima, climb and maintain eight thousand one hundred, turn left heading zero-niner-zero, contact Albuquerque Center."

At eight thousand one hundred feet, Kip keyed the transmit button, "Albuquerque Center, November-four-six-Mike-Lima, heading zero-niner-zero, eight thousand one hundred."

"Albuquerque Center, November-four-six-Mike-Lima, climb and maintain three-one-thousand. All southwest sector air traffic is on full ground stop, except by special clearance. At this time, the only traffic is military at nine o'clock, two miles. You are cleared for VFR direct approach to Newark at your discretion. Good day."

"November-four-six-Mike-Lima, Albuquerque Center, cleared for VFR direct approach to Newark at my discretion, Traffic at nine o'clock, two miles roger."

Kip keyed the cabin intercom, "We have been cleared for a VFR approach direct to Newark. You are free to move about the cabin."

Zach released his seat belt, stood up in the aisle, and stretched. He poked his head into the cockpit. "If you are cleared for an approach at your discretion, can you increase the speed?"

"Yes I can," Kip responded. "Are you in a hurry?"

"Yes, I am. I want to get my hands on that scumbag as soon as possible."

Kip reached for the throttles and eased them forward to the top speed notch.

Copper Queen Community Hospital
100 East 5th Street
Douglas, Arizona

Standing at James Templeton's bedside, Angie Templeton watched as James struggled to push himself higher in the bed, trying to find a more comfortable position. She reached out her arm for James to hang on to.

"Thanks, Angie," James whispered, licking his dry, cracked lips. "Water please?"

Angie grabbed the insulated mug from the window sill and held it so James could get the straw into his mouth. He sucked in two large swallows and spit the straw out. "Lips dry," he croaked.

Angie rummaged through the personal items the hospital had provided and located a small tube of lip balm. She held the tube out to James. He attempted to lift his arm and take the tube, but only managed to get his arm halfway there before his arm flopped back onto the bed. James turned his head toward Angie with a pleading look on his face.

"You're getting rather demanding," Angie said as she winked at James. "One of these days you will have to start helping yourself." Angie dabbed some balm on her finger and smeared it across James' lips. James lifted his right hand and gave Angie a thumbs-up signal and a weak smile.

Angie was greatly encouraged to see James beginning to regain his strength. The length of the periods he was awake and lucid had also increased. Angie looked up when Dr. Ramona Berger entered the room to check on her patient's progress.

"Well, I see my star patient is awake," Dr. Berger said. With a chart in hand, she walked over to James' bed and reviewed the latest lab results. "The blood work has improved dramatically which means the internal bleeding has stopped. You should begin to feel better soon. Now, it is just a matter of time for your injuries to heal."

Dr. Berger slipped the stethoscope from around her neck, stuffed the ends into her ears, and listened to James' chest. She moved the stethoscope several times, listening carefully to his breath sounds. She turned and looked at Angie. "Has he been using the spirometer?"

"I got him to try several times," Angie answered. "But getting the indicator halfway up was the best he could do."

"He's not moving enough air into his lungs," Dr. Berger commented. "That creates a risk he could develop pneumonia. I will have the nurses get him out of bed. When he is in the chair and sitting up, I will order some breathing treatments. All things considered, he is doing pretty well."

"How soon do you think he could be discharged?" Angie asked.

"If his progress continues, I would think five or six days. He will be very sore for several weeks, but the more he is up and moving the quicker he will heal. Do you have any questions?"

James rolled his head side to side and whispered, "No questions. Thank you, Doctor Berger." Angie also shook her head, indicating she had no questions either.

Dr. Berger made several notes in James' chart and hurried out of the room to visit another patient. James watched as Dr. Berger left the room. As soon as she was out of the room, he motioned for Angie to come over to the bed. Angie stepped over beside the bed. James rolled his head toward Angie and asked, "How is Zach?"

"I haven't talked to him recently, but I got a text from him a few minutes before Doctor Berger came into the room. It was very short. It said he was on his way to New York City."

A horrified look spread across James' face. "The name I gave him…," James choked, stopping to clear his throat. He grimaced and coughed twice then continued, "That man is dangerous…. very dangerous…. must warn him."

"I'm sure Zach knows that," Angie protested.

"Don't understand…. evil…. must call….," James gasped, falling back onto the bed, overcome by the pain from his broken ribs. He grabbed the bed rail and attempted to pull himself up again. "Angie, must warn him!" He lost his grip and fell back against the bed again, his eyes wide, filled with dread.

Angie realized James would never settle down unless she agreed to contact Zach. "Okay, I'll call him," she said. She dug through her purse, retrieved her cell phone, and called the SAT phone number Zach had given her. She let it ring twenty times and then ended the call. She scrolled through the list of contacts, selected Zach's cell phone, and pressed 'Call'. Immediately, she heard the carrier's canned message telling her the cell phone customer she was trying to reach was unavailable. Either the cell phone's battery was dead, or Zach had turned the cell phone off. She looked at James and shook her head.

James became even more agitated and pushed the bed-side table out of the way, knocking several items off onto the floor. "Must warn….," James sputtered, one leg dangling over the side as he tried to climb out of the bed. Angie ran to the bed and pushed James back.

"James, no!" Angie shrieked. "You're not strong enough. You've got to stay in bed. If you don't settle down, I will ask the nurses to sedate you."

James pushed back, still trying to get out of bed. "No, must warn….," he gasped. The fear flashing through his mind and the effort expended as he fought to get out of bed depleted what little strength he had. He fell back onto the bed exhausted. Angie punched the nurse call button.

Aroused by the racket and the ringing patient alarm, nurse Amber Peters rushed into the room. "I heard the rack-et. Is Mister Templeton okay?"

"He's agitated," Angie answered. "I'm having trouble keeping him in bed."

Doctor Berger, exiting the room next to James', also had heard the commotion. She rushed into the room and took charge of the situation. "Mister Templeton, you must relax and settle down."

Neither Angie nor the nurse nor Dr. Berger could calm James down. Out of desperation, Angie shouted at James, "I'll call Admiral Hadley. We will find a way to contact Zach."

James quit struggling and lay still on the bed. Doctor Berger glanced at the monitoring equipment and noticed James' blood pressure was rising. She ordered a sedative to calm James down. The sedative and Angie's offer to call the admiral soon took effect and James was asleep.

"What set him off?" Dr. Berger asked.

"He's worried about his son. I really can't tell you any more than that."

"I suppose it's related to the shootout here in the hospital?" Dr. Berger questioned. Angie just shrugged her shoulders. "Well, see you don't upset him again. You've got to keep him still. Another episode like that could rip lose his internal stitches."

"Yes, Doctor Berger. I understand."

Dr. Berger grabbed the chart she had dropped on the floor and left the room. Angie, also worried about Zach and as she had promised, grabbed her cell phone, punched in Admiral Hadley's number, and waited.

"Naval Intelligence, Admiral Hadley. May I help you?"

"Admiral Hadley, this is Angie Templeton."

"Angie, I wasn't expecting a call from you. What can I do for you?"

"Admiral, I have tried Zach's SAT phone and cell phone and I can't reach him on either phone. Have you heard from him?"

"No, Angie. I haven't been able to reach him either. Are you worried about something specific?"

"Zach called several hours earlier and insisted I get two names from his father. His father was not very lucid at the time, but he gave Zach one name. His father is doing better. Just a few minutes ago he asked me if I had heard from Zach. I told him I got a text from Zach saying he was going to New York City. When his father heard that, he went ballistic. He said we had to warn Zach, and he tried twice to get out of bed. The doctor had to sedate him. Admiral, is there something I should be worried about?"

Angie paced back and forth in James' room waiting for the Admiral to answer, becoming more concerned with every passing second. "Admiral, are you still there?"

"Yes, Angie, I'm still here. I'll keep trying to reach Zach. I will call you the instant I have any news."

"I'll be waiting. Call me either way, Admiral." Angie continued to pace back and forth, more worried than before the call.

Chapter Fifteen

Second Lieutenant Alvin Davis, the Duty Watch Officer, ran up to the CIA Director's office door and rapped loudly three times.

"Enter," CIA Director Sandberg called out.

Second Lieutenant Davis yanked the office door open, rushed over to the Director's desk, and announced, "Sir, there's a resource named Rojas on line one. He says he needs to speak to you.."

"Thank you, Mister Davis. That'll be all," Director Sandberg said as he grabbed the phone and punched the blinking line.

"Sotero, the duty watch officer informed me that you needed to talk to me."

"You bet, Director," Sotero Rojas answered. "After Porter got out of the cab and rushed into the general aviation terminal, we repositioned and watched departures from the duty runway as you instructed."

"What did you see?" Director Sandberg asked.

"Over the next hour, there were three private, business jets that departed."

"Were you able to get the tail numbers?"

"Yes, Sir, we got all three."

"Read them to me," Director Sandberg said, grabbing a pad of paper and a pen. Rojas read the tail numbers to the Director as he wrote them down.

"Anything else?" Director Sandberg asked.

"No, that's it. What do we do now?"

"Go back to your regular assignments. Drop by Porter's apartment occasionally to see if he has returned."

"Will do, Sir."

Director Sandberg hung up the phone, quickly picked it up again, and dialed Admiral Hadley's number.

"Naval Intelligence, Petty Officer Sanders. May I help you?"

"CIA Director Sandberg calling for Admiral Hadley."

"Sorry, Sir, Admiral Hadley is at lunch."

"Is he in the building?"

Petty Officer Sanders looked up at the checkout board and answered, "He's not marked out on the board. So, he should be in the building, Sir."

"Well, then, go find him and have him call me. Now, Petty Officer Sanders. It's urgent," Director Sandberg yelled into the phone.

"Yes, Sir. Right away, Sir."

Petty Officer Sanders dropped the phone like it was on fire and rushed off in search of Admiral Hadley.

Alternate Safe Facility - Defender Two
Location - Classified

Admiral Hadley sat in the cafeteria munching on an egg salad sandwich and potato chips. A large, half-empty fountain drink sat beside the plate. He picked up the sandwich and took a bite. About to stuff a couple of potato chips in his mouth, he stopped when he saw Radioman Second Class Donald Sanders push the cafeteria door open and rush into the room.

"This can't be good," he muttered to himself, recognizing the Duty Watch Stander. "Yes, Petty Officer Sanders," Admiral Hadley said as Petty Officer Sanders stopped in front of the table and stood at attention.

"Sir, CIA Director Sandberg called. He said you are to call him back immediately," Petty Officer Sanders advised, handing the Admiral a pink, phone message slip.

"Can't it wait," Admiral Hadley grumbled, annoyed and still chewing the bite of sandwich.

"I don't think so, Sir. He said it was urgent. He was yelling, Sir."

"That's not unusual. He's always yelling," Admiral Hadley complained, wiping his mouth with a napkin. He stuffed one more bite of the sandwich in his mouth then pushed his chair back, stood up, and started to gather up the remains of his unfinished lunch.

"I'll get that, Sir," Petty Officer Sanders offered.

"Thank you, Petty Officer Sanders. I'll keep the drink," Admiral Hadley said as he grabbed the cup and headed for the door. Petty Officer Sanders followed the admiral toward the cafeteria exit, dropping the unfinished lunch items in the garbage can before stepping through the door.

With his large drink in hand, Admiral Hadley hurried back to his temporary office in the alternate safe facility. Once inside the office, he set the drink on a coaster and dropped the phone message beside the phone. Seated in his chair, he punched in the number the duty watch stander had scribbled on the message slip and waited.

"CIA Director Sandberg."

"James, this is Hadley. The duty watch stander said you called and said it was urgent."

"You bet it's urgent," Director Sandberg exclaimed. "Our undercover resource in Ecuador called earlier and said he saw Porter rush out of his apartment building and jump into a taxi. He and his partner trailed the taxi to Quito's airport. Porter got out of the taxi and entered the general aviation terminal."

"Do they have any idea where he was headed?" Admiral Hadley asked.

"No, his movement was sudden and unexpected. I instructed them to park their vehicle where they could observe the duty runway and report the tail numbers of any private, business jets that departed."

"I assume they reported back something or you wouldn't have called me."

"Yes, he called back and reported the tail numbers of three aircraft that departed over the next hour. Unfortunately, they couldn't tell me which aircraft Porter might have been on."

"I'm guessing you used your authority to get the flight plans of those aircraft."

"Yes, I did. I instructed the FAA to monitor those aircraft to be certain they follow the flight plans they submitted to flight services."

"Has it been long enough to hear anything?"

"I haven't heard as yet. Hang on, Admiral. I'll call and see if I can prod them a little." Director Sandberg put Admiral Hadley on hold, punched an unused line, and called another number. Admiral Hadley waited, listening to the sound of soft jazz coming from the receiver. Admiral Hadley, getting impatient, began to drum his fingers on his desk. A full ten minutes passed before Director Sandberg came back on the line.

"Admiral, I have updated information. One of the tail numbers filed a flight plan for a direct flight from Quito to Panama City. Around an hour into the flight, it disappeared from the radar screen. They think it descended while making a left turn, but they can't be certain. The transponder signal disappeared and it's not answering radio calls."

"Can we assume Porter is on the aircraft that disappeared?"

"Yes, I think that's a safe assumption. The other two aircraft are on course to their filed destinations, and they have been contacted. They advise they have no one onboard matching Porter's description. To be certain, those two aircraft will be met and searched when they reach their destination."

"If Porter is on the aircraft that disappeared, can we determine where he may be headed?"

"Well, we know Porter cannot enter the United States from an international flight even if it is private. Given that the aircraft appeared to turn left, the logical destination is somewhere in Mexico, but it's not possible to pin it down any closer than that."

"I believe we have to conclude he is headed for the US. If he is onboard the missing aircraft, and it lands somewhere in Mexico, he will not have any trouble crossing the border. You know the issues, James. My ninety-year-old mother could sneak across the border wearing a bright yellow vest while singing 'Yankee Doodle Dandy'."

"Sadly, I agree Admiral. I will put out the word to the border patrol for all the good it will do. You know the hatred Porter has toward Mister Templeton. I think you had better warn him."

"I absolutely agree, James. I had a call from his wife earlier. Neither one of us has been able to reach him, but I will keep trying. Keep me apprised if you hear anything else."

"Will do, Admiral," Director Sandberg answered as he ended the call.

Admiral Hadley tapped the hook switch on the phone and quickly punched in the number for the SAT phone Zach Templeton was carrying, letting it ring twenty-five times before giving up. He tapped the hook switch again and punched in the number for Zach's cell phone. Immediately he heard the carrier's notification that the cell phone customer was unavailable.

Left with no other options he punched in the number for Zach's wife, hoping she might have heard from him.

Copper Queen Community Hospital
100 East 5th Street
Douglas, Arizona

Angie Templeton, exhausted from the day's tension, snored softly, curled up in the recliner pushed into the corner of

James Templeton's hospital room. James' wife Martha was sitting in another recliner that had been pushed into James' room, unsuccessfully trying to read a book Angie had purchased for her at the hospital's gift shop. Every few minutes she looked up to see how James was doing. The incident when he had become agitated and had tried to get out of bed had caused a serious setback. Under Dr. Berger's orders, the nurses were checking his vital signs every fifteen minutes. Dr. Berger, worried that James' attempts to get out of bed had set off his internal bleeding again, was considering taking him back into surgery.

Angie's cell phone, lying on the windowsill, rang and began to dance around. Angie struggled out of the recliner and answered the phone before it could awaken James. "This is Angie," she whispered into the phone.

"Angie, this is Admiral Hadley."

"Hang on Admiral," Angie said. She poked Martha's shoulder and said, "It's the Admiral. I'm going to take this out in the hall." She pushed the door open, stepped out into the hallway, and nudged the door closed.

"Okay, go ahead, Admiral."

"First off, Angie, I haven't heard from Zach, and I'm afraid I've got some additional information that is of great concern. I just heard from the CIA Director that an undercover operative saw Frank Porter take a taxi to the Airport in Quito, Ecuador, and rush into the general aviation terminal. Three private jets departed over the next hour. Now, one of them has disappeared from radar. The Director and I are reasonably certain he is heading for the states."

"Do you think he is coming after Zach?" Angie asked.

"We don't know that for certain, but you know Zach's history with that stinking rat. That makes me a little worried."

"Yes, I remember, Admiral. If it hadn't been for Zach's dad, Porter would have killed him. What can we do Admiral?"

"We? What do you mean we?" Admiral Hadley asked.

"Well, Admiral, when Zach's dad found out Zach left Tucson headed from New York City he went ballistic. He tried to get out of bed twice. Now, the doctor thinks he may be bleeding internally again. It's obvious he knows something we don't, Admiral."

"I nearly lost Zach once. I will not allow that to happen again. We have to do something!" Angie asserted.

"I agree, Angie, but I don't…."

Angie interrupted and said, "Admiral, I know where Zach is headed and I will warn him." The Admiral tried to interrupt Angie, but she talked over the top of him. Sensing it was futile to argue, he shut up and just listened as Angie explained exactly what she needed and what would happen.

"Are you kidding?" Admiral Hadley exclaimed during a lull in Angie's explanation. "There's no way I can do that."

"Come on, Admiral. I know you can make things happen. Recently, Zach responded when you asked him to help. He risked his life and lost his company, if you remember. Now, I'm begging for your help." Angie waited for Admiral Hadley to respond. Silence. "Admiral Hadley, did you hear me?"

"Yes, I heard you. I'm trying to decide what to do. I can't believe I'm saying this. I will make the arrangements as you requested, but only if you agree to call me if you have the slightest difficulty. I'll text you the time and place."

"Thanks, Admiral," Angie said as she ended the call and dropped the cell phone in her bag. She pulled the door open and walked back into the room. She walked over beside the recliner where Martha sat, squatted down, and whispered into her ear.

"Absolutely not," Martha exclaimed, a look of horror spreading across her face. "That's crazy. You can't!"

Angie held her finger up to her lips and spoke quietly, "I have to, Martha. There's no other way."

They argued back and forth for several minutes. Finally, Martha, unable to change Angie's mind, gave in, promising not to say a word to James about what Angie intended to do.

Angie turned and started toward the door, but noticed James was awake and motioning for her to come over to the bed. She walked over to the bed. James reached up, grabbed Angie's arm, and pulled her down toward the bed. With great effort, he pulled himself up and whispered in her ear. She smiled and kissed him on the forehead. James let go of her arm and flopped back onto the bed.

About to exit the room, Angie turned and said, "For an old man, you're pretty smart."

In true James Templeton style, he smiled, rolled his hand upward, and gave her a thumbs-up signal. Angie returned the signal and slipped out the door.

Chapter Sixteen

Admiral Hadley sat at his desk shaking his head, uncertain why he had agreed to Angie's requests. The Admiral replayed in his mind the plan as she had laid it out. He had promised Angie he would provide what she needed, and he was a man of his word. He had convinced Zach to get involved. Admiral Hadley felt personally responsible so he would do whatever was necessary. Unable to come up with a single better alternative, he reached for the phone.

"Davis Monthan Air Force Base. Airman Perez, may I help you?"

"This is Rear Admiral Charles Hadley, Director of Naval Intelligence. I need to speak to General Hart. It's urgent."

"May I tell him what this is about?"

"Sorry, it's classified. This is time-sensitive. I really need to speak to the general now."

"I'll see if he is available. Please hold."

Admiral Hadley waited impatiently. He stood up and stretched, pulling the phone toward the edge of the desk. He reached out and caught the phone as it started to tumble off the desk. The Admiral set the phone back on the desk and dropped back into his chair, continuing to wait.

"I'll connect you to the General," Airman Perez announced.

"Admiral Hadley, to what do I owe the pleasure of your phone call?" Brigadier General Richard Hart, Commanding Officer of Davis Monthan Air Force Base asked.

"General Hart, I am investigating the detonation of the nuclear device in Sacramento. What I am about to tell you is classified at the highest level. This must remain only between you and me."

"Agreed, Admiral. Go on."

Admiral Hadley spent several minutes explaining to General Hart exactly what he needed, its importance, and adding that prompt action was crucial. General Hart listened carefully to Admiral Hadley's desperate plea for assistance, interrupting only once for further explanation.

"I don't know, Admiral," General Hart responded. "What you are asking for is beyond standard protocol. Way beyond, I might add."

"I understand, General, but these are not standard times. If we do not contain this threat, violation of protocol will be the least of your worries," Admiral Hadley insisted.

"Admiral, I don't like the threatening tone of that."

"Sorry, General, I didn't mean to threaten you. I shouldn't tell you this, but we suspect more devices are hidden somewhere. In what cities or when they might be detonated we simply do not know."

"Why haven't we been notified of the threat?"

"The panic is exploding and is threatening to turn into full-blown anarchy. If this information were to get out, the panic that resulted would overwhelm law enforcement's ability to contain it. Law and order would disintegrate. The President himself ordered that information classified as need-to-know. General, can you help me?"

"Well, the 355th Air Force Support Squadron has the required resources to accommodate your request."

"How soon can you get it there?"

"If I scramble a team immediately and we don't have any mechanical issues, it can be there in forty-five minutes. Will that be acceptable, Admiral?"

"Yes, that will be acceptable. Thank you General. I appreciate your taking my call and for agreeing to help."

"I hope you round up the vermin responsible for the cowardly act. Keep me in the loop if you can."

"I'll do my best, General. Thanks again," Admiral Hadley said as he disconnected the call.

General Hart punched an unused line and buzzed the duty phone watch. "Airman Perez, get the 355th Support Squadron commander on the line immediately."

One minute later the phone on General Hart's desk rang. "Major Nesbit, Sir. How may I help you?"

General Hart explained what he needed and ordered the resources that Admiral Hadley had requested to be on-station in no more than forty-five minutes.

"General, if I may speak freely?"

"Yes, Major Nesbit, go ahead, but make it quick."

"Sir, what you are asking for violates protocol. I cannot be respon…."

General Hart cut the Major off, shouting into the phone, "Major, I will take full responsibility. You are wasting time. I want the team scrambled now! Do I make myself clear?"

"I think this is wrong, General."

"Duly noted, Major. Now, unless you want to spend the rest of your career as an airman recruit swabbing decks and painting rocks, I suggest you follow the orders you have been given! Understood!"

"Yes, Sir. As you ordered, Sir."

"By the way, Major Nesbit, you now have forty-three minutes," General Hart barked.

Back in Admiral Hadley's office, he hurriedly typed a short message on his cell phone and pressed send."

The message simply said, "45 minutes - be there"

22,000 Feet, Seventy-Five Miles Southeast
Aeropuerto Internacional del Norte
Monterey, Mexico

Anthony Sterling glanced at his watch. According to his ear-lier calculations, he should be approaching the point where he needed to radio in and get clearance to enter controlled airspace. He reached up to the instrument panel and switched on the transponder and the radio comm unit. Eas-ing back on the throttles, he slowed the Learjet to three hundred eighty-five knots, in preparation for entering the airport's approach pattern.

Anthony switched the radio to the airport's approach control frequency, identified his aircraft, and requested per-mission to land. Approach control requested he descend to eleven thousand feet and reduce speed to two hundred fifty-five knots for a vector-based approach around the south side of Monterey's main airport. Approach control requested he turn left to heading three-zero-one to remain south of Gen-eral Mariano Escobedo International Airport. Once past the main airport, approach control ordered Anthony to turn right to heading zero-two-five. Anthony complied with ap-proach control's request.

A few minutes later, five miles from his destination air-port, Anthony had the Learjet lined up on Runway Zero-Two. He reported the airport in sight and was granted final permission to land. He flared the sleek aircraft as it passed over the threshold of the runway, pulling the nose of the aircraft up, allowing the wheels to kiss the runway surface with hardly a bump.

Anthony taxied the aircraft to the north end of the runway where he was met by a beat-up, mustard-colored pickup with a 'Follow Me' sign mounted on the roof of the cab. He followed the pickup onto the taxiway toward the general aviation parking ramp. Stopping just past the parking area's entrance, an arm protruded from the pickup's passen-ger window and pointed toward the parking area. Anthony turned right into the parking area and selected an empty spot at the end of the first row of aircraft.

He shut down the engines, hurried to the forward exit door, let the stairs down, and handed his passport to the immigration official that stood waiting beside the aircraft.

"Mister Emanuel Olivares, what is your business here in Monterrey, Senor?" the immigration official asked in Spanish.

"I'm here on an emergency," Anthony lied, answering in Spanish. "My mother is quite ill. I'm hoping to get there before she passes." The passport Anthony had handed the official was a fake, but it was flawless. It was one of a dozen fake passports he had taken with him when he fled the United States after his earlier plot had failed. Each of the fake passports indicated a European country of origin where Spanish was the national language because Anthony spoke fluent Spanish.

"I am sorry to hear that, Senor Olivares. Will you need transportation?"

"No, I will not. I have arranged a limo. It should arrive soon."

"How long will your stay be?"

"Hopefully no more than a week. Can I leave the Learjet parked here and will it be secure?"

"Yes, you can leave it parked where it is. This area is very secure. You can lock the aircraft. I assure you it will not be bothered."

"Thank you. I have a few things I need to grab from inside then I will be on my way."

"I hope your mother gets better soon, Senor Olivares," the immigration official remarked as he took a small stamp from his pocket and pressed it on a blank page of the passport. "When you go, stop in the terminal at the immigration desk and tell the woman there Juan has cleared you. She will recognize my stamp." Juan handed the passport back to Anthony, turned on his heels, and headed for another private plane just arriving in the parking area.

Anthony climbed back onboard the aircraft and busied himself in the cockpit wiping down all surfaces he might have touched. In the passenger cabin he wiped down the seat belt, armrests, and back of the seat. He retrieved his weapon from its hiding place, wiped it down, and dropped it in the lavatory trash slot. He hated discarding a great weapon that had served him well. He could easily replace the weapon, and it was not worth the risk of trying to exit through immigration with a hidden weapon. Walking up and down the aisle twice, he looked for anything he might have brought onboard that could identify him. Satisfied he had left nothing behind, he exited the aircraft, closed the forward exit door, and secured it.

As the immigration official had instructed, Anthony presented his passport to a skinny, dark-haired woman seated at the immigration desk inside the terminal and told her Juan had cleared him. The woman shuffled through the pages in the passport until she saw Juan's stamp. She pressed the 'CLEARED' stamp on the page next to it and handed the passport back to Anthony. Anthony grabbed the passport, hurried through the terminal, and stepped out into the bright sunlight. He slipped on his sunglasses and waited for his transportation.

Ten minutes passed. Anthony began to get concerned. Finally, a black Lincoln Towncar sped around the passenger pickup circle and pulled up to the curb in front of Anthony, squealing to a stop. A heavy-set man with dark skin jumped out of the car and lifted the trunk lid.

"Mister Olivares?" he questioned.

"Yes, that's me."

"Sorry, I am a little late. My son was sick at school and I had to pick him up and take him home. My name is Julio. I will take you wherever you wish to go."

Anthony tossed his bag into the trunk and slammed the lid. "Let's get going, Julio. I'm in a hurry."

Julio opened the door for Anthony and waited for him to climb into the back seat. Julio slammed the rear door, hurried around to the driver's door, and wedged his large frame into the front seat. He started the engine and leaned over the seat. "Where is it you would like to go, Senor Olivares?"

"Villas De San Miguel. Just across the border from Laredo. Do you know where that is?"

"Si, Senor. I know where that is." Julio answered as he roared away from the pickup area, and took the first exit out of the airport, turning left onto Mexico Highway 85.

"I'm really in a hurry. There's a one hundred dollar bonus if you can get me there quickly."

"Si, Senor. I can do that," Julio answered, his eyes lighting up at the thought of a big fat bonus. "Here we drive as fast as we think is safe. If you pay for a fine if I get one, I will get you there in less than two hours."

"Agreed," Anthony said, leaning his head against the seat back, intending to take a short nap.

As promised, one hour and fifty minutes later, Julio shouted at Anthony, "Senor Olivares, we are approaching Villas De San Miguel. Where exactly do you wish me to drop you?"

"It's on Calle Santa Cecilla Street. When you get on that street I'll point out the house." Julio located the street sign, turned left onto the street, and drove slowly for two blocks until Anthony pointed toward a large house in the middle of the block. Julio stopped, popped the trunk, and hauled his large frame out of the driver's seat. He opened the door and waited for Anthony to climb out. Anthony retrieved his bag from the trunk and handed Julio a sizeable stack of bills. Julio's eyes grew large as he excitedly counted out the bills.

"Senor Olivares, you are very kind. If you need a ride again, please call me. I will come immediately."

Anthony turned without answering and headed for the front door of the house. The door opened before he could press the doorbell. "Senor Sterling, we have been expecting you. Come in."

"Don't use that name," Anthony snapped. "You don't know who might be listening. My name is Sandor Carrero."

"Welcome, Senor Carrero. My name is Angelino Ochao," the man said with a wink. "Can I get you something to eat or drink?"

"I don't have time. Just a bottle of water," Anthony said as he withdrew a different passport from behind the lining of his bag. He slipped the passport in the name of Olivares behind the lining and pressed the lining's Velcro closure shut. "Is the vehicle ready?"

"Yes, it is ready. It is parked in the garage," Ochao answered.

"Good," Anthony replied. "I'll be on my way then."

The man named Ochao showed Anthony the way to the garage. Anthony dropped his bag on the floor behind the vehicle's driver's seat while Ochao opened the garage door. Anthony started the panel van's engine. A sign on the side of the van read 'Carrero Fresh Flowers'. A half-dozen large tubs full of fresh-cut flowers sat in the back of the van. Anthony drove the van out of the garage, turned left onto Calle Santa Cecilla Street, and headed for his next destination.

A short time later, Anthony drove slowly down Highway MEX-2 and joined the line of vehicles waiting to cross the border into the United States. Anthony had chosen the small border crossing north of Laredo because one of the border patrol agents had a weakness for drugs and owed his dealer a large sum of money. The border patrol agent had been threatened with exposure of his habit if he did not agree to help.

Anthony inched along, the sixth car in line waiting to cross the border. When he moved up to number two in line, the border agent looked up and recognized the van he had been instructed to watch for. The car in front passed through the checkpoint and the border agent waved Anthony forward. Anthony handed the agent a packing list for the flowers sitting in the back of the van. The agent pretended to read the list, handed the paper back, and waved Anthony through.

Anthony, driving carefully and five miles-per-hour under the posted limit, drove a short distance on Texas Highway 20, turned left onto the interstate access ramp, and merged into northbound traffic on Interstate Highway 35. He drove north for fifteen miles and exited the interstate onto Texas Highway 83. Three miles south of Catarina, Texas, he turned off the highway onto a rutted dirt road. Driving slowly and dodging many, large potholes, Anthony cursed the unmaintained road. He continued driving west for three-quarters of a mile, pulling onto a bumpy lane leading to a rundown shack. Behind the dilapidated shack stood a metal Quonset hut type structure with large doors on both ends.

Anthony angled his vehicle toward the front of the shack and flashed his lights twice and waited. He waited for the signal to proceed. A small light on the porch flashed twice. He pulled up beside the shack and turned off the van's engine.

Air Force C-20H
39,000 feet over East Central Texas

An Air Force C-20H, a militarized version of a private, business jet aircraft, was flying at five hundred seventy knots, just below its top speed. By special, high-level clearance, the aircraft had been assigned a direct, increased speed flight plan straight to its destination.

An hour earlier the military aircraft had spent less than ten minutes on the ground at a small municipal airport. The frantic call to scramble the jet and its crew had come so suddenly there had been no time to stock the galley.

Technical Sergeant William Cox, the communication system operator and duty flight attendant, rummaged through the items left in the galley from a previous flight. Sergeant Cox was a small, thin man with watery blue eyes and sandy colored hair. A cloud of light brown freckles spread across his face. He hailed from Conroe, Texas, and no matter how hard he tried, he could not shake his southern Texas drawl, which was a constant source of amusement for his Air Force buddies.

"Hey, ya'll.," he shouted to the lone passenger sitting in the first row of the cabin. "All that's left here in the galley are some slightly cool sodas."

"That's fine," the passenger replied. "I prefer my soda warm. Is there anything else there? Any snacks of any kind?"

"Sorry. There's absolutely nothing," Sergeant Cox answered. He made his way forward carrying the soda and a clear plastic glass in his hand. He handed the soda and the glass to the passenger and apologized, "Sorry, ain't no ice neither."

"That's okay," the passenger answered, setting the glass aside. "I'll just drink it from the can."

"If'n ya'll need anything, just holler at me," Sergeant Cox said as he continued forward to take care of his other duties.

The passenger took a few sips of the warm soda, placed the can in a cup holder, and, lulled by the constant drone of the engines, drifted off into a fitful sleep, deeply concerned over the upcoming gamble that awaited.

Chapter Seventeen

Rundown Shack
Three Miles SW of Catarina, Texas

At first glance, the dilapidated shack, weather-beaten and in disrepair, appeared to be abandoned. The Quonset hut behind the old shack had been artificially aged to look as old as the shack. Except for Anthony's van parked beside the shack no other vehicles were in sight.

Anthony walked up onto the porch, stepping sideways to avoid the broken and missing floorboards. The door, window broken and a tattered curtain flapping in the wind, stood partially open. The door screeched, scraping the floor, as he pushed it open and walked inside. Two steps inside, Anthony stopped, taken aback by the scene of neglect. The shack appeared even more rundown and unkempt on the inside. Had it not been for the porch light signal, Anthony would have sworn he was in the wrong place. Dust and trash swirled across the floor, disturbed by the wind blowing through the missing back door. All but one window was broken out, glass scattered across the floor. A jumble of rusted cans sat scattered on shelves in the corner of the room in what Anthony assumed had long ago been a kitchen. Anthony did not see the tiny, disguised camera, nestled between some old pots and pans sitting on the top shelf, pointing directly at him.

In a hidden bunker twelve feet below Anthony's feet, two men watched his every move on a closed-circuit video display. The men spoke in hushed whispers, "Is that him?" the taller of the two men asked.

The shorter man lifted a cell phone out of his pocket, pulled up a photo, and held it up for the other man to see. "Looks like him. What do you think?"

"I believe it is him," the taller man said. "Go tell Matteo, then take your gun and go greet our guest. I will let him know you are coming." The shorter man pulled a large-caliber semiautomatic from behind his back and started up a spiral staircase set against the far wall. The taller man pressed an intercom switch and said, "Sir, do not move. You are being watched."

Startled by the sudden sound, Anthony flinched involuntarily and looked around, trying to identify its source.

"Set your bag on the floor and hold your hands out. Do as you're told and you will not be hurt."

Anthony complied, holding his hands out to his side, palms up.

"Sir, the cabinet on the north wall will move. Do not be alarmed and do not move," the taller man instructed. A stocky man of average height wearing faded jeans, a dirty work shirt, and a sweat-stained cowboy hat walked up behind the taller man and looked over his shoulder at the video display.

"That's Sterling," the stocky man said. "I know him. He's okay."

"To be safe, I sent Gordy up to check him out."

From the bunker below, the two men watched as the cabinet slid sideways away from the wall and Gordy stepped into the room with his semiautomatic pointed at Anthony's chest.

"Mister Sterling is it? Do you have any weapons?" Gordy asked.

"Yes, I'm Sterling, and no I do not have any weapons."

"Toss me the bag."

Anthony picked up his bag and tossed it over to the man as the man had instructed. Gordy threw the bag aside and walked over to where Anthony stood.

"If you don't mind," Gordy said, slipping the semiautomatic behind his back and gesturing for Anthony to raise his hands.

Anthony held his arms out to the side while Gordy patted him down. "He's okay," Gordy called out.

"Let's go join our guest," the stocky man said in the bunker below. The stocky man nudged the tall man toward the spiral stairs against the wall. They climbed up the spiral stairs and stepped out into the room.

Instantly recognizing the stocky man as he entered the room, Anthony walked over and grabbed the man's beefy hand, pumping it hard. "Matteo, I didn't expect to see you here."

"Well, after the unfortunate incident in Sacramento, everyone is a bit jumpy. I decided to hide here for a while in case I needed to make a quick departure."

"Yeah, that stupid fool Ahadi wasn't supposed to detonate the device. We were going to use it for leverage."

"Nobody has seen him, so we have to assume he activated it by accident when he connected the triggering device. If not connected exactly according to the instructions, it could have triggered early."

"Well, he should have been more careful. He got exactly what he deserved," Anthony sneered.

"I don't imagine he felt a thing," Matteo remarked. "It surprised me when I heard you were coming. If the authorities find you, you will go to prison. What is so important to bring you here during this crisis?"

"Unfinished business. I have a few loose ends to tie up and, if I am fortunate, some long overdue payback."

"Let's go downstairs where it's more comfortable. Gordy, go put Mister Sterling's van in the Quonset."

Anthony dug the van's keys out of his pocket and threw them to Gordy then followed Matteo down the spiral stairs into the underground bunker. Gordy went out the back door, drove the van around to the back of the Quonset hut, and parked it inside. Back inside the shack, he picked up an old broom leaning against the wall and swirled it around the dusty floor to obliterate any footprints they had made. He leaned the broom back against the wall, pulled the cabinet back to its normal position, and descended the stairs.

Anthony, surprised and impressed, took in the brightly lit underground bunker, comfortable furniture arranged against the walls. Two small bedrooms opened off the east and west walls. A well-appointed kitchen ran the entire length of the south wall. A large pantry built into the south wall accommodated many shelves stocked with a variety of non-perishable food items. A large freezer at the back of the pantry contained frozen meat and various other frozen items. A wide doorway in the north wall led to a room containing two desks and several large maps taped to the walls. Sitting against one wall, a large glass case displayed an extensive array of weapons.

"I am impressed," Anthony remarked. "I would never have guessed there was anything here except an old, run-down shack. It must have cost a lot of money to build this bunker."

"The cost was not important," Matteo explained. "We often house a number of very important clients here as they make their way north. They pay whatever we ask. We are prepared for almost anything. We have enough food and water to remain hidden here for several months."

"It certainly is well camouflaged."

"We worked long and hard to make it look that way. We knew you were coming when you were still a mile away. There is an elaborate system of motion sensors and hidden cameras around the property. As you would expect, our clients pay dearly to feel safe. We guarantee it."

"The old Quonset hut out back looks like it's been here forever," Anthony added.

"It is only two years old. A special chemical was applied to age the metal and make it appear old and rusty," Matteo replied. "But I assure you it would take days if not weeks to break into it. It is lined with hardened steel."

"Is that where the plane is housed?"

"Yes, and other vehicles as well."

"Is the plane fueled and ready to go?"

"Yes, it is ready, but can you fly without a flight plan?" Matteo asked. Not being a pilot, he did not understand what was required.

"No, a flight plan is not required when flying in clear weather. If I avoid controlled airspace around the large airports along the way, I won't have to get clearance until I reach my destination. What exactly will I be flying?"

"It's a Beechcraft Model D50, Twin Bonanza," Matteo answered. "It is fifty years old, but do not worry. It has been meticulously restored and has brand new engines and a top-of-the-line avionics package. The one hundred eighty gallon fuel tanks have been increased to two hundred fifty gallons. The mechanic said that should give you a range of twenty-four hundred to twenty-eight hundred miles, depending on flying conditions."

"Great, and the price?" Anthony questioned.

"For you, old friend, a special price of only two hundred grand," Matteo answered.

Expecting a higher number, Anthony quickly agreed. He opened a zippered compartment in his bag and pulled out twenty wrapped stacks of one hundred-dollar bills containing one hundred bills each and handed them to Matteo.

"How about something to eat before you leave," Matteo suggested.

"I would like that," Anthony answered.

Matteo opened two cans of soup, dumped the contents into a saucepan, and set it on the stove to heat up. He grabbed two bowls from a cabinet and set them on a small dining table along with saltine crackers and several bottles of water. The two men ate their soup and crackers in silence.

"I need to get started, Matteo," Anthony said, rising from the table.

"Safe flying, Anthony," Matteo said, holding out extra bottles of water for the trip.

Anthony took the offered bottles of water and followed Matteo to the far end of the map room and down a short tunnel. They climbed up a ladder at the end of the tunnel, emerging inside the Quonset hut. Matteo flipped on the interior lights, revealing a white Beechcraft Bonanza with a red stripe down its fuselage.

Gordy, climbing up the ladder right behind them, exited the Quonset hut through a rear door and ran around to the front of the Quonset hut. He quickly unlocked and removed the hardened-steel padlock from the center of the doors and swung the double doors open. With Anthony inside steering, Gordy and Matteo slowly pushed the Beechcraft through the open doorway, using extra caution as the Beechcraft Bonanza's forty-five foot, three inch wingspan left less than a foot and a half clearance on each side. Safely through the doorway, Gordy and Matteo pushed the Bonanza to the edge of the gravel runway.

Anthony set the parking brake and started the engines. He set the engines at fast idle and waited for them to warm up. Glancing left into the southern sky, he verified no inbound traffic approached. He released the parking brake, pushed the throttles forward, and guided the Bonanza onto the hardpan, caliche runway. Lined up on the center of the runway, he pushed the throttles all the way forward. Clouds of dust and small pebbles billowed out from behind the Bonanza as it raced down the runway and lifted into the sky.

Anthony retracted the landing gear and turned right to a heading of zero-five-three while climbing to thirteen thousand feet. He would fly direct to Richmond Virginia, skirting all the major airports, then a final leg along the coast at zero-three-zero to his final destination, Old Bridge Airport, southeast of East Brunswick, New Jersey.

Gulfstream 550
33,000 Feet Above Southern Maryland

Kip Johnson, piloting the Gulfstream G550 on a heading of zero-eight-four, keyed the passenger cabin intercom, "I'm sorry, Zach, there will be a thirty-minute delay due to weather in the Newark area. We are currently in a holding pattern over Harrisonburg, Virginia. Once Air Traffic Control releases us, we will start our descent into the Newark area and should be on the ground twenty minutes after that."

Zach looked up from the magazine he was browsing and listened to Kip's announcement. "Just once, I'd like to fly somewhere without a delay of some kind," he groused, angrily stuffing the magazine back in the seat-back pocket. His knee throbbed from the earlier spill and a growing headache gnawed at the back of his neck.

Twenty minutes later the radio in the cockpit crackled to life, "November-four-six-Mike-Lima, weather around Newark has cleared. Turn right, heading zero-niner-niner, descend and maintain flight level two three."

"November-four-six-Mike-Lima, turn right, heading zero-niner-niner, descend and maintain flight level two-three, roger."

Kip thumbed the passenger cabin intercom button, "Okay, Zach, return to your seat if you're up and fasten your seat-belt. We have been cleared into the Newark area and are beginning our descent."

As the Gulfstream passed over Chesapeake Bay and crossed into southern Delaware, Approach Control called, "November-four-six-Mike-Lima, turn left heading zero-two-seven, descend and maintain five thousand."

Kip acknowledged Approach Control's instructions, steering the ordered heading and descending to five thousand feet.

Eleven minutes later Approach Control called with the final inbound approach vector, "November-four-six-Mike-Lima, turn right heading zero-three-niner, descend and maintain two thousand five hundred. Cleared to land Runway Four Left, altimeter two-niner-point-niner-seven."

Just as promised, twenty minutes after being released from the weather hold, Kip had the Gulfstream lined up for final approach to Newark Liberty International Airport, approaching from the south. The aircraft was flying just west of Newark Bay on a heading of zero-three-nine, lined up on the centerline of runway Four Left.

As the Gulfstream flared over the threshold of the runway, Kip eased back on the throttles to reduce the aircraft's speed. When the end of the runway and the horizon line converged, Kip pulled back on the control yoke, allowing the aircraft to settle smoothly onto the runway. He taxied the aircraft to the end of Runway Four Left and turned onto taxiway Zulu. At the intersection with taxiway Zulu-Six, he turned right into the general aviation area. An airport ramp service worker guided the aircraft to an open spot on the parking ramp. Kip set the parking brake and shut down the engines.

Zach was already out of his seat and standing at the front of the passenger cabin, waiting for Kip to open the exit door.

"Welcome to Newark International, Zach" Kip greeted, opening the door and extending the stairs.

"Thanks, Kip," Zach said. "I'm not certain when I will be back. I'll try to let you know if I get a chance."

"Okay, Zach, don't worry about it. I'm used to sitting around and waiting. I'll be here," Kip answered as he ducked back into the cockpit to finish the required paperwork.

Zach exited the aircraft, walked across the tarmac, and entered the terminal. He walked straight thru the terminal and stepped out into a slate gray overcast day. A steady rain began to fall as another shower passed over the airport. Zach ducked back under a covered waiting area, looking up and down the passenger pickup area. He fished his cell phone out of his pocket, intending to call the number of the livery service Admiral Hadley had suggested. The screen was dark.

He tapped the screen and pushed the power button but nothing happened. The phone's battery was completely dead. About to walk back inside the terminal in search of a phone, two black SUVs slid to a stop beside the covered waiting area.

The driver of first SUV lowered the passenger window and hollered, "Mister Templeton, get in." As soon as Zach scrambled inside the vehicle, the driver asked, "Where are we headed?"

"Two twenty-seven West Seventy-seventh Street, Uptown" Zach answered. "Do you know the quickest way into the city?"

"Sure do."

"Do you have the requested items?"

"Yes, sir, Mister Templeton," the driver replied, pointing at the glove box.

Zach opened the glove box and peered inside. "Perfect," he said as he lifted a Sig Sauer P365 9mm semiautomatic and four extra clips already loaded with ammunition out of the glove box. He carefully pulled the slide back, confirmed a round was in the chamber, verified the safety was on, and stuffed the semiautomatic behind his back.

The driver flipped on the emergency lights hidden behind the grill and roared away from the pickup area with the second SUV following close behind. With traffic diving out of the way, the SUVs turned right onto US Highway One, also called the Pulaski Skyway, then onto I-78 and through the Holland Tunnel into New York City.

The SUVs turned left onto Henry Hudson Parkway North, speeding north along the Hudson River, heading toward Uptown. Exiting from the parkway, the SUVs turned right onto Seventy-ninth Street, drove three blocks east, turned right onto Amsterdam Street, then two blocks south, finally turning right again onto Seventy-seventh Street. Before turning onto the final street, the SUVs had turned off their emergency lights. The black SUVs slid to a stop midblock in front of the twenty-story Larstrand Building.

Zach piled out of the SUV, gazing up at the luxury high-rise building in awe. A large sign in front of the building proclaimed the Larstrand offered the absolute finest of luxury living in New York's Upper West Side. The sign listed the exceptional amenities the building offered: an exclusive rooftop lounge, every apartment featured designer finishes, chef-grade appliances, and fireproof safes tucked into the walls of each master bedroom.

Zach leaned into the lead SUV's window and told the driver he didn't know how long he would be and to wait. As Zach turned and headed toward the building, the SUVs squealed away from the curb and sped off toward the building's visitor parking. Zach slipped his hand behind his back, feeling for the weapon hidden there. He took a deep breath and walked through the revolving lobby door, unsure what to expect.

227 West 77th Street
New York, New York

A short time before Zach's arrival a Whitehurst Plumbing van had pulled into the visitor parking area. Two men in dirty coveralls exited the van, grabbed tool bags, and had entered the building. The two men had walked up to the security guard and presented a work order for apartment 2002.

The security guard had argued with one of the men regarding access to the apartment, saying he had no record of any such request from the apartment's owner. One of the workmen leaned over the counter pointing at the work order with his left hand and with his right hand stuck the security guard with a hypodermic needle. The security guard went limp almost immediately. The two men shoved the unconscious security guard into a service closet behind the guard station. In their haste, the two men failed to notice the small droplets of blood on the floor.

One of the men ripped off his coveralls, revealing a security guard's uniform identical to the now unconscious security guard lying in the closet. The other man, using the ring of keys pulled from the security guard's belt, walked into the elevator, jabbed the master key into the penthouse access slot, and pushed the button for the twentieth floor.

After the elevator door slid open on the twentieth floor, the man walked over to apartment 2002 and pushed the doorbell.

"Who is it?" asked the owner's voice from the speaker beside the door.

"Whitehurst Plumbing," the man lied. "We received a work order for a plumbing issue."

"I didn't report any plumbing issues," the owner's voice protested.

"Well, you wouldn't have, sir. The request came from the floor below. We can only access the drain line from this floor. The apartment below is flooding. It's important. We need to get in to clear the issue."

"Wait a minute," the owner's voice said.

The man listened, hearing the security chain being removed and the sound of the deadbolt being withdrawn. As soon as the door opened a crack, the man pushed the door open and rushed into the apartment.

"What is the meaning of this," the owner yelled.

"The person who arranged for you to meet the powerful woman to further your plan wants to see you remain quiet."

"I don't know what you are talking about," the owner sputtered.

"Don't lie to me," the man warned, waving a gun in the owner's face. "The woman you met at the global warming meeting. The woman you went to the bar to talk too. The woman that provided you with access to certain elements. Does that ring any bells?"

"I still do not understand what you're talking about," the owner lied, hoping it would buy him some time. The man standing there shouting at him had no idea the owner had recently completed a concealed carry firearms training class, qualifying with a perfect score. He went nowhere on the streets of New York without his firearm. Having just returned to his apartment, the firearm was still safely hidden under his left arm. The owner faked a sneeze and slipped his hand into his jacket pretending to reach for a handkerchief. He pulled out his small Glock G42 .380 caliber Pocket Pistol and shot the man in the face.

The assailant, his brain turned to mush by the jacketed hollow point slug, collapsed onto the floor, his weapon clattering across the floor, ending up against the wall under a hall table. The apartment owner frightened out of his wits never really expected he would actually have to use his Glock. In a panic, he ran out of the apartment and slammed the door shut. He waited for the elevator to return from a lower floor. When the elevator door opened, he jumped in and pressed the button for the lobby.

When the elevator door opened on the ground floor, the man peeked out, noticing a security guard he did not recognize sitting at the desk. He ducked back inside and returned to his apartment. Shaking like a leaf, he had trouble inserting his key into the lock. After four tries, he managed to insert the key into the lock. He opened the door, entered the apartment, and pushed the door closed. The assailant he had shot a few minutes earlier lay still on the floor, a large pool of blood staining the carpet around his head. A large splatter of blood and brain matter streaked the wall beside the door.

The owner paced back and forth across the foyer, racking his brain for a way out of the calamity in which he found himself, growing more anxious with each pass across the foyer. Noticing the assailant's weapon under the hall table, he walked over to the hall table and bent down intending to pick up the weapon that had slid against the wall. Still shaking and nearly hysterical from the encounter, he leaned against the wall and slid down and sat on the floor. Paralyzed with fear, he sat there rocking forward and backward, banging against the wall.

Chapter Eighteen

99 Hudson Street
Jersey City, New Jersey

Anthony Sterling glanced up at the luxury high-rise building, impressed by the staggering wealth it represented. The building at Ninety-nine Hudson Street towered nearly nine hundred feet above Jersey City's streets, giving it unrivaled views of the Manhattan skyline and the New York Harbor. Located on New Jersey's Gold Coast, the luxury building redefined waterfront living. The tallest building in all of New Jersey, located only steps from the Exchange Place PATH station and Paulus Hook Ferry, it provided a short commute into Manhattan.

Anthony was there to meet his one and only remaining associate in the US, Henry Tang. Of Asian descent, Henry had inherited his enormous wealth from his import tycoon father, Xiong Tang. Henry, an only child, had been given an American name, but had spent most of his early, formative years in Tianjin, a coastal city in northern China. He learned early that his enormous wealth and influence shielded him from the consequences of his lavish lifestyle.

Loud, opinionated, and cruel, Henry Tang dismissed anyone less fortunate than himself. Wealthy and pampered from birth, Henry had developed a self-centered and demanding character. When his father died at the early age of fifty-four, Henry did not shed a single tear. He was secretly glad because his father's vast empire became his.

Although most of his father's wealth came from America, Henry, like many ultra-rich non-Americans who prospered under America's free enterprise system, loathed America and, especially, America's working-class. He would fly into wild fits of rage whenever he did not get exactly what he wanted.

Years earlier, Anthony had met Henry Tang at a lavish party for political and foreign dignitaries. Anthony saw Henry and his vast shipping empire as a valuable source for smuggling desired items into the country. Using his former position in the FBI, Anthony had provided cover for many of the less than legal aspects of Henry's shipping empire. Anthony knew exactly how to manipulate and control Henry with false praise and adoration.

The large sums of money Henry flashed and spread around at parties and the lavish clubs he frequented, had garnered him an extensive array of contacts, many from the sleazy and unscrupulous underbelly of New York City. Anthony's current need for those unscrupulous contacts precipitated his visit. Anthony needed to make use of those contacts to locate a Mr. Zach Templeton and make him pay. His hired assassin had failed, so he needed Henry's extensive array of contacts to locate Mr. Templeton and then he would inflict his desired vengeance himself.

Anthony walked across the lobby and stopped in front of the doorman and said, "Anthony Sterling to see Mister Henry Tang."

The doorman picked up the house phone and called Mr. Tang's penthouse. He turned away from Anthony, speaking softly into the phone. After hanging up the phone, he motioned for Anthony to follow him. The doorman slipped a key into the penthouse elevator's security lock, turned it, and motioned Anthony inside. Unprepared for the sudden feeling of heaviness, Anthony nearly collapsed as the high-speed elevator raced to the top floor of the building.

When the elevator door opened, Henry Tang was standing directly in front of the door with a large grin on his face. True to his Asian descent, Henry stood only five foot four inches tall in his bare feet. His very expensive custom-made shoes, containing three inch lifts, increased his height to five feet seven inches, still short by American standards.

His dark and close-set eyes were visible under a shock of long hair so black it cast a purple sheen in the daylight. His diminutive size bore no relationship whatsoever to his inclination toward violence as those foolish enough to cross him had found out. Xiong Tung, Henry's cousin, had made the costly mistake of joking about Henry's short stature in front of several of Henry's associates. That foolish blunder sent Xiong to the emergency room with a broken nose, a broken arm, two broken ribs, and several large lacerations.

To compensate for his small stature, Henry had studied the martial arts, becoming quite skilled in several of its disciplines. Nobody was safe around Henry when his anger exploded. Word of Xiong's unfortunate '*accident*' spread far and wide. Nobody respected Henry, but everyone was afraid of him. Well aware of everyone's feeling toward him, Henry did not care in the least. He knew fear was a far better motivator than respect or friendship.

"Tony, I hear you coming. I not see you in long time," he said, sticking out his hand. They grasped each other's right hand and slapped each other on the back. For reasons, unknown to Anthony, Henry had always refused to call him anything other than Tony. Perhaps he had trouble with the pronunciation. Anthony had never asked, not really caring to know why. Occasionally, he used Henry for what he needed and that was all that really mattered.

"I had a little trouble and have been out of the country," Anthony answered, letting go of Henry's hand and backing up a few feet.

"Yes, I hear something. People I know say Tony have trouble. He disappear." Henry walked over to a dark blue, tufted sofa and sat down, motioning for Anthony to follow. Lying on the other end of the couch, a dark brown dachshund, disturbed out of a sound sleep, scurried over beside Henry and plopped down. Out of habit, Henry reached out with his right hand and scratched the happy little dog's ears.

"Why you here, Tony?" Henry asked.

"I need a favor, Henry."

"Cost you much," Henry answered, glaring in Anthony's direction.

"As always," Anthony quipped.

Henry smiled, unable to keep up the pretense. "You know me well. Please explain."

"I need information about a certain individual. His name is Zach Templeton. I know you have many contacts and not just in New York City."

"Yes, is true. My shipping company operates many places. I pay people good to keep eyes open. Where this Mister Templeton now?"

"Last I knew he was in Arizona. Tucson specifically. He might be headed this way. I'm certain he would like to get his hands on me. I sent an assassin, a highly skilled one I might add, to kill him, but somehow he killed her first."

"Man sounds like trouble. What I do to him if I find him?"

"Nothing. I just want to know where he is. I will take care of him personally."

"Okay, just find. You can describe him?"

"Better than that. Here is a photo of him."

Henry reached out and took the photo from Anthony and stared at it. "No recognize him," Henry said, getting up from the couch. He walked over to a glossy white, enameled shelving unit adorned with sculptures and hand-blown art glass and picked up a large cell phone. He laid the photo on the surface of the unit, adjusted the height of the phone so that the photo filled the screen of the cell phone and snapped a photo. He called up his email application, selected a contact, attached the photo, and pressed send.

"I know someone may help," Henry said. He opened the phone's contact list, selected a name, and pressed the Call icon. Henry stood in front of a large sliding door that provided access to a huge terrace, staring at the New York skyline as he waited. He talked with whoever was on the other end of the conversation for a full ten minutes. Anthony had no idea what they had talked about as Henry spoke Chinese during the entire call.

"How I call you, if we find this Mister Templeton?"

"Pen and paper?" Anthony asked, making a writing motion with his fingers. Henry returned to the shelving unit, pulled a pen and a pad of paper from the top drawer, and handed it to Anthony. Anthony scribbled a number on the paper and handed it back to Henry. Henry tore the top sheet off and stuffed it in his shirt pocket.

"Would you like drink and enjoy the view from terrace?"

"Yes, I would very much," Anthony answered.

Henry retrieved two crystal glasses from his well-stocked bar and poured them half full, offering one to Anthony. He pulled the sliding door open and waited for Anthony to walk out onto the terrace.

"Wow," Anthony remarked as he turned sideways and looked at the terrace that wrapped around the corner of the apartment.. Looking down, he asked, "What is that floor made of?"

"Thassos white marble from Greece. Imported special, just for this apartment."

Anthony forced his eyes away from the pure snow-white marble and walked over to the terrace's railing. "Absolutely amazing! What a view. You can see the entire New York City skyline."

"Number one reason I buy apartment."

"How long have you been in this apartment?"

"Only few months," Henry answered. "Many months delay required to get all furnishings. Come. Sit here."

Anthony followed Henry over to a circular seating area comprising six lounge chairs arranged around a circular brick structure in the middle. Henry picked up a device that resembled a television remote and pressed a button. Large blue flames erupted from the brick structure. "Maybe you like this," Henry said, pressing a different button, watching as the flames changed from blue to green.

"Truly amazing," Anthony said, leaning back in the lounge chair. "You live here alone?"

"Yes. No time for wife. You like to eat before you go? I order whatever you like."

"Sure. Sounds great."

The two men spent several minutes discussing what they should order for dinner, settling on filet mignon, garlic mashed potatoes, asparagus, and a mixed greens salad and for desert, hot fudge sundaes. Henry lifted his cell phone out of his pocket and called a steakhouse two blocks away, which he also owned, and placed the order.

The two men sat enjoying the warm sun and the stunning view as they waited for their dinner to arrive.

227 West 77th Street
New York, New York

About to step through the Larstrand Building's revolving door, the sound of footsteps behind Zach and someone hollering his name caused him to grab his weapon, swivel around, and point the weapon in the direction of the sound. He stopped dead, mouth open with a bewildered look on his face. He let his hand drop to his side.

"You weren't going to shoot me were you?"

"Angie, how….," Zach sputtered. "What are you doing here? How did you know where I'd be?"

"Partly the Admiral and partly your dad," she answered. "You didn't think I was going to let you have all the fun did you?"

"But why?" Zach questioned.

"Your dad wanted to know how you were. He was worried and said you had to be warned, so I called the Admiral and told him I couldn't reach you. The Admiral said he would try to reach you and call me back. Your dad must have overheard some of the conversation because he became very agitated. He even tried to get out of bed."

"How did you know where to find me?"

"Your dad heard me arguing with your mother. He whispered an address and a name to me as I was about to leave the room."

"But how did you get here?"

"The Admiral arranged transportation and for a driver to drop me here. I've been waiting in the small diner next door."

"I don't think this is a good idea," Zach protested.

"Well, I'm here now. We need to find out what these people know. Zach, we're a team. I need to do this."

"Okay," Zach relented. "You have to promise me you will stay back and let me handle things."

"Zach, you know I know how to handle firearms and the Admiral also arranged for this," Angie said, pulling a Springfield XD .40 caliber semiautomatic from her purse.

"Angie, put that away," Zach said, pushing her arm down."

"When we enter the building, you move off to the side and let me approach the security guard."

After entering through the revolving door, Angie walked through the lobby toward the elevators. Zach walked up to the security desk and held out his credentials for the guard. Zach immediately sensed something was off. A small shudder passed down his spine, the small hairs on the back of his neck standing on end. Events of the past few days had triggered long-buried memories from his service in the US Navy as part of SEAL Team Four. Because of the importance of his current assignment and his recent encounters with people trying to kill him, Zach's senses were hypersensitive. He perceived details that under normal circumstances would have gone unnoticed.

Perhaps it was the expression on the guard's face or the way he stood or the way he carried himself. Zach could not quite put his finger on it, but something was definitely not right. Then he noticed sweat running down the guard's neck. Why would the guard be sweating inside the cool lobby? Glancing slightly to the right without moving his head, Zach noticed several small droplets of blood on the floor leading to a door behind the security desk.

Pretending not to have noticed, Zach flopped the leather wallet closed and stuffed it in his left jacket pocket. Moving closer to the security desk to mask his movements, Zach asked, "I'm here to see Mister Leonid Borodin. Is he in?" While the guard attempted to look the man's name up in the building's registry, Zach slipped his hand behind his back, curling his fingers around the grip of the semiautomatic nestled there. With the guard's attention occupied, Zach slipped the semiautomatic out and pointed it at the guard's face.

"Do not do anything foolish," Zach ordered as the guard looked up from the computer screen. "Grab the master key and let's walk over to the elevator very slowly. If you make a sound or attempt to run, I will shoot you. Now, move!"

The guard complied, lifting the elevator master key from a hook on the side of the security desk. Together, they walked over to the elevator. Zach pressed the Up button. When the elevator door slid open, he pushed the guard inside. "Top floor," Zach instructed. Angie followed Zach and the guard into the elevator.

The guard jammed the master key into the penthouse access slot and pushed the button for the twentieth floor. When the elevator reached the top floor, and the door slid open, Zach pushed the guard out into the lavishly decorated hallway, considered to be one of New York City's most impressive neo-Renaissance style interiors. Rather than the typical commercial grade carpet, they stepped out of the elevator onto glossy black and white Italian marble. The hallway led to two penthouses, one on each side of the building.

"Which apartment?" Zach demanded, pushing the semiautomatic's muzzle into the man's back.

"Apartment two thousand two. Over there," the frightened guard answered, pointing to this right.

Zach pushed the guard toward the apartment he had indicated, keeping the semiautomatic pressed firmly against his back. As they neared the apartment's door, Zach noticed the door was not completely closed, and he detected the slight smell of cordite in the air. Zach crept over to the left side of the door and attempted to see inside the apartment. The door, nearly closed, did not offer a clear view into the apartment.

With his left foot, Zach very slowly pushed the door open a crack and peered inside. He saw the dead guard on the floor and a man sitting on the floor rocking back and forth holding a gun. "Stay here," Zach commanded Angie as he kicked the door open and shoved the guard through the door in front of him.

"Drop the gun," Zach shouted.

The apartment owner still nearly hysterical had not noticed the door being pushed open. Startled by Zach's shouted command, he dropped the gun on the floor and lifted his hands above his head.

"Don't shoot me," the man pleaded.

Zach saw the second gun lying under the table. "Get up very slowly and kick both guns over here."

The man complied. First, he stuck his right foot under the table and nudged the gun out where he could kick it with his foot. Then he kicked the Glock he had dropped on the floor toward Zach. Zach kicked both guns behind him and ordered the guard to go sit beside the hall table.

"Angie, come in here and cover the guard."

Angie rushed inside the apartment, pulled out the Springfield semiautomatic, and dropped her purse on the floor. She pointed the handgun at the guard.

"Take the handcuffs from your belt and put one end around your wrist. Then slide over to the door on your left and put the other end around the doorknob," Zach ordered. With the guard no longer a threat, he turned his attention to the apartment owner.

"Mister Leonid Borodin, I assume?" Zach said with a questioning tone, pointing his semiautomatic at the man's chest. The frightened apartment owner nodded his head up and down, affirming his name. "Well, Mister Borodin, my name is Zach Templeton. Does that ring any bells." The man shook his head back and forth, indicating it did not. "Come on, Mister Borodin. Can you not speak?"

"I…. I….," Mr. Borodin stammered, smacking his lips, trying to get enough moisture in his mouth to speak. "No, I do not know you."

"Well, that's not important at the moment. What is this other guard doing here?"

"He was going to kill me," Borodin cried.

"Why was he going to kill you?"

"I do not know."

"Come on Borodin. Don't lie to me. Maybe I should kill you," Zach threatened, taking a step toward the man.

"No. No," Borodin pleaded. "I will tell you. He wanted to silence me. I helped…."

"I already know you helped some very evil people sneak nuclear materials into the country," Zach interrupted. "You are responsible for the deaths of thousands of people. You deserve to die you lousy scum. I have authority direct from the President to do whatever I want. I could kill you both and nobody would ask a single question. Matter of fact, I think I will." Zach took another step toward Borodin and pointed the semiautomatic at the center of his forehead.

"No. No. Please do not kill me," Borodin begged. "I have information. I have a list of very important people that are involved. You will not believe it."

"I don't know," Zach said. "I'm not certain I should trust you."

"Please. Please. Let me show you. I can prove it. I have the list right here," Borodin said, pointing at a large painting hanging above the hall table.

Zach took a step back and ordered Borodin to produce the proof he claimed he possessed. Borodin stood up on shaky legs and pulled on the right side of the painting. The painting swung away from the wall, revealing a wall safe. Borodin failed on his first two attempts to open the safe because he was shaking so badly. On the third attempt he successfully entered the combination. He pulled the safe open, reached in, and extracted a small black, three inch by four inch notebook. He turned around and handed the notebook to Zach.

"Look at the names. They're all in there," Borodin panted, wiping the sweat from his face. "The first name provided access to the boosting elements that were used."

"Boosting elements? What are you talking about?" Zach asked as he opened the notebook and scanned the list of names.

"Boosting elements make the yield much larger," Borodin answered. "Only a small amount of boost and a twenty kiloton device can become forty or fifty kilotons."

A chill went down Zach's back as he read through the list of names written in Borodin's notebook. "This can't be true. You're lying," Zach exclaimed, looking up at Borodin.

"I am not lying. Every name in that book is involved in the conspiracy," Borodin insisted. "I would swear on my mother's grave, may she rest in peace."

"You may have to swear on your own grave, Mister Borodin," Zach added.

"Grab the handcuffs from the dead guard and do like I told the other guard over there except use this door over here."

Borodin did as Zach instructed, attaching one end of the handcuffs he retrieved from the dead guard around the doorknob and the other end around his wrist.

"I doubt if anyone will believe these people were involved in such a monstrous plot," Zach said to himself, shaking his head.

"Angie, you said Dad gave you an address and a name. What was the name?"

"Margot Wilcox. Does that name mean anything to you?"

"Hang on a minute," Zach said as he opened the notebook Borodin had given him. "Look at this list of names.

Borodin here had this notebook in his safe." Angie bent over and peered at the open pages of the notebook. "Look. There at the top of the list is her name," Angie pointed out.

"Yes, that is the woman," Borodin piped up. "She is a US Representative from New York. She has a very high position."

"Zach, I recognize some of these other names. This is insane."

"Yes, it most certainly is, but nobody will believe this," Zach added as he stuffed the notebook in his pocket. "Is Dad okay?"

"The struggle set him back some. The doctor thinks he may be bleeding internally again. They are monitoring him closely and may have to take him back to surgery. The next time the Admiral called I stepped out into the hall so your dad couldn't hear."

"But how did you get here? Here in New York?"

"When the Admiral called back, he was quite upset. I told him I had a plan. I explained it to him and at first, he said no. But I refused to take no for an answer. I informed him I knew he could get things done if he wanted to. I didn't give him any choice."

"Tell me the rest of it," Zach urged.

"I hitched a ride on an Air Force jet," Angie answered coolly, pretending to polish her fingernails.

"You're kidding!" Zach exclaimed, a look of disbelief spreading across his face.

"No, I am not kidding. The Admiral called the Commanding General at Davis Monthan Air Force Base and demanded he scramble an aircraft and its crew immediately to pick me up."

"You're amazing!" Zach beamed. "But why was the Admiral so upset?"

The Admiral learned that the CIA has been watching Frank Porter."

"Porter!" Zach snapped. "That miserable scum-bag traitor. Why wasn't I told?"

"I don't know, Zach. The admiral didn't say," Angie answered. "Let me finish. The Admiral said Porter has been hiding in Quito, Ecuador. One of the CIA's resources saw Porter suddenly race out of his apartment and take a taxi to the airport. He ran into the general aviation terminal. The CIA doesn't know which plane he might have departed on, but an hour later one of the aircraft disappeared from radar. The Admiral and the CIA Director think Porter is likely already back in the states."

"Porter? Here?" Zach shouted.

"Porter, I know that name," Borodin piped up, sitting on the floor with his left arm suspended above his head, handcuffed to a closet door.

"What did you say?" Zach sputtered, turning toward Borodin. "How do you know Porter?"

"I do not know him, but I do know he is part of the conspiracy as well. He arranged all the nuclear material shipments. He is a terrible man."

"Yes, he is. What do you know about him?" Zach demanded.

"I hear he is furious because the bomb went off before he could make his demands. I heard he is on his way here."

"I want to get my hands on that man," Zach snarled. "Where exactly is here?"

"If I help you, what can I expect in return?"

"I will tell the authorities you helped me. It might save you from the needle or how about this? If you don't tell me, I will just kill you now," Zach bellowed, pointing his weapon at Borodin.

"Look on the back," Borodin whimpered as he pulled a business card from his shirt pocket and tossed it toward Zach. "That man smuggles many things into the country. He will do whatever you ask if the price is right. He is the only one that would deal with Porter. If anybody knows where Porter is, that man would know."

Zach walked over and picked up the business card and turned it over. He pulled his cell phone from his pocket and pushed the power button to wake it up but nothing happened. He remembered the battery was dead the last time he had tried to use it. "Hey Angie, I need your cell phone?"

Angie pulled her cell phone from her purse and handed it to Zach. Zach grabbed the phone and thought for a minute. Unable to consult the contact list in his dead cell phone, he dialed Admiral Hadley's number from memory.

"Naval Intelligence, Admiral Hadley's office."

"This is Zach Templeton. Is he in?"

No, Mister Templeton. He is out of the building. He said he won't be back from several hours."

"Can I reach him by cell phone?"

"No. He left his cell phone here. Can I take a message?"

"No message. I will call him later," Zach said. He tapped the End icon and handed the cell phone back to Angie. "I need your keys," Zach ordered, looking down at Borodin." Borodin pointed to the hall table. Zack grabbed the ring of keys from the table, held them out toward Borodin, and asked, "Which one is to the apartment?"

Borodin pointed to a brass-colored key and said, "That one."

"I guess we're on our own," Zach said as he started to push Angie through the door.

"Wait, there's more," Borodin blurted out, hoping to buy himself some goodwill and perhaps even a lighter sentence. "I have a video of Congresswoman Wilcox. In the video, you can hear her agreeing to arrange for the border patrol agent to look the other way when the material crossed the border. She can also be heard providing the names that had access to the elements required to boost the weapon."

"What are you talking about?"

"I recorded all our meetings with a hidden video camera. The files are on a flash drive in the wall safe."

Zach walked over to the still open wall safe and peered inside. He reached his hand inside, moving items aside and looking under envelopes. A small flash drive lay hidden in the back of the safe. Zach removed the flash drive and held it up for Borodin to see. "Is this the flash drive you were talking about?"

"Yes, that is the one," Borodin answered. "There are also videos on the drive of other people on the list in the notebook agreeing to help. Will giving you that proof make it easier on me?"

"I don't know, Borodin," Zach said. "Considering, the evil you perpetrated, it will be unlikely the courts will make any deals. I will tell them you provided this, but I can't make any promises."

"Please, I will help you more," Borodin sobbed. "There's one more thing."

"Out with it," Zach snapped. "It better be good. I don't have much time. I need to go confront this Mister Tang."

"The woman in the notebook knows where more devices are," Borodin bawled. "She has an apartment only a few blocks from here. She is home. I talked to her earlier today."

Zach flipped the notebook open and turned to the page with the woman's name on it. "There's no address here. Where does she live?"

"Fancy apartment on Riverside near the waterfront. Sixty Riverside Boulevard, I think. Apartment Three-two-zero-three."

"Angie, it's critical we find out where those other devices are. Mister Tang will have to wait."

"What about these guys?" Angie asked, pointing at Borodin and then the guard.

Zach walked over and verified the handcuffs on Borodin and the fake security guard were secure. "They're not going anywhere," Zach answered. "I'll have one of the agents downstairs come up and stand guard in front of the door."

Zach pulled the apartment door closed, making certain it was latched. He and Angie hurried to the elevator still on the top floor with the door standing open and stepped in.

The elevator had remained on the top floor because Zach, in his haste, had left the building master key inserted in the penthouse access slot. He reached up, removed the master key, and pressed the button for the ground floor.

Once on the ground floor, Zach and Angie hurried through the lobby, exited through the revolving door, and ran toward the waiting SUVs parked in the visitor parking area. Zach handed the penthouse elevator master key and Borodin's apartment key to one of the secret service agents standing beside one of the SUVs.

"Go up to the twentieth floor and stand in front of the door to apartment two-thousand-two," Zach instructed. "Do not allow anyone to enter without my personal authorization code - Romeo-Alpha-Alpha-Seven. I don't care who it is. Absolutely no one gets in without that code. Is that understood?"

"Understood, Mister Templeton," the secret service agent acknowledged. "No one gets in except over my dead body." The secret service agent turned and disappeared through the revolving door.

"Follow us," Zach said to the other secret service agent. "We are going to arrest a very important and possibly dangerous woman. Once we have her in custody, you will need to guard her while Angie and I go question someone else."

Zach and Angie jumped into the lead SUV.

"Where to, Sir," the secret service agent sitting behind the wheel asked.

"Sixty Riverside Boulevard. Full lights and sirens. Go!" Zach ordered.

Alternate Safe Facility - Defender Two
Location - Classified

Admiral Hadley sat staring blankly at the wall, deeply concerned that he had agreed to Angie Templeton's impulsive plan to contact Zach. He had to admit that at the time there had been no other viable options. Zach had to be informed that Frank Porter, his archenemy, might be on his way back to the states. Left with no choice, he had given in. Still, he had a very bad feeling. Porter was a despicable traitor, depraved and driven only by his insatiable thirst for power. He would stop at nothing. Admiral Hadley was convinced Porter would murder his own mother in her sleep to get what he wanted. What chance would someone like Angie Templeton have against such a murderous thug? He hoped he had not made a terrible mistake.

The phone on the Admiral's desk rang, yanking him back from the nightmarish visions swirling in his mind. He grabbed the phone and answered, "Admiral Hadley."

"Chuck, this is Paul," the President of the United States said.

"Mister President, what can I do for you?"

"Let's dispense with formal titles. Chuck, I'm worried," President Cantwell confessed.

"Okay, Paul. Has something new developed?" Admiral Hadley asked, dropping the formalities with his friend of many years.

"No. Nothing new, but time is quickly running out. Our strategic nuclear forces will be at their launch coordinates soon. If I don't issue countermanding orders by that time, it will be too late and the world will plunge into a global war. I need more information. Have you heard from Mister Templeton?"

"No, I have not. His wife said Zach called and got a name from his dad and then headed to New York. I have been trying both the SAT phone he is carrying and his cell phone. No answer on either phone. Angie has been trying also, and she hasn't been able to reach him either."

"Chuck, I desperately need to hear from him. I can't let this happen," President Cantwell pleaded.

"There's another wrinkle," Admiral Hadley interjected.

"I probably don't want to know, but go ahead and tell me."

"A CIA operative saw Frank Porter rush out of his apartment in Quito, Ecuador, and go to the airport. They think he chartered a private jet. The FAA reported an aircraft disappeared from radar about an hour after that. The CIA Director thinks Porter is on his way to the states. Based on the times, he could already be here."

"Great, that's just what we need," President Cantwell fretted. "Where exactly does the Director think he might be headed?"

"His best guess is DC or maybe New York City. He thinks Porter may be involved in the bombing somehow. Why else would he be taking the risk to come here? And there is something else I need to tell you."

"You're kidding. There's more?"

"The last time I spoke with Zach's wife she had come up with a plan to go find Zach. She requested, or more accurately demanded, I arrange a military jet to take her to New York. I had no other options, so I agreed. I called Davis Monthan Air Force Base and commandeered an aircraft. She is likely already there."

"Good grief, Chuck, can this unbelievable mess get any more bizarre!" President Cantwell exclaimed. "What do we do now?"

"I think we just have to let it play out."

"Let it play out!" President Cantwell bellowed. "If I let it play out, I may bomb a country that is not responsible and start World War Three."

"Huh, what are you talking about, Paul?" Admiral Hadley asked. The Admiral waited but there was no response. "Paul, are you still there?"

"Chuck, you are not cleared for what I am about to tell you, so you must promise to keep this to yourself. A NEST team reported their initial analysis of the nuclear residue from the blast site. That analysis determined the weapon was deuterium boosted. The blast crater indicated the total yield was in the neighborhood of thirty to forty kilotons. The uranium had a signature indicating it probably came from stockpiles that went missing in Eastern Europe, but the deuterium to boost the weapon had to be sourced in the United States."

"What? You can't be serious," Admiral Hadley gasped.

"Yes, there is no doubt. Can you see my dilemma? Now that I hear Porter may be involved, I am beginning to doubt my initial assessment. Chuck, I need more information and I need it yesterday."

"How long do we have, Paul?"

"Not more than a few hours."

"I'll put out the word and see if anybody has seen Zach or his wife. If I hear anything, I will call you immediately."

"See that you do. The country may depend on it."

The line went dead, but Admiral Hadley just sat there having trouble accepting what he had just heard.

"Never in a million years would I have thought such a thing was possible," Admiral Hadley thought as he dropped the receiver on the desk.

Chapter Nineteen

60 Riverside Boulevard
Apartment 3203
New York, New York

Zach and Angie, followed by the three secret service agents, entered the Aldyn apartment building at Sixty Riverside Boulevard. Zach walked up to the building security desk and held out his credentials toward the old man sitting behind the desk. A sixtyish man with pasty, yellowish skin looked up from the video he had been watching. He squinted his gray-green eyes trying to focus on Zach's credentials.

"Just a minute," the man said, grabbing a pair of reading glasses from the far side of the desk. He set the glasses on the bridge of his crooked nose and squinted at the credentials again. He blinked several times, slipped off the glasses and rubbed his eyes, and reset the glasses. "Sorry, mister, I haven't been well," the old man explained. "Now let me see…. Wow, secret service. What on Earth does the secret service want here?"

Zach leaned over the counter and looked at the man's name tag. "Clifford, I'm here on behalf of the President of the United States and I really need your help."

The man sat up a little straighter in his chair and said, "Whatever you need ah…. ah…. What is your name again?"

"Templeton, Zach Templeton."

"Whatever you need, Mister Templeton. What can I do to help?"

"We're here to arrest the woman that lives in apartment thirty-two-zero-three," Zach answered. "We need you to help us make sure no one comes up in the elevator while we make the arrest. Can you help us do that, Clifford?"

"Yes, sir, I can, Mister Templeton," the man asserted, lifting a key from a hook in front of him. "Here, take this key. When you get to the thirty-second floor, open the fireman's panel, insert the key, then turn it to the right. The elevator will not move until you turn the key back to the left. I will disable the other elevator from here." The man reached in front of him and flipped a toggle switch down. "The first elevator on the left is the only one active. Anything else I can do?"

"Clifford, can you accompany us up to the apartment? I want the woman to hear a familiar voice."

"You bet. Most excitement I've had in years," the man exclaimed, beaming as he stood up, steadying himself by hanging onto the security desk. Zach watched as the man teetered back and forth as he headed for the elevators.

Zach motioned for Angie and the three secret service agents to follow him. Zach instructed one of the secret service agents to stay behind, stand in front of the elevators, and turn everyone away.

With everyone else on the elevator, Zach pressed the button for the thirty-second floor. When the elevator stopped, and the door slid open, Zach opened the fireman's panel, inserted the key, then turned it to the right. Zach took Clifford's arm and guided him to apartment three-two-zero-three, positioning him to the right of the door. Zach signaled the two secret service agents to stand to the right of the door. He pushed Angie to the left side of the door and pressed his ear against the door.

He could hear soft classical music playing and someone talking. He eased to the right behind Clifford and rapped his knuckles on the door.

"Who is it?" a voice on intercom asked.

"Okay, go ahead, Clifford," Zach whispered.

"Miss Wilcox, this is building security," Clifford spoke into the intercom.

"What is it? What do you want?"

"Miss Wilcox, this is Clifford. There is a security issue. I really need to talk to you."

The woman inside the apartment, recognizing Clifford's familiar voice, opened the door. With weapon in hand, Zach slammed the door open and pushed his way into the apartment with the secret service agents right behind him..

"What is the meaning of this outrage?" the woman screamed.

"Cover her while I explain to her who I am," Zach said to the secret service agents. "I am Zach Templeton, Secret Service, Presidential Unit," Zach advised, holding out his credentials.

"I don't care who you are. You have no right to barge into my apartment. Do you know who I am?"

"Yes, Miss Wilcox, I know exactly who you are. You are a stinking traitor."

"What? How dare you insult me. I will have you arrested," Ms. Wilcox shouted.

"I don't think so because you are under arrest. Gentlemen, if you would do the honors."

The two secret service agents stepped around Zach and approached the woman. She attempted to back up, but one of the agents grabbed her arm and twisted it up behind her back. "What are you doing," the woman screamed as the other agent took hold of her free arm, put it behind her back, and snapped a pair of handcuffs around both wrists.

"This is an outrage. I'll have your badges," the woman sputtered.

"No, you will not," Zach shouted as he stepped in front of her and shoved his credentials in her face. Had she not been supported by the two secret service agents, she would have toppled over. Before she could protest further, Zach dragged an upholstered chair away from the wall and instructed the agents to sit Ms. Wilcox down. "Now, Miss Wilcox, you will answer my questions and you will answer them truthfully or this interrogation will go very badly for you.

The next time I will not be so gentle. Do you want this to continue, Miss Wilcox?"

"No. No. Please no," Ms. Wilcox begged, strands of her once beautifully coiffed blond hair hanging in wild disarray.

"Good. All you have to do is answer my questions truthfully. We have just come from Mister Leonid Borodin's apartment. We know everything."

"Who is that? I do not know any such person," Ms. Wilcox protested.

"Come, come, Miss Wilcox. You are lying to me. I told you it would go badly for you if you lied to me again." Zach raised his arm as if he were going to strike her.

"You can't. I'm a United States Congresswoman. You will not get away with this," Ms. Wilcox screeched. She attempted to get up but the secret service agents pushed her back down in the chair.

"Well, how about this?" Zach questioned, removing the flash drive from his pocket and holding it up. "Mister Borodin had this flash drive hidden in his safe. It seems he recorded every one of your meetings with a hidden video camera. What do you say to that, Miss United States Congresswoman?"

"I told you I don't know this man, Borodin."

"I am tired of your lies," Zach shouted as he kicked the leg of the chair, knocking it over. One of the agents grabbed the chair and set it upright. "I am running out of patience, Miss Wilcox. I guess you don't believe me." Zach pulled the weapon from behind his back and gently rested the muzzle against Miss Wilcox's left knee. "Do you have any idea what a hollow point slug does to a knee?" Zach wondered if he could really pull the trigger. Doing so would violate his sense of morality, but Borodin had confided that there were additional nuclear devices hidden somewhere. If he did not get the locations of those devices before they could be detonated, untold thousands more would die and the country would be lost for certain. The vision of a nuclear holocaust, trumped his morality. *"I will do whatever is necessary,"* he convinced himself.

Terror filled Miss Wilcox's eyes as she looked down at the weapon resting against her knee. She desperately tried to scoot the chair back away from the menacing weapon. "Why are you doing this?" she stammered.

"Come now, Miss Wilcox. We know the entire story. Mister Borodin recruited you to join his murderous plan. You agreed to arrange for a border guard to look the other way when nuclear materials were smuggled across the border. Then you also provided names of individuals that could provide elements to boost the yield of nuclear weapons."

"I don't know what you are talking about," Ms. Wilcox protested, but less forcefully, glancing back and forth between Zach's face and the weapon resting against her knee.

"I am assigned to the Presidential Unit by the President himself. He granted me full authority to do whatever I believe is necessary. No questions asked. As a member of Congress surely you must understand what that means. Do you know what that means, Miss Wilcox?"

"Yes, I know what that means," she whimpered, growing more terrified with each passing second.

"Well then, you need to start telling me the truth. What do you know of the additional devices?" Zach waited but the woman, believing the man standing before her really would not pull the trigger, just sat there with a defiant look on her face. He pressed the weapon harder against her knee. "I guess you won't need this knee anyway after they give you the needle." Zach pulled the weapon away from her knee and fired into an expensive couch sitting a few feet away. He pushed the hot muzzle of the weapon against her knee. "Tell me where the other devices are or you are going to lose your knee," Zach bellowed, his finger tightening against the trigger.

"No, no. Stop," she screamed, attempting to squirm away from the hot muzzle burning her knee. "I will tell you everything."

Zach removed the weapon from her knee. Miss Wilcox went limp from the aftereffect of the flood of adrenalin that had coursed through her body and from the realization that life as she had known it was over. The expensive cars, the luxury apartment, the lavish furniture, the designer clothes, and the grand parties were over forever. Never again would she enjoy the finer things in life. The arrogant and self-important spirit poured out of her like a flood. Everything she had acquired - gone in an instant. She would answer all Mr. Templeton's questions. Nothing mattered anymore.

"Well, Miss Wilcox, there are still one or more weapons hidden somewhere. Where are they?"

Ms. Wilcox sat there panting, beads of sweat running down her forehead. Her carefully applied eye makeup smeared and ran down her cheeks. The contempt that had initially radiated from her face had turned to desperation and finally to despair. The once powerful member of Congress had been reduced to a sniveling crybaby.

"Well, Miss Wilcox, let's have it. How many devices are there and where are they?" Zach asked, reaching out and poking her on the shoulder.

Ms. Wilcox looked up at Zach with hollow, emotionless eyes, streaked with smeared mascara. "Two devices. One in Chicago and one in Washington, D.C.," Ms. Wilcox confessed.

"But where exactly? I need addresses. How long before they detonate?"

"The devices cannot be detonated. They do not have triggers and there are no boost elements," Ms. Wilcox replied. "The other device was not supposed to be detonated before a list of demands was delivered."

"I need to know where," Zach urged.

"I can write the addresses, if you remove the handcuffs."

Zack looked at one of the secret service agents and nodded his head. The agent reached behind Ms. Wilcox's back and released the handcuffs from her right wrist. She pulled her arms from behind her back and rubbed her wrist. Zach turned the notebook he got from Borodin to a blank page and handed it and a pen to Ms. Wilcox. She wrote down two addresses and handed it back to Zach. The secret service agent yanked her arms behind her back and replaced the handcuffs around her wrists.

"Why on Earth did you do this? Why did you murder thousands of innocent people?" Zach asked.

Suddenly Ms. Wilcox's arrogant and self-important spirit returned. "They're not innocent. I did it to destroy Capitalism. I did it for the betterment of the world. Now the world will continue to suffer. I hate you and your kind," she sneered. She spit in Zach's face.

Zach raised his weapon, very much wanting to hit her in the face, but he stopped. He lowered his weapon, pulled a handkerchief from his pocket, and wiped his face.

"You don't deserve it, but I feel sorry for you, Miss Wilcox" Zach said, shaking his head. "The system you claim to hate is exactly what produced the wealth you enjoyed. You have no right to mock the system that afforded you the best of everything. Look at the riches, provided by Capitalism, that you willingly accepted I might add," Zach said, sweeping his hand toward the extravagant furnishing of her luxury apartment.

"These trappings are just a useful tool to suck in the weak and the ignorant you fool," she scoffed. "One day we will destroy you and your system of riches."

"I promise you that on the day they stick the needle in your arm I will be there. I pity you, Miss Wilcox. Your soul is twisted by evil."

Ms. Wilcox struggled with the agent that had hold of her arm as she screamed obscenities at Zach. Zach tossed his handkerchief to the agent. "Shut her up," Zach ordered as he turned and walked over to where Angie stood.

"Hard to believe isn't it," Zach remarked.

"That woman is pure evil," Angie added. "What do we do with her?"

"I'd like to take her out on the balcony and throw her off, but I guess I probably shouldn't do that," Zach quipped. "I'll have one of the agents hold her down in the lobby until the FBI can get here and take her into custody."

"What do we do about Porter?" Angie asked.

"Oh, that's right, Porter. In the excitement, I almost forgot about him. Come on. Let's go."

Zach, Angie, the two secret service agents, and Ms. Wilcox, handcuffed and with a handkerchief stuffed in her mouth, climbed into the elevator and rode it down to the ground floor. Standing in the lobby, Zach instructed one of the secret service agents to wait there and hold Ms. Wilcox until the FBI arrived and took custody of her. Zach, Angie, and the other secret service agent rushed out the door and headed for the SUV parked around the corner in the visitor's parking area.

They all piled into the SUV. Settling into the back seat, Zach grabbed Angie's hand and squeezed it.

The agent started the engine and looked over the back of the seat, "Where to now, sir?"

Zach leaned over the front seat, "Ninety-Nine Hudson Street in Jersey City. Full lights and siren, again," Zach answered. "I need to borrow your cell phone."

The agent handed Zach his cell phone, switched on the emergency lights, and stomped on the accelerator. The SUV squealed out of the parking area and jumped the curb. Zach's hand slipped off the seat back, and he tumbled into the back seat because of the sudden acceleration. Angie grabbed his shoulder and pushed him upright.

"Here we go again," Zach exclaimed as he clicked the buckle of his seat belt into place.

USS Wyoming (SSBN 742)
South-southeast of Bermuda

"XO, you have the Conn," Commander Anderson announced as he stepped down off the raised platform in the center of control and headed aft.

"I have the Conn," Lieutenant Commander James Barton, *Wyoming's* Executive Officer answered.

Commander Anderson stopped amidships at the ladder leading to the deck below and shouted to those below, "Down ladder, make a hole." With both hands, he gripped the handrails, polished smooth by thousands of hands before him, and slid down to the deck below. He continued aft to the missile compartment and stepped through the hatch.

"Weps, are the missile systems back up and operating per specs?" Commander Anderson asked.

"Yes sir, Captain," Lieutenant David Murphy, *Wyoming's* Weapons Officer answered, wiping his hands with a heavily stained rag. "The two senior missile techs have run the diagnostics three times each. Every run performed exactly to specifications, Sir."

"Well then, Mister Murphy, switch all systems out of test mode and into standby mode. We will arrive in our assigned launch zone soon."

"All missile systems to standby mode. Aye, aye, Sir," Lieutenant Murphy repeated as he reached over to the missile control console and switched the systems. One by one, the 'Stand By' indicators for all twenty-four missiles changed from green to white.

"Men," Commander Anderson said, waiting for all activity to stop and all eyes to focus on him. "It is a difficult thing we are about to do. The destructive power we will release is unimaginable, but the President of the United States has given us an order to launch our missiles. Without a countermanding order, that is exactly what we will do in less than one hour. I expect you to perform as you have been trained. Is that understood?"

In unison, every voice inside the missile control compartment shouted, "Aye, aye, Captain."

"Very well," Commander Anderson acknowledged, ducking through the hatch and back into the passageway. Back in the control center, he stopped at the navigation station. "Nav, what is our progress?"

"Just over eight nautical miles from the edge of the launch zone, Sir." Lieutenant Michael Gertz, *Wyoming's* Navigation Officer replied, pointing at a cross-hatched rectangle on the chart with the dividers he held in his right hand.

"I have the Conn," Commander Anderson announced as he stepped up on the circular platform. Lieutenant Commander Barton stepped back, giving control back to the Captain. "Helm, Conn, All ahead standard, make turns for twelve knots."

"Conn, Helm, All ahead standard, make turns for twelve knots, aye."

Commander Anderson reached up and thumbed the switch for the 1-MC. "Crew of the *Wyoming*, this is the Captain. We will soon enter our designated launch zone. I want everyone sharp and focused on their duties. As soon as we enter the launch zone, verify our coordinates, and assume launch depth, we will fire our missiles. Then we will go deep and disappear. Be prepared from extreme maneuvers."

Commander Anderson kept a wary eye on all crew members in the control center, looking for any outward signs of stress.

Thirty-seven minutes later an excited voice filled the control room. "Conn, Navigator, we are entering our designated launch zone," *Wyoming's* navigation officer, announced.

"Conn, aye."

Commander Anderson's hand trembled slightly over the 1-MC as he considered the order he was about to give, knowing the unimaginable destruction the twenty-four missiles would inflict when they slammed into their targets. During countless missile drills, he had completed the launch process flawlessly every time, and without hesitation. He could recite every command from memory, but this final command seemed to stick in his throat. This was not a drill. This was the real thing. The *Wyoming* carried twenty-four deadly MIRV (Multiple Independently Targetable Reentry Vehicle) missiles. The death and destruction about to be unleashed would be unimaginable.

After completing OCS and upon entering the submarine service, Commander Anderson had undergone extensive psychological testing to determine if he could execute an authenticated order to launch nuclear weapons. Passing every evaluation, he had readily accepted the grave responsibility that came with the command of a nuclear missile submarine. The *Wyoming* had received and authenticated an order to launch its missiles. Now, it was his duty to execute that order. It really was as simple as that.

Commander Anderson stood a little straighter, took a deep breath, and with all the conviction he could muster spoke into the 1-MC, "Man Battle Stations Missile for Strategic Missile Launch. Spin up all missiles, one through twenty-four."

"Helm, Conn, all stop."

"Conn, Helm, all stop, aye," the duty helmsman responded.

"Dive, Conn, ten degree up bubble. Make your depth one hundred fifty feet. Prepare to hover."

"Conn, Dive, ten degree up bubble. Make your depth one hundred fifty feet. Prepare to hover, aye," the diving officer replied.

Wyoming's engines stopped, the deck pitching upward as the boat went shallow, preparing to launch its deadly missiles.

Several minutes later *Wyoming* leveled off at launch depth, sitting dead in the water. The diving officer engaged the hovering computer and reported, "Conn, Dive, the ship is hovering at launch depth."

In MCC (the Missile Control Center) the Weapons Officer watched as Lieutenant Jg. Bill Chambers, Assistant

Weapons Officer, and a group of missile technicians arrived. Each man had a specific responsibility for operating the missile launch systems.

"Radio, Conn, any message traffic I should know about?"

"Conn, Radio, Sir, the radio is still down. We are close though, Sir. We need maybe ten or fifteen minutes more."

"Radio, Conn, Understood, but we do not have any more time."

Commander Anderson glanced around the control center and noticed all eyes were on him. It would be far from easy, but they had authenticated orders, and it was his responsibility to see the crew carried them out. He reached up and keyed the 1-MC, "This is the commanding officer. Set condition one-SQ for strategic missile launch. The release of nuclear weapons has been authorized."

The XO, Lieutenant Commander Barton, stepped up and repeated the command over the 1-MC. "This is the executive officer. Set condition one-SQ for strategic missile launch. The release of nuclear weapons has been authorized."

In the control room, the crew's eyes returned to their consoles as they focused on their duties.

Two officers ran into the control room, one holding the CIP key. Commander Anderson accepted the key and inserted it into the Captain's Indicator Panel. Everyone waited as the missiles were brought fully online and the targeting coordinates were confirmed and loaded into the eight individual warheads in each of the twenty-four missiles.

Each position in the last column of lights on the indicator panel turned red as the missile technicians armed the explosive gas generators that would literally blow the missiles to the surface in a bubble of gas. The *Wyoming* was fully ready to launch its missiles. The only remaining step was the final order to fire. After receiving the order to fire, the weapons officer would unlock the safe in MCC and remove the tactical firing trigger, which looked like a pistol without a barrel.

Commander Anderson swallowed hard and gave the order, "Weapons you have permission to fire."

The Weapons Officer spun the combination dial to the right several times, then he spun the dial left, then right, then left, to the final number in the three-digit combination. He turned the locking lever and yanked the safe door open. With a shaking right hand, he withdrew the tactical firing trigger. The Weapons Office swallowed hard, poked his index finger through the safety guard, took a deep breath, and pulled the trigger.

75th floor Penthouse
99 Hudson Street
Jersey City, New Jersey

A black SUV with emergency lights flashing screamed down Grand Street past the Jersey City Medical Center and past the intersection with Jersey Avenue. Zach had borrowed the secret service agent's phone and had it pressed to his ear. Knowing they were approaching their destination, he ended his call with the President.

"Can I keep this," Zach asked. "I may need it later. Mine's dead."

"Certainly, no problem," the agent answered.

Five blocks later, the agent driving switched off the SUV's emergency lights and siren. At the next intersection, the SUV turned left onto Hudson Street. In the middle of the next block, the SUV slid across three lanes of oncoming traffic and halfway up onto the sidewalk. Fortunately, pedestrians passing by either heard or saw them coming and dived out of the way.

Zach and Angie threw open the SUV's rear doors and rushed inside the towering seventy-five story building. They ran past exclusive shops offering designer clothes and accessories, footwear, fragrances, and candies. Everything New

Jersey's elite could possibly want. They slid to a stop in front of the building's security guard station. Shaking his head, Zach stared at the security guard standing behind the counter dressed in an unkempt and ill-fitting uniform. A dirty, stained clip-on tie hung askew from the collar of his shirt which appeared to be two sizes too big. Zach could not see below the guard's pot belly but assumed the rest of his appearance would be no better. "*I would certainly expect a more squared-away guard in such a swanky building,*" Zach thought to himself. Before the guard could say a word, Zach pulled out his credentials and flopped them open for the security guard to see.

"We need access to the penthouse. A Mister Henry Tang's residence, I believe," Zach demanded.

"This is an exclusive building. I can't let just anyone in. Especially to the penthouse," the rumpled security guard protested.

"Look at the credentials again," Zach barked. "What do you see written under my name?"

"Secret Service, Presidential Detail. Wow!" the security guard exclaimed.

"Yes, wow is right. That gives me all the authority I need and for whatever I want. Now, you will escort us to the penthouse and you will not let Mister Tang know we are coming. Is that understood?"

The security guard hesitated, uncertain if he would jeopardize his job by allowing someone up to the penthouse without its owner's knowledge or permission.

Zach leaned over the counter and looked directly into the guards eyes. "Listen up, Benny. I will only say this once. If you do not do as I ask, and right now, I will arrest you and have you thrown in the ugliest, most miserable prison I can find where you will rot for the rest of your life. Am I clear?"

"Yes, sir," the security guard squeaked, grabbing for the elevator master key.

Zach grabbed Benny's arm and directed him to the one elevator that went all the way to the penthouse floor. Zach pushed Benny inside and waited for Angie to step into the elevator with them. "All right, let's go," Zach ordered.

Benny inserted the master key into the control slot and pressed the button for the penthouse. The elevator door screeched as it slid closed. Once the door was closed, the elevator started its high-speed rise to the top floor of the building. After a short ride, the elevator door opened to a medium-sized foyer, elegantly appointed with beautiful oil paintings on two walls. A museum quality highboy stood against the opposite wall. Twenty feet in front of them was a single door labeled 'Penthouse'.

"Okay, Benny, return to the lobby and do not allow anyone to come up to the penthouse for any reason. Tell anyone that asks, the elevator is out of service. Understood?"

"Yes, sir. No one comes up," Benny answered, rapidly nodding his head up and down.

"Oh, and another thing, Benny. Return to your normal duties and say nothing to anybody. We are not here. The same warning of prison still applies."

"Yes, sir. Normal duties. Say nothing," Benny agreed, glad to be released and headed back down to the ground floor.

Zach pointed his index finger toward the apartment's door bell about to press it but stopped and dug the borrowed cell phone out of his pocket. "Angie, I better call the Admiral before we confront Mister Tang."

Angie watched as Zach punched in the Admiral's number from memory and waited. Before the phone on the other end could ring, the cell phone chirped once and went dead. Zach looked at the dead cell phone with disgust. "I don't believe it. I just used this stupid thing," Zach complained. "Couldn't happen at a worse time. My phone's dead too. I guess we're on our own, Angie."

Zach turned back toward the door and pressed the doorbell.

Inside the penthouse, Henry Tang had just pushed a cart loaded with dirty dishes from the terrace into the penthouse's kitchen. He turned and looked at his guest who had also heard the doorbell.

"Leave the cart there and come over here," Anthony whispered, motioning for Henry to follow him. "You answer the door and I will duck out of sight.

Anthony held his finger up to his lips, pulled a large-caliber semiautomatic from behind his back, and slipped into the coat closet, leaving the door slightly ajar.

Chapter Twenty

President Paul Cantwell sat bleary-eyed watching yet another gut-wrenching video feed from the southwestern United States showing people running wild in the streets. All roads in and out of major cities in the western half of the country were clogged with desperate, terrified citizens. People, over-come with fear, had overwhelmed all the operating airports, demanding to be allowed out of the country. What few communications circuits that still functioned in the western half of the country, had become inundated with frantic calls for help, quickly becoming useless.

Shaking his head, the President became deeply dis-turbed and sickened, as he watched panic-stricken people running down streets, many carrying lifeless children. The screen on the television switched to scene after scene of desperate people, many already showing signs of radiation sickness, challenging military roadblocks. Military personnel, greatly outnumbered and fearing for their lives, opened fire on the fleeing masses.

Crowds of horrified onlookers became angry, joining in the conflicts. Civilians overran military barricades, seized their weapons, and turned on the military personnel. Gun battles raged out of control. One particularly disturbing vid-eo segment showed violent mobs running down litter-filled streets, screaming and beating looters to death. Innocent bystanders unable to get out of their way were trampled and crushed in the street by the swelling flow of the mass of fear-crazed individuals. What little remained of law and order was breaking down and threatening to collapse completely.

As people's terror and panic grew and their last hope of escape faded, the situation deteriorated even further and went from desperate to ugly. Soon any hope of restoring law and order would be lost completely. The President had grown more horror-stricken with each new scene. He picked up the remote to turn off the disgusting spectacle. About to press the power button, he stopped, frozen by a new scene of carnage that flashed onto the screen. The video showed a hysterical mob running down a street strewn with abandoned vehicles. The horrified, fleeing mass trampled and crushed anyone who tripped and fell. Children, knocked from their parent's arms, were mercilessly trampled to death before their parents had time to grab them. The President, visibly shaken, dropped the remote and turned away in horror.

"I can't watch anymore. Turn it off," President Cantwell choked, tears running down his face as he turned away and hung his head. Jeffery Williams, the President's Executive Assistant retrieved the remote from the floor and switched the television off.

On the opposite side of the country, hundreds of miles away from the zone of destruction, growing crowds of belligerent citizens demanded answers and protection. The President's beloved country was on the brink of anarchy and destruction. Soon nothing would stop the growing chaos.

"I need answers," President Cantwell bellowed to no one in particular, slamming his fists on the desk. "I need something to tell the people. The country is coming apart at the seams. If we don't do something soon, there will be no stopping the panic. We will have a full-blown insurrection on our hands."

The President looked around the room at the members of his staff that had made it to Air Force One in time to relocate to the alternate safe location. "Well, gentlemen, any ideas?" the President questioned, looking at each member in turn. No one said a word. The only responses were dismal, dejected faces and a couple of shrugged shoulders.

Except for the President, everyone stood silent, staring at the floor. The President stood up, leaned forward, and placed his hands flat of the desk. "A miracle is what I need," he muttered as he closed his eyes and tried to drive the horrible images from his mind. He jumped when the phone rang.

"President Cantwell, who is this?"

"Zach Templeton, Sir. I have some information you are not going to believe."

"Let's have it, Mister Templeton," President Cantwell said as he pulled his chair toward the desk and sat down.

"Sir, I have learned there are two additional devices. One is hidden in Chicago and one in Washington, D.C."

"My God," the President wailed. "You can't be serious. How long do we have before they detonate? We can't evacuate cities that size. It's impossible."

"Calm down, Sir. The devices don't have triggers and the perpetrators have not been supplied any more boosting elements."

"That's great news," the President replied, letting out a large sigh.

"Do you have something to write with, Sir?" Zach asked.

President Cantwell grabbed the first piece of paper he could reach and turned it over to the blank side. He snapped his fingers in the air. Jeffery Williams pulled a ballpoint pen from his shirt pocket and handed it to the President. "Go ahead," the President advised. He wrote the two addresses on the paper as Zach read them from the notebook.

"Hang on a minute, Zach," the President said. He motioned Jeffery Williams, his Executive Assistant over to the desk. "Jeffery, there are nuclear devices hidden at these two addresses. Scramble two NEST bomb disposal teams immediately and secure those devices." Jeffery Williams rushed into the outer office to notify the NEST group commander.

"Who's behind this?" the President asked.

"The mastermind behind this catastrophe is a Mister Leonid Borodin."

"I have heard that name," the President interjected. "He's a highly respected international financier. He couldn't accomplish this without help. Who else is involved?"

"Are you sitting down Mister President?"

"Yes, why do you ask?"

"The individual that arranged for a border guard to look the other way and also provided the names of individuals that could provide boosting elements is Miss Margot Wilcox."

"What?" the President gasped. "She's a respected Congresswoman. She's a member of the House Permanent Select Committee on Intelligence. There has to be a mistake."

"Absolutely no mistake, Sir. I confronted her myself. One of the secret service agents accompanying me has her in custody and is waiting for the FBI to arrive."

"I just can't believe it. This is a dark day in our country's history. Anything else, Mister Templeton," the President questioned.

"Oh, yes, there's more. Much more, but you won't believe what I have to tell you without the physical proof I have. Plus, I don't have time to go into it. We're on the way to track down a lead on Frank Porter."

"That scoundrel? I hope you learn something useful. I want to see that man pay for his crimes."

"Me too," Zach agreed. "Sir, I've got to go. We're getting close."

"Good hunting, Zach," the President offered as he dropped the phone back into its cradle.

President Cantwell immediately picked the phone back up and called NMCC (the National Military Command Center) and issued a recall order for all strategic nuclear strike forces. He ordered all strategic bomber groups and submarine forces to stand down immediately. He next called the joint chiefs and instructed them to return all military forces to DEFCON3.

The President paced back and forth across his office, waiting for confirmation that all strike forces had acknowledged the stand down order and were returning to normal conditions. Thirty minutes later the commanding general from NMCC called and advised that all bomber groups had acknowledged the recall order and were returning to their bases. The general hesitated when he had to inform the President that all nuclear submarines except one had received and acknowledged the recall order and were returning to their normal patrol areas. The general informed the President that the *Wyoming* had not as yet acknowledged the order. The general told him that COMSUBLANT was frantically trying all comm channels to reach the *Wyoming* but were unable to contact the submarine.

"What if we can't reach the *Wyoming*," President Cantwell asked, already knowing the answer he feared would come.

"They will follow their SOP, Sir," Brigadier General Robert Gordon answered. "Assuming they have reached their designated launch zone, without a countermanding order, they will launch their missiles."

"We must reach that submarine, General," President Cantwell bellowed, the veins in his neck bulging. "Use whatever resources are necessary. That launch must be stopped."

"I'm certain COMSUBLANT is aware of that, Sir. There isn't anything we can do if their communication systems are out. If she is deep as I imagine she would be, there is simply no way to contact her. We have to hope they at least can restore the long-wire communications system so they can receive the EAM traffic we are sending. COMSUBLANT has put the EAM message in a repeating loop. I'm certain they are aware of the issue with time, but I will call the admiral and pass along your orders."

"Thank you, General," the President said as he hung up the phone. He stood perfectly still for several minutes, staring at the floor. Bile rose in his throat, partly from the immense stress of the situation and partly from the gallon of coffee he had drunk. With a look of utter dread clouding his face, he looked up at the members of his staff and asked, "Antacid? Anybody got antacid?"

Jeffery Williams picked up his briefcase sitting beside a small couch positioned against the wall and laid it on the President's desk. He opened the briefcase, grabbed a plastic bottle, and shook three round antacid tablets into the President's open hand. The President threw all three tablets into his mouth. He grimaced as he chewed the chalky tablets. He returned to his pacing as he contemplated the catastrophe that would likely engulf the world if *Wyoming* could not be reached before she launched her missiles.

75th floor Penthouse
99 Hudson Street
Jersey City, New Jersey

Impatient, Zach stabbed the penthouse's door bell again. Inside the penthouse, Henry Tang walked to the front door and pulled it open. "What is meaning of this intrusion?" Henry snarled. "You not announced. Nobody allow up to my penthouse without permission."

Zach, with credentials already in hand, pushed his way into the penthouse and shoved the credentials into Henry's face. "This is all the permission I need, Mister Tang."

Henry brushed Zach's arm away and backed up several steps. "I not care who you are. Get out of my penthouse!" Henry yelled.

"I'm not going anywhere till you answer some questions, Mister Tang," Zach shot back.

"No, I not answer any you questions. Now, get out!" Henry yelled again.

"Well, maybe you would rather get dragged to FBI headquarters in handcuffs and answer questions there," Zach warned, taking a step toward Henry. "Either way, you are going to answer my questions."

Henry detested people crowding into his personal space. He took another step backward but said nothing. He stared at Zach with anger and hatred in his eyes. Angie had followed Zach into the penthouse, staying several steps behind him. She nudged the door shut and moved to Zach's left, standing beside an ornate side chair upholstered in rich peacock-blue organza brocade. Everything in Henry's penthouse bespoke his enormous wealth. If he liked something, he purchased it, never caring, or asking, about the price.

Inside the closet, Anthony was nearly giddy, hardly able to believe his good fortune. He did not have to go hunting for the man he hated, the man that had destroyed everything he had worked for. Forced to abandon everything he owned and flee the United States, Anthony's anger had grown more intense with each passing day. All because of one man. The man now standing only a few feet away. *"Payback, sweet payback,"* he thought, savoring the vision of putting a bullet in Templeton's head. Before he took his revenge, he would listen to see what Templeton, and those he worked for knew.

"Sit on the couch, right there," Zach ordered, pointing toward an odd-looking couch covered in pure white suede leather. The highly polished, curved sides, made of mahogany with a lacquer finish, shone like a mirror. The couch, tufted in a diagonal pattern, sparkled with what looked like large diamonds at four of the intersecting lines. Zach thought it looked rather garish and ugly. Zack did not know the couch he considered garish and ugly was an extremely limited Gerste Blanche Sofa, created by one of the world's most highly sought after designers. The sofa's cost, way more than double Zach's yearly pay, came in just shy of two hundred thousand dollars.

Henry sat on the couch as instructed. Zach chose a stylish opera chair, upholstered in matching pure white suede leather, and sat on the edge of the cushion facing Henry. "What do you know about Leonid Borodin?"

"I have business deal with Borodin. That is all," Henry answered.

"Don't lie to me, Mister Tang. I just came from Borodin's apartment. He is handcuffed to a door, waiting for the FBI to arrive and take him into custody. He says you are a smuggler and a very bad man."

"I no such thing," Henry protested. "I honest business man. I import many things. All legal."

"That's not what Borodin said and I'm inclined to believe him. But that is not why I am here. Borodin said you would know the whereabouts of a Mister Frank Porter. Is that true, Mister Tang?"

"I not know this man Porter. Never see him. Borodin lies! I not know Porter," Henry whined.

"Maybe you need a little persuading," Zach said, pulling the semiautomatic from behind his back and pointing it at Henry. "I want to know what you know about Porter," Zach threatened.

Henry's eyes grew large, and he began to visibly shake at the sight of the gun pointing at him. "No shoot. I know nothing of man called Porter. No shoot," Henry begged. Driving much of the criminal activity occurring in the depraved underworld of New York City, Henry was always fearful. For protection, he had several weapons hidden around his penthouse, but sitting where he was on the sofa they were all out of reach. He kept glancing at the bookcase where a Sig Sauer .380 lay hidden in the top drawer. Knowing he would never make it to the bookcase, he turned his attention back to the weapon pointed at him. "*Why Tony not do something?*" he wondered.

"This is your last warning, Mister Tang. Tell me where Porter is," Zach warned, extending his arm toward Henry.

Anthony had listened to the exchange between Zach and Henry, not learning anything useful or that he did not already know or suspect. Deciding to wait no longer for the revenge he so desperately wanted, he slowly pushed the door open just enough to see into the room, edging the barrel of his weapon around the edge of the door.

Angie, standing behind and to the left of Henry and Zach, noticed the closet door move and the barrel of a gun unexpectedly jut out into the room. "Zach, gun, behind you!" Angie screamed, her hand already in her purse holding a gun. She jerked the gun from her bag and fired at the door. Startled by the door's sudden movement and her rapid reaction affected her aim. The slug from Angie's hurriedly aimed and errant shot hit the door three inches above the barrel of the gun jutting into the room. The slug passed through the door, splintering the edge of the door, sending wood and paint chips flying into the air. Surprised by the sudden gunfire, Anthony dropped to the floor, kicked the door open, and fired at Angie. He turned and fired twice at Zach.

Alerted by Angie's warning, Zach had leaped up from the chair and had dived behind it, just disappearing behind the chair's back as Anthony fired. The second shot hit the chair and passed through it, tumbling across the room before slamming into a priceless antique curio cabinet. Shards of glass from the cabinet's curved glass front and bits and pieces of destroyed porcelain figurines rained down onto the floor. Zach cautiously peered around the edge of the chair and saw Henry standing three feet away with a bewildered look on his face, a large red stain spreading out from the middle of his chest. Frightened by Angie's scream, Henry had jumped up off the sofa, stepping right into the path of Anthony's first shot. Henry looked down at his chest in horror and disbelief, opening his mouth to speak, but no words came out. His eyes fluttered and closed as he fell backward onto the snow-white sofa. A rivulet of blood ran down the front of the sofa and dripped onto the carpet.

Zach sprang up from his hiding place, fired in the direction of the closet, and dived over the couch. Anthony fired at the flash of movement but missed. Zach popped his head above the couch and fired again. Anthony fired back, hitting a table lamp sitting on the end table, showering Zach with chunks of broken ceramic. Anthony fired twice more, hitting the expensive sofa. Zach watched as two black holes appeared in the back of the sofa less than a foot above his leg. The slugs bounced off the marble floor and passed through one of the floor to ceiling windows. The first slug passed through the glass, producing a pattern of starburst cracks radiating outward from the hole. The second slug hit the window several inches from the first, shattering the entire window. The penthouse became an explosion of chunks of glass shrapnel.

Zach fired twice at the closet as he squirmed around the end of the sofa to avoid the falling shards of glass. He assumed a position behind a white-lacquered cabinet and waited. The Penthouse went deathly quiet, smoke swirling in the air from the gun battle. The heavy smell of cordite burned Zach's nose. He poked his head around the side of the cabinet expecting more gunfire, but there was only silence.

Suddenly panicked, Zach remembered Angie had been standing beside a chair by the door. "Angie, where are you? he called out, but she did not answer. "Angie, are you okay?" he called out again, but she still did not respond.

"Angie," he screamed, jumping out from behind the cabinet, weapon raised, expecting a hail of bullets.

USS Wyoming (SSBN 742)
Designated Launch Zone
South of Bermuda

Lieutenant David Murphy, *Wyoming's* Weapons Officer, holding his breath, waited for the telltale shudder and whooshing sound that would indicate the missiles had been launched from their tubes. No shudder and no whooshing sound. Lieutenant Murphy pulled the trigger two more times but nothing happened. Without warning, the Weapons Department plunged into total darkness for a second time. After a two second delay, the battle lanterns flashed on, casting an eerie yellow-orange glow throughout the compartment.

"What happened?" Lieutenant Murphy shouted at Lieutenant Jg. Bill Chambers, *Wyoming's* Assistant Weapons Officer.

"Don't really know, Sir," Lieutenant Jg. Chambers replied. "I would say it must have something to do with the short we had earlier in the engineering spaces that forced us to the surface."

"Conn, Weapons, We have lost power in the weapons compartment," Lieutenant Murphy spoke into the 1-MC. He waited for thirty seconds and not receiving a reply, looked around the compartment for a runner. He spotted Missile Technician Third Class Peter Lefler, the newest addition to *Wyoming's* weapons department, huddled next to a control panel like the newbie he was.

"Petty Officer Lefler, over here now!" Lieutenant Murphy hollered. "We're on station to launch our missiles, but the power has dropped out. We need to know what happened and what the Captain's orders are. Make your way to control as fast as you can and find out what happened and then report back here. Understood?"

"Yes, Sir. Find out what happened and report back here," Petty Officer Lefler acknowledged. He turned and ran down the passageway, glad to have something useful to do. Twice he ran into shipmates on his way to control, knocking them off their feet. He stopped only long enough to help them up then disappeared down the passageway before they could chew him out. As he ran, he saw that the entire boat was in darkness, except for the glow of the battle lanterns.

He slowed down and cautiously entered the control center. Quickly scanning the compartment, he spotted the Captain standing beside the fire control system talking to one of the electronics techs. He ran over to the Captains' location and announced his reason for being there. "Captain, Sir. Petty Officer Third Class Lefler. The 1-MC is out and Weps, I mean Lieutenant Murphy, sir, sent me to find what happened and what your orders are?"

"Petty Officer Lefler, we haven't determined the cause of the power outage as yet. Report back to Weps and tell him to stand by in position. The instant we get power back, we will correct our position, reset the fire control system, and launch our missiles. Got that?"

"Yes, Sir," Petty Officer Lefler responded, turning on his heels and sprinting back down the passageway toward the weapons compartment.

"XO, you have the Conn," Commander Anderson shouted, turning and dashing down the same passageway Petty Officer Lefler had just disappeared into. Lieutenant Commander Barton did not bother to respond as the Captain had already disappeared.

Commander Anderson continued down the passageway and down the midships ladder. Crewmen leaped out of the Captain's way as he raced toward the engine room, the source of the earlier malfunction that had nearly crippled the boat. He entered the engine room, determined to find out what had happened. Engineman Third Class Mike Hall, having been relieved from his normal watch station as Duty Helmsman, had both arms inside an equipment bay trying to locate the source of the current electrical fault. Commander Anderson walked up behind Engineman Hall and looked over his shoulder.

Infuriated that his boat had failed its mission to launch its missiles a second time, he barked, "Sailor, why did the electrical system fail again?"

Engineman Hall, his attention fully focused on his task, yanked the test probe away from the equipment and lost his balance. Unable to stay upright he fell against the equipment. The wristwatch on his arm brushed against the terminals of the main power buss, creating a large spark. Engineman Hall screamed and jerked himself away from the equipment. Screaming and dancing in circles, he frantically clawed at the wristwatch, trying to get it off his arm.

"Get it off. Get it off," he shrieked.

"Hold still," Chief Machinist Mate Michael Warren, the Machinery Division Chief, shouted as he grabbed Engineman Hall's arm and released the wristwatch's clasp and slipped it off. With the wristwatch removed, Chief Warren turned Engineman Hall's arm over, revealing an angry-looking red welt. "Hall, go find the corpsman and have that attended to."

Engineman Hall glared at the Captain as he stepped around him and stomped off in search of the corpsmen.

"Somebody take his place, quick," Commander Anderson barked. "Are the maneuvering systems online so we can hold our position?"

"No, Sir," Chief Warren answered. "The surge tripped all the breakers. We're afraid to reset them until we locate the source of the fault."

Commander Anderson, demanding but normally calm, lost his temper. "Not acceptable, Chief," Commander Anderson yelled. "Reset the maneuvering system, *NOW!*"

Chief Warren knew better than to disagree with the Captain. He moved over in front of the master control panel and reset the two breakers for the maneuvering system. Instantly, a large flash flared from the equipment bay Engineman Hall had been working in and the two breakers tripped. Commander Anderson looked at the wisp of smoke rising from the equipment bay and shook his head.

"Let the men do their work, Captain," Chief Warren urged. "They're working as fast as they can."

"Okay, Chief," Commander Anderson answered. "Assign as many men as it takes. Let me know the instant the fault is located and power is restored. I'm returning to the Conn."

"Yes, Sir, Captain," Chief Warren responded, waving at the two senior enginemen standing at the far end of the compartment.

Commander Anderson walked back into control and straight over to the navigator's station. "Mister Gertz, are we on station?"

"Hard to be certain, Sir, with all the power out," Lieutenant Gertz answered. "I suspect we are drifting. The current here generally runs north-northwest at three to four knots. If maneuvering is not back online in ten minutes, we will have drifted out of the launch zone."

"Great, just great," Commander Anderson huffed, rubbing his tired, gritty eyes. He fretted and paced back and forth across the small raised platform, glancing at his wristwatch every few seconds. Growing more and more exasperated as fifteen grueling minutes passed, he stepped down off the platform. About to go to the engine room and give everybody a swift kick in the pants to get them moving, the lights flickered several times then came on. Once again, the normal hum of equipment filled the control center as *Wyoming's* systems powered up. The crew, uniforms soaked through, was especially thankful for the air conditioning and ventilation systems returning to normal operation,

The shorted component that had caused the total blackout had been located and replaced and power had been restored to the main power busses. Most systems appeared to have been unaffected. However, the sophisticated, and delicate, radio equipment had been severely damaged by large voltage transients created when the shorted component exploded and fell across two main power busses. Access panels hung open and rack-mounted assemblies sat on the workbench with covers removed as electronic technicians worked frantically trying to locate and replace fried components.

To avoid a replay of the previous boat-wide failure, Commander Anderson ordered systems to be brought back online one at a time, a process that took nearly thirty minutes. All systems were powered up and going through their boot-up cycles. Missile technicians were realigning the missile system, the most crucial system, and re-verifying that all targeting coordinates matched their launch order. The one system still offline was communications.

"Radio, Conn, progress report," Commander Anderson requested.

"Conn, Radio, long-wire, UHF, and VHF systems are still offline. The techs are replacing components as fast as they locate the damaged ones. No estimate on time to repair as yet."

"Radio, Conn, We desperately need comms back on line. Keep me apprised."

"Conn, Radio, these guys are the best. It shouldn't be too long. I will keep you apprised," Chief Radioman Thomas Dawson, *Wyoming's* Radio Division Chief, responded. Chief Dawson returned to the workbench and encouraged, goaded, and swore at the techs. "*Whatever it takes,*" he thought to himself.

Commander Anderson turned his attention to *Wyoming's* position compared to their launch zone. He consulted with the Navigation Officer and learned that the boat had drifted several miles outside their launch zone.

"Helm, Conn, right standard rudder, come to course zero-three-two. All ahead slow, make turns for three knots."

Helm and maneuvering responded to the Captain's orders. The crew could feel the boat heel slightly as *Wyoming* turned to starboard. The Captain and the XO started at the beginning of the missile launch procedure and ran through the required steps, stopping with only one step remaining. Commander Anderson looked over at the navigator.

"Conn, *Wyoming* is inside the launch zone," the Navigation Officer announced.

"Conn, aye," Commander Anderson acknowledged, then looked at the Quartermaster.

"Conn, *Wyoming* is hovering on station at launch depth," the Quartermaster announced.

Commander Anderson wanted to make a final check on communications before continuing. "Radio, Conn, do we have communications yet?"

"Conn, Radio, Not yet, Captain, but we're close."

"Radio, Conn, very well," Commander Anderson acknowledged. He had desperately hoped to learn there had been a countermanding order. *Wyoming* was ready in all respects to accomplish her mission. He could not wait any longer.

"Weps, Conn, are we ready to launch?"

"Conn, Weps, missiles are ready in all respects. Awaiting your orders, Sir"

Commander Anderson swallowed hard. There was no longer anything standing in the way of the Wyoming launching her missiles. He would make one final check with the navigation officer to confirm they were on station in the launch zone. And then….

Chapter Twenty-One

75th floor Penthouse
99 Hudson Street
Jersey City, New Jersey

The sound of someone shouting and pounding on the door dispelled the silence that gripped the penthouse. The security guard, disregarding Zach's instructions to tell no one he was there, had called the police when he returned to his desk.

"Open up. This is the police," a New York City policeman on the other side of the door shouted. "Open up or we'll kick it open."

After the last exchange of gunfire, Anthony had crawled out of the closet and around the corner into a hallway leading to a butler's pantry. Looking for a way out of the penthouse, he had raced into the butler's pantry. He saw just what he needed, a rear service entrance. Easing the door open just a crack, he saw three uniformed policemen standing in the hall. He eased the door shut and waited. A horrendous crashing noise echoed through the penthouse when the policemen kicked the door open and stormed into the penthouse. Anthony eased the service entrance door open a second time. Seeing no one, he slipped out into the hallway, ran to the elevator, and pressed the call button. The elevator door opened immediately. Anthony jumped into the elevator and jabbed the button for the ground floor, slipping his weapon behind his back. The door slid shut and Mr. Anthony Sterling disappeared.

After the policemen broke their way into the penthouse and stormed in, Zach held his weapon out with one finger through the trigger guard and held up his credentials with his other hand. He yelled out, "Secret Service. There's a traitor hiding in the closet."

Two of the policemen, weapons drawn, ran over to the closet while the other one kept his service weapon trained on Zach. "Throw out your weapon and come out with your hands up," one of them shouted. They waited. "Come out now," he shouted again. One of the policemen shoved the door open and pointed his weapon into the closet.

"There's no one in here," he shouted.

"What? That can't be," Zach bellowed with his weapon still dangling from his finger and ran over to the closet. "He was just here. He can't be gone."

Zach turned to look at the other policemen and saw he had crouched down beside Angie's motionless form lying on the floor. Zach dropped his weapon on the floor and raced over and knelt beside Angie. A large red stain covered the front of her blouse. "Oh, Angie, no!" he whimpered. "No. No. No," he cried as he ripped off his shirt, waded it into a ball, and pressed it against the wound to stop the flow of blood.

"Angie, Angie, can you hear me?" he pleaded.

Angie managed to open her eyes slightly. Recognition registered on her face as her eyes turned toward Zach. She tried to say something, but coughed, a thin trickle of blood ran down the side of her face.

"Angie, don't talk. Save your strength. Help will be here soon," Zach urged, looking up with desperation at the policeman.

"Yes, EMTs were called at the same time we were," the policeman answered. "They should be arriving here any second."

"Zach, important," Angie gurgled. "Love you."

"I know you do. I love you too, Angie. Don't try to talk. Just hang on a little longer," Zach sniffled through the tears beginning to stream down his face. "The officer says the EMTs should be here soon." He took one hand off the waded up shirt, found her hand, and squeezed it. She looked up at him. A faint smile curled the edge of her lips. A long, slow breath escaped through her lips as her face went slack. Zach looked down in horror, seeing the empty, lifeless look in her eyes.

"Angie, No!" he screamed just as the EMTs rushed through the door.

The EMTs sat their medical equipment bags down and dropped to their knees beside Zach. "Sir, we need to assess the patient," one of the EMTs said, but Zach didn't move. The other EMT grabbed Zach by the arm, "Sir, you need to let us do our job. Sir, you have to move out of the way," he insisted, pulling Zach away from Angie. Zach gave in and stepped away. One of the policemen put his hands on Zach's shoulders and pushed him back several feet.

"I know it's hard," the policeman said. "These guys are the best. Just let them do their job."

Zach watched in horror as the EMTs started CPR. One EMT performed CPR for several minutes and stopped while the other EMT checked for a pulse. He shook his head and the other EMT resumed CPR. Twice more the EMTs repeated the process. After the fourth unsuccessful CPR session, they stopped and turned off and disconnected the heart monitor. They stood up, turned toward Zach, and shook their heads.

"I'm sorry, sir. She was already gone. There was nothing we could do," the taller of the two EMTs offered, clenching his fists. He absolutely hated this part of his job. Looking into the face of a loved one and seeing the devastating anguish and pain, ripped at his soul. It was horrible. It was always horrible, but for some unknown reason, this time seemed so much worse than any of the others. He did not know the man standing before him, but intense, inconsolable pain flooded into his soul as he looked into Zach's face. He considered himself a tough, hardened emergency medical technician, but as he stood there with no words to say, tears also formed in his eyes and rolled down his cheeks. Violating department policy, he stepped forward and gave Zach a hug and said, "I'm so sorry, Sir. I wish I could have done more," he said, deciding at that instant he was never again going to look in the face of a devastated relative. Watching their terrible pain and suffering was too much. He was finished. He vowed that as soon as he returned to the station house, he was going to quit.

Unable to speak, Zach managed a half-hearted smile and nodded his head. The EMT returned to where Angie's body lay and consulted with the policemen. Their conversation concluded, one of the EMTs pulled a yellow plastic sheet from a bag and spread it over Angie's lifeless body while the other EMTs gathered up their equipment.

Zach's mind recoiled at the sight of the yellow sheet being draped over Angie's body. "*NO! NO! This can't be happening,*" his mind screamed, unable to accept the unspeakable sight. He raced over and knelt beside her lifeless body. He pulled Angie's hand from under the sheet and placed it against his cheek. She had risked her life to warn him and now she lay dead. Zach's world was crashing around him. He wanted to scream. Zach's anger exploded, temporarily overpowering his grief. He wanted to feel his hands around Porter's neck. "Porter? Where did Porter go?" Zach shouted. As the EMTs were about to leave the penthouse, Zach asked, "Hey, did you see anyone exit the elevator when you came up?"

"Matter of fact, we did," the taller EMT answered. "A man about six feet tall wearing a dark brown jacket met us halfway across the lobby and said there'd been a shooting and someone needed us up in the penthouse. Is that important?"

"Yes, it is. Where did he go after that?"

"We don't know. We jumped right into the elevator and came up here."

"Okay, and thanks by the way for the kind thoughts. I really appreciated that." Zach said.

While Zach had hovered over Angie, the elevator had stopped on the ground floor. Porter had exited the elevator, meeting the two EMT's rushing toward the elevator carrying medical equipment bags.

"Gun shots on the penthouse floor. They need help, hurry." Porter had shouted as he ran past them.

The EMTs had acknowledged Anthony's false plea for help and had continued running toward the still open elevator.

Porter had hurried across the rest of the lobby, had pushed the door open, and had stepped out onto the sidewalk. Fortunately for Anthony Sterling, a taxi was parked at the curb discharging a passenger. He had rushed over to the taxi and had jumped into the taxi, ordering the taxi driver to take him to the airport. The driver switched on the meter and sped away from the curb.

Anthony Sterling (aka Frank Porter) had managed to escape again.

USS Wyoming (SSBN 742)
Launch Zone
South-southeast of Bermuda

Commander Anderson had just finished speaking with the navigation officer, confirming that *Wyoming* had arrived back on station and was again hovering at launch depth. Before repeating the launch sequence for the third time, he checked with communications one last time, praying that a countermanding order had been received.

"Radio, Conn, communications check. Have you had any success restoring communications?"

"Conn, Radio, we were certain we had the systems restored a few minutes ago, but when we applied power, one of the replacement modules got fried. I'm certain we are close."

"Close isn't good enough. We've been without communication for over five hours, Chief. We need communication now! I don't want to launch our missiles if there has been a countermanding order. We need those communications systems back online."

"Understood, Captain. We're doing our best."

"Concentrate on bringing the long-wire system back online. That is the first link COMSUBLANT would attempt to contact us with."

"Aye, aye, I agree Captain. I already have the best techs in the department working on it."

Lieutenant Commander Barton, *Wyoming's* Executive Officer, tapped Commander Anderson on the shoulder. "Captain, we really can't wait any longer. Our orders are to launch our missiles once we reach the designated launch zone. We are on station in the launch zone and we are hovering at launch depth. Without a countermanding order, we are directed to launch our missiles. Sir, it does not matter if we have communications or not. Our orders are to launch our missiles."

"You're correct, XO," Commander Anderson agreed, as he leaned over and gripped the guardrail that ran around the raised platform. He squeezed the rail so hard his knuckles turned white. "I just have this itchy feeling up the back of my neck. Something in my gut tells me this just isn't right. I have to be certain."

"But Captain…"

"You don't have to say it, XO," Commander Anderson interrupted, pushing himself up and turning toward the XO. Time had run out. He could no longer justify waiting for an order that might never come. For all he knew, war could already be raging just one-hundred fifty feet above his head. *Wyoming's* Commander-in-Chief had assigned them a mission and they would complete it. He stood up straight with a resolve to complete that mission. He reached up and keyed the 1-MC.

"Crew of the *Wyoming*, this is the commanding officer. Set condition one-SQ for strategic missile launch. The release of nuclear weapons has been authorized."

The XO, Lieutenant Commander Barton, stepped up and repeated the command over the 1-MC. "This is the executive officer. Set condition one-SQ for strategic missile launch. The release of nuclear weapons has been authorized."

In the control room, all the crew's eyes turned toward the Captain, wondering if this third attempt to launch their missiles would fail again.

"Focus on your duties, men," Commander Anderson ordered.

As had occurred two times before, two officers ran into the control room, one holding up the CIP key. Commander Anderson accepted the key and inserted it into the Captain's Indicator Panel. Lieutenant Commander Barton stepped up to the Captain's Indicator Panel and inserted his key.

Everyone waited as the missiles were brought fully online and the targeting coordinates were reconfirmed and loaded into the eight warheads in each of the twenty-four missiles for a third time.

With all the conviction he could muster Commander Anderson spoke into the 1-MC, "Man Battle Stations Missile for Strategic Missile Launch. Spin up all missiles, one through twenty-four." Commander Anderson glanced over at Lieutenant Commander Barton. The XO nodded his head.

"Ready, three, two, one, NOW," Commander Anderson ordered. Both men turned their keys.

In the missile compartment, the last column of lights on the indicator panel turned red as the missile technicians armed the explosive gas generators that would literally blow the missiles to the surface in a bubble of gas. *Wyoming* was once again fully ready to launch its missiles. The only remaining step was the final order to fire. After receiving permission to fire, the weapons officer would unlock the safe in MCC (the Missile Control Center) for a third time and remove the tactical firing trigger, which looked like a pistol without a barrel. All that remained was for Commander Anderson to give the final order.

Commander Anderson wiped the sweat out of his eyes and gave the order, "Weapons, Conn, Release of nuclear weapons is Authorized. You have permission...."

Chief Radioman Thomas Dawson's excited voice jumped over the top of the Captain's communication. "Conn, Radio, Receiving EAM," Chief Dawson shrieked. "We're receiving an EAM on the long-wire, Captain."

"Weapons, Conn, hold in present position. Do not launch. I repeat, do not launch."

Commander Anderson reached up to the 1-MC again and shouted, "Radio, Conn, bring the message to Control, on the double. EAM decryption team one get the codebook and bring it to Control, *NOW*!"

Chief Dawson stepped out of the Op Center into the radio room, ripped the EAM from the radio room printer, and ran toward the control room. Chief Dawson and the two members of the decryption team nearly collided as they rushed into the control room.

"Here is the message, Sir," Chief Dawson announced, holding out the piece of paper for Commander Anderson to read. One single, three-letter sequence of letters appeared on the piece of paper. Lieutenant Bill Chambers, Assistant Weapons Officer, slowly read off the letters using the phonetic alphabet while Lieutenant Jg. Ted Mitchell, Electrical Division Officer, looked over his shoulder, "ECHO–TANGO–FOXTROT." Both officers held the codebook, while they searched through the list of codes to determine what action the EAM called for.

"Captain, we have a valid EAM requesting *Wyoming* to break patrol orders and proceed to periscope depth to receive emergency flash message traffic," Lieutenant Bill Chambers announced.

"Weapons, Conn, return the tactical firing trigger to the safe and stand down from strategic missile launch. Set normal condition."

Commander Anderson and the XO stood in front of the Captain's Indicator Panel, turned their keys counterclockwise, and removed them from the panel.

Commander Chandler thumbed the 1-MC to make an announcement to the entire boat, "This is the Captain. We are going shallow to receive flash radio traffic. Rig the boat for ultra-quiet."

"Helm, Conn, all ahead slow. Dive, Conn, five degree up bubble come to periscope depth, smartly," Commander Chandler ordered.

"Conn, Helm, all ahead slow," EM2 Mike Hall answered.

"Conn, aye."

"Conn, Dive, five degree up bubble. Come to periscope depth, smartly," the diving watch answered.

"Conn, aye."

Commander Anderson waited impatiently as the change in depth ticked off on the digital depth display. "XO you have the Conn. Maintain current depth and heading," he ordered as the boat approached periscope depth. "I don't want to stay at this depth longer than absolutely necessary. As soon as the flash radio traffic has been received and verified, I will instruct you to take the boat down to patrol depth."

Without waiting for a reply, Commander Anderson stepped off the platform and ran toward the radio room. He stuck his head into the radio room, he looked over at the senior radioman, and asked. "Is the message complete and verified?"

"Just completing now, Sir," the radioman replied, beads of sweat running down his forehead. "The message is starting verification now."

Twenty seconds passed as the communications control computer compared the cryptographic control codes embedded in the message just received to those stored in the computer's internal memory.

"Message verified sir."

"Very well. Print it," Commander Anderson ordered. As soon as the printer stopped, he ripped the paper from the printer and began to read.

```
YYYY DE XXXX 012/34
YYYYXXXX RUCBXXX3456 17118855-UUUU-
RMFRSUU
ZNR UUUUU
P 191510Z MAY 15
FM: COMSUBLANT
TO: USS WYOMING SSBN 742
BT
CLAS //N02120//
1.  NUCLEAR DETONATION OF LOCAL ORIGIN
2.  STANDOWN FROM MISSILE LAUNCH
3.  REPEAT STANDOWN FROM MISSILE
      LAUNCH
4.  CONFIRM RECEIPT ASAP
5.  RETURN TO ASSIGNED PATROL
BT
2021
```

An enormous flood of relief washed over Commander Anderson as he read the message. "Petty Officer Jiles, confirm receipt and acknowledge the message," Commander Anderson said as he folded the message and slipped it in his pocket.

Commander Chandler thumbed the 1-MC and announced. "XO, take the boat down to patrol depth. Have the navigator plot a course back to our assigned patrol area. As soon as we are at patrol depth, turn the Conn over to Lieutenant Gertz. Then meet me in the mess deck. I think we could both use some coffee."

Whitehouse
Oval Office
1600 Pennsylvania Avenue
Washington, D.C.

President Caldwell had rescinded Presidential Directive Fifty-One, returning all government operations to their normal locations. The announcement that the nuclear detonation had been perpetrated by a small group of deranged individuals had calmed the citizenry down tremendously. Slowly, life was beginning its return to normal, except for a few pockets of looting and rioting that continued in some of the larger cities. All strategic nuclear forces had received and acknowledged the stand-down order and had returned to their bases. Once the airborne strategic nuclear forces had returned to their bases and the nuclear missile submarines had returned to their patrol areas, the President had ordered the military alert level returned to DEFCON5.

President Cantwell sat limp in his chair with his head resting on his chest, exhausted by the ordeal that had finally come to an end. His staff had pleaded with him to go up to the residence and get some sleep, but he had refused. Until he received the full details of the attempted uprising, he had refused to leave his desk. Donald Walsh, the White House Chief of Staff, slipped into the Oval Office and walked over to the President's desk. Gently, he shook the President's shoulder. "Sir," he said, receiving no response. "Sir," he said again, shaking the President's shoulder a little harder.

"Huh, what?" President Cantwell sputtered, sitting upright in his chair. Recognizing his chief of staff, he asked, "What is it, Don?"

"Mister President, Zach Templeton is in the outer office waiting to see you," Mr. Walsh answered.

"By all means, send him in," President Cantwell said, blinking his tired eyes to clear the fog of sleep. Dark circles showed under the President's eyes, a physical evidence of the fatigue he felt.

Mr. Walsh poked his head into the outer office and motioned for Zach to come in. Zach pushed himself from the chair and entered the Oval Office. Mr. Walsh exited the office and pulled the door shut. The President met Zach halfway across the room and extended his hand. Zach stuck his hand out and grasped the President's hand. The President squeezed Zach's firmly, looking into Zach's face to gauge his condition.

"Mister Templeton, my deepest sympathy. I cannot begin to express to you how sorry I am about your wife," President Cantwell offered.

"Thank you, Mister President," Zach replied. "I appreciate your concern. Please call me Zach."

"Okay, Zach. Have a seat," President Cantwell said, pointing to a chair directly in front of his desk. The President sat down in his chair and rolled it up to the desk. "Before we get started, would you like some coffee?"

"Actually, I would like that."

The President buzzed the outer office and requested a coffee service be brought in. The two men engaged in meaningless chatter until the coffee service had been delivered and the door was once again closed.

"When and where is the funeral, Zach?"

"Three days from now in Tulsa, Sir."

"I will be there and I will see that all expenses are paid. Transportation costs for anyone in your family, funeral expense, whatever. Just name it, and it will be paid for."

"Thank you, Sir. That will really be a big help."

"By the way, how is your dad?"

"Thankfully, he's on the mend."

"In a couple of weeks, once the dust settles, you will be presented with the Presidential Medal of Freedom. Zach, your incredible sacrifice saved this country from anarchy. We are all very grateful."

"Thank you again, Sir. I am humbled."

"Okay, I guess we should get down to business. What can you tell me about the traitors behind this heinous act?"

"You are not going to believe what I have to show you, Sir," Zach said as he pulled a notebook from his jacket pocket, leaned forward, and handed it to the President. "I got that notebook from Mister Leonid Borodin. It has the names of all the perpetrators."

The President flipped through the pages of the notebook and stopped on one page. His mouth hung open and disbelief flooded across his face. "This can't be true!" he gasped.

"That was also my first reaction, Sir, but I assure you every name on that list had a hand in what happened."

"I refuse to believe this," the President declared, looking up at Zach.

"The first name in the list, Miss Margot Wilcox, is in the FBI's custody. She admitted to the whole thing. I have undeniable proof, Sir," Zach said, as he reached in his pocket and pulled out the flash drive. "This flash drive was in Borodin's wall safe. It has video recordings of every one of their meetings." Zach leaned over and handed the flash drive to the President.

"Unbelievable. Fifteen members of Congress!" President Cantwell groaned, shaking his head. "This is a dark, dark day in America's history. This will further shake the people's trust in Government."

The President reached over and picked up the phone and pressed the intercom button. "Send Mister Walsh in here."

The door opened and Donald Walsh stepped into the office. "What do you need, Mister President" he asked.

The President held out the open notebook. "Take this notebook and make a copy of this page. Then deliver it to the Director of the FBI and have him arrest everyone of those traitors immediately. I want to be notified the instant they are in custody."

"Yes, Sir," Mister Walsh answered as he withdrew from the office.

President Cantwell looked up and asked, "Porter?"

Zach shook his head. "That despicable traitor slipped away again. He disappeared when the police and the EMT's came in. The EMT's said a man ran across the lobby and told them there were gunshots in the penthouse. He's gone, Sir."

The President picked up the phone and pressed the intercom again. "Send them in."

All the officials that were available filed into the Oval Office and shook Zach's hand, thanking him for his great sacrifice. The buzz in the Oval Office lasted for fifteen minutes.

As the last official filed out of the Oval Office, Zach walked over to the President's desk and held his hand out. President Cantwell jumped to his feet and grabbed Zach's hand and pumped it vigorously.

"It was an honor to serve at your pleasure, Sir," Zach said, managing a half-hearted smile. He pulled his Secret Service credentials out of his pocket and handed them to the President.

"I'd like you to stay on, Zach," President Cantwell said, trying to hand the credentials back.

"I'm sorry, Sir. It would be a great honor, but I just don't have it in me to go through anything like that again."

"What will you do?"

"I don't really know at this time. I'll go home to Tulsa and get my parents set up in a house there. My dad is going to need some rehab. After that I'll try to sort out my life. I'm still numb. I just don't know....," Zach's voice trailed off, unable to continue.

"I repeat my earlier offer, Zach. If you need anything, ever, just call me."

President Cantwell sat back down in his chair and laid Zach's credentials on the corner of the desk.

"There is one more thing, Sir," Zach said as he leaned toward the President and whispered in his ear.

President Cantwell smiled and said, "Yes, sir, Mister Templeton. I'm quite sure that can be arranged."

Epilogue

Four days later a gleaming, blue and white Gulfstream 550 lifted off the runway from Washington's Dulles International Airport and disappeared into the dark night sky. Receiving its final vector, the sleek aircraft made a wide right turn to a heading of one-eight-one and climbed to its assigned flight level.

In the passenger cabin, the Gulfstream's lone passenger grabbed a blanket from a burled walnut credenza and curled up on the luxurious couch mounted on the port side of the cabin. Tossing and turning on the narrow couch, the passenger fell into a troubled sleep.

Seven hours later, the Gulfstream crossed over the northern coast of Ecuador just east of Tumaco Airport on a heading of one-seven-five. Awake for several hours, the lone passenger attempted to pick out features of the dimly lit landscape as the sun began to rise in the east. The Gulfstream passed four miles east of Quito's Mariscal Sucre International Airport, on a heading of one-eight-zero. Twenty-five miles south of the airport, approach control instructed the aircraft to turn left and intercept the downwind leg of the approach to the airport.

Crossing over the outer marker, the pilot had the aircraft lined up on the runway's centerline flying due north. The pilot flared the Gulfstream as it passed over the threshold of the runway. He eased back on the throttles to reduce the aircraft's speed and pulled back on the yoke. The Gulfstream settled out of the sky and the tires touched the pavement, creating an almost imperceptible bump.

The Gulfstream taxied down the active runway in the early morning sun and turned off onto the taxiway leading to the general aviation parking ramp. Following the visual directions of an airport ramp worker, the pilot steered the Gulf-stream to an empty space beside a small Learjet. While the airport ramp worker placed chocks in front of the wheels, the pilot set the parking brake and shut down the engines. He lifted himself up out of the pilot's seat, exited the flight deck into the passenger cabin, and opened the forward hatch.

"Great landing," the passenger complimented as the pilot extended the stairs.

"Thanks, I aim to please," he replied. "How long do you think we'll be here?"

"Hopefully, not long. A few hours maybe. No more than a day."

"Okay, I'll have the aircraft fueled as soon as I finish the paperwork. Then, I will file a provisional flight plan so we'll be ready to depart as soon as you return."

"That's good," the passenger said. "We may need to depart in a hurry. The local authorities do not know we are here. I don't want to spend any more time on the ground than is absolutely necessary."

"The aircraft will be ready," the pilot assured the passenger.

After descending the stairs, the passenger walked into the general aviation terminal, pulling a small suitcase packed with the usual items a customs inspector would expect any traveler to have. The suitcase was just for show. The passenger intended to spend only a few hours in Quito, a fact he would not share with immigration. Inside the terminal, the passenger approached the immigration desk and held out his passport to the inspector.

"Welcome Senor," the inspector said as he opened the passport and slid the edge of the front page through the optical scanner. The inspector held up the passport, comparing the photo to the passenger's face. Satisfied the photo matched the individual standing before him, he opened the passport to an empty page and stamped it.

"Where will you be staying, Senor?" the inspector asked.

"Casa El Eden," the passenger lied. "Probably no more than a day or two."

"You no like our country, Senor."

"I have important business back in the States. I just can't stay any longer," the passenger answered, hoping the inspector would not ask any more questions he probably could not answer.

"Well, maybe you come back again, yes?"

"Yes, I certainly hope to."

"You are clear to go. Have a nice stay, Senor," the inspector said as he handed the passport back and waved the next traveler up to the counter..

The passenger breathed a deep sigh of relief. He had been able to pass through immigration with no issues. He exited the immigration area and searched for a sign that would direct him to ground transportation. Unfortunately, all the signage was in Spanish. He scanned the signs trying to decipher them with his limited knowledge of Spanish. His eyes settled on a sign to his right that read *Transporte de Tierra*. Deciding the sign must mean ground transportation, he walked that way. After taking only a few steps, a familiar face emerged from the crowd.

"Zach, you old sea dog," the man beamed.

With a look of astonishment on his face, Zach answered, "Bill..."

"No, Senor. I am Sotero Rojas," the man interrupted, shaking his head and winking his right eye. "Long time no see, Senor."

Going along with the ruse, Zach answered, "I agree, Senor Rojas. It has been a long time. I was about to arrange for some transportation."

"No, my good friend. I have a car outside. Hurry, come with me," the man urged, grabbing Zach's arm and directing him toward the exit. Outside the terminal, a black SUV with dark-tinted windows sat at the curb waiting. A short, squat man with hair as black as coal leaned against the side of the SUV. As the two men approached, the short man opened the rear passenger side door. Senor Rojas directed Zach into the back seat. Senor Rojas took Zach's bag, handed it to the short man, and slid in beside Zach. The short man circled around the back of the SUV, deposited Zach's bag in the back, and climbed into the driver's seat. He started the engine, put the SUV into gear, and pulled away from the curb.

"Okay, Bill, what gives," Zach demanded.

"I'm undercover for the CIA," Bill Morrison explained. "I and two other agents have been here for a few months to watch the activities of a subversive group of dissidents. That is Nestor Guzman driving and that is Omer Herrera in the passenger seat. Several weeks ago, quite by accident, I spotted a man that looked amazingly like Frank Porter. I took several photos and sent them to my superior for confirmation and voila! Facial recognition confirmed a one-hundred percent match."

"That explains your presence here, but how did you know I was coming?"

"Admiral Hadley sent word via our emergency contact. He said the President called and told him you were to get whatever assistance you needed. Must be nice to be so important. Why are you here?"

"I want Porter. I'm going to kill him and put an end to his evil," Zach snarled. "I guess the Admiral didn't tell you. Porter murdered Angie."

"What!" Bill exclaimed.

Zach detailed the long story as the SUV sped toward central Quito. Bill grew more distressed and angry as the heartrending details of the incident at Henry Tang's penthouse unfolded. He had liked Angie a lot. Angie had always been a bright spot when the families of SEAL Team Four got together on the rare occasions when they were not on a mission somewhere on the other side of the globe. Far more upsetting was the torment and anguish he saw in Zach's eyes. Zach and Bill had faced death together as soldiers many times, forming a bond that few people could understand. What one felt the other felt. In those few short minutes as Zach shared his ordeal, Bill shared Zach's pain and an insatiable desire to see Porter dead grew inside him.

"I couldn't believe Porter returned here so quickly," Zach said. "He must think we are stupid."

"We were very careful to not let Porter see us. We always maintained a safe distance. When I reported to my superior that he left the country in a hurry, nobody approached him in any way. They only observed him. So, we have to assume he believes nobody knows of his identity here in Quito."

"That will be good for us," Zach observed. "Maybe he will go back to his normal routine. That will make it easier for us to apprehend him."

"You are correct," Bill answered. "Since he returned, he has gone to the same outdoor café for coffee every day. He is a predictable creature of habit."

"What is our destination and how soon will we arrive?" Zach asked.

"To an apartment building on Vicente Leon Street. Porter has an apartment on the fourth floor. Another few minutes and we'll be there. We couldn't believe our good fortune when we learned the occupant of the adjacent apartment moved out. We paid the landlord triple the usual rent to let Nestor have the apartment for a three-month lease. We will be there when Porter returns from the café."

The four men sat in silence for the rest of the trip through the narrow streets of Quito. Nestor stopped the SUV a block from the apartment building and let Omer out. He would watch the building's entrance and call Bill when Porter returned from his morning coffee. Nestor continued driving a block beyond the building and parked the SUV on a side street. The three remaining men hurried back to the building, rode the elevator up to the fourth floor, and entered the apartment adjacent to Porter's.

"How long before he returns?" Zach asked, eager to get his hands on Porter.

Bill glanced at his watch. "A little over an hour yet. As I mentioned earlier, Porter is a creature of habit. The time he spends at the café does not vary more than a few minutes and he always takes exactly the same route when he returns. Omer cannot miss him. He always wears a white Panama hat."

"I hope you're right," Zach fretted. "I have waited a very long time to see Porter pay for his crimes."

"Don't worry, Zach, we won't miss him. Have a seat," Bill said, pointing toward a brown leather couch. "You might need this," Bill said, sliding open a drawer in a corner cabinet sitting beside the couch. Lying in the drawer were two 9mm Beretta 92FS pistols. Bill lifted the pistols out of the drawer and handed one to Zach. Zach hefted the pistol in his hand, checking its weight and balance.

"Nice weapon," Zach said as he eased the slide back slightly to verify there was a round in the chamber. Both men stuffed the pistols behind their belts.

Zach sat down onto the couch while Bill snagged a cushioned stool from the kitchen peninsula and positioned it opposite Zach. The two men reminisced about the last time Porter had avoided capture, slipping away only minutes before the Washington, D.C., Capitol Police stormed into his office. Eventually the conversation drifted to memories of dangerous missions they took part in as part of SEAL Team Four. Bill had just started to talk about a particularly harrowing mission in the jungles of southeast Asia where they had been ambushed and only he and Zach had made it out of the jungle alive. Before he could finish the story, his cell phone rang. Omer informed Bill that Porter had just entered the building.

"He's here," Bill exclaimed. Come on. Let's go."

Zach stood and followed Bill to the door. Both men pulled their pistols from behind their belts, ready for whatever was to come. Bill turned the doorknob, releasing the latch. He pushed the door open just enough to see into the hallway. Less than two minutes passed before Porter appeared in the hallway. Bill waited until Porter passed the door and stopped in front of the door to his apartment. Bill slammed the door open and shoved the muzzle of his pistol against Porter's neck. Zach raced around to the other side of Porter and held his pistol at the ready.

"Quick, into the apartment you stinking rat," Bill barked, shoving Porter toward the open door. Zach followed close behind and pulled the door shut. Once inside the apartment, Zach hooked his foot behind Porter's leg and slammed him to the floor.

"Recognize me you murderous traitor?" Zach shouted, holding the muzzle of his pistol six inches from Porter's face. Porter just laid there, a look of fear spreading across his face. "Answer me you scum," Zach screamed, striking Porter across the face with the pistol. Porter didn't speak, frozen by fear.

"Answer me! Answer me!" Zach screamed again, pressing the muzzle of the pistol against Porter's forehead. "Remember Mister Tang's penthouse?" Zach demanded, striking him again across the face with the pistol. "That was my wife you murdered, you pile of garbage." Again, Zach pressed the muzzle of the pistol against Porter's forehead. Zach shook with rage as he stared down at the man he loathed, a man that deserved to die.

"Kill him. That scum doesn't deserve to live another minute," Bill snarled, standing beside Zach.

Zach's finger tightened against the trigger. The trigger moved backward closer and closer to the point it would release the firing pin, which would ignite the primer which would then ignite the gunpowder in the cartridge. The sudden explosion of gunpowder would propel the hollow-point bullet from the barrel with tremendous force and would turn Porter's brain to mush.

Zach's finger tightened more against the trigger. His mind begged him to just pull the trigger and be done with it.

He desperately wanted to see Porter die. A large breath of air escaped from Zach as he released the trigger. "I can't. I can't do it," he sobbed as the emotions of the past week escaped. He sat on top of Porter, emotionally drained. He simply could not pull the trigger. Zach believed in decency, the rule of law, and justice. He could only hope that when they got Porter back to the United States, the court system would order the punishment Porter deserved.

"Tie him up," Zach ordered as he climbed off Porter and stood up. "Bill, how do we get him to the plane?"

"I know someone that can help," Bill answered, pulling out his cell phone. He punched in a number and had a short conversation in Spanish.

An hour later the black SUV pulled up to the general aviation terminal at the Quito airport. Bill jumped out and ran inside. A few minutes later he stuck his head out the door and motioned at Nestor to drive around to the freight door. A man of medium height with a pock-marked face slid open the freight door and signaled Nestor to unload their package and bring it into the terminal. Nestor opened the rear gate of the SUV. With Omer's help, they lugged Porter's wrapped up body through the freight door. Inside the freight center, Adulfo, the man with the pock-marked face, waited with a four-wheeled pushcart. Nestor and Omer loaded Porter's body onto the cart and the three men pushed the cart out to the waiting Gulfstream.

Standing beside the plane, Adulfo spoke up, "May I look at him?" Bill pulled back the corner of the tarp till Porter's face was visible. "*Usted apestando credos*," Adulfo hissed as he spit in Porter's face. "Drop him in the ocean as you fly," Adulfo said as he turned and walked back to the terminal. Kip watched while the three men stuffed Porter's body through the rear access door.

Thirty minutes later, the Gulfstream lifted off the runway into the northern sky. For a long time, Zach sat motionless, staring out the window at the verdant landscape passing below the aircraft. As the aircraft passed over Ecuador's northern coastline and flew out over the Southern Pacific Ocean, Zach turned away from the window. His mind churning with wild and disconnected thoughts. After Angie's death, he had not allowed himself to think about anything except capturing Frank Porter and delivering him to the authorities to be punished for his crimes of treason and murder. For the last two days, nothing else had entered his mind. But now that his mission had been accomplished, his mind turned to the disconcerting thought of arriving home in Tulsa and walking into an empty house. His mind screamed with torment. Every fiber of his being wanted to run to the back of the airplane and beat Porter until he was dead, but he knew that would do nothing to alleviate his pain.

Even the thought of receiving the Presidential Medal of Freedom held no appeal for him. Without Angie to share it with, it would be a hollow and empty ceremony. Once the ceremony was over he would return home to Tulsa with no job and little desire to search for one. "*What am I going to do?*" he asked himself. He could not answer because he did not have the slightest idea.

The Gulfstream streaked through the cloudless sky with Zach dreading the empty days he knew lay ahead. In the back of the passenger cabin, Mr. Frank Porter lay trussed up like a Christmas Goose.

Only the passing of time would lessen the unspeakable pain and emptiness Zach Templeton felt.

Or Would It?

THE END

About the Author

Keith Hoar writes fiction that transports you beyond the mundane into worlds of intrigue and suspense, mystery and terror.

Writing that plunges you into the story, makes you hold your breath, and interrupts your sleep.

Keith began his career in the United States Navy, proudly serving his country for ten years. At his final duty station, Naval Submarine Base New London, he was responsible for daily operation of a periscope approach tactics trainer. He assisted in training crews from both Fast Attack and Ballistic Missile submarines that patrolled the world's oceans in defense of freedom.

After his military service and business career, determined to combine his experience with his creative writing skill, Keith began writing thrillers in 2011 from his office overlooking a picturesque 80 acre pasture filled with wild horses. Years later, his driving passion is to craft mind-boggling tales that transport his readers to worlds of intrigue and suspense.

Keith earned a BS in Business from Excelsior College and a Master of Ministry Degree from Louisiana Baptist Theological Seminary. He enjoyed a successful career as a certified "Business Intelligence Expert", consulting for numerous Fortune 100 companies.

www.ingramcontent.com/pod-product-compliance
Lightning Source LLC
Chambersburg PA
CBHW030656120726
47905CB00001B/244